Out There in the Dark

◆

Wesley Strick

◆

Thomas Dunne Books

St. Martin's Press ✹ New York

Out There in the Dark

THOMAS DUNNE BOOKS.
An imprint of St. Martin's Press.

www.stmartins.com

ISBN 0-312-34381-7
EAN 978-0-312-34381-1

First Edition: February 2006

10 9 8 7 6 5 4 3 2 1

For Marla, darling

Many thanks to my editor, Sean Desmond,
and Richard Abate

Out
There
in the
Dark

Prologue

What We Think of As the Legacy

In late 1988, Chester Dowling was contacted by the Harley P. Hayden Library in Columbus, Ohio. In her letter, Helen Prater (the curator) asks whether Dowling, long-retired head of production at Superior Pictures, would consider returning to the studio to sort through his archive of magazine tear sheets, interview clips, outtakes, contracts, photo proofs, notes, fan mail, and other "primary source materials" related to Mr. Hayden's years as a Hollywood actor. "This is an area in which we believe we are lacking in terms both of breadth and depth," Ms. Prater writes. She adds that, though the library cannot offer payment for this service, "we feel your research would make a marvelous contribution both to our country and to what we think of, here, as the Hayden Legacy."

She closes by expressing the hope that "this letter finds [Mr. Dowling] in good health." In fact, though he'd just celebrated his eighty-third birthday, Chester Dowling was remarkably fit, even vigorous. Even so, he was not a happy man, his wife of nearly half a century (Doris Dowling) having passed away not long before, after a harrowing battle with bone cancer. Since her death, the former studio czar, once used to disciplining unruly movie stars as though they were children, and pressuring top directors into casting actors who weren't necessarily right but were under contract—and *idle!*—now spent his days nearly idle himself, padding around his Tarzana ranch house clutching his wife's wet/dry vac as he hunted for puddles and crumbs. Aside from the vac his time was also taken up with (*a*) waiting for the Sparkletts man to deliver jugs of unfluoridated water, (*b*) taking naps from which he would wake with a start, convinced either that his wife was alive and calling for him or that he'd missed the Sparkletts man, and (*c*) trying and failing to sleep at night due to all the naps he'd taken throughout the day.

So, yes, even without remuneration, Dowling would be willing to return to the Superior lot (for the first time in over twenty years) and dig through the cartons stored on some basement shelf there. He wrote as much to Ms. Prater, and two weeks later Dowling eased his bulky—but not fat—frame behind the wheel of his tan Cutlass Supreme and drove (avoiding the freeway, taking surface streets) back into a Hollywood much changed (but little improved) since his tenure at Superior.

When he passed the Palladium on Sunset—one landmark that looked just as it had back in 1940, on the night Dorsey opened the joint—Dowling fell into a reverie set to a faint but reverberant big-band sound track. He could picture Harley Hayden, rangy and young, as well as the ex-cop Dowling had hired at Lustig's behest to "look into" Hayden (par for the course, both pre- and postwar). One syllable, something like "fork" or "shark," as Dowling recollected the ex-cop's name, a harsh sound to it like a junkyard dog's bark. No, not bark—*Roarke*. A mean mick sonuvabitch Roarke was, which figured into Dowling's decision, sic one mick on another and stand back . . . Plus that strike in the late thirties, short-lived, when Roarke, still a cop then but glad to moonlight for a little extra do-re-mi, proved his mettle with no fanfare, going toe-to-toe with those hoodlums up from San Pedro, who were they, bunch of painters and plumbers who'd decided to form a labor union—how do you like that?— tried to organize the studio, drove right up to the main gate with a gang of longshoremen muscle to find Roarke waiting with a few other off-duty cops who'd left their uniforms at home—but not their billy clubs.

Dowling must have decelerated as the memories came flooding back, because some whippersnapper asshole actually *honked* at him, and the octogenarian was so rattled by the racket, he floored the gas and lost control of the Cutlass for a moment as it skidded up onto the sidewalk and clipped a parking meter. (He had a peripheral image of the honking tailgater sailing past him in a Porsche, vindictively flipping the bird.) A miracle the veteran exec made it to Superior Pictures' main gate, but he did, a few minutes later, and the guard actually had his name down (though he looked askance at the dented Olds and made an inaudible joke to his partner as he waved Dowling through).

The cartons were arranged not by actor but by year. An improbably young woman showed Dowling to the cobwebbed corner where the boxes labeled *1940* were stacked. The old man stripped off his seersucker suit coat, rolled up his sleeves, declined the girl's offer of water and a chair, and dived in.

The first cache of faded, mildewed items he brought up were, of course, clippings and photos of Flynn—who'd done a string of Superior's boffo pix whenever Jack Warner felt like humiliating the Aussie whorehound by loaning him out. Dowling feebly blew away a cloud of dust then dug a little deeper, this time coming up with the revised production schedule of *Midnight Masquerade*. He vaguely recalled ordering a seven-page script cut to accommodate the female lead's forced two-day absence from the set, either for an abortion or a round of shock therapy.

Then Dowling remembered, as though it had happened last week: Despondent after being dumped by her director, the actress had checked herself in to Jasper Ridley's sanatorium for a long weekend of "electrical stimulation," hypnosis, monkey gland injections (no doubt spiked with morphine sulfate), and whatever the hell else that creepy quack got up out in Pasadena; Dowling made it his business not to know. Was Ridley running his clinic like a little fiefdom? Then he was the local constabulary's headache. There was always some faddist physician around (what the kids nowadays called a guru) whose role it was to relieve stars and movie-biz spouses of their anxieties along with their excess wealth. The gimmick might be narcotics, it might be sex. (Nowadays it seemed to be yoga.) Inevitably there'd be a complaint, or overdose, followed by an inquiry, a scandal, a gated compound suddenly up for sale.

It wasn't till he'd excavated the third carton that Dowling found his first Hayden-related artifact, a call sheet for Day Twelve of *Phi Beta Caper*. It wasn't *The Big Betrayal*—that was the movie they thought of when they thought of Hayden in Hollywood—but it was a start. A memo was still paper-clipped, from the set decorator, to the effect that *the kid sitting in the classroom set next to Eddie Albert* had to have the legs of his chair shaved an inch or two—*so he don't tower over Eddie.*

The note made Dowling chuckle: They may have lowered Hayden's chair to feature Eddie, but it wasn't a letter from the Edward Albert Library about "the Albert Legacy" that had brought Dowling back to Superior some forty years after the fact. But then one could argue that neither scenario made a hell of a lot of sense, except from this standpoint: Movies were stories, and lives were stories, and sometimes the two got tangled together like wires that crossed—and what happened then was a big hail of sparks just before all the lights went out.

Wrap Your Troubles
in Dreams

Dowling knew Roarke would be hungry, knew he'd jump at the offer of a civilized business lunch. But he couldn't be seen with Roarke inside the grill. So the two men ate in the parking lot, in the backseat of a Lincoln-Zephyr limousine like the Chicago mobsters rode around in, with curtains drawn across the back windows to keep busybodies and lookie-lous from peeking.

"Did Bill Fields really say, 'I never drink water—fishes fuck in it'?" Dowling began, as his driver brought out two Caesar salads and passed them over the front seat with a pair of cloth napkins from the studio's executive dining room. Dowling munched a leaf of lettuce, then finished his thought, which wasn't so much a thought as a gag: "Well, I've always been leery of Musso and Frank's. Screenwriters like the food."

Roarke laughed—maybe a little too hard, but Dowling was the only game in town these days. The ex-cop was still under a cloud, being investigated on a corruption beef not only by the Los Angeles County prosecutor, but also by CIVIC, the Citizens Independent Vice Investigating Committee. And he was newly alone, his wife having ditched him (and taken their daughters) without leaving so much as a note. (Even a scribbled screw-you would've been nice.) Roarke's meals were desultory, undelicious, just something to swallow down between scotch and beer binges.

Mostly the work consisted of showing up on sets that some would-be Wobbly was trying to organize, and threatening to bust skulls. Road-company Pinkerton-type crap. Table scraps. But Roarke wasn't complaining. Instead, he was watching Dowling as the production head munched his Caesar while running two fingers through his brush cut. Whether it was the brush cut, the thick hide, or the way he chewed his lettuce, there was something of the hand-fed farm animal about Chester Dowling. Roarke half-expected him at any moment to go *oink,* or *moo,* or even *baa.*

Instead, he said, "This one's for Mr. L."

Roarke tried not to look surprised or unsettled. But it was a very long way from the back lot to the executive suite.

"Mr. L is concerned." Dowling lowered his voice, for effect. "Some young actor's been seeing Ellie."

It took Roarke a moment. "Lustig's daughter?"

Dowling nodded. "A knockout. Not just cute—built. Best-looking sheenie chickadee I ever laid eyes on."

Roarke smiled. "And your eyes are all you'll ever lay on her, I'll bet, Chet."

"You and me both." Dowling laughed. Then: "This young actor, he's under contract with the studio. Bit parts, walk-ons, 'Tennis, anyone?' Handsome kid, though. Not John Garfield handsome, don't get me wrong. He's no Ty Power, but nothing to sneeze at either. Great set of muscles on him, too, make you think of Weismuller without the—"

"—Leopard-skin jockstrap," Roarke joked.

Dowling came to the point: "Mr. L's nervous the kid could be using his daughter to—you know, to curry favor. Or worse, chiseling her for dough. But he doesn't want to risk ticking off his little girl without hard evidence. So he sends me—the House Goy—on an errand to find out what's what with Mr. Rising Star. Is this kid on the level? Does he gamble, drink, sniff coke? Is he straight or queer? If he's queer, then it's cut-and-dried, open-and-shut, no? If he's straight, well, is he getting anything on the side, running with the chippies same time he's screwing—I mean, doing—I mean, *dating*—Eleanor?"

Roarke gestured that he'd gotten the gist.

"But he doesn't wish to know how I come by the information. That's very important to Mr. L., alright? It's vital that the boss not—how best to put it?—dirty his hands. No offense."

Roarke shrugged. "Lustig started as a glove maker, isn't that right? Stands to reason he'd be sensitive on that score."

Chester smirked, then glanced at his gold watch. "I got Lubitsch on Stage A shooting *The Man Who Wore Mink*. I got Von Sternberg on Stage B helming *Awful Wedded Wife*. On top of all that, I got Seife on Stage C, lousing up *Midnight Masquerade*."

"Fascinating." Roarke smirked in return. "Here I thought we had a beef with the Jerries, and the Jerries are all you got on the lot." With a fingernail, he freed a sliver of anchovy from between his front teeth. "Maybe you fly in the Führer himself, to guest-direct the *Follies of Nineteen Forty-one*?"

"In all fairness?" Dowling shot back. "These Kraut directors you're bellyaching about, they ran away from Hitler."

"Ran away," Roarke agreed, "to live another day and make another dollar. With which, god knows, I have no problem—just so long as these saintly refugees we're weeping for don't turn around and airmail their salaries straight back to Berlin."

Dowling shrugged. "Germany's one of our big markets. If Roosevelt's not at war with 'em, neither is Superior Pictures. Anyway, these Teutonic SOBs, you gotta hand it to them, they know how to stand up to the talent. All day shouting through a megaphone seems to come natural. Hell, maybe just as well we've stayed outta this war." He pulled back the curtain on his side, rolled down the window and stuck out an arm, waving for his driver, who stood by the front fender. To Roarke: "Let's wrap it up so I can return in haste to my private hell."

Roarke unlocked his door. "Gimme two weeks. I just need a couple of things: this matinee idol's name, and an advance to cover the first week, standard rate." (Roarke regularly asked Dowling for forty dollars a day, and invariably took twenty-five.)

Dowling had the money out before Roarke finished speaking.

The ex-cop counted a hundred and a quarter. "Want a receipt?"

Dowling shook his head. "Let's do this on the honor system. That way there's no paper trail leads back to Mr. L or the studio. I can't even give you a pass to get on the lot."

The honor system was no favorite of Roarke's: indeed, it was the very system that had tripped him up in law enforcement. But Roarke didn't object. Whenever he held cash in his hand, the former vice cop found himself incapable of making even the most elementary moral distinctions. It was the darnedest thing.

That same afternoon Roarke dropped by the lot and right away hit the expected snag at the main gate: no drive-on, the studio cop said with a grin. Roarke couldn't fault the beefy bastard: this was his one chance all day to high-hat someone else.

Roarke promptly ruined his day. "I'm from the Breen office," he announced, flashing a phony card. Joseph Breen, the movie censor, was a practicing Catholic, but Roarke had learned that in Tinseltown he was treated like the pontiff. The card had paid for itself many times over. Roarke got waved right in.

Harley Hayden was playing the third male lead in a college comedy, some B-picture fluff featuring wacky fraternity high jinks, guys in letter sweaters driving jalopies, and girls in angora and bobby socks beside them. This one, a grinding eighteen-day shoot, was titled *Phi Beta Caper*.

Today Hayden was sitting in a standing classroom set, the same set they'd used for the Andy Hardy pictures, on loan to Superior. Though he was twenty-five at the time, Hayden easily passed for the college freshman he was playing. Roarke picked him out immediately from a copy of *Photoplay* he'd skimmed at a stand on Vine en route to the lot. Hayden looked fine in the publicity photo. In person he looked even better.

He was taller, for one thing. Even seated at that desk, you could tell he was a good six feet, six one. Most movie stars were little men with large heads. A better proportion for the big screen, or so they said. Ladd, Bogie, Dick Powell . . . shrimps, all. Not Hayden (though his relatively small head might have kept him from becoming a major marquee name).

Hayden had an athlete's posture, relaxed but alert, and it worked just right in the scene—he was playing an A student whose best friend was a young drunk about to wash out of school. Harley's thick, full head of chestnut hair didn't hurt either. The natural wave created a prodigious pompadour with one strand that fell boyishly onto his forehead.

The eyes were Hayden's main asset, though. Even at a distance (Roarke stood behind the sound cart, about thirty feet from his quarry) those eyes impressed. Not just because they were a bright limpid blue. Plenty of bright limpid blue eyes in Hollywood. Besides, they were shooting black-and-white.

Maybe it was the eyebrows—their natural shape, the way they cocked and curved. Their contour gave Hayden a perpetual look of shy enthusiasm, proud self-effacement, "aw-shucks" but tempered by a faint, furtive amusement. And all this before he'd opened his mouth, hit his mark, done anything but show up.

Someone shouted for quiet on the set, they started rolling film, a third voice called "Speed," and the director yelled "Action." Roarke was pleased to note that the word was pronounced with no trace of an accent, Germanic or otherwise. Probably because it was an unimportant, low-budget programmer destined for the bottom of the bill, Superior had seen fit to entrust an American with the property.

The freshman lush stumbled through the door into the classroom. Teacher was just writing a complex trig equation on the blackboard. Now he turned around and, watching his inebriated student clumsily finding his seat, did a slow burn.

The poor hungover kid was seated next to Hayden. In a stage whisper as he plopped down, the young star asked, with exaggerated innocence, "So what'd I miss?"

Eyes front, as he copied the equation, Hayden replied sotto voce as the camera tracked in for a two-shot:

"Spring semester."

"And *Cut!* Print that one."

Hayden waited with a hopeful look as the director made his way over to the two desks.

But the director had nothing to say to Harley—because Harley was barely in this picture, a foil at best, the straight man. Still he listened hard while the director gave his notes to the star ("Take a

beat as you come in, pivot in front of the professor, *then* lunge for
your seat like this was an ocean liner caught in a gale") as though
the notes were for *him,* for Harley.

And it was plain to see, Harley *was* an A student, not in a
book-learning sense, rather in the way he was soaking up all the
moviemaking secrets being revealed here. Working hard without
putting a hair out of place. As the lights were reset, Roarke realized what it was about Hayden's eyes that reached out, appealed. It
wasn't the eyebrows. No, it was a slight squint that conveyed a look
of not-quite-getting-it mixed with wanting-to-get-it-real-badly-but-
preferably-at-no-one-else's-expense.

Not that the director noticed. But the director, after he was finished sucking around his young star, did notice Roarke—that is,
he glanced at Roarke's unfamiliar face behind the klieg lights with
a flash of irritation. The ex-cop scuttled ratlike into the shadows,
then let himself out the stage door.

And tailed Hayden for what felt like miles across the lot as the
actor ambled past prop men and girl extras, offering one and all a
wave, a smile, a warm hello. Harley never glanced back, never
gave the impression of a guy who sensed he was being followed, a
guy with anything to hide. By the time they reached his trailer
Roarke was logy and perspiring, while Hayden looked dewy and
fresh. Chalk it up to the decade Roarke had on the actor, or his
dark serge suit, or Hayden's superior genes.

Hayden's trailer was divided in half, what those racy film folk
call a double banger—Harley had to share it with another juve-
nile on another picture. Roarke waited in the shade, taking a seat
on a bench, lighting a Lucky. Much beguiling "atmosphere"
strolled by, mostly in small chattering groups. Some of the girls
dressed like Babylonian slaves, others as flappers or Okies. All of
them oblivious to the ex-cop—so displaced he might have been

another studio extra. Then along came a lone female vampire all in black, with tapered teeth and a drop of dried blood on her lips. She stopped to ask Roarke for a light. After she smiled her thanks and sauntered off, the former vice cop reflected that loitering on a studio lot was like buying a box seat at a cathouse for crazies—minus the expenditure of cash, the physical act, the social disease.

Then Hayden emerged from his trailer. Roarke almost missed him—some jailbait Valkyries had sashayed past, hefting spears. Roarke caught sight of Hayden as he took a shortcut back to the stage. Hayden now looked even younger—maybe he'd had a catnap. Or (while Roark blinked) a blow job. Or just read a good book. More likely, he'd curled up with a copy of *Photoplay* and spent his rest period admiring publicity pictures of Harley Hayden. Or maybe Roarke was being hard on the actor because gravity seemed to exert so little force on him.

Roarke decided not to press his luck with the Sound Department; in the afternoon he stood alongside Makeup and Hair. Women mostly, and a few fairies—but a big enough contingent that Roarke blended in, impervious to the bitchy glances.

The rest of the day's work consisted of take after take, in close-up, of the hungover lead asking Hayden what he'd missed. Close-up, followed by medium close-up, followed by extreme close-up. Not even a shot over Harley's shoulder onto the star. But Harley hung in there, take after monotonous take, listening to that same silly question with that same squinting, amiably baffled look, then delivering the "Spring semester" punch line with that same dead-on, uninflected inflection.

Then, without warning, there was an atmospheric shift. Someone shouted "Martini shot," voices grew hushed, they took the shine off the star's nose, ran some more film, called "Cut"—and now, as beefy men carted away cables, mirrors, and lights, and craft and crew folk packed their paraphernalia to break for the day, more beefy men wheeled a bar onto the stage complete with a white-coated colored mixologist and his array of sodas, juices, gin, vodka, scotch, and rum. The director, the cameraman, several tan, pudgy gentlemen in butter-yellow sweaters who looked like associate producers, and the young star all bellied up for martinis, mostly, poured from iced pitchers.

"They do this every day?" Roarke asked the soigné fellow standing next to him: one of the fairies with Makeup and Hair.

The fairy batted his eyes then gave Roarke a *look*, like he really was a bluenose from the Breen office. Then deigned to reply, "Liquor? It's the lifeblood of this business. Keeps the wheels turning better than a grease gun." Then walked away, twitching his high, round ass—whether as a rebuff or a provocation, Roarke wasn't sure and didn't want to know.

Hayden was also walking away. At his back, the director shouted, "Harley! Get over here and take your medicine!"

Hayden shook his head: "Mama was a Christian Scientist." And though everyone kept shouting for him to join them for a belt, he ambled off the stage with a breezy, "*Mañana*, fellas."

Hayden didn't take long to change out of his letter sweater and frat slacks into something just as casual but a little less ridiculous. All he was carrying were his car keys and script. When he came bouncing down the steps of his trailer, Roarke followed him to the parking lot—same lot where, conveniently, the ex-cop had left a spiffy little hunter green Packard 120. A year ago Roarke had borrowed the roadster from a Negro stoolie who was now in no position to reclaim it, being deceased. Both the county prosecutor and CIVIC had been angling to get their hands on the Packard, but

Roarke had—so far—stymied one and all by conclusively demonstrating that he didn't own the car.

Harley drove a powder-blue Plymouth, rusting a bit around the running boards. Roarke followed him west on Melrose in light traffic. But as the ex-cop caught a glimpse of Hayden's face in Hayden's rearview, he blinked. It wasn't Hayden! The man in the mirror wore a pair of black horn-rims with thick lenses. He looked like a junior accountant, not a college freshman. Within three blocks Roarke had managed to follow the wrong Plymouth!

But there *was* no other Plymouth: Hayden had, in the privacy of his automobile, quick-changed into Clark Kent. At Vine he turned, heading north to Hollywood and Orange: Grauman's Chinese. Hayden pulled his car into the lot (Roarke did likewise). When he exited his car, he was no longer wearing horn-rims; he'd resumed being Harley Hayden. And Roarke realized the quarry wasn't wise to him—quite the contrary, he was nearsighted! No wonder he hadn't yet tumbled to his tail, no wonder he watched the world with a befuddled squint. Myopia was Hayden's Achilles' heel—and his secret weapon as well.

As the actor paid the attendant, he started, finally, to act furtive: glancing to the east, west, north—everywhere but south, where Roarke stood. Roarke was getting cranky, and wouldn't have minded a little confrontation; he knew it wasn't the end of the world—or even the surveillance—when a subject stopped in his tracks and turned on you. A tail can learn a lot about his man when he's nose-to-nose flinging accusations, wild or on target. Just smelling the subject's breath (whether redolent of halitosis, pussy, or scotch) can speak volumes.

Hayden now moved to the theater's concrete front yard, but lurked off to the side where William Hart's gun prints, and Rin Tin Tin's paw prints, were embedded. And here he waited, head lowered to hide his face, while Roarke passed the time comparing his shoe size to Gable's, and Beery's, and Hedy Lamarr's.

Now there was some sudden activity on the periphery—a girl had darted from an Independent Taxi, then slipped through the crowd that was gathered at the pagoda-style ticket booth. The girl wore dark glasses, her hair was covered by a kerchief—studiedly nondescript, a wallflower whose costume screams, "Look at me, I'm incognito." Like a movie star, in other words.

Hayden's two-timing the boss's daughter with a movie star, Roarke thought, suppressing a snigger. But who? Rita, Greta, Ingrid, Lana? Some unattainable siren whose name and hand prints were sunk right here in cement beneath the ex-cop's Florsheims?

A ticket taker—who must've recognized one or both of the young couple—shooed them inside. But when Roarke stepped up a moment later, her thick arms were akimbo. "Ticket?"

"I'm with them," he bluffed.

She shifted her stance to block his way. " 'Them' who?"

The line at the ticket booth was snaking halfway down the boulevard by now. Roarke reluctantly joined the hoi polloi waiting to see *The Maltese Falcon*. By the time he got inside, the first picture (about a G-man called Brass Banfield versus a Nazi spy with the depraved name of Swenko) was in progress.

Roarke sat in back, dividing his attention between his mark and the movie. At the climax, Agent Banfield wrested control of some infernal death ray—the Inertia Projector!—and turned it against the bad guys, vaporizing them. Then Brass looked out at the audience and warned them to keep an eye peeled for tricky Prussian types "who may even now be making their way to our shores to threaten our freedoms, our happiness, our very way of life." He mentioned a table set up in the lobby where anyone

could sign up to join Brass Banfield's Freedom Club, get fitted for
a decoder ring, do his or her bit for Democracy.

Then, just as Roarke settled in for an eyeful of Mary Astor,
Harley and his companion swept up the aisle to the exit.

Five minutes later Hayden's Plymouth and Roarke's Packard
were headed west on Santa Monica. Harley forked right at the
Holloway split and pulled into the lot behind Barney's Beanery.

The Beanery was not Roarke's sort of saloon—too many poets
from New York City and Bruins from UCLA. He dragged himself
inside to find Harley at a billiard table in back with his Mystery
Date—who'd stripped off her sunglasses and kerchief and was
letting her hair down in every sense, all silvery laughter as she
sipped beer and took amateurish swipes at the cue ball.

It was Roarke's first real look at her, and he had to look twice.
She wasn't Bergman, or Turner, or Hayworth, or any film goddess
he'd ever seen, on-screen or in the flesh. But she was as striking as
any of them, and more memorable than some.

And all at once Roarke recalled Dowling's description of
Arthur Lustig's daughter as the "best-looking sheenie chickadee I
ever laid eyes on." He'd faltered on making the connection because the idea of a beautiful Jewess was hard to swallow on the
face of it, a claim to be taken with a grain of kosher salt. But
Dowling hadn't exaggerated. This girl, with her deep olive skin,
lustrous black hair, dark brows, high sculpted cheekbones, and
cool feline eyes, was a classic beauty who belonged on a wall in
the Louvre, not in the back room of Barney's Beanery.

So Hayden was enjoying an innocent night out with his girlfriend Eleanor Lustig, a stunning kike who just happened to be
the studio head's nineteen-year-old daughter. Notwithstanding
his naked envy and mean instincts, Roarke sensed nothing forced
or phony about their union—Harley seemed to hold the secret of

making Ellie giggle, of bringing a sudden delighted or scandalized glint to those big black eyes as he patiently taught her to play a decent game of eight ball. Still it was a long evening, what with Roarke continually ducking overfed freshman fullbacks on their way to the men's room. After three shots, he had to hit the head himself. As Roarke stood on line he heard a warm, quizzical Midwestern voice just behind and to the left:

"Say, do I know you?"

Roarke took a breath, then turned, started to speak, and approximated a double take. In that awkward moment it was obvious which one of the two was an actor. Still, he went through with the charade. "Wait, aren't you what's his name, from the movies? Sure you are. You're—Harley Hayden, right?"

Hayden hesitated, before modestly conceding as much.

Sensing that, at any moment, he'd realize Roarke had been tailing him all day (rarely at a distance of more than forty feet), the ex-cop decided to snow Hayden with flattery. "I loved you in *The Last Great Battle.*" It was the one Hayden title he remembered, though he'd never caught the picture. But he'd read a few notices and watched a coming attraction and knew it had something to do with doughboys, the Battle of the Marne, appalling casualties, soul-stirring heroism, and the sort of nurses you'd more likely find at Chasen's than Mount Sinai.

"Appreciate it," Hayden said, smiling.

"I don't think I've ever stood shoulder to shoulder with an honest-to-god movie star," Roarke was inspired to trowel on.

Hayden's eyes crinkled as he tilted his head, then shook it. "I'm no movie star," he protested, studiously modest. "Just a contract player, a glorified working stiff. Don't get me wrong, I'm not complaining—it's a great job, making movies. And I've been lucky. But don't confuse me with Gable or Cooper—*those* guys are stars. I just come on, say my lines, and get off without knocking over the light stands, if I'm lucky."

It was Roarke's turn in the toilet. When he reemerged a moment later and Hayden took his place, Roarke had the chance to drift back to the billiard tables and gape again at Ellie Lustig. Without Hayden at her side she seemed underage and helpless—and, if possible, more lovely. Maybe because she'd stopped having to giggle at his jokes and shenanigans? Her features were relaxed now, almost solemn, and classically sculpted. If Roarke hadn't known she was of the Hebrew persuasion, he'd have compared her beauty to Nefertiti's or Cleopatra's. Or one of his beloved ebony whores, now out of bounds at the Dunbar Hotel down on Central Avenue.

He must have been staring, for she slyly turned her head and looked straight at Roarke. He could tell by the clarity of her gaze that Ellie Lustig had perfect vision. Roarke quickly averted his eyes as some painful thrill ran through him. It felt like a summons and a warning, both. Roarke rose, slapped down a few bills, and walked out.

He considered dropping in on Sally, his stenographer girlfriend—but Sal's sister would be lurking; Roarke called her the Shadow. Driving home in a light rain, he felt a crushing apprehension about returning to his empty apartment. What would he do there but kill another whiskey bottle, play his new Buddy Collette and Lee Young records on the phonograph, and mentally drift back to the Club Alabam, the easy money, the respect and the fear, and the stink of sweaty jazz trumpeters and Mary Jane?

Roarke awoke at five in the morning, clammy and gasping. At ten it was back to the lot for more surveillance (security now raised the gate as the Packard approached, and they'd reserved a prime parking spot near the soundstage) as H.H. (so coded in Roarke's notepad) continued under sweltering lights to act collegiate, upbeat, and befuddled. Einstein had argued that time was elastic; on a movie soundstage, it was stretched nearly to nothingness. But a different sort of nothingness suffused Roarke's notes, solely devoted to Hayden and Ellie's *amour*:

Subj. meets E.L. corner Hwood/Cherokee, early movie at Egyptian. Dinner Brwn Drby. H.H. drives her home. G'bye kiss. (Polite, no tongue.) H.H. early bed (9:43 lights out) . . . H.H. and E.L. rowboat Echo Park lake. E.L. mts. subj. at Sepulveda minigolf. H.H. corrects her stance, lets her win ½ the holes (drives her home then straight to bed 9:51) . . . Chinese Theater then milkshakes at C.C. Brown's, hold hands under table. Chaste g'night kiss. . . .

Et cetera. Four days before the surveillance was set to end, Roarke phoned Chester Dowling to let him know the case was wrapped up in ten days not two weeks, and Superior would save a hundred clams. Dowling instructed the ex-cop not to say another word on the phone; rather, they would meet at the Beverly Hills Hotel, at the Polo Lounge, at six, "when the only people around are a half-dozen hookers and, on the off chance, Howard Hughes."

The Polo Lounge at six, in addition to being rather empty, was rather dark. Presumably the subdued lighting was designed to take a few years off patrons' faces. A perspiring Dowling showed up a good half hour late, mumbling excuses. ("Dieter Seife threw a full-scale, Reichstag-sized tantrum on the set, I had to go and babysit the Jerry prick while he fumed and shouted *'Scheisse!'* in his trailer.")

Dowling then tossed back two manhattans to Roarke's single

scotch while the ex-cop filled him in: "Hayden's on the level. I can show you all my notes, but what you'll find is a variation on this theme: He's a good boy all day every day at the studio, always knowing his lines, never breaking a sweat, and in his free time he squires little Ellie all around town, where they carry on like a couple of giggly high schoolers, Mickey and Judy but a foot taller, both, and slightly more wholesome even."

Just then, a tall, gaunt, and stooped figure entered the restaurant and loped to a booth in back with a platinum dish in tow. "Hughes," Dowling murmured. "Crazy man. Too much of everything but sense." He drained his drink. "Like Welles, but worse: without talent. Can't fly a plane worth shit." The production topper turned back to Roarke, grave and expectant.

"Nothing *on* this guy," Roarke restated. "He's so clean, he squeaks. Early to bed, early to rise, doesn't drink hooch, doesn't smoke marijuana cigarettes, observes the speed limit, wears a pair of cheaters, but he's true-blue to his Eleanor."

"You get a gander at the Lovely Yid?" Dowling grinned, wolfish. Roarke waited for saliva to drip. "Whattaya say?"

Roarke shrugged. "If you go for the type, the dark, oily skin, the coarse black hair. Probably has to tweeze all over. Wash her underarms three times a day. And a muff like a mink stole, betcha. What can I tell you? I'm a Betty Grable man."

"Yeah, sure—but what can *I* tell Mr. L?"

"Hayden's okay. Lustig wants to shake him off his little girl, he'll have to trump something up, or hang a frame. Can't help you there: I'm a choirboy now." Roarke lit a Lucky and sucked. "Or 'Mr. L' can send his daughter on a long cruise and hope she meets an eligible Vanderbilt round about Cape Horn."

Dowling was either reluctant to accept there was no dirt on

E.L.'s suitor, or he didn't want to leave the lounge on a mere two manhattans. He signaled for a third, then whispered, "They say Hughes can't get his gun off. Imagine that—with all the beautiful broads hanging off him. Must be a living hell, huh?"

Roarke's phone rang the next morning at seven A.M. It was Dowling again. "Mr. L would like to see you."

"In person?"

"That's what 'see' means. And not at the studio. Up at the estate, in Laughlin Park. You know Laughlin Park?"

"Like the back of my Bentley."

So much for the fiction that Mr. L wished to stay ignorant of how facts about Hayden were gathered—especially now that those facts hadn't met his specifications. Roarke grabbed his notebook as supporting evidence.

When he made a left off Franklin twenty minutes later, Roarke found a gate arm blocking his way. He scanned the directory for *Lustig* then picked up a brass-plated outdoor house phone and rang the extension. A butler or valet answered, commanding the ex-cop in crisp faux English tones to "kindly hang up and dial the following digits": 1-7-7-6.

Roarke snorted. These fucking movie moguls—every one a European refugee, or first-generation immigrant at best—were convinced that they, and not the Founding Fathers, had invented America.

Lustig's estate was more a gated compound than a home, what with three separate Moorish structures landscaped with date palms, agave cacti, birds-of-paradise, purple bougainvillea, and lush eucalyptus. A servant steered Roarke to the largest of the buildings, set dead center. Rather than being taken to the house, he was escorted along a winding path that led to an ornate, overscaled gazebo out back between the tennis court and swimming pool.

Dowling was already here, in his tight seersucker suit. He sipped coffee with one hand, scratched his brush cut with the other. Fine flakes fluttered onto his shoulders, disappearing into the white stripes, decorating the blue.

"What's this about?" Roarke asked.

"Mr. L would like to ask you a question."

"What question?"

Dowling sipped. "Let's wait for Mr. L."

So Roarke waited, staring up at the frescoed ceiling: portraits of angels fluttering, hovering—as though here was Hollywood's own Sistine Chapel right beside the heated pool.

"Some neighborhood, huh?" Dowling mused. "To the left you got DeMille, other side Bill Fields. Across the street, Deanna Durbin and her mom, who thinks she's some kinda medium. And I'm not talking dress size. Mr. L tells me they hold loud séances late Sunday nights, screaming and shrieking and moaning, maybe makin' a little whoopee with the ghost of Valentino—"

He whirled at a *crack!* Arthur Lustig crossing the lawn, wielding a riding crop. It wasn't entirely a prop—Dowling had noticed the Movie Jews were abandoning canasta and taking up polo this season—but surely it was meant to strike fear? Though, given Lustig's stooped posture and haunted look, the crop in his fist made him appear less of a Simon Legree sort, more like some dazed itinerant hobo with a dowsing rod. Lustig shuffled into the gazebo, fixed Dowling and Roarke with a frosty look, then came alive as he demanded: "Hayden *shtupping* her?"

Roarke sat back and complacently crossed his legs, causing Dowling to inwardly cringe. "Define '*shtupping*,' sir?"

Lustig cracked the whip again, in frustration or pique—who was kidding who?—then turned to Dowling. "Define it."

Dowling chose his definition carefully, laboriously: "Ah, consummating . . . in the sense of carnal knowledge . . . that is, intimate contact, particularly in the area below the waist—"

"Fucking!" Lustig laughed, the laugh fueled by fury.

Roarke shook his head, then made a show of thumbing through his worn leather notebook. "Not according to my records."

"You'd remember," Lustig observed.

Sensing that the boss awaited a final summing-up, Roarke offered, "I'd have to say no, sir. Though it's possible they did— *things,* in the dark, at the movies. But not—*shtupping,* though, that'd be near impossible given the setup, to *shtup.*"

"Things?" Lustig murmured, morose. Then, to himself, the mogul mused, "He would like to take Eleanor from me. . . . Harley Hayden? That . . ." Lustig went silent, at a momentary loss. Finally the apposite word came to him, and it was a word that neither Roarke nor Dowling had expected. "*Starlet.*"

At first Roarke thought Lustig meant Hayden was a cross-dresser or queer. To refute this he reached for his notebook. Then it struck him that "starlet" was meant to denigrate the way some men denigrate others with a low remark like "He's gotta squat to pee." So Roarke lowered his notebook and sat silent while Lustig expounded upon the *chutzpah* of this "second-rater" who unaccountably believed he might possibly be "good enough for the daughter of the fellow who founded Superior."

Roarke considered the name. Lustig had felt compelled to imitate the founders of Paramount and Universal, thumbed his *Roget's* and picked the best-sounding synonym, betraying an immigrant's tin ear.

Or maybe the story was true—that, back in his rag-trade days, Lustig ran an outfit called Superior Furs. Not because his furs were superior—they were probably in a range between average and counterfeit—but because the trappers brought their beaver pelts east from the Great Lakes. And Erie Furs didn't quite cut the mustard. Nor Huron Furs. Hence, decades later, the world had Superior Pictures. Based on the few Roarke had bothered to see, they didn't have a patch on the beaver pelts.

When Lustig stopped muttering, Roarke offered, "Could be worse, you don't mind my saying, sir. Your daughter could be dating Chaplin. Or Flynn. Or some colored fellow—Bojangles?"

Lustig stared owlishly. "Bill Robinson is a fine man and a personal friend, and he will not be besmirched in my home for a cheap laugh." Little knowing he was lecturing a man fellow officers had once nicknamed "the Nigger Lover." But Roarke stayed mum. He'd learned something else about Lake Superior in grade school: it was the coldest of the Great Lakes, too.

The meeting was over. "Sorry I didn't bring you anything useful to give Hayden the brush." Roarke shrugged, rising.

"Yes, yes," Lustig muttered as he flailed the riding crop in midair, but without cracking it; he seemed to have tired of this crude effect after the initial, shocking explosion.

Dismissed, Roarke nodded a brisk goodbye to Dowling then exited the gazebo and strode across the lawn, back the way he'd come. The servant who'd shown him in appeared again, but Roarke waved him off. Halfway up the narrow path, he heard, "Hello?"

It wasn't the servant's voice, but the voice of a girl. Roarke already knew the voice, from ten painful days of hearing its peals of gay laughter. He stopped; his stomach flopped as he turned around. Ellie Lustig stood here, panting, flustered.

"You're that man, aren't you?" she breathed. Roarke supposed she'd just dropped her croquet mallet and come running after him. "The one who's been investigating me? And Harley?" Seeing her face like this, so close, Roarke realized she was the model for one of the prettier angels painted on the gazebo's ceiling.

"If I was investigating you," Roarke hedged, "I'd have gone through your garbage and steamed open your mail. All *I* was doing, was *watching*. Was my job, y'see, that is, I was hired—"

"By Father. Yes, I know." Ellie glanced behind her, in the direction of that stooped patriarch. But they were alone on the narrow path, protected by an adobe wall on one side, thick row of palms on the other. "And you don't need to apologize. People have to make a living. Times are tough all over."

Then a self-conscious, almost melancholy laugh at the absurdity of such a statement, here, in Laughlin Park. "And of course, Father is not a trusting man. He wants proof, of—well, everything. And he's happy to pay top dollar for that proof."

Top dollar? Roarke let that one go by. "I didn't tell him anything," he volunteered, backing to his car. " 'Cause there wasn't anything to tell." Meantime he drank in her tawny good looks out here in daylight—he'd mostly watched Ellie in the evenings and at night—and could only marvel at how little she resembled his wan, freckled wife, the woman who'd bundled up his daughters and disappeared the very day Roarke was stripped of his badge.

As he surveyed her impassively, Ellie pursed her full lips and, with a sparkle in her eye, shook her head—Roarke wasn't sure in response to what, the statement he'd just made? That seemed unlikely. Why would she reject his acquittal of Hayden? Roarke turned away and continued on to his car. Ellie followed. "And I thank you for being truthful, Mister . . ."

"Roarke." He climbed into his Packard, backed down the

winding driveway and swung the car toward the gate, all the while resisting an impulse to check his rearview, see whether Ellie was watching.

Roarke drove south. He had no heart to go home and wait till the clock said it was time to decently start drinking. Anyway, all the scotch in Roarke's cupboard wasn't enough to slake his blues, nor would his collection of race records do the trick today. He stayed on Western past Washington, Manchester, Imperial . . .

At El Segundo Roarke went east, to Central Avenue—Brown Broadway—where he drew stares from early-bird black bucks in conked dos and pinstripes, strutting with their high-yeller mamas. Some openly hostile, others curious, all frankly interested in the green Packard. As if to imply that the car was not legitimately his. Roarke stared back—the old LAPD stink eye—and those jigaboos turned away, wanting no trouble.

Finally Roarke found the alley he was looking for, off Central at Forty-second. Across from the Hotel Dunbar, adjacent to that jazz club, the Alabam—closed, of course, at this hour. But there was an unmarked, rough-hewn wooden door across the way. Roarke pulled the Packard into the alley, parking behind a Dumpster that more than half-hid his car, then hopped out and approached the door. It swung open on screechy hinges.

Guarding the door from inside was a big, brawny coon, splendiferous in his blue velveteen tux, born PeeWee Bledsoe Jr., but he'd long since remade himself as the Emperor Jones. "My favorite peckerwood!" he exclaimed, thrusting forward a thick, calloused hand that felt to Roarke like a catcher's mitt. As they shook, the Emperor observed that Roarke's pink puss had not been seen on Central "since Fletch got hisself swore in."

"Fletch" was Mayor Fletcher Bowron, a former Superior Court judge and fanatical do-gooder whose landslide victory had sparked the resignations of twenty-four veteran, high-ranking cops. And whipped up a tidal wave that washed Roarke—among other seasoned officers—out to sea like so much flotsam.

In fact, the last time he'd been down here, Roarke had enjoyed a waived door fee at the Club Alabam as well as a dollar bag of fine, potent Black Maria weed. After sampling said weed in the alley behind the club, he'd watched Coleman Hawkins blow umpteen choruses of "Body and Soul" while the Hi-Hatters Dance Trio did its crazy synchronized stuff. If Roarke closed his eyes he could see daisies and daffodils spontaneously sprout, then explode in a silent, slow-motion detonation of petals and hues. When he opened his eyes again there was Hawkins, so slick with sweat his forehead and cheeks resembled sealskin, still chasing a slithery melody—a stud who couldn't quite climax.

"Well, I'm not here on police business," Roarke replied—unnecessarily, since the Emperor was well aware that this Irish piece of shit, who'd shaken down all his hookers and touts but in return permitted his whorehouses and gambling dens to thrive, had since been unceremoniously busted down to *civilian*. But the Emperor knew better than to rub Roarke's nose in his disgrace, the Emperor knew how to humor white guys like Roarke—in fact, he excelled at it—and as his grin widened, he asked in a tone pitched comfortably between solicitous and Steppin Fetchit:

"So what sort of business is it you are here to conduct?"

And Roarke, the sort of cracker who'd beat the black off a man just to prove he had the legal sanction to do so, replied, "The business of pleasure, Jones."

The Emperor displayed teeth that looked like two rows of chicklets. "If you're Jonesin', well, you come to the right pleasure palace." He then took Roarke's forearm and walked him down a narrow unlit corridor to a second corridor that led to a room even darker and suffused with heavy, perfumed smoke: stinkweed this was, the white-haired lady, Mary Jane herself.

Roarke couldn't see the smoke, but he could feel it snake down his throat, wrap around his clothes, and stick to his skin. All he could discern were pinpoints of red light around the room like planets, like stars. Whole constellations and galaxies, dimly aglow. But as Roarke's eyes adjusted to the gloom, he realized that these were not heavenly bodies, rather the glowing goof butts of so many vipers lying sprawled and content on mattresses that quilted the floor. Nor was the music he heard the Music of the Spheres, rather Art Tatum on wax, tickling the ivories. The only ofay in the entire tea pad, Roarke took a seat in a vacant corner, reached out a hand—and the Emperor laid a joy stick on him. Roarke inhaled greedily.

Waiting for the daisies and daffodils, he saw Ellie Lustig's face instead. Just her face, floating, larger than life and illuminated from within, a guardian angel to watch him and watch over him. Roarke relaxed on the thin mattress, feeling the cheap, slack springs beneath, while Ellie's face floated up to the ceiling, gazing down—just as in the Lustig gazebo—and a body formed, but it was the body of an angel.

Roarke wanted to tell her that, any time she felt too heavy with the sins of this world, she could descend from the ceiling and rest her wings on his mattress awhile. But what issued from his mouth was a dull gray doobie cloud. Ellie laughed at that, she whispered to him: "Wrap your troubles in dreams, and dream your troubles away"—and then she flitted off somewhere and Roarke tried to follow, but was dead on his feet.

Someone took Roarke's hand. A woman, no angel. She led him to another room, airless and windowless as well, but they could be alone here. Without a word she unzipped Roarke where he stood, swaying unsteadily beneath a single yellow bulb. Pulled out his cock and with artful lips and tongue made of it a club, a pork sword, a battering ram. He stroked her nappy hair that looked like Brillo but felt soft as lamb's wool as she took him down to his ball sack without blinking. Roarke guessed the Emperor was still repaying him for all those years of profitable partnership and racial tolerance, and he was glad. He let his lids close and soon the woolly hair he held magically changed, in his mind's eye, to the thick, straight, sleek tresses of Arthur Lustig's daughter, and the busy lips and tongue were Lustig's daughter's also. And when it was over—too soon, too soon—the dusky fellatrix licked Roarke clean then skulked out like an alley cat before he could put away his prick or fumble a sawbuck from his wallet as a gratuity—whereupon the ex-cop collapsed, curled up, and dreamt for an hour or more of Eleanor.

A year would pass before he'd see her again.

Two months after Roarke's midday visit to the viper's den, everything changed: The Japs bombed Pearl Harbor and most of the local jazzmen were drafted into the Tenth Cavalry's band at Camp Lockett; Central would still swing, but never quite the same.

And Harley Hayden? For a while, anyway, he would show a generation of GIs how to Slap the Jap and Stun the Hun.

. 2 .

Perilous Passage

Hayden dons his uniform, every stitch: the boots with the rough leather cuffs, the wool trousers tucked into the boots, the field jacket with the four outer pockets filled with rations. He buttons up the field jacket, despite the heat. Hoping, if he's humping it behind enemy lines, that he can subsist on a single chocolate bar till night falls and he can send up a flare, maybe get spotted by a British Spitfire returning from the mission.

When his B-17 with its RAF escort, swooping low on a bombing run, got hit in the tail by Luftwaffe interceptors—a pack of Messerschmitts—Harley'd miraculously managed to bail, somewhere near Wilhelmshaven, must've been. And damned if he didn't graze a tree, then land upside down, tangled, still dangling from his chute a few feet above the ground, blowing like a wind sock in the breeze. Hilarious. But how believable was it? He'd snapped a couple of ribs. How believable was *that*?

He tightens his web belt to help with the pain of the cracked ribs. Then tightens some more, to *simulate* pain. A canteen hangs from the belt, but what he wishes was hanging there instead is some kind of digging tool. To hide his chute, before he and Johnny try to make for the Swiss border. Say, doesn't that make sense?

As he dresses, and double-checks supplies and provisions, Harley sings: "*Ain't no use in going home, Jody's got your girl and gone.*" It's the song the soldiers chant when they're marching. There is a knock. Harley doesn't appear to hear it. "*Every time you stand retreat, Jody gets a piece of meat.*"

There is a rustle. Though the rustle is softer than the knock, he responds to it, looking over to its source.

Someone has slipped pages under the door. Even from across the trailer, Hayden sees that the top page is studded, pocked, with asterisks. Asterisks mean changes, last-minute revisions. Slapped together late at night by overtired studio contract writers under the gun.

Harley marches across his trailer—left, right, left, *right*—and bends down with a groan to scoop up the new script pages. His eyes scan the lines of additional dialogue:

JOHNNY
Our Flying Fortress was doing just under two eighty-five when the flak started flying. So if my calculations are correct we must be—

MIKEY
—up to our keisters in Klaus?

JOHNNY
(nods)
Up to our heinies in Heinz.

Christ, how cutesy, Harley muses. If I were Danny Kaye, playing opposite Virginia Mayo, and this was a dogface romantic comedy, well, then, the scene would quickly segue into a novelty song-and-dance number, a chorus line of grinning buxom milkmaids in the background, shimmying, and the next couplet sure to go:

> Shot down by some goose-stepping louse;
> Fell in love behind enemy lines . . .

Harley dries his forehead with the sleeve of his field jacket, reminding himself that It's Only a Movie. But of course it is also More Than a Movie—it is a morale booster and a shot across the bow, and that must not be forgotten either, Mister.

Harley startles at the next knock. A production assistant's voice, muffled: "We're five minutes away, Mr. Hayden." That's when Harley realizes he's still wearing his eyeglasses! He yanks them off, vigorously kneads the twin indentations (in close-up, on the big screen, they'd be more conspicuous than Jane Russell's tits) made by the nose pads.

"Thanks," Hayden calls, then speaks the next revised line aloud—not as Movie Repartee but something real, the Real Deal:

"Hope to hell the bombsight wasn't left intact, for those Nazi insects to swarm all over."

"Those what, sir?" That officious P.A., lingering outside Harley's trailer.

"Be out in a jiff!"

Scrunching the rest of the revised pages into his field jacket, Harley checks his reflection and, with a practiced backsweep of his right hand, raises his pompadour a half inch.

Strides out of the trailer.

The sun, directly overhead, is a bitch alright. But screw it.

Harley smiles at the P.A., then starts to jog. At first the P.A. thinks he's jogging toward the soundstage, but then he sees that Hayden is jogging *around* the soundstage, how do you like that? In weather like this, full costume and props?

Like boot camp, Harley figures, but more grueling, even— Parris Island, say. Two, three laps. More P.A.'s have been dispatched to reel him in, he can hear his name repeated over their walkie-talkies. They watch him jog past, but don't dare stop him outright. He spends the time thinking about Ann Sheridan. Scratch that: thinking about Norma, Frank's girl, his tail gunner's girl. And how tough it'll be, 'cause his tail gunner never made it out of the flaming B-17. And when he gets home, it's gonna fall to Harley—to Mikey—to comfort her. Tell her about Frank's final mission, his last moments, some casual affectionate comment he'd made about her just before the shit started to fly. Mikey will insist Frank didn't suffer, never knew what hit him—and Norma won't quite believe it, but she'll accept it, and soon she'll come to depend on Mikey not just for sustenance and strength, but companionship, and love, and *sex*—

Wrong. Cut. Take two, Harley remonstrates with himself as he swelters, jogs, prepares. And, presently, sprints onto the set— pouring sweat, his pompadour limp, face powder congealed. Hair and Makeup spot him, start to swarm, but he ducks around them all, waves them off, he doesn't need them, that's the *point*.

It's the Black Forest set. The electrical cables are cunningly hidden under a blanket of fake leaves. Lights are concealed behind phony pine trees. And there is a backdrop, beyond the tree line, of a bucolic village "below." So detailed, convincing, you can almost smell the fresh salted pretzels and Wiener schniztel. Movie Magic, Harley reflects, with pride and satisfaction—the set, that is, including the backdrop, excluding the script. Certainly not the new pages.

H.D. is busy lining up the next shot. Not H.D. as in C.B. (as in DeMille), but amid all the P.A.'s and A.D.'s milling on set, H.D. stands in Harley's mind for Hack Director. Harley ducks behind Hack Director to reach his canvas deck chair, where he can read today's revisions in (relative) peace.

MIKEY
    How wide a berth we need to give the place?

JOHNNY
(shrugs)
    I'm tempted to turn tail, is how wide.

MIKEY
    Guess I've never understood you, Johnny.

JOHNNY
(a grin)
    And you never will, for sour apples.

There's a pencil in the saddlebag hung on his armrest. Harley grabs it and, in the margin, scribbles: *Would Johnny say this?* Meantime he's wondering: Why does Johnny get all those bonus parentheticals? The *nods,* the *shrugs,* the *grins?* Whereas Mikey, he just gets the lines, the flat, straight, bozo lines—

"Jeez, Harley, you smell something awful."

Hayden looks up, at the script girl.

"What're we shooting today?"

"Scene fourteen. Johnny starts toward the village. Mikey follows." She finds the pages from her own binder.

Hayden reads with growing incredulity. Johnny is described as "racing" and "skipping" down the mountain, toward the German village, *energetically kicking rocks and clumps of dirt as though on a Sunday outing.* Mikey tries to stop him.

MIKEY

Before you can say Jack Robinson we'll be swinging in the town square. And I don't mean swinging like Glenn Miller or Dorsey.

Johnny just picks up the pace, *like he's a returning hero— Lindbergh, say—running late for his own ticker-tape parade.*

Hayden blinks at the page. "What is this . . . crud?"

It gets worse. Mikey follows him to the village, trying all the while to get Johnny to turn back. Inevitably, the Yanks are surrounded by curious locals. A hideous crone—Harley'd seen her in Makeup this morning, they were applying a wart and some whiskers to her chin, crazy Wicked Witch of the West stuff, no idea she'd turn up on his set, for goodness' sake—pushes through the crowd, comes right up to the two and demands: "*Amerikanischer Soldat?*" And Johnny, Mikey's bosom buddy Johnny, answers, "*Nein, nein.*" Then, introducing himself as "*Johann,*" he starts to answer the villagers' flurry of questions in fluent, conversational . . . *German.*

Harley looks wide-eyed at the script girl. "A spy? I don't believe, I *can't* believe . . . My pal Johnny, a *Jerry spy?*"

"I'll get him," says the script girl, something wild in Harley's eyes seeming to disturb her. She backs toward H.D.

Harley watches as the script girl draws Hack Director aside for an emergency conference, then H.D. wearily signals a gaffer . . .

The bulbs hidden behind the pine trees go dim as the safety lights come on and Hack Director crunches across the carpet of fake leaves to his own canvas deck chair beside Harley's.

"Harl, you look like hell."

"I feel like hell."

"And you don't smell much better."

"So I'm told."

H.D. laughs, a manly laugh. He'd started out on Howard Hawks's crew, and after lighting and building and rigging and shooting second unit on *Dawn Patrol* and *Scarface,* what he'd mastered was Howard Hawks's laugh. H.D.'s breath—even in the morning—is cigar stale. (Maybe Hawks munched stogies for breakfast? Well, but he was Hawks!) "Don't tell me. Out late, carousing? 'Seen at Romanoff's, squiring Joan Fontaine'?"

Hayden shakes his head. "I was home early, in bed at a decent hour, pair of fresh pj's, all set to study my lines—"

Before Harley can work up a head of steam, H.D. sensitively surmises: "Wait a sec, you're worried that when Johnny starts to spout in German—hell, that's gonna steal your thunder?"

Harley blinks. *Is* that the problem? He honestly doesn't think so. They're making a movie here, he's a professional, a costar, second-billed at that, he's got no illusions, it's not about who's the bigger hero, Mikey or Johnny . . . On the other hand, what *about* all those parentheticals for Mikey? "Why can't *I* shrug?" he yearns to demand of H.D. "Why can't *I* throw up *my* hands?" Or maybe it's the Lindbergh reference to Johnny, not Mikey, maybe it *is* about who's the bigger hero? Except Johnny can *have* "Lucky" Lindy, that apologist, that appeaser—

Stymied, Harley picks up his previous dialogue, backing up for continuity, just like he'd learned from the Script Girls:

". . . Pair of fresh pj's, all set to study my lines, 'cept instead I get a message from Stanley, once again there's no lines to study!" He laughs, but the laugh is hollow: he remembers a college acting coach grimacing at his laugh, and telling him: *Don't mimic—find the mirth.* "No pages till morning, new scene'll be in my trailer. Well, I don't know, I'm sorry, maybe . . . I mean, I've been working on Mikey's 'interior life'—his thoughts while he's walking through the woods, about Frank's girl, how conflicted and balled up he's feeling—he's sweet on her, I think . . . The camera can read your thoughts, I believe, but if the script changes then the interior life is all wrong suddenly, and maybe some actors can work like that but I can't work like that. At least I can't do my best work, that much I can tell you."

H.D. frowns. "Think *I* like it? Every day, not knowing what-all I'm gonna shoot, whether it's good or bad, whether it even makes sense? Or *stinks out loud?*" He lowers his voice, brings his mouth closer to Harley's face, so Harley feels dizzy from the sour smell. Confides: "Every day I drive to the set, feeling like I need to pull over on Sunset and *puke my guts.*"

A pretty P.A. offers a cup of coffee, though Harley didn't ask for one. He takes it anyway, thanks her, has a sip: it's cold and bitter. He swallows it regardless, to prove himself a Good Sport, then groans: "Who do we talk to? This can't go on."

"Talk to Lustig. Talk to your—" H.D. was going to say "father-in-law" but held back, maybe bad taste, inaccurate to boot: there'd been no wedding bells, not yet. But those hoped-for bells had figured heavily in H.D.'s casting choice. Getting any picture off the ground was tough enough, why not grease the wheel, goddammit? "I've already put in my two cents and see what good it did? But that's where the buck stops, am I right? Stops with the almighty Arthur Lustig?"

Harley, resigned: "I'll do it. At lunch."

Hack Director nods at first assistant, who shouts: "*Lunch!*"

Hayden changes back into civvies, then dials his agency. A girl answers, giggling, "Good morning, Music Corporation of America." He's noticed, with some annoyance: they're always giggling, these receptionists. Working the MCA switchboard must be the most fun job in show business. He asks for Moe Kasher.

Moe comes on the line. They say if your agent takes your calls, you need a new agent. But half of what they say about agents is hogwash. "Harley? I thought you were shooting."

"I am shooting, on my lunch break, and . . . I'm thinking of popping in on A.L. Y'see, there's script problems, Moe, and—"

"Harley. Honey. Pester a studio head about a line of dialogue rubs you wrong, you're back in Bumfuck, Ohio, before—"

"It's not a line of dialogue, it's *script* problems, it's—"

"For eye problems they got eye doctors, for script problems they got script doctors. *Harley*. Listen to Moe, please. Are you listening?" Before Hayden can affirm that he is, in fact, listening, Kasher has vigorously launched into a plot synopsis:

"So this guy—young, handsome—wanders into a small town up in Sonoma County. Wine country, okay? He's looking for work, he's able-bodied, he meets this gorgeous local girl, 'Leora,' she stomps grapes—for a living, how they make wine. He falls in love. 'Cept he's not sure how he landed here, who he is, he's got a head injury—amnesia! She nurses him back to health and as he starts to feel better, he remembers his name—Tony—and that he's a stockbroker from Frisco, rich guy with a Pacific Heights penthouse. Something of a playboy, bon vivant, okay?"

Hayden grunts: okay. Either Moe is several dazzling career moves ahead of him, or Moe has adroitly changed the subject.

"With the harvest over, Tony brings Leora back to Frisco, all the hot spots in his fancy convertible, sweeps her off her feet. But someone spots him. Follows him, and spells it out: How Tony bumped his head, see, he'd gotten stewed one night and, driving too fast down by the bay, plowed into some poor working stiff just off the late shift on the wharf. Fatal accident. And one witness only: this sonuvabitch, lowlife, blackmailer. He warns Tony if he don't pay, he'll wind up in Alcatraz—or worse. Tony has no recollection of the accident, but he's so sure the stinker's lying, he refuses to fork over a nickel. But the pressure of hiding it from the girl starts to build, plus his family thinks this rustic Sonoma gal's not good enough for Tony—they're pushing him to marry some iceberg from the Social Register. Tension's giving Tony these throbbing headaches, plus he's tortured by terrifying memories—fragments, really. Gets so bad, one night Leora hops in his car to buy some medicine at an all-night pharmacy. What she don't know, the blackmailer cut the brakes. Girl winds up in the hospital, paralyzed below the waist. Now she can't be a real wife to Tony—but she can't go home and stomp grapes, either. What does she do? Drags herself to the window and throws herself to her death. You with me?"

Hayden checks his watch. "Yes, but . . . Moe, I gotta—"

"After the funeral, Tony agrees to marry Miss Snob Hill. 'Cept the night before the wedding, he resolves to hunt down the blackmailer, shoot him dead, avenge Leora. But when he points the gun on this scum, the awful truth Tony's suppressed comes flooding back—*why* he got stewed that night, *who* he ran down, the blackmailer's identity! Worst of all, his fiancée's role in it all.

Suffice it to say, there's stock fraud, union corruption on Fisherman's wharf, an adulterous love triangle, the works. Instead of pulling the trigger, Tony turns around, walks into a police station, and confesses. Rats out his rat buddies, but like a *mensch:* he puts his own name at the top of the list. It's a final scene every movie mogul will sit up and notice. All across America, men will applaud, and women will weep—"

"Moe, look, I really have to—"

"Book's called *Meet Fate Among the Clouds*. Superior's betting it's a best-seller. They've assigned their top scenarists to adapt the material. I firmly believe that by the time it's on the production schedule you'll be seasoned enough to play Tony."

"I'll be in the service by then, Moe, on my way to—"

"Maybe you will, kid, and maybe you won't. Meantime it's *Tony* I'm talking about! Not Tony's business partner, not the rookie cop he confesses to. This is *Dark Victory,* it's *Kings Row,* it's *Petrified Forest*. But you don't get the part if you don't play ball—and you don't play ball if you're not a team player. So Harl, y'gotta ask yourself: *Am I a team player?*"

· 3 ·

The Man You Love
to Hate

The middle-aged German shifted, uneasy, in his chair. It was a large quilted leather chair, plenty of room, one could almost toss and turn in a chair this size. (An insomniac like Dieter Seife was always looking for a comfortable place to toss and turn.) But big as it was, the chair was only in proportion to the desk opposite—a prodigy, a leviathan of a desk, truly something preternatural. Yet so far as Seife saw, the main effect of the huge, heroic desk was to reduce the desk's owner.

Further reduce him, for he was already stooped, scooped-out, and, perhaps only a decade older than Dieter, prematurely aged.

He was Arthur Lustig, founder and president of Superior Pictures. And Dieter Seife's employer. No, more than Seife's employer, as Chester Dowling was wont to remind Seife, his *benefactor,* more accurately: the refugee director knew he was a charity case, of a sort all the studios had taken on nowadays. Heinrich Mann was over at Warner's, under contract as a screenwriter at a hundred-fifty a week. Bargain basement price for the

Blue Angel author, but Seife knew Heinrich was happy to get it. And then there was Seife's former colleague Detlef Sierck, also under contract—at Columbia—as a writer, though he'd directed *La Habanera* among other big films for Ufa, and countless prestige theatrical productions as well. But Sierck, too, was just scraping by here in Hollywood, glad for any leftovers tossed him by these crude and scrappy self-made Movie Magnates with their peculiar brand of noblesse oblige.

Lustig had been staring down at his notes for an excruciating length of time, seeming to have trouble focusing on the typed words. Finally he looked up at Seife. "So you want to make a Technicolor picture here at Superior?" he asked.

Indeed, Seife had approached Dowling with this request after his second picture for the studio, *The Gal from Altoona,* was unexpectedly held over at the Roxy and did fifty thousand in Chicago in a single week. And now, it appeared, Dowling had seen fit to broach the matter with Lustig.

"It isn't so much a question of the color process, or the color stock," Seife responded, carefully parsing Lustig's query, aware that his limbs and torso were twisting on the big chair. Writhing was alright, Seife decided, just so long as he didn't appear to be blatantly *cowering.* "Whether the picture is made using the three-strip Technicolor method or even the TruColor technique for that matter, is not for me the central—"

"What is it then, *Dieter?*" Lustig interrupted, drumming gnarled fingers on the maple expanse of that immense, immaculate, and nearly empty desk.

Before answering, Seife paused to reflect whether Arthur Lustig had just, shall one say, overpronounced his name, emphasizing its foreignness? And if Seife hadn't imagined this, well, then, what on earth did Lustig mean by it?

"A question of, as I would put it, values," Seife said.

Lustig, if he'd heard Seife at all, registered bemusement at best. Which made Seife doubt himself—his command of the language, anyway—at once. "Is that the word I'm precisely searching for, then, Mr. Lustig? 'Values'?"

"Damned if I know," Lustig answered, looking distracted. Indeed, he'd become aware of faint scurrying sounds. "Is it?"

Seife squirmed some more. Maybe if he squirmed enough—and not until then—would Lustig help him get to the point of this meeting. "I have made two black-and-white pictures for the studio, sir—for which I am most grateful. To have had the opportunity," he added, torturously. One must, he knew, pay obeisance to one's master. Not that Seife had had a master back in Berlin, *Gott Seir dank*. Bosses, of course—masters, never. But he'd read about such figures in the English-language novels he'd begun to devour in hopes of grasping the language—starting the day the Gestapo arrested one of his actors for improvising a Nazi joke in some second-rate Düsseldorf cabaret.

Dickens's works, for instance, were filled with these mysterious patrons, backstage sponsors who'd settle several hundred pounds a year on some orphan who might otherwise starve or freeze to death but who was barred by some obscure codicil from ever learning his savior's name. And if the orphan were, somehow, to penetrate the mystery of his patron's identity, that stipend would instantly vanish. To Dieter, *this* was the perfect system: one in which the humiliation of accepting desperately needed funds was to some small degree softened by veils of secrecy, intrigue, romance, mystery.

But there was nothing mysterious about Lustig, alas. His beneficence, his paternalism—so prominently displayed—surely masked the fact that every dollar paid, every favor proffered, was meticulously noted in a ledger somewhere. Seife found himself speculating: Was this, finally, a Jewish characteristic? Was this, and not the Crucifixion, the real reason why mankind loathed the Jews down through the ages?

"It's true you have made us two successful little pictures," came Lustig's reply. "But let me ask. In Germany, did you, ever . . . ?" He trailed off and gestured, ambiguously.

"Did I, ever . . . ?" Dieter wondered. What self-indulgence, what depredations, was the man hinting at? And then, reacting to Lustig's bland expression, he realized that the question was a simple one. "*Ach!* Make color films? *Selbstverständlich!*"

Not until Lustig winced did Seife realize he'd spat out some German—and not the most musical German word, either. "Of course," he amended, flushing. "In fact, not just color, but large productions, big budgets—fantasy sequences, musical numbers, special effects like George Méliès." No, too foreign, too esoteric a reference. Seife scrambled for another name, something quintessentially American. "Epic crowd sequences with bravura cross-cutting, like David Wark Griffith." A glaze of boredom coated Lustig's eyes—plainly visible even behind the thick round lenses. Yet, like an aging Mercedes sedan with worn-through brake pads, Seife couldn't quite come to a dead stop. "At Ufa," he blathered on, self-consciously, "I was entrusted with a very big property, titled—you wouldn't have heard of it, but it's a well-known tale in Germany, a sort of fairy tale—no, more a retelling of the Scheherazade myth, the Scheherazade figure in my version a seductress called Gretchen, hauntingly played by black-haired beauty Sybille Schmitz."

Lustig reached under his desk—to itch his privates, most likely—but Seife half-expected a trapdoor to open beneath his chair, dumping him into the steaming open sewer he imagined ran beneath the studio, directly below him. Seife quickly came to the point: "So, yes, the simple answer is *yes*."

"I see." Lustig drummed his fingertips again—then his knuckles (which Seife saw were quite raw) for variety. It was almost as though there was something on his desktop—something invisible, and moving, and multiplying—that Lustig was trying to crush with those gnarled, nervous fingertips. Suddenly the drumming stopped and Lustig leaned forward. "Listen, Dieter," he began, "it's not out of the question I'd give you a crack at one of our A projects. I have confidence in your abilities, your track record." Then, either out of politeness or a need to postpone the dropping of the second shoe (was that the colloquialism?), he asked, "This German title, Scheherazade-Gretchen thing, can we get our hands on a print? I want to run it for my daughter, Ellie—she likes all that crazy kinda stuff."

Seife shifted again, this time involuntarily. "I don't think it was ever released in this country, the tone wouldn't necessarily . . . travel," he hedged. "If you're very curious, I suppose you could cable Berlin, but . . . Ufa, as you may know, is now overrun with Nazis, the whole outfit, what a shame . . ."

Lustig, nodding, made a small, obligatory what-a-shame noise, low in his throat, as Seife elaborated:

"But it was a great success back home in thirty-eight. Afterward, I was given a nickname by the critics." He started to say the name, *Der Phantasie Erz–* Then stopped himself before finishing: no more German, today. "The, ah, approximate translation would be, let us say, something on the order of 'Yarn Spinner'?"

Lustig looked vexed again. So Dieter offered a more pleasing translation: " 'The Man of Make-Believe.' Perhaps comparable to your Mr. Disney. Anyway, it is how I was known."

Lustig's lips twitched. Was it the name "Disney" that had caused this? Because Disney was no Jew lover? Or had Lustig screened the new film *Bambi,* and was he still mourning the doe's murdered mother? Implausible though it seemed, Lustig now looked on the brink of tears. But instead of breaking down, the mercurial tycoon was standing. As though the point of all that power and money was to gain the privilege of shifting moods on a whim.

"Look, Chester and I have talked this over. We're willing to entrust you with one of our big titles. We *want* you for it." He squeezed shut his eyes, and mouthed two words. Seife couldn't be sure; he thought the words were "greedy" and "grasping." "But we don't want you using that name of yours—Dieter Seife—let's face it, in this atmosphere, clouds of war blotting the sun, the great American public—and you *will* reach a large segment of the public with this title, I guarantee—the great majority of that public"—Lustig's arms energetically swinging now, ironically he resembled a tin-pot dictator—"might experience feelings of disgust, revulsion at a name they'd naturally associate with—sorry to say this but it's incontrovertible, Mr. Seife, a name they'll associate with—"

"Germany."

"You got it." Lustig sat again, winded.

"But it is my name," Seife reminded him, without conviction.

"Yeah, and what kind of a name is it, anyway?" Lustig mused. " 'Seife.' It's an ugly little name, isn't it?"

Seife was not a pretty name, true—but then what German name *was* pretty? Farben? Siemens? Mauser? Schmeiser?

" 'Seife' means 'soap,' in fact."

Lustig coughed.

Seife shrugged. "Well, you know, *your* name in German means 'merrily,' " he informed his patron. And wanted to add, At least Mr. Soap keeps himself clean. Whereas *you,* Mr. Merrily, all I have seen you do today is grimace, wince, and mumble.

Instead, perhaps a tad cheekily, Seife joked: "So! Would Superior Pictures prefer to bill me as Dieter Soap?"

Lustig merely looked down at his notes and began, unaccountably, to read, in a crisp, businesslike monotone: "Raymond Bannister, Clifton Brown, William Grayson, Jennings Powell, Seymour Langston, Aaron Carr."

Then looked up at Seife—who wondered aloud: "A list of my competitors? Other directors under contract to Superior, contending for this—important A title we've discussed?"

Lustig shook his head. "Other names we've cooked up. For you, Dieter. Better ones. For the coming, all-important phase of your American career." He waved the sheet. "You want me to read 'em through again, one more time, before you decide?"

Seife was too stunned to feel offended, or hurt. " 'Decide'? But I . . . Mr. Lustig, may I say . . . Having been Dieter Seife for—well, some forty-odd years . . . though I respect the efforts of the studio to help me to . . . fit in here . . . I am most concerned that, were I to try to take a new and different name, *now,* during my adjustment period . . . this might precipitate a split. Of an interior, psychic sort. Do you see? A potentially catastrophic split of the personality, not unlike *The Strange Case of Dr. Jekyll and Mr. Hyde.*"

Lustig snorted. "Jekyll and Hyde? Don't be a schmuck."

"No, I mean it, Mr. Lustig. It is a fear." He thought of mentioning Dr. Ridley, and Ridley's theory of the bifurcated ego, then thought better of it. "It is a specific fear of the Germanic soul, perhaps. You are familiar with the concept of the doppelgänger? We believe—some of us do, anyhow—that each man has his double, you see, somewhere, walking the face of the earth. And if at any given time we should have the bad fortune to encounter that double, then one of us must swiftly perish."

Lustig nodded—in sympathy, Seife thought at first. "Not a bad idea for a horror picture, psychologic horror—something for Jacques Tourneur, but he's over at RKO, so the hell with it." Lustig abruptly leaned forward again, with that list of names. "Take these home with you, Dieter, you don't mind, and look 'em over. We're flexible: if you come up with something better . . ."

He waved the sheet.

Seife shook his head. "I must go now, Mr. Lustig. I will think about all that we have discussed." And the director stood, straightening to his full height—suddenly a stiff-backed Prussian cavalry officer. He had not taken the sheet of paper.

Lustig was about to jump up and force the names into Seife's hand, but Seife's ramrod posture—so much prouder than his own—kept the mogul pinned to his seat. Meantime Seife turned on his heels (did he click them first?) to leave the office, passing Adele, Lustig's longtime executive secretary, here to tell the boss: "Harley Hayden."

Lustig didn't respond. He was focused on his door as it shut with a muffled thump. Then: "Did you see how that SOB practically goose-stepped his way out of my office? If he ever washes up as a director, he can go after Von Stroheim's roles as 'the man you love to hate'—or better yet, wing back to Berlin and get himself a *real* job again with the New German Order—"

"Harley," Adele reminded.

Lustig handed her the list of studio-generated names.

"Make a couple of carbons, save one for my file, mail one to

Dieter Seife's home address and one to his agent. Then shoot a
wire to his lawyer: New name by Monday, or he's out."

Adele took the sheet of paper. Once again: "Harley?"

Then she flinched as Lustig belatedly leapt from his chair and
raged at the closed door: "So long as those hooligan Huns are
rampaging across Europe, there is no way in hell this studio will
release an A picture directed by somebody named *Dieter!*"

Out in the reception area—so vast, Seife hadn't yet reached the
exit—the director stopped, stunned. Out here, the tirade, only
half audible, sounded like the declaration of a lunatic.

Simultaneously a tall, young, rangy actor who'd been waiting
for an audience now rose, unfazed. Apparently these flare-ups
were nothing new to him, and not remotely terrifying. All that the
muffled rant seemed to signify to Harley was that the previous
meeting had now officially adjourned.

Seife paused, noting Hayden's lanky physique, his athlete's
grace—and the incongruous element of those glasses, which
would have lent an intellectual air if Harley had possessed even a
faint trace of intellectuality. But the actor's presence seemed entirely physical, and pleasingly so. Hayden would make a convincing screen cowboy, or soldier, or baseball player.

For his part, Harley wondered who this big, perturbed-seeming,
older (than Harley, by a good fifteen years) fellow might be. First,
he must be foreign: the tweed jacket and corduroy pants were not
just ridiculously heavy for Southern California, they were *wrong*.
Here was a man either unfamiliar with L.A.'s balmy climate or
perversely unwilling to enjoy it.

As Hayden entered Lustig's office, Seife spoke to Adele: "That
good-looking boy. An actor?"

Adele nodded. With a touch of the maternal: "Harley Hayden.
Nice kid. Hails from Ohio. He's under contract here."

Seife made note of the double initial, believed by some to be a sign of good luck. At the very least, the alliteration sounded good, and looked wonderful on posters and marquees.

Lustig collapsed into his quilted leather chair. Finally the spiders had stopped scurrying across his desk. He'd scared them off with his hands, his fingertips—if only he'd brought his whip to work today—and now he composed himself, awaiting Harley's entrance. Jokes like "the son-in-law also rises" wafted through his mind. Actually just the one joke, and not original—a gibe coined for use against David Selznick, son-in-law of Louis Mayer. Not only was the gibe unfair (Selznick knew his onions) but it wasn't even strictly applicable here: Hayden hadn't yet married Lustig's daughter.

Though nuptials, it must be said, seemed inevitable.

Lustig still wasn't sure how he felt about the suitor of his only child, his little girl. "My boyish, goyish albatross" were the words in his head when Lustig thought of Harley. He was even ambivalent about the clean bill of health that scummy bottom-feeder gave Hayden—what kind of young fellow (especially one as handsome as Harley) wouldn't sow his wild oats in this brothel of a town? Why was this two-bit, would-be leading man such a monk? It irked Lustig. An entry or two on the sin side of Harley's ledger would help balance the books, if only a bit.

Hayden entered, striving to break the ice with a breezy, "Little hot under the collar, there, A.L.?"

Lustig disliked A.L., found it not nearly as convincing as L.B. or B.P., to name two famously initialed studio heads, but never mind. "Just doing a little acting," he claimed, with a sly grin. "How can I be around you actors all the time and not give it a try myself?" And then, before Hayden could start in with whatever litany of complaints he'd rehearsed, the boss preempted him: "I got a call from the stage, young man. Said you couldn't shoot the scene, said you got light-headed?"

"Not light-headed, Mr. Lustig, the point is I can't—"

"I see by this morning's production report, you were running around outside, overdressed. That is a *messhugah* thing to do, but let's not get into that now. When you're light-headed, you should always bend over with your head between your knees, let the blood flow into your brain. Did you try that, Harley?"

Hayden shook his head. "Sir, what's happened is I—"

"Or it may not be a matter of blood flow, but rather a vitamin deficiency. Do you eat balanced meals, young man?"

As Hayden defended his diet, Lustig stopped listening; this freed him to think about that fancy-pants Pasadena headshrinker and his theories about the ego, and depression . . . when Lustig knew full well that Depression meant breadlines and dust bowls and bad musicals; whereas, what plagued Lustig were *spiders,* hordes of furry black arachnids that infested his beach house and crowded his desk but finally, inevitably, wound up inside his head, crawling across his very consciousness.

"I'm fine—physically. I just can't perform up to snuff under these circumstances. New pages every day. Changes slipped under my trailer door. And I don't mean changes like 'Mikey cuts his chute loose.' I'm talking about 'Mikey turns to Johnny—who's suddenly spouting in *Deutsch!*' I'm talking about, 'Mikey's best pal Johnny is a goddamned Nazi spy!'"

Lustig gazed up at his future (barring a tragic death in combat, not inconceivable, and not necessarily more than a few months out) son-in-law. "Well, there's a war on, and these are the realities.

Spies, saboteurs, plants, impostors, double agents, fifth columnists, traitors of all stripes. . . . The less said the less dead. Keep it
under your Stetson." He shrugged.

"I know there are spies. Of course there are spies. I read the
L.A. Times. I listen to Lippmann. But in *Perilous Passage,* there
weren't spies, not as recently as *yesterday* . . . In yesterday's script
pages, Johnny was just the same as Mikey—a scared Midwestern
farmboy behind enemy lines. He got wounded by Jerry shrapnel,
or strafed by a Messerschmitt, I forget now. But today it turns out
Johnny's a graduate of Hamburg High? My first thought was,
some other picture's pages got mixed up in Mimeo. But acting
under these conditions feels like an earthquake under my feet
while I'm trying to do a Roseland foxtrot." Harley took a breath.
"Every day I drive to the set, feeling like I need to pull over on
Sunset and *puke my guts up.*"

Even as he made this assertion, Harley silently registered that
his route to the set took him nowhere near Sunset. But Lustig
didn't pull out a Los Angeles street map as Harley had feared for
a moment; he was recalling a conversation with Rabbi Rosten in
which the rabbi had made this surprising statement: Jewish elders
held that a long life was a lucky thing, but to never have been
born was luckiest of all. Weighing this, Lustig drummed the fingertips and knuckles of both hands. He switched extremities,
tapped the toes of his wingtips. His desk, solid as a sarcophagus,
muffled the sound. "Fact of the matter, we had to rush into production before the script was finished. And not, as you might assume, because we agreed to loan out Ann Sheridan next month
for . . ." What was the name of the project? Presently the title and
cast (and the fee for loaning out Sheridan, which he kept to himself) came back to him: "*Navy Blues,* some nonsense with Jack

Oakie, Jack Carson, Jack Haley, and Jackie Gleason—a regular jack-*off*." He smiled at Hayden, but Hayden was waiting for the rest. "No, because you'd received your induction notice. So! *Perilous Passage* has to be in the can before you get called up for active duty. Let's work backward, okay? Take a look at my calendar."

His desk calendar: an oversized, leather-bound item that Lustig now wedged and wrestled sideways, so Hayden could look on as the studio head counted the days, weeks, months, in reverse.

Adopting the slow, simplified, patient tone he used with "talent," Lustig elaborated, "The script would've been all set to go . . . here." His finger landed on a certain Tuesday. "But if we'd waited till that date to start principal photography, by the time the cameras were ready to record Mikey's big homecoming scene . . ."—that same finger moved down three rows—"you'd be in your barracks, pompadour snipped off, second week of basic training. And that wouldn't do, would it now?"

Hayden stared at the calendar, fiddled with his horn-rims, and said nothing.

"So, in view of the fact that you'd received your induction notice, Superior opted to jump in and start shooting before we'd dotted every last *i*, crossed every *t* in our script. For my money, it's the lesser of two evils. Shit, did you read in the trades, where Metro replaced Hank Fonda when he went into the navy? Big picture, big payday, I'd hate to pull a stunt like that on you, Harley. Why, I almost think of you as family."

Hayden was still gazing down at the days, weeks, and months. In a soft, almost delicate voice, he said, "I know what you mean. You're like a father to me, A.L. Almost more than my own natural father. Hardly ever saw him. He was a night watchman."

The spiders were marching in formation, burrowing into Lustig's brain. He closed his eyes, silently intoning the two words—"greedy," "grasping"—that sometimes dispersed them. Then popped his eyes open again. "So tell me what it is specifically that you have such a big problem with, in the new script pages?"

"Only that I don't believe a word, A.L.! We've spent forty minutes of precious screen time establishing that Johnny's an A1, all-American kid from Topeka, Kansas." He looked up from the calendar, tilting and shaking his head. "*And* he's my best pal; we sailed overseas together. Now what kind of soldier would I be— I'll rephrase that, what kind of *nincompoop*—not to see that this guy was a ringer? If he really was, that is?"

"For all you know," Lustig countered, "it'll turn out Johnny-the-*Nazi* is really the ringer. A double twist, get me?" Something new, some more powerful presence certain to overwhelm the spiders, was coming into focus as Hayden looked blankly at Lustig, who explained it another way: "All the Heil Hitlering's just a— whaddyacallit? A ruse." Lustig distractedly answered his own question. He'd noticed a creature decidedly not a spider, standing in the wings of his awareness.

Hayden nodded, excited. "Okay, okay, I get it! Johnny studied German at Kansas State. Now he's pulling the wool over Jerry's eyes. And after they haul me—Mikey—off to a labor camp, Johnny's gonna come get me, all dressed up like a Storm Trooper . . . and free not just me, but a whole bunch of rowdy Yank and Limey POWs, am I getting warm here, sir?"

"Pretty darn warm, alright," Lustig replied, beginning to see the outline, then the form, then the face, of a woman.

"And while we're behind enemy lines, we'll perpetrate some mischief?" Harley persisted. "Make saps of the Krauts, stick it right up the Führer's fanny, show Goebbels he's got no balls?"

"Slow down." Lustig laughed. "You're starting to sound like one of your scripts, least before the Breen boys louse it up." He grabbed his phone. "Get me Story." Then smiled at Hayden, not because he was enjoying Hayden's company today, or relished issuing commandments to the Story Department, but because the woman in his mind's eye had now stepped from the shadows and revealed herself as the former Theodosia Goodman of Cincinnati, renamed Theda Bara by the Fox Studio's publicity people.

"I'm ringing you right through, Mr. Lustig," came Adele's voice, with pleasing promptness.

"Consider the matter taken care of," Lustig assured Harley, waiting for his call to connect. And then, in case the actor missed his cue, Lustig dismissed him with a fluttering hand.

As soon as Hayden was gone, he spoke again into the phone. "Adele? Hang up on Story."

"Right away, Mr. Lustig."

"And then come in with your steno pad."

"Right away, Mr. Lustig."

Lustig hung up and sat back, envisioning Theda Bara (who drank in the mogul with blazingly black, kohl-ringed eyes, then leapt catlike onto his conveniently vast and empty desktop, arched her back, and flared her nostrils silent-movie style).

"I've got a notion for a horror picture," Lustig announced, reluctantly banishing Bara as Adele strode in with her fountain pen and pad. "But a classy horror, perfect for Jacques Tourneur, if Legal can get him out of his RKO contract on a suspend-and-extend." Swiveling his chair to face the window, Lustig began, sonorous, "A guy walks down the street and spots another fellow, sitting in a restaurant, who looks just like him! Amazing, right? See, turns out everyone's born with a double, a counterpart of some kind, somewhere in the world." He watched out his window as Harley ambled from the Administration Building with that graceful (Lustig had to admit) almost animal stride. The "animal" association brought with it an unwelcome image of Hayden atop his daughter, humping away (notwithstanding the conclusions of the fly-by-night fucker Dowling had hired).

Lustig swiveled back, suddenly, dramatically, to face his secretary. "Turns *out*," he added, "that once you *see* your double, one of you will die—inside of twenty-four hours!"

Adele gasped.

Lustig leaned forward and patted her knee. He hadn't meant to frighten his secretary. To Lustig, as the "double" idea had begun to percolate, there was nothing frightening about it—and maybe that was a problem the Story boys would have to lick.

Already Lustig found himself musing about his own double, feeling a pang of envy toward the man, wherever he might be living and whatever he might be doing. Even if his counterpart were a lowly farmer, back in the old country—*especially* if he were a farmer, Lustig decided—it was almost certain he would not have suffered a blow the likes of which Lustig had endured. For Lustig's was a blow that snuck in with good fortune like a plague-bearing rodent in the belly of a luxury liner. The sort of blow that was custom-made for the greedy, grasping, and altogether ridiculous greenhorn Lustig knew himself to be.

"Mr. Lustig?"

On the other hand, he also knew that this farmer (perhaps Lustig was picturing his dairy-farmer father, left behind in the old country) had never heard of Theda Bara, had no access to a print of her first and finest film, *A Fool There Was,* and would never know the ecstasies of sitting alone in a private screening room and watching the vamp lead Victor Benoit to his doom.

"Mr. Lustig."

"What?" He'd finally noted that Adele was addressing him.

"Mr. Lustig? My knee."

Lustig looked down. Indeed, he was still patting Adele's lump-ish knee. Mortified, he pulled back his hand as though from a hot spike. Then swiveled again, back to the window. Staring out, Lustig murmured, "Get me Projection," to break the silence and minimize their mutual embarrassment.

Anyway he'd need a projectionist tonight to keep the black furry spiders from swarming Laughlin Park. For Ellie would be off, gamboling with Harley Hayden—though not before padding up silently behind him as he sat at the table, taking his supper. She would place her hands on his shoulders, and that would be his cue to lean back his head and, doing his best Victor Benoit, accuse her: "You have ruined me, you devil, and now you discard me!"

And Ellie (doing her Bara, which was immeasurably better than his Benoit) would vamp as she stroked his cheek: "Kiss me, my Fool!"

Lustig would kiss her. When she was gone, and it was just the movie tycoon and his projectionist, the screen would roll down and the living room lights dim, and the old film would unspool. And Lustig would feel safe, for a little while, in the flickering dark.

· 4 ·

Dieter Seife

Seife awoke late. Without looking at the clock, he could sense it was already well after ten. He lay in bed, on his back, still wearing padded eyeshades. With his left hand, he felt for the radio on his nightstand. It was a chunky wooden Philco, big and powerful, and it pulled in stations up and down the coast. Seife turned the knob: Nelson Eddy, Fibber McGee, Hedda Hopper, Hopalong Cassidy—and a song, a new Tin Pan Alley atrocity featuring some insanely optimistic youth, warbling:

"Goodbye, Mama, I'm off to Yokohama . . ."

Seife turned the knob again, and found the news. War news (the only news). "Nazi troops are on the advance," a lurid voice insisted. But details were vague: the Hun was, apparently, at the gates of India, nearing Cairo, and taking Stalingrad, all—improbably, apocalyptically—at once. And the Nippos? Not only were they swarming Malaya and the Solomon Islands, but the Yellow Peril was right here in Southern California, *at this very moment walking freely down the streets of Los Angeles!*

This came as a mild shock to Seife, who'd never noticed anyone but the occasional elderly tourist from Topeka walking down the streets of his adopted city, lost. All others drove.

Seife wrenched the knob once more, and he was sorry: The Andrews Sisters (those three desperately plain women; Seife had known prettier, daintier transvestites in Bavaria) were singing that diabolical song about "the apple tree"—as though the Home Front were some elysian paradise, not a hell of cloying sentiment and close harmony. Seife snapped off the Philco.

And lay stiff as a mummy in his purple silk pajamas, eyes still blind courtesy of those quilted eyeshades, loath to let the California sun invade his consciousness with its banal, insistent heat and light.

It was always like this for Dieter when he found himself between movies. Back in Berlin he would sink into despair with unaccountable quickness—a mere week after locking his last picture, say. How fast the exhilaration would fade: whether or not the film was previewing well, whether or not he was still carrying on with the beautiful leading lady (or, when the leading lady was unavailable, the willing wardrobe mistress).

Here he had none of those erotic distractions. In the way of females, Seife had only Hilda (formerly Hilde) Biederhof, the efficient cleaning woman who came in on Mondays, Wednesdays, and Fridays. Hilda was certainly no object of lust, but she was of German extraction and was, with her bun and bustling manner, a familiar and comforting type to the deracinated director. A rosy-cheeked figure out of Central Casting, mother of two burly young men, buxom she was, and sexless. Seife enjoyed watching her wash, and clean, and cook his sauerbraten.

But *ach,* she would not be in today: today was Saturday. Seife had nothing on his calendar, no script to read, no notes to make, no thumbnail storyboards to sketch or revise. He couldn't even drive to his office at Superior and sit behind his desk, feigning activity: due to wartime security concerns, the lot was shut down on weekends. And so the day yawned before Seife with a terrifying sun-bleached blankness.

Still wearing his eyeshades, he stumbled out of bed to the bathroom. And pissed into the toilet, only missing the bowl for the initial blast, which soaked the carpeting (Hilda's problem).

He tore off his eyeshades and flung them away. The sun—though he was ready for it, or thought he was—stabbed at his pupils. Seife blinked and cringed like Max Schreck in *Nosferatu,* pulling off his pajamas as he staggered out of the bathroom to the walk-in closet, where all his heavy suits hung. Though he couldn't sit in his office today, Dieter decided, he would don one of those suits and at least simulate the sensation of "developing" a project as he paced his porch, feeling "purposeful," feeling "busy," sipping schnapps.

Or perhaps he would sort through his notes, the battered books he'd thought to bring with him from Germany (lugging his collection across an ocean and a continent) in which he'd jotted outlines, sketches, characters, and synopses for potential films over the past decade. Most of these, he knew, were obsolete in this curious subtropic, having been hatched under the chilly aegis of Goebbels and the Universum-Film Aktiengesellschaft. The majority of these highly stylized, wholly artificial, and—no, not National Socialist, but distinctly Central European, scenarios— well, like Scheherazade, they simply wouldn't (as he'd alerted Lustig) *travel.*

So perhaps, instead, Seife would spend the day bringing his diary up to date. Musings, anecdotes, and mundane weekly reminders that, one hoped, might someday be published—or, at least, pored over by film archivists and students. Seife would be remembered by history, he was certain; maybe only a footnote, maybe a whole chapter, depending on the kindness of men like Lustig. In any case, he was part of a wave, a movement, one of a number of distinguished émigrés, such fugitives from the Führer as the Mann brothers, Stravinsky, Schoenberg, Ophuls—brilliant men caught up in stupid circumstances. And there were more, some of them neighbors here in the parched canyons above Hollywood. Werfel was just down Los Tilos with his famous, once-delectable wife, Alma. (Although a faded drunk now, and legendary slut, Alma, compared to the She-Wolf, was an angel, saint, Mother Mary herself. Seife had foolishly flirted with her, six years ago, a world ago, at the Berlin premiere of *Das Schönheits-fleckchen,* all about the Marquise de Pompadour, the first German color picture, a garish bore.)

Seife chose a dark tweed outfit, despite clear evidence that the temperature would rise to the mideighties by early afternoon. The discomfort he would feel, all day, was part of his plan of self-abnegation, a carefully calibrated suffering that would stand in for actual work. After lacing on a pair of heavy oxfords, Seife lumbered downstairs toward the dark, messy study, where his notebooks and diaries were stored. But in the hallway, he stopped. His problem with the diaries was that he could not sit down with them to make a simple entry without encountering earlier, angrier entries to do with the She-Wolf and her Cub. (And not *that* much earlier: just last month, Seife had drunkenly scrawled another rambling diatribe—in crazy, incoherent Germlish.) The thought of adding even an innocuous item in the same volume where such nutty screeds were scratched made his bowels constrict. He swiveled, stiffly, as his plan changed: he would fix himself a simple breakfast of coffee and a kaiser roll, instead.

As he entered his kitchen, Seife could see out onto the street, where the mailman had just stuffed several envelopes into his mailbox. Immediately he was seized with curiosity—letters, for Seife! From whom? But pride kept him from striding out to retrieve his mail in sight of the mailman, who would probably snicker at this poor refugee with his nose pressed to the window-pane, pining for news from home, photos of loved ones, schmaltzy avowals of fidelity and yearning.

He forced himself to consume breakfast, first, brewing his coffee till it was tar black, chewing each bite of roll a dozen times. Only then did he venture outside, peering up the road first to be sure the mailman had vanished down Castilian Drive.

Seife pulled out the envelopes. In fact there were just two. One from Superior Pictures. A check? Seife's heart rate accelerated slightly—till he remembered that, here, checks came only from the Directors Guild, or his agency—and even so, the studio had given him no work in several months. He tore open the envelope, regardless. And stared—blankly, at first.

It was a list of names, neatly typed: Raymond Bannister, Clifton Brown, William Grayson, Jennings Powell. All familiar, yet he knew he'd never met any of these men. And then it came back to him: of course, these were the proposed names—the "better" names—that Lustig had suggested, to remake the expatriate German into a new, more palatable (or at least less repellent) A-list director.

Simultaneously, as though in a movie, there was music in the air—dire, dramatic music, perfect underscore for the upsetting moment. At first this seemed so natural (that is, so cinematic) that Seife didn't question it: he just eagerly went with the mood, feeling darker and more aggrieved, but then, beginning to wonder from whence these notes were wafting, he recalled that just down the hill stood the Hollywood Bowl. And that Leopold Stokowski was scheduled to conduct the Hollywood Bowl Orchestra tonight. Something, Dieter recalled with revulsion, to do with both Mussorgsky and Mickey Mouse. Undoubtedly Seife—*ja,* lucky Dieter—was hearing a rehearsal.

Leopold Stokowski. Seife was told, once, by someone at least moderately reliable, that the white-haired ham was born Leo Stokes in England, and had made his name Polish and polysyllabic in an effort to sound *distingué.*

In short, the *very opposite* of what Lustig was trying to foist on Dieter Seife! In a petulant rage, Dieter tore up the list of ridiculously phony pseudo-Anglo-sounding names. Then, having nowhere to put the resultant scraps, he awkwardly stuffed them into his suit-coat pocket. Took a deep breath, hoping to calm his nerves—then turned his attention to the other envelope, lightweight airmail paper, Generalissimo Franco stamp.

The address was handwritten in carefully characterless block letters. Conspicuously, no return address. The postmark, Seife saw—and he did not venture to open the envelope until he'd examined all this—was Madrid.

Seife meant to slit open the envelope with a fingernail but his hand was shaking a bit, and he raggedly tore the thin paper instead. But he didn't unfurl the letter—not here, outside the house, in full view of nosy Los Tilos Drive. Instead he retreated back into the kitchen, closed the screen door, unfolded the sheet, and scanned the note.

It was written in English, using the same phony lettering style—like a child trying to imitate a typewriter. It read:

My Dear Friend:

You have been working hard. Now you could well use a vacation. The Hacienda Hotel on Harney Street in San Diego would be a very good place to relax. It is conveniently near the Greyhound Station. Spend a pleasant weekend and forget all your troubles, would be our kind suggestion. Everything is arranged so that you may relax.

All best wishes, your friend, Mr. Smith

P.S. If the room becomes stuffy, as it very well may, then please open a window, or else use the fan.

Seife read the letter twice. He lingered on the postscript with its doggerel rhythms, the beat scheme reminiscent of a cute children's poem he'd committed to memory early in his efforts to learn English, " 'Twas the Night Before Christmas."

Then he repeated Hacienda Hotel, Harney Street, and considered the significance of that name—Hacienda—cropping up again. Coincidence, a doubling, a portent of some kind?

When he was certain he'd memorized each word, he ripped up the sheet, just as he'd shredded Lustig's list of names, though not in a rage this time.

Then Seife strode into the powder room and flushed away all the irritating (letter one) and incriminating (letter two) confetti.

The day had become a very different proposition: instead of contriving to kill it with stratagems and distractions, Seife now had to move quickly—and with focus—so as not to lose more time. In the next moment he was back upstairs in his bedroom, hauling an overnight bag off the upper shelf of his closet while muttering, "Raymond Bannister, Clifton Brown . . ."

With the bag open on the bed, Seife threw in a change of underwear, a fresh undershirt, a pair of socks. The bare minimum of toiletries—toothbrush, tooth powder, comb.

Then he was backing from the garage in his oversized Buick Roadmaster that Superior leased him at—so Business Affairs assured him—a bargain rate. Perhaps. But the Buick was a beast, guzzling gasoline that was increasingly hard to come by (thanks, one must concede, to the success of German subs in the Atlantic sinking Uncle Sam's tankers). Therefore Seife confined his driving to his daily (if lately pointless) commute to the lot. Except for the rarest of occasions—like this one.

Seife took La Brea down the hill. *La brea,* he was told, meant "the tar" in Spanish, and the name suited the street, with its sticky black surface that seemed, in the heat, to melt under his wheels, maybe one day to swallow him *and* his dinosaur-sized car. Heading west on Sunset, Seife found himself wishing, as he maneuvered this boat on wheels, that he was driving one of those sleek Volkswagens, scaled to the human form, truly one of Hitler's (and, to be fair, Ferdinand Porsche's) bright ideas.

Forty minutes' worth of dizzying curves later, Seife reached the Pacific Coast Highway. He rolled down his window, breathed in the cool and salty air. This was the only time and place the California sun was aesthetically acceptable to Seife: when it dazzled and dappled the ocean's surface, kitschy though the effect might be.

Seife blanked his mind as he drove to San Diego, responding instinctively to traffic but thinking of nothing—not the past with all its injustices and gripes nor the discontented present. It was the most peaceful way to spend four hours and, perhaps, the safest. For Seife could grow emotional when his memory roamed from Bavaria to Berlin, then to the weeks of hide-and-seek in Paris, followed by the slippery and terrifying Pyrenees, and finally Los Angeles. In the grip of that emotion, the director might be tempted to do what, as an audience member, he'd likely deride as *melodrama:* steer directly into the path of an oncoming truck, perhaps—or, no, far better, drive off a cliff into the ocean below. Though, it must be admitted, there were no such cliffs between Los Angeles and San Diego. One would have to motor north, to Big Sur, for such a grand finale.

Presently Seife reached the outskirts of the dull border town— it was late afternoon, but the heat was holding—and he stopped at an Esso station to refill the greedy bastard Buick.

Here he asked the attendant for directions to the Hacienda Hotel, on Harney Street. "That's down in Old Town," the polite boy told Dieter, while puzzling over the accent, trying to place it: friend or foe? He described the quickest route, Dieter thanked him, paid him, tipped him a quarter. And saw, in the rearview as he pulled back out, that the young man was watching him, watching his Buick, perhaps noting the license plate number. Seife was sure he could read the words behind the gas station attendant's eyes: *Kraut, Jerry, Fritz, saboteur . . .*

He left his auto with the hotel valet, but didn't check in right away. Maybe it was that inquisitive attendant. In any case, Seife thought he'd stroll this Old Town, stretch his legs—and make sure no one was watching his movements.

Old Town was a small, dusty, dingy affair—several mock-Mexican plazas stuffed with curio shops and outdoor stands hawking jewelry and pottery, plus cheap restaurants crowded with beer-swilling sailors on shore leave with their brazen V-girl dates. So far as Seife could tell, the area had at one time—not so long ago, less than a century?—been just another sleepy Mexican business district. Which the American conquerors had seized, and reworked, and improved, not satisfied till they'd made it entirely false, turned an old town into an Old Town.

Retreating from the falsity, the forced revelry, Dieter found himself in a small, overgrown cemetery dense with crumbling tombstones. Something in the air here—or was it the damp, freshly shoveled earth?—made his eyes water. Haunted as he already was, by ghosts (though Seife's were living), he continued on to the Bazaar del Mundo. As it was a Saturday, raspa dancers swirled, hopped, and stomped across the square, and the garish colors made Seife's eyes ache. He bought a burrito and a glass of lukewarm lemon soda, consumed both standing, then crossed the trolley tracks back to the Hacienda Hotel. By now Seife was satisfied he'd neither been followed nor observed.

The Hacienda was just like any Southwestern-style, sun-bleached, adobe-walled structure between Santa Barbara and Ensenada. Dieter entered the lobby, at best two degrees cooler than outdoors, and asked the desk clerk whether there was a reservation for Mr. Seife. He was far from certain there would be. Yet the clerk brightened at Seife's name: "We've been waiting for you, sir. Pablo will show you to your room."

Dieter now followed a humpbacked porter up an outdoor stair. He found another quarter in his pants pocket and gave it to the poor malformed man in exchange for a room key. As Seife entered the stale-smelling room, he saw that his overnight bag had already been brought up and was resting at the foot of the bed. Then he looked around. The room appeared empty, except for the few sticks of inferior furniture.

Seife tried the desk drawer first. It was empty. So was the

drawer by the nightstand—even Gideon had passed up this place. That left the dresser: Seife found nothing but a dry, curled length of flypaper here. Next, he felt under the pillows on the bed.

Where else? The bathroom. But the medicine chest was empty and nothing was taped to the inside of the water tank.

Seife retreated to the center of the crummy little room. Had he been hoodwinked? If so, to what end? A lone trumpet, blasting mariachi music, brought him over to the window. He could hear the weepy repetitive chorus of "Cielito Lindo" but couldn't see much from here, only an alley where chicken fat and chicken feathers from the kitchen were dumped.

Standing at the window, he was reminded of that two-line postscript in this morning's letter about opening a window. Just as in the child's Christmas verse he'd memorized: "Away to the window he flew like a flash, tore open the shutters and threw up the sash . . ."

Of course: the inner sill is where it's hidden! Feeling foolish, Seife forced open the seriously out-of-plumb sash. And found . . . numerous paint chips, and several desiccated mosquitoes.

Again he backed to the middle of the room, reciting, in singsong, the letter's last line: "*Open a window, or else use the fan.*"

Then he slapped his forehead while muttering, "*Dumm,* Dieter."

The electric ceiling fan was suspended directly above his head. Actually, four feet above, too high to reach. And there was no chair in the room—doubtless to discourage guests from hanging themselves. Seife flipped the fan switch. As it creaked then whirred to life, a metallic object flew off the upper surface of one its wooden blades and hit the wall with a dull *ping.*

Seife knelt to retrieve it: a rusted locker key, the number twenty-seven painted on it. A line in the letter's main body, about a convenient Greyhound Station, returned to him. In a moment he'd grabbed his overnight bag and was descending the outdoor stairs, two at a time.

Seife stopped at the front desk to settle up.

"Was the room not to your liking?" asked the clerk—who appeared, or purported to appear, astonished at the idea.

"In fact, the accommodations were superb," Seife replied, then handed over the valet stub for his Buick.

Ten minutes later he stood in the Market Street bus station in Central San Diego. The lockers, several rows' worth, were at the far end, by the restrooms. Seife crossed slowly and—he hoped—casually, head lowered, watching the shadows of other men nearby, waiting for those shadows to stretch and shift in his direction. The shadows stayed still. There was a sharp urine stench as Dieter reached his row, and found locker 27. The key fit right in, though the old lock needed some encouragement.

Seife paused a moment before opening the locker door. One more small surge of panic, that this was all a frame-up, as they said in the excitable States. That a horde of FBI agents—led by Hoover himself—would pop out of some hiding place, waving guns and shouting "Drop it, Kraut! Walk away from that carton!" Maybe they were all concealed in the men's room. But no, the stink was too terrible—no one could lie in wait in that cesspool, not even the most hardened lawmen.

Seife took a breath, regained his equanimity, and swung open the locker door. Within, a large box was tightly wedged. Cardboard, reinforced with packing tape. Dieter had to wrestle it free, his grunts drowned out by the P.A.'s announcement of a bus leaving for Anaheim, with stops in Mission Viejo and Tustin. The *heim* in Anaheim caught Seife's attention: *home,* in his mother tongue.

Fitting, that he was fighting to extract this particular package while *heim* blared over the loudspeaker. Now it was out—and, *verdammt,* but it was heavy, too, even heavier than Seife had expected; he almost dropped the package on the linoleum-tile floor. Then, straining, he carried it out to the parking lot.

One last look around reassured Seife he was still unobserved, anonymous, safe. He unlocked and opened the trunk, revealing his bag, which lay open. The package *just* fit inside the nearly empty canvas valise, leaving the slightest ugly bulge as Seife snapped it shut. Then he got behind the wheel of his Roadmaster.

Seife made the trip back to Hollywood without stopping. He felt he'd spent the four hours in a tingly trance of anticipation. Los Tilos was dark and cool—it was after nine P.M.—as he pulled back into his driveway, shut the garage door behind him, then popped the trunk and lugged the overnight bag inside his house via the garage.

He'd run out so fast, he'd forgotten to leave a single bulb burning. Now he lowered the bag with one hand while feeling along the cool plaster foyer wall with the other, till he found the light switch. The chandelier blazed on brightly.

Seife let out a shout. Standing beneath the chandelier, in its pretty pool of crystal-refracted light, was a small, compact man with thinning red hair carefully combed, natty in a finely tailored gabardine suit. He remained impassive, wearing a half smile, as though posing for a photo. Then he extended a manicured hand. "Mr. Seife. I'd begun to worry."

Seife knew this man, but was so startled to see him—here, in his home, uninvited—that he couldn't get his right arm to obey, and give a handshake. Instead he could only mutter, "Dr. Ridley. How did you—what did you—how did you get in here?"

Dr. Ridley's half smile stretched to three-quarters. "You left the kitchen door unlocked. It's a wonder you didn't leave it wide open. You were in such terrible haste to do your—errand, Mr. Seife, were you not? Now remember how we've talked about those moods of yours, how you must master them or they can pose a grave danger to you?" He spoke mildly, soothingly, as though to a neurotic wife, or someone dangerous as Dillinger.

Seife made an effort to master his current mood. Though he couldn't match Dr. Ridley's calm, he came close: "Sorry, but I didn't expect you, Doctor. Is there something you need from me?"

Jasper Ridley's smile vanished. He nodded, down, at Dieter's feet.

"The contents of that bag," he said, referring to the valise Seife realized he was now trying to conceal, stupidly, by standing in front of it. "I believe, quite firmly, that the bag's contents should right away be transferred to my possession, for reasons I trust you'll understand."

"But—Dr. Ridley—are you sure," Seife stammered, stalling, "you even know what the valise contains?" He knelt down, and elaborately undid the stays and locks and opened his luggage. "I myself, as you can see—" He removed the homely, asymmetrically bulging cardboard box, with all its packing tape intact. "I myself have not even had the opportunity to open it, to examine it." He stood again and shrugged, all innocence.

Dr. Ridley scowled. "We're not little boys in short pants, playing a game, now, are we? No, we're two adult men, and we both ought to behave as such." But Seife gazed at the floor like a scolded child as the doctor concluded, "It's for *your* benefit, Dieter, that anything you do with this . . . *material,* be done under my supervision. For I am trained in these matters, and you, sir, are decidedly not."

Seife looked up again, his face flushed, about to protest—when he heard two knocks on his front door. Seife stiffened, Dr. Ridley relaxed. He strolled to the door and opened it, wide enough to allow two burly men in white lab coats to sidle in.

One positioned himself in front of Seife and folded his tree-trunk arms across his chest while the other squatted and hefted the heavy box.

"Thank you, Tommy. Take it out to the car."

Seife could only—barely—peer around the heavyset man who was guarding him as Tommy carried the precious carton outside to Dr. Ridley's Lincoln Continental.

"I'll phone you first thing Monday morning," promised Dr. Ridley as he glided, backward, to the door. "We'll discuss the proper time to examine the . . . material. In private, together. As you're well aware, I have the appropriate facilities for doing so—comfortably, securely."

Then the doctor and his twin bodybuilder bodyguards were gone. Seife stood listening to the Lincoln's powerful purr as it disappeared down Los Tilos. Soon everything went quiet but for the howl of a coyote higher up in the canyon.

And a more mournful howl, right here in the house, from deep in Dieter Seife's own throat.

From *Daily Variety*

Hayden Found 4-F; Erstwhile Grappler
Sidelined by College Injury

Actor Harley Hayden, 26, currently under a 3-pic-per-year contract at Superior Pictures, has been found unable to serve in the U.S. Armed Forces due to a hamstring injury suffered seven years ago as a star wrestler at Ohio State University. Thesp—known on the team as "Flip" for an ability to turn the tables on opponents just when they thought they'd pinned him—released this statement through the studio: "Uncle Sam may keep me stateside, but he won't keep me out of this war, you watch."

. 5 .

Fumpoo

Way down in Culver City, they were building Tokyo and Berlin and bits of North Africa—the same studio artisans who had constructed perfect models of Tara and Manderley and Xanadu were now constructing superdetailed, 1:100-scale versions of the Mitsubishi plant and Berchtesgaden and French Morocco out of scrap balsa and rubber and tin. There's a line in "Brother, Can You Spare a Dime": *Once I built a tower, up to the sun* . . . Well now the tower was eight inches tall, tops, and these ingenious old union fellas from the Camera Department at Columbia had mounted a rig above it, and upside-down dolly tracks, and they were pushing in the camera, overhead, to give an authentic bombardier's-eye view of the Nip, the Hun, and the Wop below.

Then they'd take this footage and intercut it with close-ups of a guy in the cockpit shouting orders. It didn't have to be Olivier or Barrymore—just a kid who looked more or less of draft age and knew how to yell, *"Get set back there, boys, we're going in!"*

without sounding like some sissy from Manhattan, or an amateur they'd recruited out of summer stock. Because that's how desperate things could get in forty-two, that's how slim the pickings were, with half of Hollywood in olive drab.

It was Hal Roach's studio, in Culver, and the clever boys who labored here nicknamed it Fort Roach. Or maybe that was sour grapes, because there was a war on, and instead of humping it at Guadalcanal or Wake, these poor feebs with flat feet, ruptured spleens, and punctured eardrums were stuck grinding out training films for the First Motion Picture Unit, a.k.a. "Fumpoo."

And do you think it was easy, sitting in some cramped cockpit made of composition board, candy glass, and spit, as six tubby grips rocked you back and forth to simulate turbulent flight and motion, while shouting—as though you meant it: "Strap in tight, boys, we're flying in low to stun the Hun"?

That's where pros like Harley Hayden came in handy. Here was a guy who *looked* every inch the part of GI Joe—no, GI Joe might've been modeled after Harley himself; they could've dubbed the soldiers Harleys like they called life vests Mae Wests. But despite being born the Platonic ideal of our brave men, Harley was hobbled, Harley was 4-F, Harley was fucked.

"We could probably swoop in and blast the Jerries before they knew what hit 'em. But what's the hurry, let's just cruise around awhile—keep our eyes open for a break in the clouds."

That was Harley Hayden in *How to Make a Sour Kraut*.

"Gather round, men! Now don't ignore the five telltale symptoms of foot fungus. Here, let me roll down my sock . . ."

Harley Hayden in *Rah Rah Jungle Rot*.

"These old torpedo bombers may be obsolete—but they're the best we got and we can use 'em to make Yamamoto wag the fantails of his Jap carriers, keep the Nips from getting any planes off!"

And *cut.*

They were just finishing up *Let's Keep Those Zeros at Zero.* Grunting, the grips set down Hayden's cockpit. The biggest of them let out a wet fart. The smallest laughed. Hayden squinted out through the glass—they'd have to find another way to manufacture the stuff, sugar was scarce now—at the dim face behind the camera. "How was that, Pete?"

Pete, a creator of short subjects who prior to Pearl Harbor was generally deemed incapable of directing traffic, stared back at Harley for a moment as though he hadn't heard him. And maybe he hadn't. Harley was loath to appear like he was trying to teach Pete his job, but . . . hell . . . "You want another? Same reading for safety, or something different?"

Pete grimaced. "Why don't you get your head out of that medieval torture chamber, Har," he suggested. "The old brain must be starting to bake."

Hayden ducked free of the cockpit contraption, only then realizing what a vile little sweatbox he'd been stuck inside. He pushed his wilted pompadour back off his forehead. A smear of makeup stuck to his palm. "Next setup or one more?"

Pete nodded Hayden over to a corner of the cramped stage. "Thing is, Har, the corporal says he wants to see you soon as we get this shot in the can. Which, for my money, we got. Only allowed to print one take these days anyhow, so . . ." He checked his watch. Nodded to the first (and only) assistant director.

"That's a wrap!" the A.D. cried.

Instantly, cables were dragged clear. Harley nearly lost his footing as the ground shifted beneath him.

"Well, good," he told Pete, "because I want to see the corporal." Actually he hadn't, not till that moment, anyway—but now, as soon as he said it, Hayden really did want to see the corporal, and badly.

. . .

"Who writes these damned scripts anyway?"

Hayden sat opposite the corporal, a.k.a. Walter Grube, on leave for the duration from his position as head of physical production at Disney. Corporal Grube was one of the few Fort Roach enlistees who wore his uniform (which he'd taken to his Rodeo Drive tailor to have the waistline let out, the shoulders padded) on a daily basis, and kept it crisp, pressed, perfect.

"Glad you asked me, Hayden. We call 'em the Flying Typers." Grube tilted back his chair and chuckled.

Hayden managed a polite but curdled smile. "Seems to me," he said, "that the Flying Typers are just that: typers, not writers, who've mostly copied old combat scripts, cut out all the good parts, and pasted in every single chestnut, end to end. Do you have any idea how tough it is, Corporal, to sell a line that's worn-out as a . . ." He groped for a suitable comparison.

"Five-buck hoor?" Grube supplied. And then, before Harley could continue, Grube began to rhapsodize: "Sure, I know it's tough, but you make it look so easy! That's the key to your success, Hayden—throw you a curveball, throw you a sinker, you swing, you connect, *crack,* just like that, out of the ballpark!"

Harley waved this away. "Only 'cause I've had some practice, that's how come I can tell when a line of dialogue isn't working." He demonstrated, woodenly shouting a line from the recently wrapped *Don't Be a Sap, It's a Jap*: "*Say, that's no P-40. That's a Nip Zero painted to look like . . .*" Harley shrugged. "When it feels like sawdust in your mouth."

"Ah, c'mon, seems to me like you got some magical gift for stepping in between raindrops! Hayden, you're a pip!"

The poetry was contrived, evoking mediocre Hallmark and subpar Saroyan, but Harley hung in there, figuring Grube would come around to the point sometime before the Axis surrendered.

"I tell you, it's just a matter of doing it enough—and god knows I've made my share of pictures, this past year, at Superior," Harley responded, to keep the conversation flowing.

The corporal poured out whiskey from a thermos into two Dixie cups. He pushed one across the desk. "Yeah, you sure have, Harley, haven't you? Not necessarily the starring roles, but there's nobody better for the best friend, the sidekick, the fifth wheel, the second banana . . ."

Hayden sipped the cheap warm whiskey, which went down his throat like liquid sandpaper. "Not having the burden of carrying the picture yet," he croaked, "I guess it's given me a good opportunity to watch, to learn, to study and hone my craft—if that doesn't sound too highfalutin." Harley's cheeks bloomed red from embarrassment, the booze, maybe both.

"You? Highfalutin?" The corporal refreshed their Dixie cups, and bolted his. "You got the common touch, Hayden, in everything you do. And that's something can't be faked. Take it from me."

Hayden nodded, enjoying the hooch's effects—for one thing, his tongue felt amusingly cotton-coated. "Thanks, Corporal, but let's cut the soft soap—you're making me blush like a jane."

Corporal Grube nodded. "Alright, Harley, no more beating around the bush. I think we've been circling the problem here, you and me, so why don't we talk turkey, like a coupla men?"

Hayden had an eerie sense of where this was heading. *Find the mirth.* He laughed—an octave higher than normal.

The corporal reached for his thermos again. "Refill?"

Hayden shook his head. But Corporal Grube brought the thermos to his Dixie cup, still half-full. Though Hayden put his hand over the cup, the corporal started to pour anyhow, so Hayden spread his fingers, let the whiskey level rise an inch.

"We get mail. Scads of it, actually."

"Mail?" Hayden sucked at the soggy rim of the Dixie cup. "Fan mail, y'mean?" His nerves subsided a tad. Hayden's fan mail customarily ran ten to one in favor. Well, maybe not quite so high, since news of the 4-F.

"*Just* like fan mail," Grube smiled, faintly patronizing. "But not from bobby-soxers in Boston or Kansas City, these letters come to us from Fort Benning, Fort Bragg—from our boys in boot camp, see."

Hayden sipped more whiskey, despite the now-disconcerting sensation that his tongue was steadily thickening, like an unaccountably aroused sex organ. "And?"

"And the problem, in a word, is *exposure*." Having said the word, the corporal sat back, giving the word some room, some time alone.

Harley swallowed. "Is there a water fountain in the building?" He was parched.

The corporal held up an index finger: hang on a sec. "What we're hearing, Harley, is the boys'll be watching our flight training footage, they'll be paying close attention, memorizing the terrain, the tail fin of the Messerschmitt, the markings of the Zero, making mental notes, then we intercut a shot of *you* in the bomb bay, or the cockpit, and it . . . *violates the reality*. On account of the . . . *recognition factor*. See, Hayden, here's a case where all that stupendous, god-given *star quality* you've got is working against you, and that's it in a nutshell."

Harley could hear him, but Grube was a blur—not just on account of the hooch, but because Harley'd shoved his glasses in his trouser pocket twenty minutes earlier, for the martini shot. Now he fished them out, balanced them on his nose, straightened them out, then returned the corporal's steady gaze. And softly enunciated a single syllable—all he was capable of just now:

"Wow."

Corporal Grube nodded: yep, wow. Then, as his gaze fixed on a patch of Hayden's cheek bare of makeup, the news got worse:

"Sometimes they start laughing."

"They what?"

"The boys. They start to guffaw, sometimes. That's what we've been hearing. Y'know, 'Look, Tommy, it's Errol Flynn's good pal, what's-his-name!' Or, 'Hey, Jim, ain't that Joan Leslie's next-door neighbor?'"

Before he had to endure one more lousy impression of a chortling GI, Harley stood. "What're you suggesting, Walter?"

Corporal Grube, who hadn't been called Walter by anyone but his wife in at least six months, set down his whiskey and lit a cigar. He didn't offer Harley one. "I'm afraid the First Motion Picture Unit requires fresh talent, actors with skills approaching the equal of yours but without faces quite so darn familiar from the the-ayters. I'm thinking of fellas on the order of Arthur Kennedy, or Van Heflin—you know, like that."

"Then I'm dismissed?" Harley, dizzy, reached down to the desk for support. His hand landed beside his Dixie cup. With his other hand he raised the cup and polished off the hooch.

"Don't be sore, I'm setting you free—free to go back to making your patriotic features! That's priority work, Hayden—not me saying it, comes straight from the War Production Board!"

Hayden started to giggle. "What's worse than a SNAFU, but not as bad as a FUBAR?" he asked the uncomprehending corporal.

"I dunno, Harl, but—"

"A Fumpoo!" Hayden crushed the empty Dixie cup in his palm. "My patriotic features, so-called," he murmured. Then, voice rising: "They're swill, they're bunk, they're . . ." He swayed. Grube edged his chair back, in case Hayden toppled over. "D'you know the last five quickie-cheapies we churned out—last *five*—were all to do with spies, German spies sneaking around the West, plotting to dynamite the Golden Gate Bridge, plotting to dynamite the Hoover Dam, plotting to dynamite every goddamn national treasure 'cept the one goddamn national treasure deserves to be dynamited."

"And that would be?"

"Hollywood." Hayden yanked off his horn-rims and violently rubbed his eyes.

"You don't mean that. Sit down," the corporal urged, half-heartedly. Hayden stayed standing. He shook his head.

"I mean it! The stuff is crud. On every streetcar there's a German Bundist with a stick of TNT under his hat. Baloney!"

Corporal Grube shot back: "For your information, a U-boat off Long Island managed to land eight Nazi saboteurs on our shores who, thanks to the unstinting efforts of law enforcement, got nabbed pronto—or don't you read the daily papers?"

"Well let's make a movie about *that*!" Harley shouted, stamping a foot. "Not some cardboard concoction with Lorre as a Nippo—when he isn't playing a Nazi—or Flynn winning the battle of Burma with one hand tied behind his back. I joined up at Fort Roach to get away from all that claptrap and cliché, help the war effort by doing something—something—something real!"

Corporal Grube clucked his tongue. "This isn't real, either, m'boy. Get that through your thick skull. It's just a whole lotta celluloid, that's all, see?" He stood, walked to the open door and closed it. Then confided: "We gotta do our bit here, gotta play ball with the Production Board so's they don't take away *all* our film stock, 'stead of just a third of it. Not to mention the razor blades we use to *cut* our pictures, the nails we need to build our sets. Dammit, Hayden, sets are in such short supply, Hitch is shooting a picture that takes place in New Jersey, and the sorry bastard actually has to go *shoot* in Jersey!"

"Helluva thing," Hayden offered.

Grube clapped Hayden on the back. "It's all about boosting morale," he reminded the younger man. "Bet your spy-pic 'swill' does more to buoy spirits and win this war than the next *ten* shorts we crank out: ditch-and-live, when to pull your rip cord, crash-land safely in the desert, proper way to interrogate an enemy airman, and wake me when it's over."

Hayden blinked at the corporal. "Is there a pay phone in the building?"

Corporal Grube flung the door open again. "Straight down the hall to your left."

Harley fed a nickel into the phone, then dialed. The phone rang and rang—and rang, maybe fifty times before he hung up.

Then he changed, in what passed for a dressing room, back into mufti, first rinsing off the rest of his makeup and resculpting his pompadour into something a star could wear in public.

Stepping outside, Harley was startled to find it already dark. Fort Roach's windows were coated in blackout paint, and one could easily lose track of the day. And now it was night.

Where was Eleanor? Was she, could she be . . . it pained Harley to even hypothesize . . . out, with that other fellow?

And not entirely parenthetically, where was Harley's car?

He was drunk, dismayed, disoriented, and the parking lot was—for national security reasons—dimly lit. Hayden loped unsteadily down the aisles of gleaming coupes and sedans and road-sters, hunting for his Plymouth. It wasn't where he could've sworn he'd left it. Maybe, Hayden thought with grim humor, some Axis spy with a top-secret invisibility serum had moved his automobile to another row: to confuse, delay, and demoralize a decent American.

Then he found his car. Whether it was where he'd parked it or not didn't much matter. What mattered was steering it out of here without dinging some brass hat's LaSalle.

Harley must've managed, because in the next moment he was speeding east on Venice Boulevard, muttering, "I'm free, I been set free." He almost believed this, he almost felt fine. At La Cienega he headed north. He'd never driven while tight before, and was astounded at the control, and confidence, that a little whiskey conferred. Traffic seemed to part for him.

At Sunset, Hayden caught the lights of the Trocadero in his rearview—and, on impulse, did a squealing U-turn as dramatic as anything Cagney'd ever managed hightailing it from the coppers. Harley knew he wasn't quite dressed for a night out at the Troc, but he hoped no one would stop him from having a quick one at the bar and using the phone. He pulled up to the Mexican valet.

"I'll just be fifteen minutes."

Inside, he spotted Myrna Loy in a booth with her hubby, Arthur Hornblow. Loy, in a plunging silk nothing, was sipping a sidecar, evidently on hiatus from her war bond and Red Cross work. Hornblow looked elegant, if stiff, in his tux. Harley wondered whether he should breeze over and say hi to Arthur, who'd been an executive producer on *Phi Beta Caper,* but he didn't know Myrna and he wasn't wearing a monkey suit and . . .

"Flip?" A hand tapping his shoulder pad. Harley turned.

"Tough break, huh, Flip?" An older, soigné man stood there:

thin William Powell mustache, slicked hair, the gimlet gaze of a Warner Bros. gangster. Before Harley could register amazement at the speed with which bad news spreads—even in the small town of Los Angeles, and smaller town of Hollywood—the stranger explained: "I mean your classification—old wrestling injury and all."

Hayden shrugged. "Gotta roll with the punches."

The man with the mustache nodded, all the while looking Harley up and down. "Good height for a boxer, speaking of . . . Little tall to be a wrestler, though, huh?"

Hayden took a step back, abashed at the hard scrutiny, but smiling still. "Lot tall, I guess."

He started to turn around again, now dying for a drink (Ellie could wait, Hayden had a powerful craving to wet his whistle) when Mr. Mustache added, "Should've given *us* the story. We'd have played it way bigger than *Variety*. Played the sympathy angle—kid wants to serve Uncle Sam, kid gets slapped in puss by heartless draft board."

Then, off Hayden's increasing bewilderment, Mustache stuck out a damp hand. "Billy Wilkerson. *Hollywood Reporter*."

Feeling back on solid ground, Harley joked, "I know it."

Wilkerson's eyes sparkled. "I own it." He pumped Hayden's hand, and Hayden pumped back. Then Wilkerson transferred his grip to the actor's biceps, lightly spun him like a dance partner, and escorted Harley two yards to the bar. Here, grandly: "Give the boy one of whatever he wants." Harley started, out of habit, to demur, but Wilkerson assured him, "No skin off my ass, Flip— y'see, I own this joint as well."

With that, Wilkerson skipped off to welcome Norma Shearer as she walked in with a man who wasn't Irving Thalberg. Now Shearer's husband was relatively youthful, but this fellow was younger by a decade at least, and far more fit than the famously neurasthenic producer. Meanwhile Hayden (brooding that faithlessness was rampant, contagious, unchecked this season) found himself alone with the bartender and the inevitable, unsettling question: "What's your pleasure?"

An hour later, Harley stood by the hatcheck stand at Ciro's, on another pay phone, listening again to Ellie's line ring and ring. One could easily lose oneself in the repeated rings, which hypnotically blended with the music, a live swing band blaring in the background, but wasn't it a little early for "Milkman, Keep Those Bottles Quiet"?

The hatcheck girl threw a pitying glance at Harley, who figured he must look like some poor sucker who ought to be surgically separated from the receiver. Perhaps she didn't recognize him with the horn-rims. He took off his glasses, stuck them in a pocket. She still looked sorry for him, but less distinctly now. With reluctance, Hayden hung up.

Wilkerson owned Ciro's as well, and he'd called ahead, instructing the house to stand Harley to another scotch and water. Hayden sat sipping at a tiny round table, alone, watching the parade of blurry starlets and fuzzy producers and smudged executives—like some flashy fantasy sequence in which the camera crew had neglected to properly pull focus. But hell, it was easier to survive Ciro's this way: the busy baroque decor became a bright, cozy cave.

Occasionally he'd hear a "Hi there, Harley" or "Care to join us, Hayden?" Nobody called him Flip, thank god. After draining his drink he got up to leave, bumping into one of those many colorful moving splotches as he navigated toward the door.

"He made me spill my highball," a woman's voice whined.

"Watch where you're going," a man's voice blustered. Harley didn't want a fight (or else he knew he was too soused to win one). He kept walking, toward the honking horns on Sunset. Just before he stepped outside, Harley heard, muttered, behind him: "He's just a contract player for that dirty Jew Lustig."

At least that's what he thought he heard, though with the car horns and a chorus of "We're the Janes Who Make the Planes" from inside the club, Hayden wouldn't have testified to it under oath. But he was also pretty sure he recognized the Tasmanian accent of the man who'd said it, the clipped, conceited tones of a movie star who'd stolen most of Harley's few good lines from a picture he'd lensed last year, about two GIs trapped behind enemy lines, a thin slice of tripe called *Perilous Passage*.

Harley turned back around, swinging. His fist made contact with Errol Flynn's jaw. Actually he wasn't sure it *was* Errol Flynn, but he was certain that Flynn (or not-Flynn) had shifted his weight fast enough to deflect most of the impact of Harley's fist and that Flynn (or not-Flynn) impressively counterpunched.

Harley staggered back, and probably would have slammed his keister on the sidewalk if several concerned citizens hadn't caught him. Moreover, he would've charged back at Flynn (*was* it Flynn or something worse, an Errol Flynn type?) had those same citizens not held him fast, dragging Harley away while the valet pulled up with his Plymouth and he was bundled into it, after mumbling "Yeah" to the obligatory "Say, y'sure you can drive?"

Within minutes he was at the third—and final—nightspot in the Wilkerson collection, the jewel in Billy's crown, the Mocambo, deliriously done up south-of-the-border style, the horn blasts and cymbal splashes of the big band onstage competing with the squawks of parrots and macaws fluttering above.

"Pay phone," Hayden muttered, as he searched for same. He found one on the wall by the men's room, and then after a while he located a last nickel in his trouser pocket. Harley was about to dial Ellie's number when the cacophony suddenly subsided, the lights in the club dramatically dimmed, a cool blue spot came up onstage, and a girl began singing:

"I can make the angels cry, make the devil turn and run . . ."

The setting for the song, which Harley'd never heard before, was a slow, bluesy, agonizingly erotic vamp. The chanteuse was dark and slinky, and her voice wrapped around the melody like a silk dress cinched at the waist. Hayden let go of the telephone receiver and drifted toward the nearest banquette from which there was an unobstructed view.

"I can make a statue sigh, make a soldier drop his gun . . ."

Hayden had no doubt that all the foregoing claims were true. He squinted at the girl who swayed, almost imperceptibly, at her mike stand, elegant as a willow in a cool summer breeze.

"But when it comes to soothing you with my touch . . ."

With a start, Hayden placed the voice: it was Eleanor! Right here! The Mocambo's chanteuse was his girl!

He patted his suit—every pocket—for his horn-rims, just to be sure, but, dammit, he'd left his glasses in the Plymouth, tossed on the passenger seat. So he'd have to squint, straining to see her features a little sharper, as she wound up the verse:

"I can only do so much . . ."

"No," Harley blurted, because *this* disclaimer was certainly *not* true, but he was shushed by rapt patrons all around him.

The chanteuse waited through the instrumental break, gyrating her slim hips, head thrown partway back and eyes squeezed closed like an opium fiend savoring her high.

Harley tried to move closer, closer to Ellie. But the floor was crowded with busy waitresses dressed like Carmen Miranda and as pretty as Rita Hayworth in her earlier more "exotic" (fuller eyebrows, lower hairline, browner skin) Margarita Cansino incarnation. They frowned at him, shook their tropical headdresses, pushed him back up the aisle.

Harley called out to the singer: "Ellie! Eleanor!"

"Shut your trap," one customer prompted.

"Put a sock in it," another proposed.

Harley ignored them. "Honey, I've been phoning, trying to reach—" as the singer slid, suggestively, into Verse Two:

I'll be here to break your fall down below on bended knee
If you need me to stand tall, if you need to lean on me . . .

Harley found himself starting to swoon, the way the girls swooned for Gable, for Frankie. But *his* swoon wasn't one of sexual hysteria; rather, it was a deeper, dizzying realization that one's lover led a second, secret life, moreover, a second, secret *public* life—on top of it, a second, secret public life singing to perfect strangers about her and Harley's (heretofore private) love affair and all of its purported problems.

"But when it comes to being your lover and not your crutch I can only do so much."

Which was wounding! Unless she was singing of her romance with . . . that other guy . . . which was *more* wounding! Either way, why did all these chic drunkards have to hear about it?

Except, wait, as Hayden's pickled brain made its sluggish, soggy connections, he remembered that Ellie's hair was black, and he could see well enough that the woman onstage had an auburn mane, and that she was taller and rather more svelte than his beloved, whose figure might best be described as voluptuous.

In short, it struck Hayden all at once that he was the victim of a delusion. A mirage, caused by scotch—and, maybe, that stunning haymaker delivered by Mr. Flynn (or an equally objectionable lookalike). Or maybe he'd never really mistaken this nightclub singer for Ellie; maybe all he was, was lonely, and playing a harmless game with himself? In any case, as the truth dawned, Harley felt a profound, glandular—cellular—need to get out of the Mocambo and find her: his elusive Eleanor, who *wasn't* here—and who, therefore, was someplace else. But where?

And (Hayden couldn't help but wonder again) with *whom*?

There was applause, at Harley's back, as he left the club. Was it for the chanteuse—or for him, leaving?

Hayden may not have been sober, but he *felt* sober for the first time in hours as he darted expertly from lane to lane, between Studies and Mercs, even though he'd forgotten to stick his glasses back on his face! Driving blind, but effortlessly, and with precision! The goddamned stupid army didn't know what it was missing. He'd heard (and told) all the jokes about movie star GIs winning the war single-handed. Well, tonight, Hayden knew he could do it, for real! All he'd wanted was a chance!

He reached Laughlin Park's south gate in fifteen minutes. Grabbed the phone, to dial the gate code. Which was . . . what? A four-digit date out of history. That he couldn't quite think of, right now. And then, like that, he thought of it. And tried it—the Battle of Hastings. 1-0-6-6. Nothing happened.

Try again, 'nother date . . . Okay . . . The War of 1812, of course! Harley dialed the numbers, 1-8-1-2. More Big Nothing.

He was annoyed now. What other dates were there? Then it hit him—of course, the code was all about *America* . . . Moron!

Whistling the tune to *Columbus sailed the ocean blue,* Harley dialed 1-4-9-2 and waited for the gate arm to rise. But there was no response. He slammed down the receiver and started to curse. Hayden had learned a lot of curses—from the Greeks at Ohio State, from the grips and gaffers on the back lot—but he'd never used them himself till now. He was astounded—even as he muttered the words, in a foul sequence—at how many curses he'd picked up over the years, and how fluent he was.

Then a light appeared from behind Harley, splashing off his mirror onto his face. Swell, he thought, a policeman. He'd spend the night in the pokey on a Drunk and Disorderly. Billy Wilkerson would get his Harley Hayden story after all.

He straightened up, smoothed his suit coat, looked alert.

"Harley?"

Turning, he saw Eleanor in her tan Caddy convertible. She pulled in next to the Plymouth.

"Ellie?" He tried to look calm, reasonable, even suave—not like a guy who'd been drinking and driving and swearing and brawling and hallucinating. "Where've you been all night?"

Ellie gave him an odd look. "At school. Studying. You knew that. I stay late every Wednesday night."

Wednesday night! How could this be a Wednesday night? Wednesday nights were so tame, and dull, Harley was always in bed by ten on Wednesday nights learning tomorrow's lines and here it was nearly twelve and he'd learned nothing.

"Studying? This late?"

Ellie took a second look. Harley wasn't joking, he was jealous! She laughed. "You think I'm seeing someone else?"

"I know you are." He went silent as did Ellie, too stunned to refute him. Then he forced out: "A few months ago there was some guy following us around, fairly good-looking, older guy—"

"You mean to the movies, miniature golf, the soda shop?"

Spoken so innocently, yet here was an implicit admission of guilt! My god! His girl—

"To everywhere. I didn't say anything, just hoped he'd go away. Which he did—so I thought. Figured he was some swain you met at UCLA. Teaching assistant maybe? Junior professor?"

Ellie smiled. "Cop. Ex-cop, actually. Disgraced," she added, for drama. Then: "Father hired him to follow us around and make sure you weren't some—I don't know, some . . . beast?"

Harley stayed silent. Stared at his dashboard.

Ellie leaned out her window. "Hon, I'm with you all the way, up or down, make or break." It was a line from a movie Ellie'd seen, a line she'd remembered, stored away, hoping to use some-day. What better time? "How could you ever think—"

"Guess I *wasn't* thinking." Hayden tugged off his glasses. "Least not thinking *straight*. I've been driving around, stopping at the hot spots, behaving like a . . . beast."

She smiled, indulgent. "You could've come to the library. I'd have left you a pass at the LeConte gate. But the stacks're so dusty, and last time you went you sneezed for days, don't you re-memb . . ." Eleanor trailed off. "Harley, you're crying."

He was, but he hadn't realized till she saw it, said it—which made him even sadder, made more hot tears spill down his cheeks. "Ellie, I'm sorry, just . . . Oh, honey, I've tried so hard here in Hollywood, to do my best, to *be* my best, but . . . Maybe I'm just not cut out for this . . . this crazy . . . this town, it's too . . . for a regular Ohio boy, it's too darned—"

"Sweetie." Eleanor sprang out of her convertible, lithe and ath-letic as Hepburn. Now she was sitting beside Hayden, stroking his strong, trembling jaw. Since he'd been turned down by the draft board—as relieved as Eleanor felt about that—she knew her beau was feeling shaky and unsure. And of course she understood. But thank god he had his work with the First Motion Picture Unit to keep him involved in the war effort. And now she voiced this aloud, to remind Harley that all wasn't lost: "I know you had your heart set on serving, but your training films, don't forget how crucial a service *they* are to our—"

A hoarse sob exploded out of Hayden's throat. Then he tried to speak, but his lips just smacked together wetly.

"What? Harley? Has something hap—"

"They threw me out on my ear. They . . . fired me, El!" he gasped, and snot ran from his nose.

She'd never seen him like this. She could smell booze on his breath, which would account for some of it, as Harley wasn't a drinker and undoubtedly couldn't handle hard liquor but . . .

"*Fired* you? For what possible—"

Behind them, a car beeped. Ellie stuck her head out the window as the driver shouted, "What's wrong with you young people? Can't you see you're blocking the whole—"

"Go peel an eel!" Ellie yelled at the driver, whose mouth fell open almost comically, and who then backed up and sped away, doubtless circling to the Los Feliz gate just north.

Ellie turned back to Harley and ordered: "Lie down."

"What? Why?" Were the cops here *now*?

"Lie down," she repeated. "In my lap."

Harley sucked the snot back into his sinuses as Ellie forced his head onto her thigh. "Why?"

"So I can comfort you. Dopey." She began to stroke his head, his hair, even his big, lightly brilliantined pompadour. "There, there. Mama's gonna make everything okay for Harley."

An almost imperceptible whimper escaped Hayden's lips. Then

more words started to form: "They say I'm too—well known, or something? The soldiers don't believe in me, or something?"

"There, there. It's not so bad."

"It's not? Maybe I'll go back to Ohio."

"No, Harley Hayden. Ellie won't let you leave her."

Hayden looked up at Eleanor looking down at him, her olive-skinned features framed by thick, black hair. In this light, she could almost be an Indian squaw. Which made Harley think of cowboy movies. "I won't do 'em," he murmured, defiant.

"Won't do what, dear?"

"Those lousy . . . those cheap . . . I won't go back to making B pictures, El, not while there's a war on. I'd rather—" He sat up. "Hell, I'd sooner get my job back at Hillcrest again than churn out one more cheapjack oater or gangster flick."

"The hell you will," Eleanor said with a laugh, then urged Hayden's head back down onto her upper thigh where it belonged. "Ellie Lustig will make sure," she declared, "that Harley gets treated as Harley deserves. Do you hear me, Mr. Hayden?"

Hayden heard. Even swathed in self-pity, he registered the tempered steel in her tone. He'd heard it before, on occasion, and assumed Ellie was doing Scarlett O'Hara, or Judy Garland in the scene where she tells off the Cowardly Lion—the way he, Harley, when at a loss, would do Sergeant York, or Tom Joad, or Ronald Colman in *A Tale of Two Cities*. Whether Ellie really had the moxie, or was merely mimicking her favorite Female Movie Role With Moxie, was something Hayden hadn't thought much about.

Because it made no difference. Either way, Eleanor Lustig was an emblem of his good luck, and bringer of same. Hayden's living, breathing—and ravishing, raven-haired—rabbit's foot.

· 6 ·

The Bronze God of
Summer's Sunglasses

June was bearable. So, usually, were July and August—just. If you kept open enough windows and stayed in the shade or the gazebo. (Though the gazebo featured her face on the ceiling, a fresco of herself as a fluttering angel, which was so mortifying—if she'd had friends, she could never have let them set foot inside.) But by September, L.A. could turn stifling, deadening. Yellow smog would settle not only below, south in the flats, but above, in the hills of Griffith Park. Ellie would watch from her bedroom window as it enveloped the observatory like some lethal airborne poison, like a cloud of mustard gas.

But Father would not take her up to Malibu. He had a hundred excuses, always changing, always the same—"Goddamn Wyler is a week behind," "Lousy labor union's trying to pull a slowdown," "Superior board meeting in New York"—most of which sounded urgent and imperative to a young girl worried about her father's nerves, his heart, his finances. Though he was just fifty then, or maybe not quite, he seemed old to her, and frail.

"Maybe after you get back?" she'd suggest, or "When Wyler catches up?" Father would agree: as soon as the current crisis had passed. Forgetting—or not—that a new crisis always came right along, as though on the very schedule Father's directors seemed habitually to ignore. And Ellie was never surprised.

At the Westlake School for Girls, they'd put on *Peter Pan,* with Ellie as Wendy. Father attended. She saw him in the audience, watching her. He seemed to be smiling, he looked a proud dad. But as soon as "the Lost Boys" were mentioned, Father stood and walked out. Eleanor forgot her line—someone had to whisper it from the wings. She never performed again.

Father no longer drove out to the Malibu Colony on summer weekends. Or spring, or fall. Only occasionally on winter weekends, on days when swimming was out of the question, would he venture west of Hollywood to look in on his beachfront property. He'd check for signs of pilfering by the loyal groundskeeper, whose job it was to safeguard the slowly moldering home. Ellie would sit on the sand those Saturdays or Sundays and watch her father through the porch window, in a three-piece suit, poking through the silver drawer (occasionally he'd count forks), running a finger along the sideboard to test whether *schmutz* had collected, peeking at the sheets to make sure the place wasn't being rented out overnight for quick cash right under his nose. Father wouldn't come to the beach. When he was satisfied the house was in order, and that no hard-hearted swindle had been perpetrated against the Lustig family, or what remained of it, they'd drive back into town.

But one spring day a real problem presented itself: an infestation of spiders, large, hairy-legged black arachnids that, mysteriously, appeared throughout the house—hiding in corners, under couches. Some brazenly dangled from wood beams. They weren't tarantulas or black widows. The man from Western counted six, as opposed to eight, eyes, and speculated that they might be Apache recluses, which he'd never seen in Malibu—but a rival exterminator said absolutely not. (Beyond that, though, he was stumped.) And the infestation persisted, despite the efforts (various vapors and toxic powders) of a dozen pest-control companies. Father even brought a crew out from the studio. They tented the place (which mortified Ellie but Saul would have loved it; the material's fat red and brown stripes made it look like Barnum had come to the beachfront) and "bombed" it with pressurized gas. When, two days later, the gas had dispersed and it was safe to go back inside, hundreds of spiders were found lying dead. But by the next weekend it was clear: an equal number of the hardy critters had somehow survived.

The past few years, Father wouldn't even go to the Colony on raw winter days. As far as Ellie knew, he'd been to the beach house exactly once since 1938, when a temblor in late May knocked out power for nearly a week in Laughlin Park. (Other than the outage, the only damage the Lustigs sustained was cracked plaster, piles of it, which Ellie liked to pretend was snow, till Fausto swept it up.) Father had packed Eleanor into his Cadillac convertible—the one she drove now—and the two of them had taken the Coast Highway north together. At the beach they played gin rummy and hearts, and at night Father inspected every corner, declared her room spider-free, then sat by his daughter in her bed and read *Return to Oz,* doing all the voices, or trying to, though she was already fifteen and far too old for L. Frank Baum.

But she hadn't complained. When she finally yawned after fifty pages, Father put on a pained face and proclaimed: "You have ruined me, you devil, and now you discard me!" Ellie had breathily commanded, "Kiss me, my Fool!" Which Father had done—on Ellie's forehead—before turning out the light and retreating to his bedroom. These were the finest few days she'd spent with her father since Ellie cared to remember.

But whenever September rolled around, and the town got not just hot but muggy, there was little relief. Father wouldn't hear of spending so much as a Saturday afternoon at the Colony. His all-purpose, single-word excuse? "Spiders." (Nor would he consider selling the white elephant, either, for no reason Ellie could discern.) If she wandered into one of his story meetings or budget meetings held in the living room on a Saturday morning, looking conspicuously miserable, Father always had but one suggestion—another single, two-syllable, and final word: "Hillcrest."

Ellie was too young to remember the humiliations of the California Club, and the University Club, and the Los Angeles Country Club, and there were more, all those restricted old-money bastions. Father never spoke to her directly about the policies that prohibited her from playing tennis, sunbathing, or practicing the backstroke with her best friends from the Westlake School for Girls. In later years, she realized, he'd only wanted to protect her from a self-perception as something "other," something "lesser," something "dirty" or "bad." So instead of simply explaining that the Lustigs were Jews, and most private clubs were Christian Only, he left her to wonder why she could only swim at Hillcrest, at the farthermost edge of Beverly Hills, among people she barely knew, rude girls in packs who'd whisper about her, ignore her, or giggle at her. If this was equality, if this was acceptance, she'd almost rather stand at the gates of the Lakeside Country Club or

Santa Monica Beach Club and watch her friends from Westlake worship the sun. But Fausto, Father's valet, was instructed to take her to Hillcrest, only Hillcrest. (Actually, he was permitted to make a stop at I. Magnin first, if Ellie felt in need of a new bathing suit, or bathing cap.) On the long drive, Eleanor would let her imagination run riot. Why *wasn't* she frolicking with her school friends? Did she . . . did she have a disease, some contagious, chronic illness that her father was too frightened to tell her about? But that would mean everyone at Hillcrest had a disease—and though some people there looked ill-shaped in their bathing suits, overweight or bandy-legged or weirdly matted in thick body hair, there was an almost primal life force about the members, too; that is, nobody, not even the little old ladies, looked as if they'd be dying anytime soon. Nor, for that matter, did Ellie feel in the least bit ill. So if she wasn't a leper . . . what was the unspeakable secret? "Fausto," she asked shyly, talking through the tube in back one humid September day as the chauffeur drove the Caddy west on Pico, "Do you know why I have to go to Hillcrest to swim, instead of the country clubs where all my girlfriends go?"

The dark-complexioned driver, whose patent-leather black hair and even blacker beard stubble fascinated Ellie, considered the question for several blocks. Then, fixing those sad, coal-dark eyes on his passenger in the rearview mirror, he answered: "It is because you killed Christ the Savior, Miss Eleanor."

Ellie was confused. There was some mistake. "*I* killed who?" In some ways, she'd already seen a lot. In other ways, Ellie'd been sheltered. From an early age, Lustig had let her listen in on bruising, bare-knuckled negotiations with the town's most vulgar, profane lawyers and talent agents. At ten, Ellie could tell you that net points were "monkey points." Her father had revealed to her the mysteries of first-dollar gross, restrictive covenants, negative costs, and the Wagner Act—but at the same time, he'd diligently kept his daughter ignorant of the Trinity, the Eucharist, Transubstantiation, and the Last Supper.

"Jesus Christ, God's only son." Fausto let Eleanor brood on this. When they'd reached Westwood Boulevard, she spoke up again. "You mean . . . you don't mean . . ." Ellie trailed off, then weakly murmured: "I wasn't even—" Born, she wanted to say. In point of fact, she'd missed the event by nearly two millennia. If that wasn't an airtight alibi . . . And even her father, who at fifty was fairly ancient, even *he* couldn't reasonably be implicated in the Crucifixion. Could he?

"It is something for which your people must pay," Fausto explained, as though reading her thoughts. "A sort of historical curse."

"A curse forever?" she inquired shakily, amid grim visions of her whole life passed at Hillcrest, surrounded by loud, unglamorous women and men with lox, onions, and liver on their breath, and interminable affairs and charity dinners to raise money for "our friends and relatives in Hitler's Europe."

"Till Christ is risen again." He lapsed into silence. But he'd left Eleanor with hope, however tenuous. She'd be sixteen soon—probably her best year for beauty, that's what the magazines said—and if Christ were risen again, say, in the next six months or so, that would give her plenty of time to switch to the Santa Monica Beach Club and show herself off.

They'd reached the Hillcrest entrance. Fausto drove the Cadillac down to the clubhouse, where the driveway ended. Ellie grabbed her beach bag, waved goodbye to the valet, and started to skip down to the ladies' locker room when she noticed a gaggle of girls, the girls who never acknowledged her, laughing and whispering and nodding toward the far end of the pool.

Ellie stopped, and looked. There was a new lifeguard on duty, she quickly saw, perched on that raised chair beside the high-diving board, with a parasol on top—a mini observation tower, but a kind of throne as well. And the young man installed there, even with the bright smear of zinc on his nose, looked much like a prince or minor deity. Even more so than his predecessors.

It must now be explained that the procession of stunning, physically flawless lifeguards was, in a sense, Hillcrest's Revenge. For if no amount of money could buy the Jews the privilege of swimming with the Christians, then they would hire a Christian— not just anyone who applied, but a perfect specimen of Christendom—to watch over the Jews in their Jewish pool, to keep those despised pariahs, "the Chosen," safe from harm. Which is why Eleanor had nursed a series of crushes on Thomas, then Richard, then Alex, then Stephen, four summers of Bronze Gods. And now there was . . . no one knew his name, yet. But as he stood, scanning the pool through dark glasses, it seemed possible that this was the finest example yet, of what was euphemistically known as the All-American type, employed here at Hillcrest.

In previous seasons, Ellie had been too young to do more than worship from afar. Though once she'd pretended to be stricken with a cramp, hoping Alex would dive in, enfold her sinking body in his pale, sinewy arms with their prominent blue veins, and kick them both back to the surface. Maybe mouth-to-mouth would be attempted. But either Alex didn't notice the bony pubescent Ellie as she went under, or assumed she was just playing, or knew she was faking. So Ellie, after holding her breath at the bottom, was forced to swim back up, unaided, and ingloriously drag herself over to a chaise longue—rejected, waterlogged, queasy from chlorine.

But this season Ellie was on the cusp of sixteen. She'd changed in ways one needn't be a lifeguard to notice. It was hard to imagine her sinking to the pool bottom—even the shallow end—without half the Hillcrest men diving in to rescue her while their mottled, sagging wives looked on with helpless envy. But because of her new shape, and consequent new power, Ellie no longer had to stage a near drowning. She had to do little but walk, toss back her hair, adjust her bathing suit, sit with her legs drawn up, lie down with her legs flat, roll onto her stomach to even out her tan (in the process, causing her breasts to bulge beneath her, just *enough*). Predictably, the whispering and catty jokes from the other girls only increased.

But Ellie paid them scant attention, this season. Mostly she was aware of the Bronze God on his high wooden throne. And he, she could see, was similarly alert to Ellie—her comings and goings, her sittings and standings, the cool, languid way she stroked and smoothed Ambre Solaire (a suntanning lotion she'd purchased on a whirlwind Paris trip that spring with Father) on her thighs, and pinned up her hair to fit under a bathing cap.

They'd never spoken—it was so much more thrilling that way—but his name was *Harley,* she'd learned that much. Last name Hayden, Irish name she'd overheard from some pinochle player in the clubhouse. Actually, the pinochle player had said, "Mick name. Hope he doesn't show up for work three sheets to the wind." Which, to the best of Ellie's knowledge, was a sailing term, and of no relevance in this landlocked country club.

The summer was almost over when they finally had their first conversation. Fittingly, the pretext was Harley's dark glasses. (Fitting, because two months were spent with Hayden's tinted lenses trained on Eleanor's tinted lenses. A miracle none of Hillcrest's children perished that season.)

Ellie was lolling one morning on her chaise, stretched out like a lazy cat while reading *The Good Earth*. Then she started to squirm—perhaps because she'd finally gotten to the notorious passage about foot-binding—and as her body shifted with uneasy empathy, so did her gaze: to the swimming pool, where little Seymour Lowenthal was attempting a backflip off the far edge.

Lots of other kids were watching too, standing around Seymour, urging him on. Inspired by the bigger-than-usual crowd, Seymour launched himself higher than ever before—and came down faster, harder, *smack,* his skull striking the cement pool ledge before he slid, limply, into water that sent up pink rivulets to the surface. A few toddlers, who thought this was part of the act, applauded.

Eleanor was up before she knew she was up, dropping Pearl Buck as she raced barefoot with great graceful strides to the pool. Harley was even quicker—he yanked off his sunglasses, dived from his throne, reached Seymour with three mighty strokes and, cradling the boy, brought him up at the shallow end.

He laid Seymour flat on the concrete and began to administer mouth-to-mouth. Seeing that the situation was well in hand, and that Seymour would survive (his chubby chest with its pubescent-girl's breasts rising and falling), Ellie backed from the gawking bathers all the way to Harley's wooden throne.

Nobody was watching her. For once she could have climbed to the top, stripped off her suit, and done the Dance of the Seven Veils in complete privacy. Instead she stopped below and peered up at the one item, here, of Harley's: his sunglasses, hastily discarded. They were dangling from a high wooden strut by their left temple. They might easily fall; the lenses might shatter.

Ellie reached up, grabbed them. Nobody saw. There were all the expected shouts: "Call an ambulance!" and "Any doctors here?" and "Give 'im air!"—just as in a movie—as she strode back to her chaise and slid the sunglasses into her beach bag, tucked in the folds of a clean, dry towel.

Then she lay down again and languidly worked Ambre Solaire into one upper thigh, then the other.

Later, as she ate lunch, alone as always, back to reading *The Good Earth* and feeling a little weepy (O-Lan had just died, leaving Wang Lung to realize, too late, how much he'd depended on her), a shadow fell across the picnic table. She looked up. Harley stood here, looking down.

Ellie met his gaze, unafraid somehow. "You were wonderful, this morning. So quick, and confident. But . . ."

Harley waited for her to finish, but she'd strategically trailed off—so he prompted: "But?"

Ellie smiled. "But shouldn't you be watching the pool right now, instead of me? Someone might be drowning again." She knew she was being provocative. She'd never tried before.

Harley smiled back. "The pool is closed for the rest of the afternoon. On account of the accident."

In a day of firsts, it was the first time she'd heard Harley speak. She liked his voice—gentle, though not in the least effeminate. She wasn't much on American regions, but she sensed something Midwestern, maybe in the vowel sounds.

"Oh." Ellie slid the bookmark into her book and closed it. Then noticed that Harley's bathing suit was just about at eye level. There was a bulge. And the suit wasn't quite dry yet—there was an outline as well. The bulge, the outline, both were disturbing and riveting. Ellie looked away, asking, "So how did it feel, putting your mouth on . . ."

"A boy's mouth? It's not like kissing, I think of it as medical. He's going to be okay, by the way. A few stitches, and maybe a lesson learned about showing off around a swimming pool." He still hadn't sat down opposite her, which is what she was trying to get him to do. Maybe Harley knew that.

"No, not that he was a boy. But that he was . . ." She lowered her voice, though there was nobody within a six-picnic-table radius. "That he was a Christ killer."

Harley looked startled to hear this. "Seymour Lowenthal?"

Ellie shrugged. "I mean in the sense of the, you know, the 'historic curse.' "

Harley shook his head. "Historic curse? You sound like Madame Ouspenskaya."

"Who?"

"You know, in *The Wolf Man*. The tiny gypsy lady who speaks in a heavy, phony, accent, of ancient spells, and hexes . . ."

"My father won't let me see *The Wolf Man*."

Harley sat. (Ellie celebrated, inwardly.) "Why not?"

"He *says* because it's vulgar. I think it's because another studio made it."

Her way (subtle, or not-so-subtle, she'd decide later) of letting him know of her Hollywood pedigree. Now she waited for Harley to ask the next question: "Who's your father?"

But Harley's next question was: "Did you by any chance take my sunglasses?"

"Oh, maybe I did," Ellie answered, casually, reaching into her beach bag. She pulled them out, waved them. "Are these the sunglasses in question?"

Harley reached for them.

Ellie pulled the glasses back. "Wait, I want to try them on first."

"No, don't do that."

Ellie'd never had a man wrapped around her finger before—and one so nearly naked! It was fun, and terrifying. She felt on the brink of running out of teasing jokes, witticisms, and irreverence. She suddenly knew that, if today's flirtation didn't conclude quickly, it would end not in triumph, but in farce. "Why shouldn't I?"

"Look, why'd you take them in the first place?"

"They were dangling. When you threw them down, before you dived in. They might've fallen. The lenses might've shattered."

Harley looked happy with this explanation. But he looked distinctly *un*happy as Eleanor slipped them on, then reacted:

"Oh my gosh! Oh my gosh, you're *blind*!" She whipped the sunglasses off her face and blinked furiously, trying to reestablish a sense of depth, focus, space. "Oh my *gosh*!"

Hayden grabbed his glasses back, unmasked as something less than perfect. "I warned you. You'll have a migraine for days. If you're lucky—months, if you're not."

She stared at him, wide-eyed, then saw he was kidding. "So that's your big secret," she teased.

"That's it," he agreed. "And by the way, miss? If you keep shouting that I'm blind, I'm liable to lose my job."

"Which means you're at my mercy," Ellie pointed out—then stood up, with her beach bag and her book, and flounced away.

Triumph.

They didn't speak again, that summer, at Hillcrest. Ellie turned sixteen, became even riper and maybe a little more confident, then impatiently waited through the winter, spring, and early summer. (Christ failed to reappear, meanwhile.) But when Fausto dropped her off in late July, and she took long leggy strides toward the locker rooms, and glanced over at the pool (heart pounding), she saw at once that, atop the wooden throne, a new Bronze God had been installed. He was handsome, even taller than Harley, and in time she learned his name was Brian. All the Hillcrest girls were crazy for him. But he never did a thing for Eleanor. Her heart belonged to Hayden.

But Hayden was gone (Where could he be? Excommunicated back to that Midwest from whence he'd been plucked?), so Ellie spent the rest of the summer managing her tan and reading books by the Brontë sisters (she couldn't decide whether to emulate Virginia Bruce in *Jane Eyre* or her Malibu neighbor Merle Oberon, soon to appear in *Wuthering Heights*) and forgetting her adolescent crush on last year's lifeguard. Two months later she entered her senior year at the Westlake School for Girls and made straight A's as always.

One Saturday night, Father screened a new Superior film and she watched it (she didn't always: never the Sagebrush stuff, never the Gangster stuff, rarely the Spy stuff, but this was Light Comedy). Chester and Doris Dowling were there, and the youngish star, who insisted on sitting next to Ellie and, in the dark, kept "accidentally" pressing his trouser leg against her bare thigh. Just when she thought she would start screaming—at the masher beside her *and* his celluloid image, going through its phony motions—the film cut to a party scene, wherein a grinning fellow cut in on the star's date.

"Mind if I twirl her once around?"

Ellie almost fell out of her frock. The fellow was Harley

Hayden—it took her a moment because of all the makeup, and the dance and elocution lessons, plus she'd never seen him wearing clothes before. Anyway, who knew he'd harbored dreams of stardom? (Or even Second Banana–dom?) Ellie'd assumed his only aspiration was to save the drowning Jews. She was so entranced, she didn't notice that the star's hand was now resting on her knee. Till she *did* notice, and swatted it off.

Next day she phoned the studio, identified herself, was quickly connected to Payroll. It was against company policy, of course, but they unhesitatingly gave her Hayden's home phone number—of course. She barely had to make up a story. "He left his sunglasses at our house" was all it took.

Then she snuck into Father's liquor cabinet, found a bottle of crème de menthe (the only hooch she thought she could stomach) and downed some, for courage. Then she phoned Harley.

He answered in that soft breathy voice she hadn't forgotten: "Hello?"

"It's me," she breathed in turn.

"Me who?" He sounded wary. Perhaps it was a fan who'd somehow found his number. Perhaps it was a practical joke.

"The girl who knows your big secret."

There was a long silence on the line.

Ellie started to panic, started to think she'd made a huge mistake, miscalculated; he'd hang up and it would be curtains—she'd lose her lifeguard as fast as she'd found him again.

She quickly clarified: "You're blind."

All at once it came back to him—the summer before last, why sure, the pretty, insouciant girl who'd sounded like Madame Ouspenskaya but looked—a bit, anyway—like Theda Bara, though without the vampiness.

"*You!*" he roared, delighted.

• • •

On their first date a week later, Harley asked Ellie where she wanted to go. He started to add that he meant *anywhere*—San Francisco wasn't out of the question if that's where she had her heart set, or Tijuana for that matter—but before he could convey any of this, Ellie answered, "Malibu."

He assumed there was a wonderful restaurant out there, perched on a cliff, maybe, with a view of the Pacific at sunset. Eleanor wouldn't say. A woman of few words, suddenly, she directed him to the Colony, where the guard waved them through. Then, when Harley'd cruised down Colony Drive to the beach house, she instructed him to sit in his Plymouth and wait for her. She promised she'd be about twenty minutes.

Once inside, Ellie found a broom, then did what she'd waited to do for several years: She went from room to room, calmly and methodically swatting, crushing, annihilating every last six-eyed, hairy spider where it hid. This took closer to forty minutes than twenty, and was also twice as much fun as anticipated: she let out screams of rapturous retribution as she crushed the little beasts, but never quite loud enough for Harley or the neighbors to hear.

When the massacre ended, Ellie cracked the broom in half over her knee and stuck both ends in the trash. (The bristles were ruined, caked in sticky gray spider matter.) Then she spent another five minutes in the powder room freshening up, catching her breath. By the time she reappeared outside, Harley had gotten out of his car and was nervously pacing the empty road. "Y'okay?" he asked the young woman, whose faced seemed flushed not so much with exertion, as with the satisfaction of a cold vengeance taken at last.

"Never better," Ellie answered. Then: "Would you come inside and help me clean up? There's the most awful mess."

Harley assented. Indeed, it was a mess the likes of which he'd never seen. He was impressed. He was her slave. He swept it all up.

From *Daily Variety*
Sykes Set to Helm "Fate" Flick

Director Derek Sykes has pacted with Superior Pictures for what studio describes as a "top-drawer suspense-melodrama" based on the current best-selling novel *Meet Fate Among the Clouds*. Project aims for a mid-fall start pending A-list star casting. Chester Dowling, Superior's production prexy, estimates the budget at "a million-five. This is a big picture for us, make no mistake." Sykes is repped by Sid Cohn at the Morris Office.

· 7 ·

The Lost Boy

Hayden went straight from the stage to his dressing room. They'd just wrapped Scene 24 and were "moving on" to the Tony's Office set. The crew would need at least an hour to light: perfect time to give Roarke a bell. But first Hayden had to do in private what he struggled to avoid doing on set, throughout each shooting day, in the presence of colleagues: fall to his knees and heave, such were the depths of his distress.

When the retching subsided, Hayden left a message, then huddled in a corner and waited, hoping Roarke would return his call before he was summoned back to the stage. The process of shooting a movie was known as being "on the floor" and that was just how Hayden felt, shooting this one: on the floor—sprawled, in fact—and kicked in the ribs for good measure.

Sally Racine took the message. (The stenographer had recently quit her sister's place to shack up with Roarke and share the rent.)

Roarke had gone downstairs to grab a sandwich, he'd said, but Sally suspected there might be another transaction involved along with the roast beef, something to do with a bookie, maybe, who took bets on the corner of Argyle and Selma. She recognized Hayden's name, of course. She'd almost blurted, "You're one of my favorites," but something stopped her. Maybe it was the fact that Hayden *wasn't* one of her favorites, having a collegiate quality she didn't care for. Also, though she wasn't sure how her boyfriend earned his money (when asked, Roarke would mutter that "plenty of people" still owed "plenty of favors," or that he was someone "who wasn't afraid to scramble some eggs, get things done—like Mussolini"), Sally sensed that where business matters were concerned, discretion was a big deal. Still, it was a thrill to hear Hayden's shy, hesitant, slightly breathy, and almost feminine (though not *effeminate*) voice in her earpiece, the same voice she'd heard over loudspeakers at the Egyptian. A thrill to know that a star (well, a sort-of star) was calling her apartment (well, her boyfriend's place). She could hardly wait for Roarke to walk back in and hear the news.

Roarke's reaction was muted. "How about that." He assumed he'd never hear or see Hayden again, except when a new picture opened. Roarke figured Hayden had another five years in pictures. Maybe a bit longer if he could manage the transition from best friend to beloved uncle, nice neighbor, or loyal business partner.

"How soon can you meet with Mr. Hayden?" she prodded. "I think he thought I was your secretary. I didn't disabuse him. In fact, I played along for fun, and said I'd let him know."

Roarke gazed pensively at Sally. She was far from his erotic ideal, yet she'd met him at his lowest point and declared her loyalty, if not her love. Whatever she saw in him, Sally clearly regarded Roarke as something more than the hapless casualty of a mayoral clean-up campaign. *And* there was the weekly paycheck.

"He say what this was about?"

"He couldn't talk. He was calling from the set."

Of course he was. Line-perfect, camera-ready Harley Hayden.

"He leave a number?"

Sally shook her head. Carefully: she washed and set her hair every morning, whether or not she was leaving for work at the county courthouse—at least she did in those early days as Roarke's common-law wife. "He said he'd call back as soon as he finished the next scene."

"Mm. How'd he sound?"

Sally shrugged. "In a rush. Under pressure. Or both." Then, to round out the portrait: "But friendly, and nice. Not flirtatious at all, a real gentleman."

Roarke made a faint snorting sound. "Harley? A gentleman to one and all. Even to me, even after he got the word as to why the hell I was following him around town for ten days."

Six months earlier, Hayden had surprised Roarke with a phone call. The ex-cop figured he was about to be threatened with a lawsuit, an invasion-of-privacy complaint. But Hayden, after identifying himself, sounded apologetic, not belligerent. "You may not remember me," he began.

Roarke forced a laugh. "Nuts, you're my favorite movie star."

It was a nod to the previous—and only—time they'd spoken: in line for the toilet at Barney's Beanery, fall of 1941. But Hayden, nervous and tentative, didn't pick up on it. "Look, Ellie— Eleanor—explained to me about how you tailed the two of us, a while back, on behalf of Mr. Lustig, and . . ."

"No hard feelings, I hope?"

"Hey, man's gotta live. And the way Ellie tells it, you played square with her—with us. I appreciate that."

Roarke murmured something that sounded like a thank-you.

"You'll get a laugh out of this," Hayden went on, "but I actually thought you were some would-be swain of Ellie's from UCLA."

"UCLA? How do you figure?"

"She studies there. Psychology major, junior year. Smart cookie, she is," Hayden yammered. "Anyway, I had you pegged for a teaching assistant with a thing for coeds, clever grad student who could come up with his own sparkling dialogue, not just memorize some movie script . . . Pretty funny, dontcha think?"

"Funny"? "Painful" sounded closer to the mark. "Sure," Roarke agreed, hoping to speed Hayden to the point of his call.

There was static on the line; Roarke thought Hayden had hung up, till he heard: "Know what a yar's-eye candle is?" At least that's what it sounded like, to Roarke: *yar's-eye.*

"Not a clue."

More static. Then: "Well, d'ya think you could find out? For a fee, I mean. I'd pay you the same as Mr. Dowling did."

Roarke didn't know which figure Hayden had in mind: the forty a day, or the twenty-five. Nor did he feel comfortable with the proposal, which sounded distinctly iffy even to a forcibly retired cop on his uppers. "Why don't you get yourself a dictionary," he suggested. "Look up 'yar.' Maybe it's like a yak or something. Maybe they scoop out its eye, melt it down with wax, stick a wick in it and presto: yar's-eye candle? There! I just saved you a small bundle."

Hayden cleared his throat. "I don't think you heard me right," he said. "It's spelled . . ." And here he paused, perhaps to consult his notes. Then: "Y-A-R-H-Z-E-I-T."

"Nothing's spelled like that," Roarke rejoined.

On the other end, Hayden faltered. "Yeah, you could be right, I think I switched the *h* and the *r*." Off Roarke's continued silence, he explained, "It's a Jewish word."

"Then why not talk to a rabbi?" suggested Roarke, a note of irritability creeping in.

Hayden cleared his throat again. "I don't know a rabbi. My mother was a dyed-in-the-wool Episcopalian."

"I thought your mother was a Christian Scientist."

"Where'd you get that idea?"

From you, Roarke wanted to say. "Look, we're going around and around here. You don't know a rabbi, but your girlfriend does. If she doesn't, her daddy does. Don't all those—" The ex-cop restrained himself from making a religious slur. "All those— big shots belong to some fancy Beverly Hills temple where they sacrifice a gentile boy on the High Holy Days?"

"That's the blood libel," Harley shot back, instantly outraged. "That's a dirty Nazi hoax. I hope you're kidding, Mister."

Roarke chuckled. "Yeah, I'm kidding. Seriously, Hayden— Harley—why can't you just ask the Lustigs about this, ah—"

" 'Cause it's *their* yahrzeit candle. It's their secret. And I . . . Well, I'm not good with secrets. I'm from Ohio."

Roarke transferred the phone from his nightstand to the floor and stretched out there. His lower back had been aching, and Hayden wasn't helping.

"Look, this is getting too balled up for the telephone. Tell you what: you know Lucey's, on Melrose?"

"Sure! Right down the street from Superior."

"Exactly. Meet me there at five for a drink. I'll buy, and you'll tell me what this is all about."

· · ·

At Lucey's, late that afternoon, there were just a few unemployed character actors, stretching out the single drinks they'd rationed themselves by slowly sipping melted ice. Perhaps they hoped to get spotted by Arthur Lustig, Chester Dowling, or the stable of directors under contract to Superior—but today they could only preen for a fellow thespian and a former peace officer.

Hayden looked even edgier than he'd sounded on the phone, which was all the inducement Roarke needed to bait the young star. "So what're you still doing stateside? Isn't Hank Fonda on his way to the South Pacific by now? Didn't Wayne Morris already shoot down a couple of Zeros?" Harley blinked across the table, apparently puzzled. "Wasn't Bob Montgomery driving an ambulance for the Frogs before FDR declared war?" Roarke continued to badger, while grinning broadly. "What's the matter with you, Hayden, chronic case of piles?"

By now Harley looked miserable. He ordered a cup of coffee, then fished in a battered little briefcase he'd brought with him and pulled out a dog-eared copy of *Daily Variety*.

Roarke took it from him. "Page two," Hayden said.

Roarke felt Hayden watching him with his big blue eyes, that seemed bigger, and bluer, and somehow more unreal, than they'd looked the year before. On page two, Roarke found an item about how an old college wrestling injury had sidelined the actor. He looked up at Hayden. "Tough break, huh, Flip?"

Hayden reddened. "They called me that in college."

"But not since?"

Hayden shrugged. "Folks back in Ohio. Few close friends."

"May *I* call you Flip?" Roarke couldn't resist teasing him again; it was the most pleasurable way to scuff up Hayden's overly earnest exterior. "Well, if it's any consolation, *Flip,* I figure that even without the bum hamstring, they'd have flagged you for being damn-near legally blind." At this, Hayden took back the *Variety.* Which is when Roarke realized: "You're not wearing your cheaters. How'd you find your way to the table?"

Hayden flushed even brighter. "I'm wearing these new-fangled . . . Contact lenses, they call 'em. Big disk-shaped doohick-eys that fit directly over your eyes." He blinked again, balefully, at Roarke. This time Roarke blinked back, surprised; straining only a little, he was able to make out two translucent cones pasted over Harley's eyeballs.

"Y'gotta pry 'em off at night with some kind of suction cup. Sometimes it feels like they're gonna take my irises off with 'em. Right now they're itching me something awful. I've seen the future and it stings. Think I'm about to give 'em up."

"Can't say as I blame you." Then Hayden's coffee came, and Roarke's rye. Roarke offered him a smoke but of course the actor declined. "So, this 'yahrzeit candle' question—let me guess, is it perchance connected with your girlfriend's family?"

Hayden sipped his coffee, then set down the cup—heavily, so it clattered. Then, staring into the tepid, muddy beverage, as he stirred it with a teaspoon: "It's just the two of them, Mr. Lustig and Ellie. On this big estate with three houses. Well, plus all the butlers and chauffeurs and valets and gardeners and cooks. I guess you've seen it. And I guess you know how I feel about Ellie." He looked up, with those uncannily magnified orbs. "But they've very . . . secretive, those two, even with me—and I've known them both for three years now. Look, the mom's never around. But I don't think she's divorced from Mr. L. Or separated, even. She's just . . . never around. Where she is, though, I've got no idea. But on the rare occasions Ellie mentions her, it's in the present tense. So I figure she's alive. But when I ask even the simplest question—" He mimicked Ellie's brusque, dismissive gesture. "And then there's a brother. Younger, I gather. His name is Saul, I know that much. There's pictures of him displayed on the Steinway concert grand. Cute little guy, with a cowlick, in a tiny coat and tie. But Ellie *never* mentions him, in any tense. And when I even *think* about bringing up his name, it's like she's a mentalist, it's like she's Mandrake the Magician, or Lamont Cranston, or . . . The girl just stares at me with those big black eyes of hers and . . ." He pursed his lips and shook his head—the way Ellie would while, presumably, reading Hayden's thoughts.

Roarke recognized the pursed lips and headshake: she'd given him the same, that day in Laughlin Park, fall of '41. Roarke knew he'd been staring at Ellie, but hadn't recognized that he was ogling her. Clearly, she had—and, with that curt little look, rebuffed him. The belated realization made Roarke flush with shame and thwarted longing. He gulped at his rye.

Hayden was speaking. "Which leads me to believe—I hate to say this, Mr. Roarke, but . . . I've got a hunch Saul's dead."

"I've got a hunch you're right."

Hayden trained those outsized eyes directly on Roarke. The enlarged pupils registered something akin to panic, even horror.

"On the way over," Roarke explained, "I stopped off at Temple Israel of Hollywood. They've got a new building on Martel. Rabbi Rosten was busy, they said, but they also said there was a reading room upstairs. All welcome—even a poor paddy like myself, evidently. So I found a reference book and jotted some notes." He dragged out his notepad and read aloud:

"Jews commemorate the anniversary of a loved one's death by lighting a small candle, called a yahrzeit candle, which burns for twenty-four hours on the death anniversary. The flame represents the flame of life that once brightened the lives of those who mourn. . . . Traditionally, we light the yahrzeit candle for parents, spouses, siblings, and children."

Roarke looked up.

"There's more, but it's kind of technical. About what to do when the anniversary falls on the Sabbath, what prayers to say when you light the thing, and how there's this nifty new *electric* candle for sale at selected retail outlets in the Fairfax district. But so far as Brother Saul goes? The smart money says he's no longer with us."

Hayden nodded, downcast.

"As to how he passed away, or where Ellie's mom disappeared to—sure, you could pay me to find out. And I'd take your money in a flash. But the catch is, I'm not that kind of detective and I never was. Never been licensed to do that sort of work, never even had an office. Now let's not kid each other, I could probably find out fast, just dialing a phone. But I say this as a pal: If Eleanor's truly the girl of your dreams, and the feeling's even halfway mutual—then *you* have to find the right words, and the right moment, to get to the bottom of things. Because when it comes to certain . . . puzzles, mysteries that need solving, Flip, sometimes a man has to solve that stuff himself."

Roarke sat back, hopeful that with this uncharacteristic burst of candor and wisdom, he'd gotten the actor off his back.

Harley nodded again, momentarily silent. Then: "I just thought . . ." he began. "That is, I'd hoped—"

Roarke waved for the check, then leaned forward. "What does it matter how the boy died—*if* he died? What? You want to know whether some disease or other runs in the family? Cancer? Rickets? Heart murmur, maybe?"

Hayden didn't answer, so Roarke went on: "Or the mom who

disappeared? Hey, maybe you're worried there's a strain of insanity runs in Eleanor's maternal line? That'd be normal, Harley, if you're thinking about marriage, and children. I'm a family man myself." He paused to clear a wad of phlegm from his throat, swallowing it down. "Anyone who didn't worry about that sort of thing ought to have his head examined."

"I just want to understand Ellie better," Hayden insisted. "On those occasions—rare occasions—when it's kind of hard to reach her. She has these . . . these blackish moods sometimes."

The check arrived. Harley tried to pay, but Roarke was quicker. "Everyone has blackish moods sometimes," he observed as they walked to the exit together. "Except maybe in the Buckeye State?"

Harley smiled. Now that the questions were asked and the check settled, he'd managed to relax a tad. It made Roarke soften too. "Hey, count yourself lucky those occasions are—as you put it—rare. With some women, I can tell you firsthand, Flip . . . the blackish moods are the *good* times."

They were out in the parking lot. "Thanks for seeing me, all the same," Hayden offered, with a brisk handshake.

By now Roarke was feeling almost sorry for the actor— between his draft status, private fears about his girlfriend and her family, even those painful cones affixed to his eyeballs . . . Appearances to the contrary, this dreamboat really *didn't* have the world by the tail after all. It was enough to make Roarke want to behave with a smidgen of empathy. "So what do you have lined up? I mean, your next movie?"

Hayden's smile calcified. Perhaps this was another sore point? "There's a picture at Superior, not a sure bet, not by a long shot, but I've got my eye on it, alright. *Meet Fate Among the Clouds*— classy title, huh? Comes from a poem, I think. They say the book was a little soapy, but the scribes on the lot worked their voodoo. British director is helming, can't think of his name but he's top of the line—"

"Alfred Hitchcock? David Lean?" Suddenly Roarke wanted to demonstrate he wasn't just some crude defrocked cop, a complete ignoramus about the company town in which he grubbed his money.

"No. But this director's right up there, from what I hear. Anyhow, I'd be perfect for Tony, the male lead, if you ask me. Which you didn't but—thing is, I'm angling for a screen test."

The son-in-law also rises, Roarke thought. "Best of luck," he said.

They got in their cars and drove off in separate directions. Having politely brushed off the actor, Roarke again believed it was the last he'd see of Flip. And that was fine.

In fact, though Roarke had been polite to Hayden, he hadn't been truthful. Between the phone call and the appointment at Lucey's, his day had been more productive than he'd let on. To start with, Roarke *had* made a few telephone calls. His first thought was Chester Dowling, naturally—till it struck him, a moment later, that Dowling would be unhappy about Roarke's unauthorized contact with a Superior Pictures contract player. Especially if the studio topper sensed that lowly Roarke was fishing for blackmail material—which, given the ex-cop's history and reputation, wouldn't be an unreasonable suspicion.

So Roarke tried Dowling's opposite number at Metro, Eddie Mannix, an old acquaintance from his days at the track. Mannix knew the whole Saul Lustig story, and he didn't even ask why Roarke wanted to hear it. "The boy drowned out in Malibu, ten years ago, must be. His folks were having a big blowout, 's what they say, not twenty yards off, but nobody noticed when the kid wandered in for a dip. They were all too tight."

"That's tough," Roarke offered.

And Mrs. Lustig? "She dropped out of sight after that" was all Mannix would say on the subject. "Shame, really, 'cause, between the two of them, Ida was a lot more lovable than Arthur. Not to mention easier on the eyeballs. Kind of a Theda Bara type—if you like the type."

Roarke was about to claim—again, and falsely—his preference for Betty Grable. But remembering that Mannix was a busy man, he pursued his line of questioning: "Ida, right. . . . Is she alive or dead? And if she *is* alive, where—"

Mannix cut in: "Gotta run, L.B. wants me. But hey, don't be a stranger. Haven't seen you at Santa Anita since—"

"Kayak won the handicap prep race, and I lost my shirt?"

Mannix laughed, and the line went dead.

Damn.

So Roarke stopped by the Cahuenga Branch Library on Santa Monica Boulevard, where they kept twenty years of the *Los Angeles Times* on microfilm. Nonetheless, he failed to find an item about little Saul Lustig's drowning. Only an announcement of the memorial service for the only son, seven years old, of Arthur and Ida Lustig, at Temple Israel of Hollywood. That was July 11, 1931. Ellie would've been about nine. No mention of a wild party, or the Pacific. Saul might've died of Spanish flu.

Mr. L had at least one friend on the newspaper, no surprise.

Roarke backtracked to the complex on Martel and Hollywood, went inside (the reception area, not the synagogue), and asked for Rabbi Rosten. "Who may I say would like to see him?" asked a pudgy, heavily powdered secretary.

The ex-cop hesitated a moment, then told her, "Mrs. Arthur Lustig's personal physician."

Roarke gave the word "physician" a certain dire emphasis. Her tone suitably hushed, the receptionist suggested that Roarke leaf through a magazine while she rang through to Rosten—and then, into the phone, she repeated "physician" with the same weighted intonation. In a moment, the receptionist was walking Roarke down the hallway to the rabbi's study.

Rosten was a trim and delicate-looking fellow, surprisingly youthful for a man of his position: the movie moguls' hand-picked high priest. He was writing in longhand when Roarke walked in—this Saturday's sermon, most likely—but immediately set aside his legal pad, looked up at Roarke, and smiled. He spoke with the faint but distinct and cultivated accent of a German Jew. "Sit down, I'm Max Rosten. And you are Doctor—"

"Burberry," Roarke said, sitting opposite. There was an advertisement for a Burberry topcoat in the *Saturday Evening Post* he'd been skimming two minutes before.

"If I may say so, you look rather young," the rabbi observed, "to be Mrs. Lustig's primary . . . caregiver?"

Both men were being cautious with their euphemisms.

"You look pretty fresh-faced yourself," Roarke countered, "to be Hollywood's big—" He almost committed a religious slur again, but caught himself in time. "Big spiritual leader?"

Rosten modestly waved a hand.

Roarke continued: "Anyway, I'm new on Ida's . . . case, which may account for my relatively tender years. And I guess also explains why I came to see you. I assume you gave her—sustenance, succor, after the terrible loss of her beloved son."

Roarke was laying on the sanctimony, perhaps moved by the

print of Moses frowning down at him from Rosten's paneled wall, and the plaster facsimile of the Ten Commandments tablets propped on the desk. "Any insight I might glean from you, about that painful time, would be far more helpful than a thousand pages of doctors' and nurses' notes, Rabbi."

Rosten clasped his hands together with the elegant precision of a neurosurgeon. "The truth is, Ida Lustig wouldn't see me. She sent word through her husband that she was not a religious woman. Arthur passed on the message, then sailed for Europe on some sort of 'talent search,' or so I was told."

"Abandoning Ellie, at a time like that?"

"There were servants," the Rabbi allowed. "An Italian husband and wife, fine and caring people so far as I could tell. Anyway, I spent time alone with Ellie. A bit of talking—about Jewish concepts of death, fate, justice. But mostly holding her, quite frankly, while she wept and screamed." Rosten looked sorrowful all over again as he relived it. "She'd stayed in town, that weekend, for a grade school slumber party. I think she believed, if she'd only been there, at the Malibu beach house . . . She shouted at me that there couldn't be a god who'd let her baby brother die." Grimacing, the Rabbi added: "And if there was a god, Eleanor said, she hated him."

Roarke shrugged. "She was a kid. Who could blame her?"

Rabbi Rosten shrugged in turn. "I haven't seen Eleanor in years, she only comes to *shul* with her Father on Rosh Hashana. Our Jewish New Year. And we have many celebrants on that occasion . . . But some congregants who know the Lustigs have told me that Eleanor changed. As a survival strategy, I suppose—but that would be more in your line, wouldn't it?"

For a moment, Roarke forgot he'd represented himself as a psychiatrist. But before he could stammer a credible response,

Rosten continued: "Ellie calls herself the Woman Who Doesn't Care, or so I'm told." The rabbi looked up at Moses' portrait and sighed, "Maybe Ripley's approach is the more effective, in this modern age. Who knows, maybe it's the *new* New Testament."

Roarke was floundering now. "Ripley as in Ripley's Believe It or Not?"

The rabbi looked surprised. "I'm speaking of Ida Lustig's longtime mental health advisor. Psychoanalyst. Wise counselor to the stars, Filmdom's own faith healer. Or whatever he'd be called. Isn't the famous Dr. Ripley your senior colleague?"

This time, Roarke—now annoyed with himself for blundering in here and botching it so badly—began to stammer aloud.

If Rosten noticed, he chose to see Roarke's unease as proof *he'd* been mistaken: "Hang on, I got the name wrong, didn't I? You're quite right, Dr. Burberry, it isn't Ripley at all."

Before Rosten asked what the doctor's name really was, Roarke stood. He started to back out of the rabbi's study.

"Have you seen our synagogue?" Rosten persisted, either out of plain friendliness tinged with pride, or the fund-raising habit.

Roarke shook his head, still moving in reverse.

"Would you like to? The interior was designed by some of the finest production people over at Fox." And then, reading Roarke's reluctance, Rosten let the ex-cop off the hook: "With a name like Burberry, I don't suppose . . ."

"I'm a dyed-in-the-wool Episcopalian," Roarke said, surprised to find Hayden's line from earlier that day coming out of his own mouth. "In fact, it's fair to say the only temple I'm familiar with, is Shirley Temple."

Rosten offered a wan smile. "That's very good. I'll try to remember that one." He turned back to his sermon.

. . .

En route to Lucey's, Roarke made two calculations. From his years on the force, he'd learned that knowledge was to be hoarded, not shared; if properly deployed, information was a weapon more deadly and coercive than a gun. No idle insight, this was a Law of the Jungle: the moment you stopped preying on others, you were preyed upon, victimized, hung out to dry. Roarke would tell Hayden nothing of what he'd learned today.

Roarke's second calculation was based on a second reality: The fact that Hayden had been in touch, and that Roarke had done some Hayden-related digging, would get back to Chester Dowling. If only because it was Dowling's job to learn these facts—and, should they threaten the stability of the studio or of Mr. L personally, act upon them. What made the situation especially sensitive was Hayden's close connection with the Lustig family. Determined to protect his Superior sinecure, Roarke resolved to write up the details of his latest contact with the actor and subsequent conversation with Rabbi Rosten. Write them up in the form of an investigator's case notes, to be submitted in confidence to Dowling. Then there'd be no misunderstandings or recriminations later. A preemptive ass kissing was the best form of ass covering, Roarke had learned the hard way. So he did as he'd resolved—the very same day. And, indeed, Dowling seemed reassured by these case notes. There would be many such documents sent on to Chester Dowling over the next six years.

At War With One's Self:
A Fragment

Humpty Dumpty is universally visualized as a short, ovoid, i.e., egg-shaped, middle-aged, male. Though he is in many respects a ludicrous character to be pitied, he is also represented as a figure of power and authority, as evidenced by the fact that "all the king's men" are busily engaged in the process of trying to fix him after his "great fall." In Hollywood, California, certainly, an abundance of this type may be found among the ranks of producers, financiers, and studio executives.

But at the same time, and in the same place, there are countless Humpty Dumptys who fit quite another description altogether: they are young (in their twenties to midthirties), unusually attractive, and more than half of them are female. They can be found working as actors and actresses primarily. Though they may be the idols of millions, and the objects of the public's avid albeit repressed sexual fantasies—and though, on the surface they may appear to resemble the Pretty Maids All in a Row familiar from Old Mother Goose—these "Hidden" (as we shall call them) Humpty Dumptys are prone to suffer from a full complement of ego confusions, feelings of self-loathing, self-despair, suicidal ideation and, often, morbid addiction to a variety of stimulants, depressants, and hypnotics, e.g., Benzedrine, alcohol, opium, cocaine, marihuana, morphine, laudanum, and heroin to name but a few from the pharmacopoeia.

Movie directors and movie writers are also greatly susceptible to these selfsame lures and traps. Commonly, the problem is attributed to the enormous and peculiar stress, competition, and "deadline pressure" found in the picture-making community. But the true culprit, in fact, is the so-called creative urge, often referred to by film practitioners as the Muse. This is a superstitious, even pagan, mode of description, but what it alludes to is a legitimate and proven mental pattern endemic within Hollywood circles. In truth, what is generally regarded (and legitimized and encouraged by grossly inflated salaries) as the so-called creative mind is a distinct category of psychological disorder, manifesting in mania, melancholia, and hallucinations.

Dr. Sigmund Freud has written that "the artist has . . . an introverted disposition and has not far to go to become neurotic." We contend that Dr. Freud—perhaps naively, and perhaps not—severely understated the problem.

Dr. A. A. Brill, a disciple of Freud's who lived and worked in Hollywood in the 1920s and '30s, perspicaciously identified the drive to compose poetry as a symptom of oral eroticism, further observing that poets are found "among the neurotic, the psychotic, the child, and the primitive." He understood poetry to be a "sensuous or mystic outlet through words" comparable to the "chewing and sucking of nice words and phrases." Though few would equate Hollywood's typical screenplay with poetry, one must acknowledge the connection from a clinical, if not an aesthetic, standpoint.

In later chapters, we will examine at greater length the origin and treatment of the foregoing problems, as well as their proper scientific terminologies and range of diagnoses.

. . .

Another fascinating if more obscure, less well understood category of the Hidden Humpty Dumpty syndrome is the spouse—generally speaking, the wife—of a film industry professional: for example a studio executive or associate producer.

These women tend to be highly educated (two years of college or better) and highly verbal, with a finely developed (some would call it snobbish and pretentious) sense of "style" and "taste." Notwithstanding their glamorous and privileged lives, these women are often profoundly unhappy, deeply neurotic, beset with buried erotic conflicts as well as unresolved guilt and fear over infant toilet-training issues and other deep-seated, latent child-developmental anxieties.

In "Beyond the Bifurcated Ego," part two of this updated and expanded edition, you will find a detailed case history of one such wife who has been in treatment under my care for over ten years.

. 8 .

Derek Sykes

A nd that column out there?" Derek Sykes pointed to the backdrop hung beyond the main window of the living room set.

"That's Coit Tower, Mr. Sykes," said the art director. "It's a major San Francisco landmark. Sorta like Big Ben, in London, get me? It'll help orient the audience right away to the city where the picture takes place."

Which only irked Sykes, reminding him of a question for which he couldn't seem to get an answer—from Lustig or Dowling or anyone at the studio. So he asked the art director: "Why can't we actually shoot this picture in San Francisco, Jeff? I saw in the trades where Hitchcock was permitted to go shoot in . . ." He had to think hard, summon the state's name.

"New Jersey," Jeff, the art director, supplied.

"Correct, Hitchcock has a picture that takes place in New Jersey, and he is actually shooting it in New Jersey—which, I understand, is all the way on the opposing coast. Whereas here we are on a Hollywood soundstage, striving to replicate a city that is only a few hundred miles to the north. Why is that?"

You're not Hitchcock was the first thing Jeff thought of saying. The second thing—but it wasn't an answer at all, more of a nagging doubt, was, Where the heck was this Sykes from? He had a Limey name, but he talked and carried on just like Jerry.

Meanwhile Sykes, waiting for an answer, paced the floor, frowning. Jeff saw that Sykes was wearing jodhpurs, for chrissake! The only other living director who still wore jodhpurs was DeMille, who had a good twenty years on Sykes—he was from the Pleistocene era, that'd explain C.B.'s dress code.

"Actually," Jeff offered, "we'll have a helluva lot more control of the look of the picture—the design of it—on the stage. In other words, we can take what Frisco's got—which, granted, is plenty—and actually improve on it! Let's say we matte in the Golden Gate Bridge, for instance . . . We can make it even longer, wider, and taller, if we want to. More majestic."

Sykes stopped pacing. He turned. His frown softened, as he envisioned the possibilities. "More golden, even."

Jeff blinked. "That won't read in black and white."

Sykes stared at Jeff through narrowed eyes. "There is some mistake. *Meet Fate Among the Clouds* is a color picture."

Jeff shook his head. "That's not what my department was told, sir." Then, on instinct, he took a step back. Something told him this strange Limey-Kraut combo was liable to lash out.

But Sykes just stood here, immobile as Coit Tower.

"Personally I prefer black and white," Jeff tried. "It's much more realistic. I know that sounds cockeyed, since we see in color. But we don't see in Technicolor, that's for sure! And thank god for it, dontcha think? The hues are so sweet and rich, we'd be walking around with toothaches all the time."

Sykes cleared his throat. "Excuse me. I must speak with Chester Dowling at once."

"Sure, boss." Jeff edged away from the living room set. "But I can show you Tony's office first, if you want, since we're right here, and the carpenters have just about . . ."

Sykes turned on his heels. Jeff heard the director click those heels. Aside from Judy Garland in *Wizard of Oz,* Jeff couldn't think of another non-Kraut heel-clicker.

"Mr. Sykes," he called out to the director, as the director marched over to the stairs that led down from the living room set, "Truth is, you *can* read gold in black and white—talk to your cameraman. Heck, we can make the bridge more gold than Jean Harlow's hair, if that's the way you want it, Mr. Sykes!"

What concerned Jeff, of course, was that this high-strung character would make the proverbial Big Stink with the front office—succeeding only in getting the picture shelved, with Jeff and his underpaid staff the first to be laid off, as always.

Sykes stopped, and turned, at the foot of the stairs. "The way I want it," he responded, "is in color. Every creative decision I've made thus far—be it to do with script, cast, camera—was made with a color picture in mind."

Tell it to the marines, the art director said to himself. But out loud, he called, "Break a leg, boss!"

As Derek Sykes trekked from the soundstage across the steaming lot to the Administration Building, he muttered: "What would Dieter do—what would Dieter do—what would Dieter do—"

Perhaps he was more than muttering. A multitude of dress extras, bizarrely costumed in torn, bloody muslin (they were making another biblical epic on the lot, and Christian martyrs were everywhere nowadays) stopped, turned, gawked as he passed. One wag flapped his arms like wings, shrieking, "Cock-a-doodle-doo," while a second smart aleck joked, "Say, Kaiser Wilhelm's gone screwy." The fellow done up as Barabbas laughed wildly.

Chester Dowling's Dictograph buzzed. "It's Derek Sykes to see you," his secretary said.

"I'm still at lunch," Dowling shot back.

But too late. "He's coming in. He swept right past my desk," the secretary warned, "and he's hopping mad."

"*De*-rek." Dowling rose from behind his desk to greet Sykes, who'd rushed in looking pale and agitated, more like a potential assassin than a picture director.

"Dieter," Derek corrected. "My name is Dieter."

"Whatever you say, Dieter." Dowling sat back down, wearing a loan officer's bland how-can-I-help-you-sir smile.

"My art director tells me that *Meet Fate Among the Clouds* is—"

"Oh, yeah, the new title. Y'didn't get a memo?"

Sykes froze.

"*Meet Fate* didn't go down so well with our exhibitors. Too . . . something. And since the book never sold that many copies . . ." Dowling took a dramatic pause, then boomed: "*The Big Betrayal.* Whattaya think?"

"*The Big Betrayal?*" Sykes laughed, darkly. "I should say so! Now I'm told you're taking away my Technicolor?"

Dowling held up his palms in a gesture of helplessness. "We're tightening our belts, Derek. Dieter. There's a war on."

"Is that so!" Sykes raged. "And now I suppose Superior is sending its spare Technicolor to the troops overseas! So they can lob brighter green hand grenades, perhaps? To bleed the enemy a deeper crimson?"

Dowling chuckled. "Got ants in your pants, Dieter?" He

leaned his chair back. "Look, pal, if I was you I'd settle down—no point getting all worked up over *color* when the fact is you don't even have a *picture*—"

"I *what?*" Dieter demanded. "Would you repeat that, sir?"

"No," Dowling parried, "but I'll finish what I was saying." He leaned forward again. "You don't have a picture till you've cast the star role. Who's playing Tony? That's more important than all the Technicolor stock in the Los Angeles basin, Sykes."

"Seife." The director stared at Dowling.

Dowling stared back. This was known, outside of Mexico, as a Mexican standoff.

Nearly a minute passed before Dowling spoke: "We just got the tests back from the lab. Matter of fact, I was gonna call you. So why don't you cool off a little, then you and me can stroll over to the screening room and run 'em. Whattaya say?"

Dieter said, "Why not?" in the tone of profound resignation only a refugee from the heart of the Sick Soul of Europe could hope to pull off. The two men started out of Dowling's office.

And the Dictograph buzzed again. Dowling backtracked. "We're not here, Agnes, we're running the 'Tony' screen tests—"

"It's for Mr. Seife. It's quite important, apparently."

Dowling sighed. "Okay, put the call through."

He handed Seife the phone.

An irritable, suspicious "Yes?" was Seife's special way of greeting his mystery caller. He heard nothing for a moment.

Then: "You make quite a spectacle of yourself when you're in high dudgeon, Dieter—did you know that?" came the voice at the other end: calm, deceptively so, and deceptively friendly.

"How did you find me here?" Seife wondered, lowering his voice, turning away from Dowling.

Jasper Ridley reminded the director: "I am your doctor, Dieter.

I consider you an outpatient. Therefore it's my responsibility to keep tabs on your whereabouts at all times. And, of course, being Hollywood's Unseen Healer, I have friends on all the studio lots, men and women I've helped through all manner of crises: medical, sexual, spiritual, professional—"

"I'm in a meeting," Seife interjected, constricted.

"As I'm well aware," Dr. Ridley assured him. "It's why I'm calling. To remind you again that, in your dealings with the Hollywood executives for whom you work, you must take care to be conciliatory, accommodating, collaborative always. And I don't mean 'collaborative' in the Marshal Pétain sense of the term."

"I really must go now." Seife had turned back to Dowling, who was tapping his toes on the deep pile carpet. He could hear the doctor's insistently mellifluous voice starting up again, and disconnected. "Apologies for the interruption, Chester. Please—let's now look at the tests."

"Who was that?" Dowling asked, on their way out.

"*Niemand*. No one." Off Dowling's look: "Okay—the art department."

They sat together in the dark, watching a long succession of would-be Tonys. Seife hadn't made the tests—these preliminary screen tests were supervised by the studio casting department and shot by a (genuine) British "lighting cameraman" on loan. The Girl was a secretary from the lot, drafted for her medium-length blond hair and the slim shoulder over which the single locked-off shot was made.

What a dreary bunch of contenders! It took Seife a few tests to realize that what he was watching were the strenuous, even desperate, efforts of a whole spectrum of actor *dregs*.

At one end were the untried and untested (and unfortunate)

prospects like Sonny Tufts, former college football star. At the opposite end were leading men held to be over the hill till the War Effort had thrown Hollywood's scientific, mathematical male casting system into chaos. Now Maurice Costello was back—but the camera, alas, couldn't get back quite far enough to camouflage the awful, craggy truth. In the middle were Western stars who'd been persuaded to trade their leather vests for velvet smoking jackets. Which accounted for Johnny Mack Brown, swaggering bowlegged into frame, sucking on a cigarette as though it were a cheroot, and reading the line, "Why don't we get out of here—just the two of us, and fast?" as though he were wrangling a favorite steer, not seducing a debutante.

"May we please pause just a moment?" Dieter pleaded, afraid that watching one more cowpoke or college athlete might cause a cerebral hemorrhage. The screen dimmed, houselights faded up.

"Who do you like so far?" Dowling asked, disingenuously. "Adolphe Menjou, maybe? Or d'ya think he's too . . . seasoned?"

The telephone between them rang.

"Dowling here," the production chief growled into the mouthpiece. A pause. He turned to the director. "For you."

Seife took the call with misgivings. "Yes?"

"Never do that again," he was admonished, in a voice that was chillingly modulated, controlled. "Never hang up on Jasper Ridley, for as long as we maintain a professional relationship. Do you fully understand me on that score, Dieter?"

Seife swallowed. "I'm so sorry. Can we continue the conversation later, this evening perhaps? I'm in a swamp."

" 'I'm swamped,' " Dr. Ridley corrected him. "Though you . . . you may *be* in a swamp, I fear, a swamp of your own making."

Seife chanced a glance at Dowling, who was watching and listening with undisguised interest.

Which Dieter tried to counteract with dull phraseology. "I was in the wrong, sir, I concede your point," he answered in a monotone. The gambit worked: Dowling turned away, instantly bored, and Dr. Ridley wrapped things up:

"I want to see you out at the Hacienda this evening. We're having one of our Healing Circles, seven-thirty on the dot. And I want you to bring me what you owe—in cash. Don't fail me, Dieter, for if you do, you've failed yourself." Dial tone.

Rattled by Ridley's apparent omniscience, Seife set down the phone and tried to get back to business. "Again, my apologies, Chester. Who's left on the list, please?"

"Just four more." Dowling read them off: "Gig Young, Guy Madison, John Hodiak, Harley Hayden." He looked up. " 'Less you'd rather wait till Jerry waves the white flag and Gable, Stewart, and Fonda come marching home?"

"Thank you, no. Can we skip directly to Mr. Hayden?"

"I said Harley, not Sterling," Dowling warned. Eddie Griffith had just made two pictures with Sterling Hayden, and the one with Madeleine Carroll was apparently sneaking well.

"I would like to see this Harley Hayden," Seife insisted.

Dowling was surprised. "You a fan of Hayden's stuff?"

"I've not watched any of it," the director replied. "But I chanced to see Mr. Hayden outside Mr. Lustig's office, months ago. It seemed to me he had a natural quality, a certain ease."

" 'Ease' he's got." Dowling smiled. "What could be easier than making the boss's gorgeous mockey daughter?"

But Seife was in no mood for gossip this afternoon, even the salacious sort. (Nor did he have the slightest idea what "mockey" meant, nor did he believe he'd find it in his English-Deutsch dictionary.) "Show me Hayden, then, if you would."

Dowling arched his broad back halfway over the seat, and

shouted toward the projection booth: "Joe! Run the Hayden test."

The lights dimmed again. Seife sat up straight, lips drawn taut, as the screen glowed once more. He watched intently over the secretary's shoulder (she'd never turned around, but Dieter had stopped wondering whether she was attractive twelve tests ago) as Hayden entered frame. In costume and makeup, he looked every inch the leading man. A tad young for the role, his "dramatic" expression maybe a shade callow, but handsome and graceful as Seife remembered him from their one encounter. He approached the secretary with confidence and conviction (his height conferred a relaxed authority, bush-league Gary Cooper), unerringly finding his key light as he stopped for his first line: "You came into my bedroom last night, didn't you?"

His voice, Seife noticed, was a bit thin, and not nearly deep enough. Maybe with a voice coach, he could learn to . . .

"I heard sounds, and got scared. You were tossing, turning, and shouting: accusations and names. A woman's name. Not mine," the secretary answered. (Seife *did* notice that her line readings had been steadily improving. She wasn't bad, really.)

"Well, at night, the pain seems to worsen." Hayden had an accent, some sort of regional accent, that Seife couldn't quite place. Whatever it was, it tended to flatten his words, make them all sound the same somehow. "It's like a bell in my head, a bell someone keeps clanging. Somehow I finally got to sleep."

Hayden grinned. It was a handsome grin, to be sure, but it was not necessarily the proper facial expression for the line.

Dieter leaned toward Dowling. "Does he often grin like that on-screen?"

"And once asleep, well, hey: 'What dreams may come?'—as some English guy once wrote." Hayden didn't seem to know who that "English guy" might be. With Sonny Tufts you expected this, but . . . *Scene preparation must be improved,* Seife noted.

Dowling shrugged. "On-screen, off-screen. It's the Harley Hayden grin. He could take out a patent on it, f' chrissake."

Seife studied the screen. The grin was still fixed across Hayden's face—like a rictus, or something glued on. In any case, the effect was most unnatural.

"Y' gotta admit, though," Dowling remarked, "the kid looks damned handsome when he does it. If I had a grin like that, I'd grin from sunup to sundown, while fighting off the dames."

Seife ignored this, concentrating again on the screen as Hayden now sat opposite the secretary. Sitting, Seife saw, severely reduced Hayden's screen presence—so much of it had to do with his lanky physique. The grin was still in evidence.

"Well, now that you're awake, if there's something you want to tell me—about that other woman, about anything at all," the secretary recited (no, that was unfair, she was actually feeling the words, it seemed to Seife—perhaps she was in the midst of an unhappy love affair or divorce, poor thing), "I'm willing to hear it. In fact I *have* to hear it, don't I, Tony, darling?"

Hayden wasn't listening. He was waiting for her speech to end, so he could deliver his next line. While such a tendency in a movie actor could be covered with skillful editing, it was painfully apparent in a screen test, in which the camera never cut away but only scrutinized, unblinking.

"Now that I'm awake, all those accusations and names have scattered to the four winds," Harley/Tony intoned. He was pitching his voice a little lower, to add weight to the line—but in the process, Hayden's voice lost nearly half its volume. "And that other woman?" Hayden scoffed. Unfortunately it sounded more like a cough. "She's just a night terror, Leora."

Then he stared straight into the secretary's eyes. No, not quite straight . . . Hayden was tilting his head, just slightly, as though to adjust to an angle he knew was his most flattering.

Then the test ended, and the lights came up.

"The kid doesn't stink" was Dowling's placid judgment.

Seife folded his hands across his lap. " 'Stink'? No. But he's more than a bit wooden, don't you agree? Disappointing."

"Ah, he was nervous, Derek. Dieter. Jumpy, and who could blame him? A picture like this'd be a big break for Harley. Chance to work with a director of your stature."

"Yes, I suppose a younger actor with not too much experience might feel that way," Seife allowed. "But there are other problems. The grin, for instance. It is a particularly annoying mannerism, I find."

"So tell him to can it. He grins, call 'Cut.' Maybe he'll be sore, the first couple times. In the end, he'll thank you for breaking him of the habit, when he picks up his Oscar."

Oscar. Another word, often used in Hollywood, to make movie people automatically start seeing (to quote the third couplet of "The Night Before Christmas") visions of sugarplums.

"Then there is his voice," Seife went on. "It has no . . ."

"Oomph?" Dowling suggested.

"Oomph" was a word that meant nothing to Seife. "The voice is thin," he pronounced.

"Hell, the *kid* is thin. Put some meat on Hayden's bones, five'll get you ten the voice gets fuller, richer. Like Welles. Better yet, we got a dozen dialogue coaches on the lot could work with him while you're prepping. By the end of four weeks he'll sound like Barrymore. And I don't mean Ethel."

Seife turned to Dowling with a frown. "Are you trying to sell me Harley Hayden?" It sounded like an accusation.

"Hell no." Dowling chuckled. "I'd just as soon try to sell you the Panama Canal. Anyway, it's no skin off my ass if you take Harley or John Hodiak, Costello or Menjou. It's just—"

"Just what?"

"Excuse me, Mr. Dowling, sir?" Joe the projectionist called from back in his booth. "We'll need the room now to run Miss Lamour's makeup and hair tests, if that's okay."

Dowling stood, started up the aisle. He looked relieved to be out of there.

Seife followed, and repeated, "Just what?"

They were outdoors again, in the grayish glare. Both men started to sweat as they began walking. "Just that, like I told you, Hayden's—well, *dating* Ellie Lustig, Eleanor, the boss's daughter. If you catch my meaning." He glanced over at Seife—who didn't seem to be on Dowling's wavelength, for some damn reason. "What I'm trying to say, it wouldn't exactly be a disadvantage to have the boss's daughter's boyfriend starring in your picture. Any of this getting through that noggin? Derek?"

Seife wore a faraway look. Was it the heat? No, the director had something on his mind: "Once, back in Germany, I knew of a young person who became involved in the film industry because of a close relative already in that industry. It turned out quite badly for all concerned."

Dowling nodded, wearing an "interested" look. But, like Harley Hayden in the screen test, he wasn't really listening.

Seife's face was now glazed with sweat. No wonder, thought Dowling—the sonuvabitch was dressed for the Octoberfest. What a piece of work! Where did Mr. L dig up these crazy SOBs?

"Dieter, hear me out. Hayden's *in* pictures already. Hell, *Photo-*

play's placed him in their Top Ten Young Male Leads for four years running—and for two of those four years, Harley made the Top Five!" Dowling had no idea whether any of this was true, but Christ, it easily *could* be true. "So maybe he still needs some grooming to make the leap into A pictures. That's where *you* come in. After all, what did Dietrich have except her gams, answer me that, before Von Stroheim took charge of her career?"

"Von Sternberg."

"Exactly." Then: "You'd be doing yourself a favor, that's all I'm telling you. 'The son-in-law also rises.'" He glanced at Seife, whose features remained grim, severe.

"I don't understand you," the director complained.

They'd reached the Administration Building, and Dowling was too overheated to explain the gag. "Think it over, will 'ya?" he urged, thrusting out a damp hand. "And bear in mind what you've got in the way of alternatives while you're at it."

This was Seife's opening. He'd been waiting nearly an hour to spring his ideal casting suggestion on the production head.

"Fred MacMurray."

"Huh?"

"Fred MacMurray would be perfect for Tony. *Perfect.*"

"No soap," Dowling shot back—and, though Dieter wasn't familiar with this idiom, he could easily infer its meaning.

"Why not?" he demanded. "And don't tell me he's in basic training or on a troopship bound for Europe. I checked this morning, I have sources. MacMurray's right here in Hollywood."

"He's right here, alright," Dowling agreed, too readily for Seife's liking. "Fact, he's on the lot. But he's committed."

Seife didn't believe this, not for a moment. "To what?"

"Nothing you'd be interested in. Psychologic horror . . . besides, there's already a director assigned to the picture, a French fella, Jacques Tourneur. Heard of him? And we got DeWitt Bodeen working on the scenario, so you can't have *him,* either," Dowling added, intending this as a humorous aside.

"What is the picture?" Seife would not be hoodwinked.

Dowling shrugged. "It's called *The Double.* MacMurray'll play a dual role—a guy who's walking down the street and sees himself, or a carbon copy of himself, then has twenty-four hours to be sure the other fella dies—the carbon copy, not him, see."

Seife's facial muscles twitched. For a moment he was afraid he'd collapse right here on the lot, from the effects of a heatstroke exacerbated by unchecked rage. He brought out a handkerchief and mopped his face. Dowling was inspired to do likewise. The two men stood a few feet apart, both drying their cheeks, in another variation on the Mexican standoff.

Ten, fifteen seconds ticked by in silence. Then: "I have to go," the pair said, simultaneously.

Seife spun around and started toward the parking lot. But within two strides he stopped and spun back, shouting at Dowling just as the production topper was about to reenter his building: "Matters to do with the casting of this picture are far from settled!" His shout dissipated, wilted, in the heat. "I still want Fred MacMurray!"

But Dowling had already ducked indoors.

Seife drove home in a state of fury and panic, intermingled. Lustig had played a shameless game of bait-and-switch, luring him into a color picture that had then been drained of pigment; Lustig had, moreover, taken a chance remark of Seife's, fashioned another movie from it—without asking permission or offering credit—then stolen Dieter's dream casting element into the bargain! Seife would not be surprised to find that *The Double* would, as a final insult, be shot in Technicolor!

The temperature inside Seife's automobile seemed to be rising fast. He opened his window, only to feel his sticky face hit with a blast of scorching air. He closed it again and resumed baking in his rolling oven of a Roadmaster. If this was how business was conducted in Southern California, Seife thought, well, would I really fare much worse back at Ufa, dealing with Goebbels, making movies with Nazis?

And then, in the midst of his turbulent meditation on Lustig and Hollywood, Seife remembered Dr. Ridley—and his enslavement to this man, both financially and psychologically, not to mention Ridley's grim insistence that Dieter go see him, this very evening, with cash Ridley knew Seife didn't have.

By the time he pulled into his garage, Seife's unseasonable clothes had fastened to his flesh like a tropical disease. He kicked off his heavy shoes and yanked down his argyle socks in the foyer, then removed his jodhpurs and climbed the stairs, hurling aside his jacket and stripping off his shirt and tie with crazy desperation.

As he burst into his bathroom he was now blessedly nude. Seife charged toward his shower stall, threw the pebbled glass door wide. The woman standing inside the shower whirled on him, and screamed.

Seife screamed, too, startled as he was. Then he saw it was only Hilda, who'd been scrubbing the purple deco tile and grout.

"Herr Seife!" She dropped the scrub brush and pressed her palms over her eyes, launching into a heated monologue, the gist of which was that she was today a respectable wife and mother, a religious person, a woman who had once been a sinner, yes, she would admit that, had committed numerous sins of the flesh but had finally been saved by Jesus Christ our Lord and was now someone of substantial character and standing in the community.

All of this in German, as Seife hastily wrapped a bath towel around his waist. Then he entreated her, in English:

"Please stop, Hilda. The crisis has passed, my private parts are now concealed. And no more German, *bitte,*" he added, quietly. "Voices carry in these hills. Nosy neighbors who overhear two people conversing in German are likely to pick up their telephones and call the police, isn't that so? Have you noticed, Hilda, how this country is full of do-gooders, men and women who are absolutely certain that everything they carry out and believe is for the best, even though it's only for their benefit? These Americans, it seems to me, are so beholden to an image of themselves as good and decent, always . . . and, above all, innocent. I wonder if that comes of their being so young?"

Finally Hilda uncovered her eyes and regarded Seife with incomprehension. Realizing he'd been a trifle digressive and overemphatic, Seife thought to simplify things: he took Hilda's hands in his own and gently drew her out of the shower stall.

"I must rinse off. I have an appointment this evening."

"Then I will go downstairs and cook your supper, Herr Seife," said Hilda in careful English, her blush subsiding.

A half hour later, she watched a showered-and-shaved Seife bolt his sausages and sauerkraut, glancing at his watch between bites. Then, joylessly swallowing down the last morsel of meat, he leapt from the table, toward the garage.

"Was the meal not satisfying, sir?" she asked.

"The meal was delicious, Hilda," Seife assured her. He hesitated. "But the smells, the cooking smells, as they waft from my kitchen down into the canyon . . . I become afraid."

"That someone will sniff my cabbage and call the police?"

Seife nodded. "Or the FBI."

His eyes, Hilda noticed, looked a bit wild this evening. Perhaps he wasn't sleeping enough. Certainly, he worried too much. "Herr Seife—" she began.

He cut her off. "I must go." Then turned, and hurried—fled, really—into the garage.

When Hilda was sure he'd gone, she picked up the phone and dialed a number. A young man's voice was heard saying hello.

"Heinrich, it's me," she said in German, making no effort to mute her voice. "I'm awfully worried about Herr Seife."

Unlike her fearful employer, Hilda cared not a whit whether some vigilant neighbor might overhear the distinctive consonant clusters, palatal fricatives, diphthongs, and strange guttural sounds of the Enemy.

From *Daily Variety*

Hayden Pacts for Lead in
"Big Betrayal"

Harley Hayden, one of Superior Pictures' most in-demand male contract players, has inked to star in studio's upcoming meller, *The Big Betrayal,* it was reported today. Pic, based on the best-selling novel *Meet Fate Among the Clouds,* is looking at a mid-November start. "It's quite a thrill to have Harley aboard," British helmer Derek Sykes is quoted in studio's press release. "He's one of Hollywood's brightest young stars." Lead fem role remains to be cast. Hayden is repped by Moe Kasher at MCA.

· 9 ·

Flip

It was during those sweltering, grueling, at times interminable sessions in front of the not-so-secret grand jury that Roarke first realized the stenographer was eyeing him as she typed. He hadn't paid her much attention—if anything, he was intrigued by the steno machine, a snappy-looking gizmo, but the woman who worked it wasn't his style: bottle blond, bumpy-skinned, coarse-featured. Though maybe she was hiding some kind of a *body* beneath the drab work clothes, and maybe her ordinary face would make her more of a go-getter in bed, in contrast with the sort of gal who believed she was doing you a big favor by lying on her back with open legs. But if Roarke gave any thought to this, it was merely something that flashed across his brainpan in less than two seconds. He was, after all, in the process of giving sworn testimony about his "activities" as a vice detective on Central Avenue between the years 1936 and 1939. He was, after all, trying to stay out of prison.

About two weeks into his testimony, while on lunch break,

Roarke ducked into a liquor store. His stomach didn't feel up to food, but he thought he could handle some whiskey or rye, provided it was mixed with a little milk. While Roarke was browsing the shelves, someone tapped his shoulder and said, "I feel like you're getting a raw deal."

It was the stenographer. Later it occurred to Roarke she'd followed him the twelve blocks from county courthouse to liquor store. (Sally wasn't one to steal a nip on her lunch break.) Roarke was impressed by her impetuosity—recklessness, some might say. Following him, talking to him, either one could have cost Sally her job. And steady office jobs were scarce then.

On top of that, Roarke was hard-pressed to see how Sally had reached the conclusion that he was being persecuted by the D.A. The lengthy accounts he'd been forced to give, under oath, about extortion, bribe taking, the confiscation and resale of narcotics, and the exploitation of prostitutes: that was rough stuff by any standard. And the stenographer had had to get every word of it into the record. It told Roarke that, never mind the "raw deal" angle, what Sally was really saying was that she had a yen for a "bad character," a "rotten apple." She must have liked what she was hearing: it gave her a thrill. Perhaps she saw Roarke not as some species of sleazy criminal cop, but rather a defiant outlaw hero: Pretty Boy Floyd, say, or Bogart in *High Sierra*. Maybe all the talk of whores, dope, and payoffs sounded manly to her, added up to the rap-sheet equivalent of a big swinging dick. Later, after they'd been to bed, Sally confessed she'd been married and divorced before the age of twenty-three, and described her former husband, Glenn Racine, as a "little no-count weasel." And Roarke had to concede to himself that whatever he was, he wasn't *that*. A wolf, maybe. A coyote, a hyena. An anteater, even—but no weasel.

. . .

And here they were playing house—with Sal playing secretary when Hayden unexpectedly called that second time. What the hell, it made Roarke's operation seem a little more professional.

"He said he'd call back as soon as he finished the next scene."

"Mm. How'd he sound?"

Sally shrugged. "In a rush. Under pressure. Or both. But friendly, and nice. Not flirtatious at all, a real gentleman."

"Harley? A gentleman to one and all. Even to me, even after he got the word as to why the hell I was following him around town for ten days."

One thing about Sally: by training, she would register information, file it away, but she'd never push for more. "He said he'd leave you a drive-on at the main gate."

Roarke much preferred to fake his way onto the lot, but grunted agreement. "If Flip wants me there at five," he muttered, heading for the bathroom, "I'll be there at five."

"Flip?" Sally looked intrigued, and Roarke suddenly felt annoyed and trapped. In such a mood he was liable to go out prowling for the treat he liked best: black meat. But in this segregated section of town, one often had to settle for Mexican girls, preferably the swarthier Aztec, Mayan, or Mestiza types.

"Nothing, Sal. Just a nickname."

She giggled. "Is he a personal friend of yours? 'Cause if he is, boy, what I wouldn't give for a signed autograph."

Roarke tried to imagine, for a moment, what an *un*-signed autograph might look like, then promised, "I'll bring you back some kind of keepsake from Hayden, if you're such a big fan."

"Oh, I *am*. I just *adored* him, in . . ."

Her heavy eyebrows crept toward each other like mating caterpillars as Sally tried to summon a single Harley Hayden title, past or present. She drew a blank.

The air was stagnant, and though the sun was still up, the light it gave off was the color of lead. As Roarke walked from the parking lot to Hayden's dressing room, he reflected on just how upside down the world had turned since he'd last seen Hayden. Half of humanity was at war, Carole Lombard was dead, Harley Hayden was a movie star. What Roarke couldn't begin to guess was what Hayden wanted to see him about, *now,* in this strange, inverted new world. He half-hoped the matter would concern Ellie again. Perhaps this time he'd share his information.

Harley had just returned from the soundstage, greeting Roarke in full camera makeup. The effect on Hayden's already handsome face was to make him appear to be a perfect-looking human specimen—or a May Company mannequin come eerily to life.

"Mister Big Shot," Roarke teased, as the men shook. "Hey, no kidding, good to see you again. I felt kind of funny, a few months back, whenever that was . . . ? Having to turn you down."

Hayden gestured for Roarke to sit on a hard, narrow couch as he drew up a chair opposite.

"Ever get the answers to your questions?" Roarke asked.

"Never tried," Hayden admitted. "But if you really did feel funny," he went on, sensing an opening, "I've got a fine way to get rid of the feeling." He took a pause—an actor's pause. "Help me out, *now.* I'm begging."

In Roarke's Central Avenue heyday, whole shifts were spent fielding the supplications and importuning of anxious citizens. A statuesque Negress working the Dunbar Hotel would offer sexual favors if only Roarke would promise not to tell her pimp she'd stashed a john's payment in the hollowed-out high heel he'd re-

trieved from the foot of her bed; but Roarke rarely had the urge
for sloppy seconds. Hophead jazz musicians backstage at the Alabam would plead with Roarke: "Don't flush my stash, man, it's
righteous shit, and I'll go fifty-fifty on it wit' you." Roarke would
scoff, pocket the whole fix, then resell it—works and all—a block
down Central, at Ivie's Chicken Shack, to a toffee-colored
chanteuse with chronic stage fright. But several years had passed
since anyone had begged Roarke for mercy, or favors. It wasn't
just that he was now a freelancer without a private license. It
wasn't just that he had no juice with local law enforcement.
Roarke was damaged goods in Los Angeles, a pariah—a leper,
even. Though he'd never been indicted, he'd remained under perpetual investigation by a special prosecutor, and that was worse:
no one would touch him but Chester Dowling. And the jobs
Dowling offered were beneath the dignity (and wages) of any retired police officer or licensed PI. Even at that, the work was
dwindling as the war was expanding; Dowling had hired Roarke
exactly once in the past five months, to scare a lecherous teamster
off a frightened hairdresser. Unfortunately, the teamster, though
large, was a bully who scared easily—Roarke could only bill Superior for two days' labor. Sometimes it seemed to Roarke as
though the only luck he'd had since Mayor Bowron's purge of the
LAPD, was that his wife had chosen to fall off the face of the
earth rather than divorce him and sue for alimony, child support,
and half of Roarke's possessions.

"As it happens," Roarke said, taking care not to rush his
words, "I'm just winding up a few matters, and could possibly set
aside some time for you." He hoped he sounded even halfway
credible, and not like a guy who'd been sponging for months off
his nose-to-the-grindstone girlfriend. Christ, when he thought of
how he'd disdained those Central Avenue pimps, shamelessly liv-

ing off their stable of women, and look at Roarke now—wishing
he had a *stable,* not just some hourly wage stenographer.

Though Hayden had drawn up a chair, he hadn't sat. Instead,
he paced the dressing room like a POW in solitary. "The picture
I'm making—remember back at Lucey's I told you there was a
British director attached?"

"What of it?"

"First of all, he's not a Brit, he's a Jerry." The well-mannered
actor corrected himself: "A German, I'd swear it."

"Okay, he's a German. Superior's always had a soft spot for
German directors, I seem to recall. Something about their author-
itarian temperament. Dowling once explained it to me—"

Hayden interrupted: "It's not that he's German, it's that he's
masquerading, this director. He's using another name."

Roarke realized it was time to show some vague interest, lest he
lose Hayden's business. "What's the name he's using?"

"Derek Sykes. They claim he's directed a bunch of pictures
back home and here, too, but damned if anyone can tell me what
they were. Or if they were any good at all, but that's another conversation." Hayden traversed the tiny room several more times,
perhaps waiting for Roarke to respond.

When Roarke didn't respond, Hayden stopped pacing and
turned to the ex-cop. "I know what you're thinking: what the hell
does that matter, whether you can track down his . . . his screen
credits? And maybe it doesn't. But it doesn't add up."

Roarke had been looking around the dressing room while Hayden had paced. He'd noted a photo of Eleanor Lustig taped to
the makeup mirror: a casual snapshot, the kind that makes everyone look average. But not Ellie: she glowed from the matte print
like a special effect. And then there were Hayden's street clothes,
neatly hanging. No other personal touches, just numerous scripts

scattered, open to various pages and heavily marked in ink. The notes were underlined, circled, emphasized with multiple exclamation points and question marks.

"You're working awfully hard there on your role, I see."

Hayden looked confused. Roarke gestured at the avalanche of annotated script pages.

"Oh." Hayden sat. He looked deflated, and sounded tired. "Those aren't my notes. They're Mr. Sykes's." He plucked the script nearest him off the coffee table. And read, at random, "*Just say the line. No acting.*" He looked like a pup who'd just had his muzzle struck by a rolled newspaper. "*No acting?* Then what the heck'm I doing here, would you tell me that?"

Roarke picked up another script, lying open at his feet—as though it had been hurled there from across the room. The top of the page was covered in Derek Sykes's heavy hand printing:

Don't indicate! You don't know what Leora is about to say!

Roarke looked up at Harley. "Who's Leora?"

Hayden sighed. "Girl in the movie. Someone I destroy, by accident. She's played by a newcomer, that Sykes discovered. Mary Oakley. Cute kid." He seemed melancholy about Mary, too.

"What—don't tell me *she's* a Jerry?"

There was a warning knock, the door swung open, and a young assistant stuck his head in. " 'Scuse me, sir, prop master's looking for Tony's lighter. Any chance you still got it?"

Frowning, Hayden patted his costume, then came up with a silver-plated Dunhill from a pants pocket. "Sorry if I caused Sam any bother," he said, handing it over.

When the door closed again, Roarke asked, "What, were they scared you were gonna steal the lighter? Hock it, maybe?"

Hayden flashed a tight smile. "No, I think they were scared I might burn down my dressing room. For starters."

"What's the trouble with Mary Oakley?" Roarke tried again.

Having removed the Dunhill from his suit, Hayden began removing his suit. For such a self-effacing man, he had little physical modesty. Perhaps it came of working at a profession in which one regularly stood around in skivvies while a director, a costume designer, and the designer's staff stared at, critiqued, and measured one's bare body. Or maybe stripping down came naturally to people paid to reveal themselves to strangers—namely hookers and actors. Or maybe it's the stark fact that an actor is his own merchandise, his product is *himself:* the person standing before you. "Mary? She's no trouble at all." Then, incongruously, the handsome young man wearing nothing but boxers and stage makeup asked the former cop: "Wanna go get a drink?"

"Isn't Ellie—Eleanor—waiting at home for you?"

"Actually, I'm a carefree bachelor tonight," Harley said, sounding anything but carefree. Then he sat at his mirror and began rubbing off his makeup with cold cream and a hand towel. "It's Wednesday, Ellie's working late in the UCLA stacks."

"Right . . . And she's majoring in—what, again?"

"Psychology."

"How come?" Roarke prompted. One part of the ex-cop (the frustrated, impatient part) wanted Hayden to start asking Ellie some questions—the right questions. But though he adored his girlfriend, Hayden was an actor. And just as an actor's only merchandise is himself, so must his first love be himself, too.

"Beats me," Hayden said, with a shrug.

Roarke wound up following Hayden down Wilshire to the Ambassador Hotel. It was still early, but the Cocoanut Grove—Hayden's choice—was already jumping when they arrived.

Though it was a world away from Barney's Beanery, the Grove

wasn't Roarke's sort of saloon either: its palm trees were papier-mâché, and stuffed monkeys hung from the leaves. Worse, photographers were allowed to roam freely with their Graflexes, popping flashbulbs in customers' faces on the off chance they were incognito film stars out on the town. Roarke'd had his fill of flashbulbs back when he'd been compelled to testify before the secret grand jury that, clearly, wasn't secret enough. (Anyway, he loathed how he looked in flash photos printed on cheap newsprint—his cheekbones, the orbits of his eyes, everything simultaneously stretched thin and drooping, puffy and hollow.) But Hayden was in his element now, quietly pointing out, as they were shown to their table, "Walter Winchell . . . Loretta Young . . ." and a few others whose names were clearly supposed to register with Roarke, but didn't.

"How the hell can you tell without your cheaters on?"

Roarke could see the actor had given up his bizarre contact lenses—Hayden's eyes no longer looked like cobalt saucers.

"If I squint hard enough," Hayden confided, "it looks like I'm thinking—when all I'm really doing, is *seeing*. Or trying to."

Now it struck Roarke that he loathed the Cocoanut Grove because, unlike his drinking partner, he could see the room in sharp relief. See the stitching on the stuffed monkeys. The peeling gilt on the stars painted overhead. The ill-fitting toupee on the aging screen idol getting plastered at the next table. Were he even half as myopic as Hayden, Roarke might've had a few laughs here. Too much clarity killed the joke.

As the two settled in with a couple of scotches, Roarke wondered, "If this Mary Oakley is no trouble at all, how come you were in the dumps about her, back in your dressing room?"

Awaiting an answer, Roarke lit a Lucky. Hayden surprised the ex-cop by reaching over and shaking one out for himself.

" 'Lucky Strike goes to war,' " he read off the pack, pointlessly evading Roarke's question for another few seconds. Then: "Look, today was the . . . let's see, eighth day of principal photography. I'm in most every scene, and Mary's been in most, too. But Sykes hasn't given her one single note. Not even a technical one, not even 'Find your key light.' 'Cause she doesn't, always—but hell, that's no sin, she's new to the game. And he only does two, three takes, tops, of her close-up. After that it's 'Okay, print it. We've got it. Next deal.' "

Hayden looked as though he might weep. And suddenly Roarke understood why the actor had dragged him all the way down Wilshire to this swanky supper club. Harley'd been humiliated on his own movie set, and now had to amplify that humiliation by sharing it with a near stranger. But he'd damn well do it in the company of big names, big spenders, and big stars, to remind Roarke—and himself—he was one of them still, a lifetime member of the club, Derek Sykes notwithstanding.

"Whereas, with *your* close-up?"

Hayden sipped his drink. Puffed Roarke's Lucky. Like the tyro drinker and smoker he was, he fought to suppress first a gag, then a cough. "With me, we do four, five, six takes. Then Sykes goes a little screwy. 'No, no, no! That's precisely what I *don't* want!' " He made Sykes sound like a vaudeville Prussian, or Bismarck on laughing gas. "So he gives me some note I can't understand. 'Stop smiling!' he shouts at me. When the fact is I'm *not* smiling, I swear it—the guy is seeing things. For a while I thought maybe he was coming to work soused. I've been through that before, not kidding, some big directors. But there's no booze on his breath . . . though I sometimes could swear I smell cabbage."

"If he's as wound-up as you say he is," Roarke suggested,

"maybe Sykes has a weakness for Happy Dust. L.A. snow." Off Hayden's blank look, Roarke used the civilian term: "Cocaine?"

Hayden looked shocked. "I don't know anything about ... dopers. All I know is, he yells and stomps and then we start all over again. Takes seven through ten. And Sykes, he stands right next to the camera, staring at me—through me—like I'm the heartless murderer who killed his wife. Or his movie."

Roarke shrugged. "What do you want me to do about it? Break Sykes's jaw? Put the Heinie louse in the hospital?"

Hayden puffed again, coughed again, then stubbed out his Lucky. "Jesus H.," he said. "I wasn't thinking anything like that." He looked around, as though worried Winchell might have overheard, and this embarrassing business would wind up on his radio show as "meow of the week." But Winchell's table was now empty.

"Just having a little fun, Flip," Roarke assured the actor. "But all seriousness, what the hell *is* it you want me to do?"

And Hayden explained, in a hushed but steady voice (the urgent yet studiously unexcited tones he'd used when instructing GIs on Slapping the Jap and Stunning the Hun): "The guy's a phony, I know it. He's hiding something—*lotta* things, could be. It's not just that his studio bio doesn't hold water—hell, I could clear that up with Mr. Lustig, or Mr. Dowling, if that was all that was eating me. And I'm not the only one with a Sykes Problem. Crew can't stand him either. Sykes gets under their skin, way he orders them around like he's First Kommandant of the Second Panzer Division. C'mon, tell me, what Brit do you know that says '*Ach*'? 'Blimey,' sure. 'Dear me.' But '*Ach*'?"

"Okay, so you and the crew don't much care for the director. That can't be anything too novel in Tinseltown?"

" 'Don't much care' doesn't begin to cover it. I'm telling you, I think the crew . . ." Harley lowered his voice to a near whisper. "Yesterday I overheard a couple of gaffers talking. Up on the catwalk overhead. One of 'em said to the other something about 'Say, wouldn't it be a crying shame if a ten-K lamp should come loose and tumble down right on top of Sykes's fat head?' "

He waited for Roarke's reaction. Roarke didn't have one. He just smoked, drank, and watched while Hayden dodged and feinted.

"Don't you get it?" the actor exclaimed. "An accident like that would kill Mr. Sykes, no laughing matter! Those kliegs are hung forty feet up, they must weigh a minimum of—"

"Don't go simple on me, Flip. You want me to believe the crew of *Big Betrayal*—professionals, family men—have hatched a plot against Sykes's life? How wet behind the ears do I look?"

Harley shook his head. "Not the whole crew; I overheard two guys. And who knows if they were horsing around, just letting off steam? But I sure as hell don't want to find out the hard way that they meant it. That'd be tough on my conscience. And yours, I'd think, since I've let you in on it."

"Okay, Flip, I'm starting to get it. You want me to shadow Sykes, do a little digging, find out why he seems to have it in for you in particular? And if it turns out he's not a right guy, he's mixed up in something dirty, then I try to throw some kind of loop over him, blow the whistle. Am I in the ballpark?"

Hayden looked around again, then nodded.

"Fine. I'll see what I can come up with. But it costs, Flip. I get forty bucks a day. I know that sounds like a lot but it's what I pulled down on the force, four years ago—"

"Mr. Dowling only pays twenty-five per day. On account of your not being a licensed investigator or anything like that."

Roarke wasn't sure whether to laugh or overturn the table. "You checked my rate with Chester Dowling?"

Harley smiled, pleased at his business acumen.

"Dowling gets a discount," Roarke insisted, annoyed. "Chet was the one guy in town who could see his way clear to hiring me despite the clouds of suspicion and innuendo hanging over—"

"We've all got problems," Harley airily allowed, then waved his arm. "Check, please?"

"Twenty-five," Roarke relented. Then, miffed at Hayden's tactics: "But two weeks, minimum, or it's not worth my time."

The check arrived. This time, Harley paid. "Two week guarantee," he cheerfully agreed. "So where do we start?"

"On Day Nine." Hayden looked confused. Till Roarke added: "Of principal photography. Leave me a drive-on, will ya, Flip?"

As Roarke strolled to the soundstage, he wondered whether the making of *The Big Betrayal* could really be the ordeal Harley'd described the night before—or was this an actor doing what an actor did, in a word, *dramatizing*? Unless Derek Sykes was a raging psycho (unlikely—studios might be run by raging psychos but those selfsame psychos rarely hired other raging psychos to actually make their pictures) then, Roarke reasoned, the atmosphere couldn't be as poisonous as Hayden had claimed.

In fact it was worse. Roarke heard Sykes well before he saw Sykes. Such a voice carries: off the set, across the stage. What Roarke heard him say—shriek, more precisely—was: "There is no camera in your living room! Therefore you cannot—must not—pose for one! Do you grasp that?" He sounded as much like an Englishman as Crown Prince Rupprecht, or Reinhard Heydrich. At that volume, Roarke assumed he was using a megaphone—though why he'd use a megaphone indoors, who could say?

Then Sykes came into view. He was a largish man, Roarke

noted with surprise: not one of those dwarf tyrants that famously terrorized Hollywood, no Hebe Napoleon. Not that Sykes was Max Schmeling, either, but the man looked capable of backing up his bullying. And no, he didn't need any megaphone. Sykes was projecting solely on the basis of lung power.

The getup was hilarious. Jodhpurs? And some sort of military jacket with epaulets and colossal brass buttons? Who was Sykes trying to kid? Certainly not the crew—Roarke caught a few semi-suppressed snickers from the sidelines as Sykes strutted the stage, waving a script as though it were a scythe.

He waved his paper scythe at Harley Hayden. In the same costume as yesterday (and, of course, the full camera makeup) the leading man looked suave and urbane, a touch of Cary Grant without the fey, distracting, continental dandyisms. Catnip for the ladies, and the envy of men . . . with the minor incongruity that Mr. Wonderful was getting a new asshole drilled for himself in front of some fifty technicians (who conveniently formed a sort of human barrier, behind which Roarke took cover).

Roarke's gaze flitted from Hayden to his costar. Though the ex-cop had never seen her before, he knew this was Mary Oakley as sure as if she wore a sign around her neck that read BRIGHT NEW-COMER. She stood off to the side, watching Hayden's latest dressing-down with pained embarrassment and fellow feeling. With every exclamation of Sykes's, Mary Oakley would wince. Roarke pegged her as a virgin who stayed intact by giving away everything to anyone who'd help her along, whenever they asked for it. Everything, that is, but the Grand Prize.

"Do you see a camera?" Sykes demanded. "Do you, Mr. Hayden, when you look this way?" The director stood beside what was, unquestionably, a thirty-five-millimeter motion picture camera.

"What do you want me to say?" Hayden asked.

"This is not a trick, nor a riddle," Sykes insisted. "I simply want an answer, an honest one. Do you see a camera?"

"Yes," Hayden said.

"Right there is your mistake," Sykes scolded. "There is no movie camera. Nor is there a mirror. Nor a reflecting pool, for that matter." He glanced at Mary Oakley, to see if the jest made her smile. But Mary Oakley kept her eyes trained on Harley's black-and-tan wingtips.

"Okay," said Hayden. "I got it, Mr. Sykes."

"Do you? I'm so glad. Then you will finally stop posing, you will stop grinning, you will stop acting, and you will start to respond to Miss Oakley *in the moment,* in a truthful, altogether human way."

Hayden nodded.

"Are you ready to do that for me, Mr. Hayden?"

"Born ready, sir."

"Good." Sykes turned, rather grandly, toward his camera crew. "Shall we roll some film, gentlemen? It would be nice to have a usable close-up of Mr. Hayden in the can before lunch."

This was the cue, apparently, for a makeup girl to sneak onto the stage and add a little powder to Hayden's face (which, quite naturally, had reddened) and a hair girl to primp his pompadour (which nearly always looked perfect, no matter how dire the situation). Stage lights were dimmed, the painting out the window was lit (Roarke recognized Coit Tower) and suddenly everyone on that cavernous, gritty soundstage was transported to a ritzy, spacious, yet cozy Snob Hill penthouse. Someone shouted "Quiet!" though a mausoleum couldn't have been quieter.

"Find your marks" came another voice from somewhere

nearby, and Mary Oakley calmly stepped into place, nearly blocking the camera lens (or so it looked from where Roarke stood)
while Hayden planted his shoes on an X made on the floor in
front of him by two strips of gaffer's tape. Somebody measured
the distance between the tip of his nose to the tip of the lens, then
a few more technical orders were given before Sykes barked the
word "Action" and Hayden's face became a strange, handsome
mask. He locked eyes with Mary's.

"And that other woman? She's just a night terror, Leora."

Hayden, in that moment, was more self-possessed than Roarke
had ever seen him. And his focus on Mary was (given what the ex-
cop knew of Hayden's poor eyesight) a major acting feat.

"Well, the sun's up and she's terrifying *me,*" Mary cut in.
Roarke was startled—Harley was doing fine, and the girl had
stepped on his line! In the next instant he realized this was the
script and not a mistake, so urgent and awkward and real did her
interruption seem. "Till you tell me who she is—and what her
hold is over you—well, I won't sleep nights, either."

Hayden didn't say anything. But the camera kept rolling. What
was wrong, had he forgotten his lines? Five seconds felt like an
agony of silence. Finally: "Who she is? Sure, that'd be swell, for
starters." Hayden laughed, so quietly it was like a private joke.
With dread, Roarke waited for Sykes's shriek. But Sykes watched
from his position beside the faintly whirring camera, holding still,
as Hayden continued: "Hey, if I hadn't hit my head, I'd have all
the answers. But then again I'd never have wandered up to that
vineyard, spotted you in that vat, and . . ." He looked down, as
though resigned, as though he knew he'd failed again, forgotten
his dialogue, lost the thread. Sykes uttered "Cut" and Roarke
braced for the next blowup.

"Print that," the director said. Then: "Lunch, everyone."

The stage lights came up, obliterating the scenic San Francisco panorama. Hayden blinked, as though coming out of a trance— or else, like a kid who'd gotten used to being knocked around, he was just passively waiting for the next sock in the head. It didn't come. Instead, Sykes smiled curtly at him. Then, imperious, the director swept off his set.

Mary Oakley took a tentative step toward Harley, around whom technicians were busily striking lights and mirrors. Roarke couldn't hear what she said, but Hayden looked pleased. More than pleased, in fact: like a working stiff who'd won the Irish Sweepstakes. A storm had—for the moment—passed.

Roarke realized he'd been holding his breath. He wasn't sure for how long. He'd come unstuck in space and time—a most un-likely sucker for that fabled Movie Magic.

"Okay, Flip, let me save you two-and-a-quarter," Roarke offered, later, as he perched on the edge of Hayden's couch.

An assistant stuck her head in. "Choice of Southern fried chicken, baked filet of sole, or Salisbury steak, Mr. Hayden?"

"None of the above, thanks." The assistant lingered for a moment, doubtful, then disappeared. Hayden collapsed onto the chair, turned to Roarke, and confided, "Anything I tried to put in my stomach right now'd just come up." He shut his eyes, kneaded his facial muscles with his thumbs. "Save me some dough, huh? Okay, I'm intrigued. What's your proposition?"

"Apt choice of words." Roarke made sure the dressing room door was shut, then offered his interpretation, based on long sor-did years of LAPD experience of busting into private clubs and after-hours joints to roust perverts of every stripe.

"Sykes is a homo, and he's crazy in love with you. Maybe he's a secret homo, maybe he doesn't even know he's one, maybe he doesn't realize he's carrying a torch for you—that would explain the temper, the explosions, all the crazy behavior."

Hayden absorbed this, then shook his head. "Good try, but it won't wash."

"Why not?" Roarke pressed. "You don't think there're men who—"

"I *know* there're 'men who,'" Harley interposed mildly. Then, for Roarke's amusement: "Even in Ohio. But not Sykes. That's what my gut says. Sorry, but this time you're off base." He kicked off his wingtips and began massaging his toes.

There was something oddly intimate about watching another man stroke his own feet, particularly in such close quarters. Roarke searched the cramped room with his gaze, found Eleanor's photo again, and rested his eyes on her face. "All the same, what if I phone a friend on the force? Old Roarke can still pull a string or two down at Vice." This was a lie, but somehow Roarke felt justified in telling it—perhaps because, by rights, it should have been true. "For instance, this friend of mine can tell us whether Sykes ever got picked up in a homo raid."

"Go right ahead," Harley agreed. "If that's your idea of a swell afternoon."

"You'll change your tune, Flip, when we find that one photo in the files, of mean, manly Derek out of his jodhpurs, wearing a dress—and a long blond wig combed peekaboo style."

Hayden laughed. "He's twice the size of Veronica Lake, easy. The dress'd have to be custom-made, by the best in the business. Maybe I should ask Edith Head if Sykes ever—"

"Look, why can't you just walk into Lustig's office and raise holy hell? The man's practically your father-in-law."

Harley nodded, somber. "That's exactly why I can't, don't you see? If I ask Mr. L for special treatment, I'd lose what self-respect I've got left, not to mention"—he shook his head—"I tested for this part. Tony wasn't handed to me on a silver platter. Sykes wanted me over John Hodiak, Gig Young, and Guy Madison, I have it on good authority."

"Then why's he raking you over the coals like this?"

"Who, Sykes, y'mean?"

"Yeah, Sykes, I mean. You don't think Arthur Lustig would knowingly subject you to this kind of misery?"

Hayden looked puzzled, depressed, and (was it the face powder?) pale. "Sometimes I wonder whether Mr. L's heard any scuttlebutt from the stage." Then, apparently attempting a joke, "It's said the Hebrew God watches over us, and sees all, but doesn't intervene." Hayden turned solemn again. "Or just maybe A.L. thinks I've got this—punishment, coming to me."

Roarke nodded. "Payback, for"—what was that ugly, funny foreign word?—"*shtupping* his sweet little Ellie?"

"Don't put it like that, please."

"Sorry, Flip. But that's your point, isn't it?"

Hayden shrugged, embarrassed. The veiled motives of other men were not his forte. He was, after all, from Ohio.

Roarke stood. "Look, I've seen enough here. Lemme do whatever it is I do. Try to find out what makes Sykes tick—if, perchance, I'm wrong and he's *not* bewitched, bothered, and bewildered by Pal Harley. In the meantime I'd suggest you eat something, even if you've lost your appetite. Fortify yourself, for the hot lights and Sykes's temper, too."

Hayden nodded a vague assent and waved a weak farewell. Roarke knew he'd eat no lunch today. But he'd said his piece, and now he left the dressing room—and neither of the two men mentioned that, after being abused by Sykes on set, Hayden had turned in a brilliant performance.

Chester Dowling wasn't in his office, which was locked up, so Roarke tried the executive dining room. It was a big, dark, pretentious Deco extravaganza, built in the early thirties when the studio was flush from a series of shrill screwball comedies and cheap but popular horse operas. And it was filled with overpaid producers and VPs, untalented cousins and greedy nephews, plus glorified yes-men and errand boys in cashmere.

And Dowling, who looked surprised to see Roarke standing out in the open, not skulking across the back lot.

"This seat taken?" Roarke asked, sliding out the empty chair beside him. Flustered, Dowling started to make halfhearted introductions to the suits at the table, but Roarke cut him off. "Who's Derek Sykes?" he asked quietly.

Dowling switched into studio-flack mode. "Derek? He's a veteran British director we've just brought over, real class."

"Well, if he's a veteran, how come his credits are zilch?"

A thin, glistening line of sweat had already formed on Dowling's upper lip as he turned to his associates. "Gotta get back to my desk. Talk to you boys at close of business."

Roarke followed him out.

"This wouldn't be Harley, again, with a bellyache?" Dowling wondered, as the two men walked back to the Administration Building. Roarke shrugged, as though he wasn't sure. Dowling heaved a sigh. "Your little—communiqués, they're appreciated, it's nice to be kept abreast. But . . ."

"Sorry if I embarrass you with my physical presence, Chet, but it happens I was on the lot and I figured if I found you, I could save some ink and paper—there being a war on, and all."

Dowling gave Roarke an owlish look—a new expression in his repertoire he must've learned from Mr. L. "If you—or Hayden—has got a question or a problem concerning Derek Sykes, ask it."

"Okay, here's the question: He may be a director but he's no Brit—so who's Derek Sykes, *really?*"

Dowling pulled out a hankie. "Roarke? I want you to think of a picture studio as a profitable kind of kindergarten. The actors are the *kinder,* right? They got to be well rested, well fed, kept happy and amused. Naps, snacks, singalongs, and games. Long as they're happy, they're relatively harmless. When they get cranky, we get concerned. 'Cause we run the kindergarten."

"Who's Derek Sykes?"

Dowling mopped his face. "He's a Kraut, okay? His real name's Dieter Seife. The boss doesn't wish to put Kraut names up on the marquee at this juncture, for reasons I trust you can work out by yourself."

"Makes perfect sense."

"I tell you that in confidence."

"Seife's secret's safe with me," Roarke said with a smile.

His cool assurance only made Dowling more nervous and excitable. "This *is* coming from Harley, right? C'mon, Roarke," he began to wheedle, "you can tell Chester."

"Actually it's John Q. Public," answered Roarke, who found his mood improving as Dowling grew more addled. "John Q. Public wants to know with confidence he's not putting any of his hard-earned cabbage into the pockets of Nazi directors. John Q. Public would rather Back the Attack and buy war bonds."

Dowling stopped and turned to Roarke. "Look, Seife's no Nazi," he said with some vehemence. "He had quite a career at home in Berlin, but he gave it all up to get away from Hitler. Had to start from scratch here in Hollywood, three years ago. Hasn't been exactly a walk in the park, for your information."

Roarke dabbed at an eye. "Can I borrow your hankie? Think I'm starting to tear up." Dowling made a face. "So he left, when, thirty-eight, thirty-nine?" The production chief nodded. "Why so late?"

"What do you want me to tell you? Seife was diddling Eva Braun while Adolf was away on business? Suffice it to say, Arthur Lustig would not put a Nazi under contract on this lot. Now it's your turn to answer a question. Who's paying you to nose around in this? If it *ain't* Harley, can I assume it's one of those agitator-type screenwriters?" The way he said "agitator," Roarke noticed, it sounded like *child molester*. "Who, Ben Hecht? John Lawson? Just tell me, I'm curious."

Roarke backed away, shrugging and smiling.

He drove off the lot, but not far. First he found a place to buy a fifth of bourbon, a fresh pack of Luckies, and a copy of *The Racing Form* strictly for nostalgia's sake. Then he circled back and located a shady spot across the street from the main gate, but halfway down the block so the studio police wouldn't have to worry about him. He sat in his Packard with the windows rolled down. Read, sipped, smoked, felt nostalgia, and waited.

Roarke watched two genuine movie stars, three actors who thought they were stars, and countless nobodies come rolling off the Superior lot around five-thirty. At six, a Buick Roadmaster left the main gate and made a right onto Melrose. Derek Sykes—or Dieter Seife, depending who was asking—at the wheel.

Roarke pulled out and fell in behind the director. Seife didn't live far, less than a mile up Highland. Roarke followed him the back way into the Hollywood Hills, winding upward toward Los Tilos. This was Outpost Canyon, though it hadn't been for long. The first houses, big Mediterraneans, had been built here less than ten years earlier by a developer called Toberman. When he'd bought up the land, the area bore the discouraging name of Rattlesnake Canyon. So the enterprising Toberman hauled in five-hundred king snakes to prey on the rattlers. It was, Roarke reflected, a distinctly Hollywood solution.

He pulled over several houses down and strolled up to Seife's place, which seemed too big for one émigré Kraut; the net effect was lonely, spooky, as though the director had brought more than a touch of Teutonic gloom with him to sunny L.A. Looking up, one half-expected to see a lone Gothic-gray thundercloud hovering over Seife's adobe *casa*.

Through the living room window, Roarke watched Seife pace as he gnawed on a hunk of brown bread. He was still in his jodhpurs and military jacket. Then the director sat, paged through his script, began scribbling. Roarke envisioned the notes:

Not like that! Terrible! Do it twenty more times!

When Seife went upstairs, Roarke drove home. He hadn't learned much, only his mark's real name and current address. The rest of the week went the same way. Just like tailing Harley—these movie people, with their risqué reputations, kept banker's hours. Roarke stayed in touch with Hayden, to be sure things hadn't changed; maybe Seife had backed off, or cooled off—warmed up, even? But according to Harley the tussle continued, a perfect microcosm of the worldwide struggle then raging, worse some days than others. Shooting ground on as Harley was ground down. (Meantime, let it be noted, no klieg lights had landed on Derek Sykes's skull.)

Roarke didn't tell Hayden he'd been right about Sykes's origins, that (as he wrote in his notes) "the beef's been unmasked as bratwurst." Roarke had to know more first. So it was back to Los Tilos Drive, night after night. But Seife's routine, after-hours, proved maddeningly unrevealing. The only variation was the appearance, on Friday, of a fat housekeeper who bustled around but didn't seem to get much done. Roarke was starting to feel the same way, except he didn't even bustle.

Until Saturday. The director slept in—no great surprise; he'd spent a grueling week tormenting Roarke's client—then fixed himself a modest little breakfast and, afterward, drifted outside to pick up his mail.

From down the street, it appeared he'd received a single envelope: one of those lightweight all-in-one airmail letters from abroad. Seife stared at it, then furtively glanced up and down Los Tilos. Roarke was standing about twenty yards away (in a beige shirt and a pair of khaki work pants that vaguely suggested a Southern California Power and Water uniform), pretending to rewire a street lamp. Gripping the thin blue envelope as though it might squirm out of his hand, Seife hurried back into his kitchen. *Ransom note?* thought Roarke.

Five minutes later, Seife came roaring out of his garage. Roarke sprinted down Los Tilos to the Packard, then gunned it down Outpost. Even so, he nearly lost his man. But luck was with him: Roarke picked up Seife on Sunset, speeding east.

A half hour later they'd reached Union Station, downtown. Roarke followed Seife to the ticket counter. North or south? North was Frisco, of course, and Frisco had its share of blackmailers and pervs. Tijuana, on the other hand, boasted pervs and

Mary Jane both. Roarke's money was on north, though he longed to sip margaritas on the beach (while enjoying a mild tea buzz) while watching Seife frolic with an underage hooker of either sex (Roarke no longer cared which). In the event, Seife bought a round-trip ticket for San Diego. Roarke followed suit.

Finding a seat in the same car wasn't easy: the Southern Pacific was packed with tourists, soldiers returning from furlough to Camp Pendleton, and their wives who weren't supposed to come along but couldn't bear to say goodbye, Roarke supposed with some resentment. A nice smooth road trip in his Packard would've been far preferable—but neither an expatriate German masquerading as an Englishman nor a disgraced vice cop came close to qualifying for C-sticker gas rations.

Once squeezed into a row behind Seife, Roarke had ample time to enjoy the ocean view (marred only by the fact that the beaches were patrolled by mounted Coast Guard) while speculating: What was down in San Diego that a man couldn't find in Los Angeles? Why the big rush? And what was in that letter?

The train grew more crowded with each stop. At one point Roarke lost sight of Seife altogether and thought maybe he'd "made" his tail—and ditched him in San Clemente. Roarke leapt up, drunk on adrenaline. Started to pull the emergency cord—but no, Seife had merely been visiting the bathroom.

Seife disembarked at the Santa Fe Depot, a Spanish Mission–style dowager of a station in downtown San Diego, its waiting room lit by sixteen chandeliers of bronze and glass. A thousand stragglers—but most in uniform and the rest female, so it was no trick to keep Seife in his sights. He got in line at the hack stand, and Roarke fell in behind him, tipping his driver a dollar for not losing Seife. At the Broadway pier Seife bought a ticket for the ferry. Roarke followed. Soon the two were crossing San Diego Bay. Seife paced the deck, Roarke had time to smoke two Luckies, then they'd docked at Coronado Island.

There were fishermen here reeling in mackerel and jacksmelt. But they sold fresh fish in Santa Monica—and, for that matter, the Hollywood Farmer's Market. Seife dodged the fishermen on his way to the Hotel Del Coronado. Roarke had enough cash for a room at the YMCA, whereas the smallest single at the Del was pricier than a *floor* at the Y. So, as Seife headed for the reception desk, Roarke ritually patted his thin wallet and cursed himself. While Seife might be spending the night, Roarke would be lucky to scrounge lunch on the island.

But Seife wasn't spending the night. All he did, in the Coronado lobby, was pick up another envelope held at the desk in his name. He tipped the clerk and turned around; soon the two were on the ferry again, returning to the mainland. From the pier they cabbed in tandem back to the train station as Roarke puzzled: all the way to San Diego for an envelope? But there was more—Seife looked around to ensure nobody was watching him (a precaution at which he was no more effective than Hayden at Grauman's Chinese), then strode to the Baggage Express building.

From the envelope he'd gotten at the Del, Seife removed a locker key. Roarke watched from a safe distance half-hidden by a Tuscan column, sipping a cup of coffee that wasn't just watery but phony to boot—made from soybeans, he was grimly certain. (The Battle of Stalingrad may have been bad, but the coffee ration ran a close second.) Meantime Seife wrestled a package from a locker that was jammed tight. Made of heavy cardboard, reinforced with packing tape, about twenty by twenty, and fifteen inches deep. And heavy, to judge by the strain on Seife's features as he lugged it over to the train tracks.

A porter told Seife he'd have to check the package, and Seife refused. In the end he had to pay the porter two bucks *not* to stow the carton for him. He sat with it on his lap all the way back to Los Angeles. Roarke wondered that the package didn't cut off circulation below the waist, costing Seife his legs.

Around Oceanside, Roarke walked to the bar car to stretch his legs and lubricate the machinery. After a few belts, as he ambled back to his seat, Seife and Roarke locked eyes. The ex-cop flashed a grin, just one congenial fellow to another. There was no spark of recognition or amity on Seife's side. He regarded Roarke with all the interest one would accord a gnat. The main thing—the only thing—was to hold on to that box.

Three more hours passed, uneventful, as the train rocked and clattered up the coast. Meanwhile Roarke considered Seife's package: it had either been smuggled through the Port of San Diego or Ensenada Harbor. Ensenada was his guess—the customs inspectors were mostly crooked; what's more, one could bribe them with pesos and tequila. If the pesos were plentiful enough, and the tequila aged enough, they wouldn't give a damn whether the carton was packed with dynamite or dirty postcards.

At Union Station, Seife stowed the carton in his trunk and took off. Roarke kept a car length behind. But the director had one final surprise up his sleeve today: instead of heading west to Hollywood, he drove to Pasadena on the new Arroyo Seco Parkway. No, actually they were calling it a freeway: miles of smooth, wide, fresh-paved road, and no tollbooths (which was fine and dandy, though when Roarke heard the word "free" he always patted his pockets). Seife drove to the swankest neighborhood, which bordered San Marino. Roarke followed.

It was dark by the time Seife pulled up to a low, sprawling, Spanish-style estate. Bougainvillea and palm trees camouflaged a high stucco wall surrounding the property. Shards of colorful glass were embedded at the top of the wall, a sight simultaneously festive and forbidding. From the road, one could hear the yips and grunts of hungry Dobermans on the prowl.

Roarke parked down the street and approached on foot, staying near the wall as Seife rolled down his window and spoke to the gate guard, who waved him through. Then he watched through the opened gate as Seife rolled up the driveway to the portico of the Moorish main house. In terms of scale this compound made the Lustig estate look like servants' quarters. The grounds were large enough, and sufficiently manicured, to do double duty as a nine-hole golf course.

Seife got out of his Buick, then stood beside it and waited. In a moment, two big men in white coats emerged. One flipped open the Roadmaster's trunk, the other lifted out the carton. It didn't look heavy in this behemoth's arms.

Next, a third man ventured from the oversized front door, a much smaller man, but even better tended than the perfect lawns. Thin reddish hair was meticulously arranged to cover his pink scalp. He shook hands with Seife, they exchanged a few words (of which Roarke only caught two unrevealing ones: "fried egg") and then, as the burly white-coated men reentered the mansion, the small fellow gave Seife a prissy farewell handshake before disappearing inside.

Roarke noted the address, then let Seife go his merry way—home, presumably—as the ex-cop drove back to his apartment.

Roarke hoped Sally would be sleeping when he came in. He was in no mood for sex or small talk. His plan was to record the day's events in his notebook, plus a few ideas as to how to proceed. In fact his lady friend *was* asleep, half naked and snoring under a twisted sheet in need of laundering. Roarke poured himself a scotch and sat at his kitchen table, but, even after several swallows, found he was too agitated to sit still for the length of time required to jot his recollections and impressions. He felt compelled to talk to Harley—fill him in, get the actor's reaction. Roarke reached for the telephone.

His index finger figured it out before his brain did: he didn't have Hayden's home phone number. Hayden had always called Roarke, never the other way around. And the rising star would not be listed in the local directory.

So Roarke grabbed a chicken leg from the icebox, splashed water on his face, changed into a shirt marginally fresher than the one he'd worn on his stakeout. (Though passable company and steadily employed, Sally as homemaker consistently fell short.) He crept out of the apartment, got back in his car, and sped the short distance to Hayden's bungalow in the flats. Chances Hayden would be home on a Saturday night were nil, he knew.

But as Roarke cruised down Formosa, he saw that Hayden's living room light was on. He could even make out the actor's silhouette (capped roosterlike with trademark pompadour) in profile, and Ellie's, opposite, on the white shade drawn over the front window. It was like one of those early lantern shows, shadows thrown for paying customers. Roarke lingered on the lawn, like a rube gawking at a forerunner of the first film.

This film wasn't silent, though. Roarke could hear the lovers' dialogue—muffled, but the words were clear enough:

HARLEY
I'm sick of waiting. What're we waiting *for,* anyhow?

ELLIE

> I don't know. I thought you still had reservations
> about me, that maybe I—

HARLEY

(a low laugh)

> The only reservation I could have, concerning you,
> would be a reservation for the penthouse suite, with a
> bottle of bubbly delivered to our door, after that a DO
> NOT DISTURB hung on the—

Ellie laughed. It wasn't the silvery trilled laugh Roarke re-membered from the Beanery, but Ellie was a year older now and maybe she'd had a drop too much tonight. Even so, Roarke suddenly needed to see her as much as he needed to see Harley.

He backtracked to his Packard. Turned on the interior light and checked his face in the rearview. Okay, so he'd never be in pictures. His hair had thinned and his nose had thickened. The last time he'd passed for boyish would've been around his first Communion. The Southern California sun had done his skin no favors. Nor had his fondness for whiskey been kind to the whites of his eyes—they looked a shade less yellow than his nicotine-stained teeth. Yet, looking at his reflection, Roarke saw a real guy, not an idealized guy, not some Jew mogul's concept of the Hand-some Christian Boyfriend, Best Buddy, or War Hero. More than a few women both white and black who'd crossed his path had seemed to support this view. Hell, Roarke thought, at least he hadn't run to fat yet, like most big-boned men his age. Reason-ably satisfied, he killed the light, hopped out of his coupe, strode to the door, and buzzed.

Harley answered, looking flustered. "Hey. Didn't expect to see *you*. Well, c'mon in."

"Hope I'm not interrupting," Roarke said, following Hayden into the living room, "but I just spent the day with our friend Derek Sykes—"

He stopped. It wasn't Ellie alone in here with Hayden: it was his costar, Mary Oakley. She was straightening her skirt as the two men entered the living room, and by the time Hayden started making introductions, she'd managed to look almost prim.

"Mary and I were running lines," he said as Mary hurriedly stood, and announced: "It's getting late, anyway, and I really should be going. So nice to have met you."

Her diction was painfully perfect. She offered Roarke a hand—it was a little girl's hand, with gnawed fingernails.

After Roarke shook with her, she turned and grabbed what *looked* like a script, then gave Hayden a wave and started out.

"Wait," he said. "I'll walk you to your car."

While he was gone, Roarke poked around the living room. There wasn't much: a radio-phonograph console in the corner; a sad potted poinsettia; a large framed photo, this one a formal portrait signed by George Hurrell, of Eleanor (stunning, of course, but Roarke preferred Ellie unposed); a photo of Harley in uniform (that, on closer inspection, proved to be a publicity still from *Perilous Passage,* with the legend *Property of Superior Pictures* only partly concealed by the frame); and a library that was skimpy even by Hollywood standards.

Roarke crossed to the single shelf. There was *Penrod,* by Booth Tarkington, and *Struggling Upward,* by Horatio Alger, and *The Autobiography of Andrew Carnegie,* and a dog-eared copy of *Our Town* by Thornton Wilder—and, hidden behind these four, was the obligatory *Butterfield 8*. Aside from this slim assortment, there was the one volume that actually interested Roarke, the 1937 Ohio State University Yearbook. Harley's yearbook.

Outside, he could hear Hayden quietly conversing with Mary. This time he couldn't make out what they were saying, nor did he want to. All Roarke wanted, right now, was to find the OSU wrestling team, see Flip as he'd been six years before—before Hollywood, before getting mixed up with the Lustigs, before defending our freedoms alongside Errol Flynn and signing on with Derek Sykes . . . back to a time when Harley Hayden was a real guy, too.

Roarke rifled to the section that featured the sports teams. Baseball, field hockey, football, swimming—and wrestling last. The wrestling team photo looked as Roarke had thought it would: a winning bunch of bare-chested young men, most of them blond, all of them smiling for the camera. Roarke scanned the faces of the few dark-haired "grapplers," searching for Hayden's distinctive grin. Or his squint. His pompadour. Anything. Then he checked the caption—twice. There was G. Hearn, and D. Graham, and L. Moxley, and J. Ranson. But no H. Hayden.

"Sorry." Hayden was standing behind Roarke now. "It's just, Mary, she's been so good-hearted, during this tough time, the movie and all, sticking by me while Mr. Sykes . . . well, you know. Least I could do was run next week's scenes with her." As though Harley'd read Roarke's mind, he added, "Eleanor's out with her dad. All-night poker game over at Jack Warner's."

Roarke couldn't picture it. "Ellie plays poker?"

" 'Course not, she's just there to be sure Mr. L doesn't lose the house. I mean the *house,* in Laughlin Park. Joe Schenck's at the table tonight. Schenck's got a poker face belongs on Mount

Rushmore. Last month he lightened Mr. L by forty-eight grand." And then, as though to make doubly sure Roarke knew Mary Oakley was no more than a current costar, added, "You'll be proud of me. I asked Ellie about her mother again. This time I wouldn't take no for an answer. And guess what? El told me the story." He left the room for a moment, Roarke heard the clink of ice, then Hayden returned with two glasses of scotch, rocks. Roarke set down the yearbook (Hayden's absence from the team photo momentarily forgotten) and sipped as Harley spoke:

"Thing is, her brother passed away, like we figured. El didn't say how, and I didn't press her. But Ida—that's her mom—had a nervous breakdown not long after. Mr. L couldn't handle it, guess he was grieving pretty hard himself, so he packed Ida off to a sanitarium somewhere back east. And she's been there ever since." He sipped. "Pretty sad story, huh?"

Roarke was making mandatory clucks and sighs when Hayden noticed the tome on his coffee table.

"Oh! My college yearbook. You were looking through my college yearbook?" Then he grinned, as he guessed the reason for Roarke's interest. "Yep, Jesse Owens ran track for OSU, his picture's in here somewhere." Hayden picked up the book and began to leaf through it. "Old Jesse sure showed—"

"*You're* not in there," Roarke said. "In the photo. Of the wrestling team."

Hayden cocked his head and squinted at Roarke, friendly but curious, the way a nurse might check to see if her patient was running a temperature. "I wasn't *on* the wrestling team. I'm way too tall to be a wrestler, even a college wrestler." He started a new search, through the yearbook pages.

"But didn't you show me some big press release, an article about how you tore a hamstring, wrestling for the team? And everybody called you Flip on account of how you'd literally flip your opponent, just when he thought he had you pinned?"

Hayden found the page he was searching for, devoted to the Drama Club. It featured a few photos from the senior-year production of *Our Town*.

"There I am," Hayden said, pointing to a character in a white wig. "I tried out for George, but got cast as the Stage Manager. Which was fine—the Stage Manager basically narrates the whole story, he's sort of omniscient. D'you know the play?"

The last live theater Roarke had seen was a titty show at the Orpheum downtown, starring Lola Linton, sometime in the late thirties. He shook his head.

Hayden grinned, stiffly. "You put your finger on it. 'Press release.' When an actor—a young actor, who looks fit—hell, who *is* fit . . ." Something akin to anger flashed across his face. "When that actor is found to be 4-F, it does not sit well with the American public. Anyway, the Great Minds at Superior Pictures thought the wrestling story'd sound a little less . . . *pitiable* than the real reason: these soft-boiled eggs." He gestured mournfully at his myopic eyeballs. "I mean, I'm just about legally blind in the left one. And who's kidding who? Does that sound like movie-star material to you, or would the public just die laughing if they knew the real story?"

Roarke shrugged. "So I should stop calling you Flip?"

Hayden pointed to the caption beneath the photo of himself as the Stage Manager. *P. Hayden,* it read.

"The P is for Philip. Harley was my mom's maiden name. 'Harley Hayden' had better marquee value than Philip Hayden."

Roarke sensed Hayden was quoting others. "The Great Minds at Superior?"

Harley smiled. "It's the alliteration, of course. Like Greta Garbo, Greer Garson . . ." His head tilted as he thought of other names. "Dan Dailey, Dan *Duryea* . . . Donald Duck—"

"But your folks, your friends back home?"

Hayden patted his back, as though to reassure Roarke he wasn't party to a fraud. "Philip was just fine for the student drama club. But my people? Called me Flip, alright. You can rest easy on that score." Then he plopped down and looked up. "So what's going on? Any news on Herr Direktor?"

"Plenty," Roarke began. "First of all, you hit the bull's-eye about Sykes."

Hayden's eyebrows rose. "He doesn't come from London?"

Roarke lit a Lucky. "About six-hundred miles east of London, in fact. Your lord and master was born Dieter Seife. Apparently, the last couple years, before Pearl Harbor, he made a couple of nothing pictures for Superior under that name."

Hayden's eyes flicked to the floor while he turned over the name Dieter Seife. Then he looked up at Roarke. "So why'd he change it?" Harley-born-Philip asked, with no trace of irony.

"Good question. But there's more. Seife got a letter this morning. Next thing you know, we're at Union Station. Would've bet we were heading for TJ, but our destination turned out to be Dago. San Diego. Next our friend leads me on a treasure hunt to Coronado and back, then the train station where Seife picks up a package crammed in a locker. Big package. Heavy, too."

Hayden's eyes widened.

"Seife seemed scared to bring it out in public, even more scared to let it out of his sight. The look on his face said he half-expected everyone from Melvin Purvis to General Patton to nab him on the spot. By the same token, this didn't seem like the first time he'd been on the receiving end of a drop. Seife didn't open it or bring it home. Instead, he left it at some ritzy South Pasadena property sealed up as tight as Fort Knox."

Hayden let out a breath. "So it *is* dope, then?"

"I seriously doubt that. If Seife was a hophead like I'd thought, he'd have found a place to pull over, open the package, and have a taste, at least. Or gotten a shot of the stuff as his fee when he handed it off in Pasadena. That didn't happen."

"What do you make of it?" Hayden looked as excited as a grade-schooler signing up for Brass Banfield's Freedom Club.

"Beats hell out of me," Roarke conceded, draining the scotch. "But let's say, just for argument's sake, that box of his was packed with nitro. There'd be enough powder inside to blow the Lockheed plant."

Hayden whistled. "Right over the hill, in Burbank."

"Just as an example. Hell, half the defense industry is out here now . . . not just Lockheed. There's Northrop, Douglas, North American, Consolidated. Crazy Hughes is building a balsa 'Buck Rogers ship' that'll 'fly in the stratosphere' . . ."

"The budget on his Jane Russell pic is already *in* the stratosphere," Hayden cracked, to cut the tension.

"Or maybe you don't blow the plant, maybe you hit softer targets."

Hayden sucked in a breath. "People who work in the plants?"

Roarke nodded. "Then it spreads to their families—"

"Spreads?" Hayden looked perplexed and alarmed.

"If it isn't nitro packed in that box, could be something worse. Something . . . contagious."

"German measles?" Hayden was doing his best to keep up.

"In the fourteenth century," Roarke informed him, "the Tatars catapulted corpses of plague victims over citadel walls to infect Christians." Roarke liked to read military history; Clausewitz, not Carnegie, had been his muse since a college-educated desk sergeant down at Central had loaned him a copy of *On War* with this advice: "You want to survive your tour of duty, Roarke, read up on the Napoleonic wars. And whenever you see the word 'Prussians,' substitute the word 'pickaninnies.'"

Roarke continued: "Lemme jump ahead. Six years ago, in Manchuria, a Nippo army medic called Shiro Ishii cultivated all kinds of deadly bacteria—anthrax, dysentery, typhoid, cholera, even bubonic plague. He tested it on the Chinese. Today the Japs and Krauts are asshole buddies. Would it surprise you if Doctor Ishii was happy to share his bug bombs with the Nazis?"

Hayden looked ready to faint.

"At Pasadena, two men came out to carry the box inside, and they were wearing white coats. Not dinner jackets. Lab coats."

"Jesus Christ. *Now* what? Do we call in the Feds?"

Roarke shook his head. Sure, they were dealing with a Kraut posing as a Brit, a case packed with explosives or lethal bacteria, and a walled-in, well-funded hotbed of fifth columnists right in their own backyard. But seen from a slightly different perspective? A German film director with a British name, a plain cardboard box, and a gated estate in Pasadena.

"I want to find some way over that wall," Roarke said, "and look around before we call anyone or do anything. Meantime, your job is to keep acting—I mean acting the role of Tony, and acting the role of a guy without the slightest idea his director might be a saboteur on the side."

"Dunno if I bargained for this," Hayden muttered. "I wasn't expecting to uncover any Jerry spy ring here in L.A."

"You and me both," Roarke rejoined. "I hoped to catch Derek in a clinch with some choirboy, snap some photos, show him the prints, then get him to give you an easier ride for the rest of the shoot. Not my fault things aren't shaping up that way."

He started for the door. Hayden followed him out.

"It's just . . . something like this could mess up the movie. Superior might pull the plug. And that'd be— Dammit, that'd be a disaster. This role, it's . . . my . . . breakthrough role! My first serious, starring part in a movie of . . . real substance." He was clinging to Roarke's sleeve, pulling at it like a child.

"The hell is this *Big Betrayal* anyway?" Roarke grumbled. "From what I can see, you're a Frisco lounge lizard trying to make some virgin. Your head hurts, and you can't sleep. But to hear you talk it's *Gone With the Wind,* for chrissake."

"Oh, no," Hayden pleaded, "it's better than that. It's an—an allegory. Tony's too rich and spoiled to bestir himself for Good. Plus he's lost his memory. In other words, Tony's Democracy, he's Freedom, he's America before the Japs hit us." Roarke had never heard Hayden so impassioned and astute—off script, anyway. "In the course of the story he comes around, discovers the better angels of his nature. Not just through the love of a woman, but her death. It's an attack on our moral complacency, our smug isolationism, the *historical* amnesia that made a surprise attack not just possible, but inevitable. It says the biggest betrayal, the worst one, has nothing to do with Nips or Krauts. The *big* betrayal is when we betray ourselves—our best selves. Like Tony says, very heartfelt, at the picture's finale: 'No more lies—we'll all sleep better.' "

"And that's what the movie's about."

Hayden let go of Roarke's arm. "More or less." Then: "Sorry if I got carried away, but this picture means a lot to me."

Roarke nodded. As he edged to his car, he promised, "We'll keep everything under our hats, at least till I've got a solid lead. Maybe nothing happens before the picture wraps, right?"

Then he drove away, watching Hayden standing on his lawn, a dim, almost spectral reflection in Roarke's side mirror.

Getting inside the grounds wouldn't be easy, short of calling in the marines, but then Roarke remembered they were bogged down in Guadalcanal. So he started working on plan B, which in any case would likely have to wait until the weekend.

Meanwhile he dropped by the *Hollywood Reporter* to check in with Billy Wilkerson. Wilkerson had contacted Roarke a few years earlier, around the time he was opening a club on the Strip called Ciro's. Apparently, a few Sicilians wanted a piece of Billy's new business—boys from the Purple Gang, bootleggers called Lucido and Zerilli who'd come west after losing their foothold in Chicago. The wily Wilkerson surmised that a former cop with a reputation as a hothead and a ruffian might scare such fellows off. For his part, Roarke figured it was another job for the Marine Corps, who weren't quite as busy then.

Even so, he thought he'd recruit some local talent as a first step. A couple of pachucos from Carmelita Street in East Los Angeles, Enrico and Mario, who ran a gang called El Hoyo—the Hole, which served as an apt, concise description of Carmelita Street.

Enrico and Mario weren't in the liquor trade. They didn't particularly enjoy violence. What they enjoyed was parading around town in zoot suits, pissing off white people. (The more pleats, they discovered, the more pissed-off.) It wasn't so difficult to convince El Hoyo to hang around Ciro's till the remnants of the Purple Gang got the message and moved on. And that is how Wilkerson and Roarke became fast friends.

Roarke was led into Wilkerson's office by a sashaying receptionist who surely moonlighted as a cigarette girl at one of his numerous nightspots. Roarke shut the door and plucked a Cohiba off the desk. Billy cheerfully lit it for the ex-cop.

"What can I do you for, Roarkie?"

"I need some info on a Kraut director called Dieter Seife."

Wilkerson's brows knit. "Under contract to Superior? What ever happened to him, anyway? We deport the bum or what?"

Roarke shrugged.

"Okay, who wants to know?" Roarke remained silent. Billy studied the ex-cop, then opened his desk drawer and pulled out a little black book. He started leafing through it, murmuring, "We got stringers and sources from coast to coast. Dependable people, peddling reliable poop." He stopped on a particular page, and smiled. "Here's a guy in New York City, a good pal. His number's RH4-0284. Know what the RH exchange stands for?"

Roarke took a guess: "Rhinelander?"

"Very good. Now, people with the Rhinelander exchange tend to live in the Yorkville area of Manhattan. *German Town,* if you will. Carl Schurz Park, the Brauhaus, the Heidelberg . . . I could call this good friend, and ask him about Seife. But you'd have to scratch Billy's back."

"Call first. Scratch second." Roarke puffed on his cigar.

"Deal." Billy dialed, then purred: "*Schatzi?* It's William R. Wilkerson. Nice to hear your voice. I got a question for you, little background, not for print, no attribution. The film director, Dieter Seife, what can you tell me, *mein Freund?*"

Next, he muttered *uh-huh, uh-huh, uh-huh, uh-huh,* jotted a few notes on a slip of paper, then signed off with *Schatzi.*

Most of what *Schatzi* told Wilkerson—or what Wilkerson repeated to Roarke—could be found in Seife's studio bio. There were just two small facts the Superior publicity department had left out: Seife had a wife in Berlin, an attractive woman not in the film business. In fact she wasn't in *any* business—as one would define business. Yet she was a prominent *Frau,* apparently—a proud, card-carrying member of the Nazi party and personal favorite of that perennial charmer Dr. Joseph Goebbels.

The second small fact? She and Seife were still married.

"Now scratch me," Wilkerson reminded.

"Where?"

"Hey, keep your shirt on, Mr. Roarke. Wilkie just wants to know who wants to know about Seife—who, not why," he bargained.

"Harley Hayden."

Wilkerson grimaced. "You didn't happen to catch that bogus item planted in *Variety,* did you? That thick slice of baloney about how the All-American Boy couldn't serve because he'd pulled a hamstring while on some college wrestling team?"

"Ohio State U.," Roarke said.

"Ohio State B.S.," Billy retorted. "The kid's six-one if he's an inch. Who the hell'd put Hayden on a wrestling team?"

Roarke stubbed out the Cohiba. "Since when did you become an expert on athletics, Billyboy?"

Wilkerson leaned way back in his chair. "Since when? I can't remember the exact date. You'll have to ask my bookie."

Roarke stood. "Look, thanks for the dope on Seife. Most of it had mold growing, but what the hell—you tried." As he opened the door to leave, something compelled him to add, "By the way,

Hayden *was* on the wrestling team. You don't believe me, look in his yearbook, class of '37. They called him Flip."

"Oh, yeah?" Wilkerson called out, lazily.

"Yeah," Roarke defiantly insisted, as he always did when caught peddling a falsehood. "I saw the team photo myself."

· 10 ·

Movie Death

"Cut! Cut, cut, *cut!*"

Derek Sykes's tantrums had lost their novelty over the preceding three weeks, but the *Betrayal* set was still a zone of misery. Nobody complained much—maybe it assuaged the cast and crew's guilt at being in Los Angeles and not El Alamein?

Hayden had settled into a routine of stoically withstanding Sykes's public browbeating, doing his work (which everyone who watched rushes agreed was his best), and then, between setups, strolling to his dressing room and casually closing the door—just as his guts erupted upward. He'd puke in the sink, rinse everything down, then huddle, shivering, in a corner, hugging his flanks while taking deep, ragged breaths till an assistant director called, "Mr. Hayden, we're back," through his locked door. Whereupon the actor would get up, gargle with Listerine, flash a fresh grin at the mirror, then stroll once again to the set.

Mary Oakley, between camera setups, and during her lunch break, would sit in a lonely corner of the soundstage and answer mail from fans who'd seen her in her previous—and, to date, only—film, *Mr. Moto and the Seven Deadly Sins,* already in production when Pearl Harbor was attacked. Most of the fans, after praising Mary's beauty and poise, went on to question how she could have costarred with a yellow ape like Mr. Moto. Miss Oakley, in her perfect hand, would patiently explain, in letter after letter, that Peter Lorre, who played Mr. Moto, was not a yellow ape at all but a white man, in fact—and a very kind and decent person to boot.

Derek Sykes, during *his* lunch break, would . . . well, today (Friday, Day Fifteen of principal photography) Sykes had scheduled an urgent appointment with Arthur Lustig. He instructed his second assistant director to supervise the prelighting for the next scheduled shot—a moving master, on the Tony's Office set—in case he was late returning. Sykes anticipated a difficult and contentious meeting. But he was confident that, in the end, Lustig would be brought around.

As soon as Sykes strode off the soundstage, Hayden reappeared. This was a surprise to the crew, among whom it was well known (if discussed only in whispers) that their star normally spent lunch not eating grub, but bringing up bile in his dressing room. But today Hayden was looking for somebody—and he soon found him: the art director, Jeff, who was often seen with Sykes, discussing the features and geography of San Francisco (the city where Tony made his home).

Harley discreetly drew Jeff aside.

"Say," he said, quietly, "I know you and Mister . . . Sykes are always jawing about Frisco. I hear you, between takes—"

"I'm terribly sorry about that, sir," Jeff returned. Movie stars could get all bent out of shape, he'd learned, about any distractions on "their" sets. "It's just that Mr. Sykes is such a . . . stickler, as you know, a real Nazi about detail. I hope it hasn't been too much of a bother." Darned if Jeff would get himself fired by some crumb-bum actor, just because the damn director was obsessive about every little thing. He'd go to his union boss, make a stink that'd reach high heaven, before . . .

Harley silently registered Jeff's use of the word "Nazi." Then, casually: "Listen, just between us two, has Mr. Sykes been asking specifically about any . . . landmarks, or military installations up in Northern California? For the movie, I mean. . . . Has he requested that extensive photographs or measurements be made, for background plates or anything like that?"

Jeff tried to make sense of the question. No matter what a movie star asked—however cockeyed—you had to at least appear to treat it, and him, with deference bordering on brownnosing.

"You mean like—what, the Presidio?"

Hayden snapped alert. The Presidio, of course, was the centerpiece of San Francisco Bay's seacoast defense. "What has Sykes asked about the Presidio?"

Odd duck, Jeff thought. Handsome, but maybe not playing with the full fifty-two cards. "Sykes hasn't mentioned the Presidio. I just thought that was the sort of thing you meant, sir." To assuage Hayden's disappointment, he quickly added, "We did talk quite a bit about the Golden Gate Bridge, though."

"You did? Really?"

Jeff nodded. "Sykes seemed sort of fascinated by it."

"Did he ask that it be photographed?"

In truth, Jeff was a little vague on this, but it was a dangerous thing for a department head to act vague about his job, especially with "the talent." "I'm pretty sure, sir."

Hayden nodded. Then, briskly: "Thanks, Jeff. This is just between us, okay? You're a good man." He shot out a hand, shook with the art director. Then headed for his dressing room.

Jeff watched him go then turned to his set dresser, who'd been observing the whole odd interchange, and shrugged. Actors.

Lustig sat at his large desk, not speaking, just cutting his flank steak into neat, nearly perfect squares. In those few private sessions, right after . . . just before Ida committed herself and Lustig fled to Europe . . . Ridley had advised the mogul to submerge his rage in the precise completion of rote tasks. More than a decade later, the approach still seemed to work. Lustig chewed with his head down, studying his plate, slicing as carefully as a diamond cutter while Seife droned: ". . . consistently, from the beginning, covered the scenes with clean close-ups of Miss Oakley. And my framing of the over-the-shoulders is such that one can't see Hayden's hair."

Only when the director stopped nattering did Lustig look up from his lunch. "What about it?" he asked, bone-weary, though he'd slept well last night, and even though it was just noon.

"What about it? What about it, Mr. Lustig, is that if we recast the role of Tony over the weekend, we will have only six days of shooting to make up. I've reviewed the schedule with my first assistant director. Because one can't see Hayden's hair in the over-the-shoulders, even, we needn't restrict ourselves to a new dark-haired lead. The replacement could be blond, for instance, if it came to that. We'd have to redo only the masters and Hayden's two-shots, which I carefully kept to a bare minimum." Seife folded his arms across his military jacket, awaiting Lustig's response.

Lustig removed his spectacles and rubbed his eyes, then looked up at Seife. There was a large gulf between them (made manifest by his desk) and a peculiarly parallel, though private, loss. The two were as different and as similar as the Yiddish and German they spoke. "Have you ever experienced a spider infestation, Mr. Sykes?" Lustig finally asked the director.

"A— What?" Seife looked nonplused.

"In your home. Back in Berlin. Here in Hollywood. An infestation." Seife still looked confused, as Lustig dourly elaborated: "Something that has no business being in your life. Something obscene. But it won't go away. Have you had that?"

Seife frowned, tried to think back, tried to imagine what Lustig might be getting at.

When, abruptly, Lustig began speaking again: "You're aware Hayden is my daughter's boyfriend? They're very close—and have been for some years."

"Yes, yes," Seife responded, annoyed at having to address the topic yet glad at least to be back on solid ground. "But—"

Lustig raised his voice, and cut him off: "What you may not know is that my Ellie campaigned quite vigorously on Harley's behalf. It was her fervent wish that he play the role of Tony. Eleanor's belief in her . . . fiancé, was, without a doubt, the key factor in Superior's decision to cast Mr. Hayden."

Seife dimly recalled Chester Dowling on this subject. "With all due respect to the young Miss Lustig," he said, "I contend that this picture, *The Big Betrayal,* is of much greater importance than Mr. Hayden's romantic life, even insofar as it involves your daughter. I believe that this picture could have an impact greater perhaps than *Dark Victory,* which received three Oscar nominations, I believe." (Seife had made some calls to confirm this last night.) "But only if Hayden is replaced."

"By who?" Lustig sighed. "Bette Davis?"

Seife's thin lips twitched. "There are numerous leading men available, actors who are capable, I believe, of inhabiting the role of Tony, not merely mimicking the mannerisms of such a figure. You must understand, Mr. Lustig, that this is no mere melodrama we are making here. *The Big Betrayal* is a fable, about a man—

Tony, of course—who represents Europe. Why else would he be named Tony, Antonio, Antony, all the way back to the Romans, you see? And this man, this Tony, under the cover of his great sophistication, the veneer of civilization of which he is so very proud, seduces and ultimately betrays all that which is idealistic and pure—in the person of Mary Oakley, who stands for this great young country, America—and, in the end, of course, he brings about her tragic demise. So you see, *The Big Betrayal* is much more than an entertainment, it is a warning bell to this nation, Mr. Lustig!"

Lustig pursed his lips. "And here I thought we were making a three-hankie women's picture, a weepie like *Dark Victory*. Maybe I was wrong? It's always possible. I'm not infallible."

Suspecting he'd overplayed his hand, Seife decided against bringing up the matter of *The Double* as he'd planned, and hastily agreed: "There will not be a dry eye when Mary Oakley breathes her last." When Lustig appeared unmoved by this prediction, Dieter decided to resort to humor, which he knew was not his strong suit—but desperate times call for desperate measures, *nein*? "I know that I may appear a bit . . . demanding and difficult, Mr. Lustig," he said, trying to sound playful, "but you should be aware, sir, that I come from a town in Bavaria with the perhaps fateful name of Bad Füssing. Truly."

Lustig peered at him, confused or bored, Seife wasn't sure. Afraid the mogul might resume his babbling about spiders, and opting to abandon humor in favor of a more direct approach, he put on his stern face again. "Anyway, I'll say this once more—"

"The hell you will!" Lustig bellowed. It was a startling outburst; there was no run-up, no prelude to it. Seife actually took two steps back from the desk, two reeling steps, as though he'd been punched in the gut. Meanwhile Lustig coolly resumed eat-

ing his steak, reflecting how at times the rote tasks would keep his fury in check, while at other times the unfettered release of his rage had a tonic effect comparable to the morphine injections Ridley'd administered to help Lustig try to sleep on those first nights, those first weeks, after . . .

By using rage, not morphine, he could banish the sensation that his skin crawled with spiders, a sensation that had made him snivel with fear, barely able to dial the phone and whisper to Dr. Ridley that the spiders were—*everywhere,* till Dr. Ridley reassured him that he was experiencing only "mental clouding" and "itching skin": classic side effects of the narcotic.

With his mouth full of masticated meat, Lustig continued, "I have seen the rushes—I watch *all* the rushes of *all* my pictures— and it is my considered judgment that Harley Hayden is turning in a fine performance. Therefore you will complete this picture with Harley Hayden. If reshoots are required, Harley Hayden will appear in them. Harley with the brown pompadour. No blond replacement. I want to hear no more about blonds, if you don't mind. As to who would direct those reshoots, that's an open goddamn question. Maybe back at Ufa you were a big fish, Seife. Well, at Superior, you're hired help. Got it? And if you ever wish to make another picture at my studio, there'll be no more discussions like this one today."

Then, his teeth finding a piece of gristle in the steak, Lustig spat a raw, bloody chunk onto his plate. The director interpreted this (correctly) to mean that the meeting was over.

On his fifth attempt in an hour, Hayden finally reached the woman he assumed to be Roarke's secretary—who identified herself only as Sally and explained, cheerfully apologetic, that she'd been out having her hair set. Between calls, Hayden tried to occupy himself by browsing the day's *Times*. But there was little within its pages to soothe him—mostly war news, mostly dire. Not only were the marines getting pummeled on Wake Island, but at the bottom of page one was an item about two undocumented German nationals—spies, presumably—found sneaking around Bandalier National Park in New Mexico, near what was rumored to be a supersecret scientific research facility in a place called Los Alamos. The story nearly drove Hayden wild with terror and excitement. He dialed Roarke's number again.

Finally an answer, though not the one he'd hoped for. "I don't know when the boss will be back, Mr. Hayden," the secretary said, exaggeratedly melodious. It was all too clear she was thrilled at having a Matinee Idol on the line. "He didn't say where he was going. I'm afraid he never does!" She giggled. "But I can pass along anything you'd like me to . . . ?"

Hayden knew he'd be called to the set at any moment, and was panicked that his message might be missed. But could this scatterbrained female be entrusted with a secret of such importance, a secret with implications for national security, the War Effort?

The knock came, as anticipated.

"We're back, Mr. Hayden," a muffled voice warned.

Harley made a quick calculation. "Just say 'Golden Gate.' "

"Golden Gate?" Sally sounded bewildered.

"Golden Gate Bridge," Hayden muttered, and hung up—not sure whether he'd just revealed too much, or too little.

Seife wrapped Day Fifteen at exactly five o'clock—perhaps 1700 hours would better convey the military precision with which the director concluded his week's work. Normally, after Friday's martini shot, he'd pause to shake hands with his stars and department heads, thanking them all for their efforts. This evening, though, he called, "Cut, print!" and made for the exit as he shouted over his shoulder, "See you all Monday morning."

"Any special plans this weekend?" Mary Oakley asked Hayden.

"What?" Harley hadn't heard her. He was watching Derek Sykes rush off the set. His first impulse was to dash back to his phone and dial the local FBI office. But he held off.

Traffic was light, and Seife reached his home at 5:15. As he let himself in through the garage, he had a sixth sense something wasn't quite right—something out of place, but what? Had his books, or his clothes, or his scripts been disturbed? Then at once he remembered: Hilda was here, today. *Dummkopf.*

Seife showered and changed. He knew he should eat—a light supper, at least; undoubtedly Hilda had left a full-course meal in the icebox from which he could pick. But Seife was too excited to eat. Anyway, it might take a while to reach Pasadena on a Friday evening. He would leave early, to be on the safe side. Best not to provoke Dr. Ridley, if it could be helped.

He thought he heard a noise as he entered his garage. "Calm down, Dieter," he told himself, aloud, then slid behind the wheel of the Roadmaster, and backed out onto Los Tilos.

In fact, the drive to Pasadena was quick and easy. Seife found he was approaching the Hacienda before he'd had a chance to compose himself, prepare himself. Maybe it was better that way—let Dr. Ridley take control, stage-manage the situation.

On the first, and previous, occasion—was it last spring already?—Seife had if anything been overprepared, had spent far too long in a state of tense anticipation. The result was an emotional cataclysm followed by a prolonged depression. He could ill afford to repeat that disaster, especially given the battle he was fighting for *The Big Betrayal*. Too many battles, altogether, in this lotusland, this Dream Factory.

"You're early. That's okay, you can sit in *La Mezquita*." The guard opened the heavy wrought-iron Beaux Arts gate. "Drive up to the front door, as usual. Leave the engine running and someone will park your car for you."

Seife did as he was told, feeling both exhilarated and sick, just as though he were arriving at the premiere of one of his own films. The front door opened as he parked, and he was gestured inside by one of those two white-coated, burly fellows (they weren't twins, really, but they might have been brothers, and Seife had begun to think of them as the Brothers Grim).

The main house seemed dead. As Seife was led along the hall, he glanced left and right: in the sitting room, done semi-French Provincial, the *chaises* were empty; in the music room with its vaguely Oriental décor, there was no one at the piano; in the library with its bold Turkish touches, nobody was sunk in a book; in the art studio, the easels stood naked and stark. "Where is everyone?" Seife asked, feeling suddenly spooked.

"Supper," Grim Brother One said.

Then they were outside, behind the main house, moving down a gravel path, under an awning of swaying palms to a building that looked to Seife like a farmhouse such as one might find outside Seville, but transformed by white stucco and scads of cash into an elegant guesthouse.

Grim Brother One steered Seife inside; this building also appeared empty—and was dark, as well. "Take any seat," the white-coated orderly instructed. Seife was reluctant to move until his eyes had adjusted somewhat. In a moment he could make out the shadows of seat rows, but the only light came from a sliver of moon shining through a Spanish baroque dome above. He felt his way down the aisle to a seat in the second row.

"Are you ready, Mr. Seife?" came a voice from behind. It wasn't Dr. Ridley's voice.

Stiffening, Seife replied, "I am."

Then the mosque reverberated with music: stirring martial music, starting with a solo snare drum, rat-a-tatting, then trumpets, then a full horn section playing simple but heraldic triads. Seife swallowed. He felt overheated suddenly.

Then a shaft of white light shot across the room, as though from a giant ray gun, and Seife realized it had been the projectionist, of course, who'd called out to him. He sat up—he could feel his spine violently straighten as though a steel rod had been thrust up his rectum, all the way to his skull—as the movie screen in front of him lit up and the title appeared:

Hans Munson Und Die Hitlerjugend
mit Martin Volker

Seife realized he'd been holding his breath only when he thought to release it now. After that his heart beat as hard and staccato as the snare drum, and he thought of nothing at all— nothing but the hypnotic picture unspooling before him.

In the moment, every frame seemed to sear into his brain, to be stored as a still photograph. But later, when he tried again and again to mentally reconstruct the movie, he found to his surprise that he could summon only a blurry series of images that felt more like a fever dream than an actual feature film:

A drunken, violent veteran of the First World War, out of a job, slapping his wife around, terrorizing his young son . . . That young son—blond, clear-eyed, tall for his age, and stoic, joining a Communist youth group, at the urging of his parents . . . The youth group on a weekend outing in the woods, where they frolic—sexually, drunkenly, immorally, all but the blond boy (the others, the hard-core Communists, were portrayed by dark-haired actors, most with pronounced, beaky noses), who appears saddened and disillusioned . . . Breaking away from the dissolute group, he walks through the forest alone. As darkness falls, and he feels lost, and frightened, the boy— Hans Munson, by name—happens, as in a fairy tale, upon another group, a better-looking group, of youngsters. He watches from behind a tree as they engage in a strange, exciting, moonlit ritual. The film shifts from a sort of grubby realism to a style more fantastic, and cleaner—hygienic, somehow. This new group (it is revealed) are Hitler Youth, and they are all fair-haired, well groomed, perfectly disciplined as they form a human swastika . . . Watching, Hans finally falls asleep in a pile of leaves. He wakes in the morning to find two beautiful Nazi teens—a boy and a girl, Fritz and Ulla—standing over him. At first they are suspicious, but Hans fervently explains he'd abandoned his Communist youth group in disgust and would give anything, even his life if necessary, to join the *Hitlerjugend* . . .

Seife's reverie—he'd been watching in a fugue state—was broken by a woman's piercing shriek, somewhere outside. Then there was a moment of silence followed by voices, shrill voices raised

outside *La Mezquita*. He tried to ignore the shouting, tried to focus only on the film:

> he convinces the skeptical young Nazis of his sincere admi-
> ration, is eventually presented with a crisp new uniform and
> boots of his own . . . Soon he is hiking through the forest
> with his new comrades, all of whom are completely, ro-
> bustly, thrillingly in tune with the natural world—but Seife
> had become distracted, around the moment Hans's mother
> finds her son's uniform in his dresser and, in despair, turns
> on the oven late one night, in a desperate attempt to gas her-
> self and the misguided Hans, but—

"Over there!"

"Who? Where?"

"Behind the stable! Look! He's getting away!"

It was like dialogue from another movie, a detective movie, but
it was live, and it was all around him, around the mosque—and
now the dogs were barking and howling, then a siren whined, all
this cacophony drowning out the sound track of *Hans Munson*—
and to add to the confusion, the inside of the mosque became in-
termittently brightened by roving searchlights, that washed out
the image of young Hans waking up, groggy but dewy-eyed, in
the hospital where Fritz and Ulla had been sitting vigil and—

"Goddammit!" "Got your gat?" "Grab that twerp!"

Alarmed—for one irrational instant, Seife believed it was *him*
they were hunting—the director stood, as if to flee the scene of
some indescribable, inscrutable crime. And then—this was even
more startling—a hand reached from behind, to clasp his shoulder, and Seife heard: "Sit back down. Don't worry."

As his adrenaline surge subsided, Seife recognized the professionally calm voice of Dr. Ridley. And he sat again—docile, almost Pavlovian in his blind and speedy obedience.

Outside, the siren had quieted, but the dogs were still snapping and there was a loud groan, of pain—and then a new voice, a male voice Seife hadn't heard before, growling: "Sonuvabitching bastards! Get your stinking mitts off me!"

Seife glanced, nervous, in the direction of that growl, but Jasper Ridley, seated behind him, gently placed both palms on Seife's jaw and redirected his gaze to the screen before him.

"Watch the film, Dieter. Everything is well in hand."

Indeed, the noise outside abated as

Ulla breaks the news to Hans Munson that his mother has died from the gas. But all is not lost—the boy can come live with Ulla, Fritz, and the others in a Nazi dormitory. Here Hans thrives on the friendship and support of the other *Hitlerjungen,* staying up late every night to print leaflets for the coming election . . . One day Hans is distributing the Nazi leaflets in his old neighborhood, and he runs into his old Communist acquaintances. A chase ensues, Hans is cornered, he fights valiantly, but the swarthiest of the Communist boys (the boy with the longest, boniest beak) stabs young Munson, who falls, mortally wounded. By the time Fritz and Ulla find him, Hans is able only to murmur: "I cannot go on any longer, I have lost too much blood. . . . But the party will go on, and there will be new blood, the blood of youth, so—"

Hans Munson dies. As his lids close, the camera tilts upward toward a clear sky . . . which dissolves to a fluttering Nazi Party flag . . . and the trumpet triads are reprised as the picture fades to black over the words DAS ENDE UND DER ANFANG.

It was the finest movie death Dieter Seife had ever seen.

"The end and the beginning," he muttered as the house lights came up, unsure whether to cackle or weep—but unable, in the event, to do either. He turned around, to Dr. Ridley. "Well . . . that was . . . I'm not certain how to . . ."

Dr. Ridley squeezed Seife's meatier hand. "Don't speak about it, Dieter, don't try to put it into words. Just . . . sit for a moment, gather yourself, then go home. Spend the weekend resting quietly. You have another big week ahead of you. You'll return next Saturday for a Healing Circle. Won't you?"

Patient and comforting though the doctor was striving to sound, Seife had the sense that Ridley was rushing out of here—and rushing Seife out, as well. On the previous occasion, he'd been invited to linger in the sitting room, just Seife and Dr. Ridley, both men quietly reflecting on the nature, as well as the repercussions, of what Seife had just witnessed.

But not tonight. After one more reassuring, therapeutic hand squeeze (Seife hoped he wouldn't be billed for it as an extra, à la carte, service) Ridley stood and glided to the rear of the mosque. "I'll have your car brought right up to the back of this building. The driver will beep."

Then he was gone, leaving Seife to wonder what chaos had erupted inside the Hacienda's gated grounds, how serious—and whether it might possibly have any connection with *him*. More to the point, he found himself pondering the deeper meaning of what he'd just watched on the mosque movie screen:

Was it a ritual of rebirth?

Or simply one more funeral?

. 11 .

The Healing Circle

It was cool in the garage—and damp, and musty. And dark. Roarke thought he'd better leave the light off in here, so long as Hilda the Kraut Cow was grazing and lowing around the house.

Why wouldn't she pack up and go? It was Friday evening, after all, and surely Hilda's husband was alone in their Canoga Park cottage crammed with Bavarian bric-a-brac, wondering when his Frau would drag her fat ass home and fry him some sausage.

Roarke checked his watch—he could faintly read its phosphorescent face, and he knew Seife would be home soon. Whether Roarke was right about "fried egg"—it hit him only this morning when he'd filled in Hayden on the latest, hung up, opened the paper, and saw that this was Fri-*day* . . .

Hilda finally quit around 5:15. Moments after she set off on foot down the hill, Roarke heard the Roadmaster's roar. He ducked into the hiding place he'd prepared—rake, shovel, some stacked cartons. He'd arranged just enough room to squat in the corner behind this humble barricade. Roarke figured Seife would see him only if he was looking for him, but the way Seife had glanced at him on the train made it clear Roarke didn't exist.

Seife pulled into the garage, then disappeared into the kitchen—not bothering, as Roarke had gambled, to lock the Buick. Uncertain what kind of hurry Seife was in this time—or if he was planning to drive anywhere at all—Roarke popped Seife's trunk and climbed in. He brought down the lid, careful not to let it click shut. Then held it that way: actually open, looking closed. This wasn't easy, but it was essential.

Within minutes, Seife was back. Roarke's second gamble was that Seife wouldn't use the trunk: his cardboard package was already delivered. Indeed, Seife went straight behind the wheel and the Buick was moving—headed, Roarke hoped, for Pasadena.

A half hour later they'd come to a full stop and Roarke heard, muffled, through sheet metal: "You're early. That's okay, you can sit in *La Mezquita.*" Another five minutes, and Roarke raised the trunk lid an inch to check for guards, orderlies, and other annoyances. Then he climbed out. In the black clothes he'd worn for the occasion, Roarke was nearly invisible—at least, that was the idea. In a crouch, moving swiftly, he surveyed the layout.

The main house looked uninhabited. Beyond it were a number of elegant *casitas,* for staff. And a large, low structure from which wafted the cloying scent of cheap institutional food. In the opposite direction stood an oddly shaped, domed building. It was the only structure in sight that might have been called *La Mezquita*—the Mosque.

Keeping one eye on the Dobermans—as he'd guessed, they were trained to patrol the perimeter, not the grounds proper—Roarke sidled across the lawn to the domed building. There were tall, narrow windows here, but heavy drapery blocked most of the view. However, the dome itself was unobstructed. And it could be reached by shinnying up a palm tree planted beside it.

Presently Roarke was crouched at the dome, peering down at rows of plush velvet chairs. He'd picked the right building: Seife was sitting alone, toward the front.

The moment he noticed the white, suspended screen—even before the screen lit up, came alive—Roarke realized Seife's carton wasn't packed with dynamite sticks, or beakers filled with bubonic plague. Dieter Seife had smuggled in a movie.

As soon as the movie began, Roarke saw what sort it was: a clumsy piece of Nazi propaganda. If the images had been violent or pornographic—women ravaged, children tortured—Roarke wouldn't have felt any more offended. But at least he wouldn't have been bored. *Hans Munson,* among its other crimes, was guilty of the sin of tedium, too.

So Seife was an ardent Nazi. Roarke had already deduced that. But why would even the most pathological Führer lover go to the trouble and expense of getting his hands on this cornball, clichéd, contraband love letter to all things Adolf?

Maybe one had to be a pathological Führer lover to know the answer. In any case, Roarke couldn't stomach the scene wherein the perfect-looking Aryan Boy watched, wide-eyed and radiant, as the Hitler Youth formed a human swastika out in the forest. The moment was Busby Berkeley by way of Beelzebub.

Having seen enough, Roarke climbed back down the palm, then started across the lawn. Then stopped at a peculiar sight.

A white-haired woman in a light cotton bathrobe was drifting aimlessly around the grounds—alone in the dark, like a ghost who'd gotten lost between the blurry borders of death and life. In an instant, just watching the way she swayed and twirled and bobbed her head, Roarke realized where he was: not a clandestine scientific research facility, not a hotbed of Nazi saboteurs and sympathizers . . . but a very high-priced nuthouse.

So he didn't bother hiding as she turned to him with a vague, disarming smile. She was surprisingly pretty for a woman in her fifties, but there was something else about her: the lady was an oddly expressionless and aged version of someone Roarke knew but couldn't quite place. He brought a finger to his lips, silently asking her to not sound the alarm, then continued on his way, searching for a wall to scale, a wall with no guard dogs sniffing and snapping. But he'd gotten less than thirty yards when he heard, from behind, a gruff male voice:

"Hey, where d'ya think you're going?"

Roarke froze, poised between running for it and putting up his hands, when he saw that the man (one of the Two Burly Men in White Coats) was addressing the lady, not Roarke. The man hadn't noticed Roarke. He grabbed the lady's wrist, not as gently as one might expect a professional hospital orderly to take hold of a patient, and she resisted as he tried to lead her across the lawn to the dining room. "Don't gimme any more trouble, Ida, I've had a bellyful already." His tone was just threatening enough that the white-haired woman relented and the two figures moved away. Roarke released a breath, withdrew deeper into shadow, started backing toward the wall.

He was almost there, almost out of the compound, when he realized who it was the lady reminded him of, who she resembled. The name helped him make the connection, of course: Ida.

Roarke didn't know any "Ida" personally but he'd heard about one recently. She was in "a sanitarium, somewhere back east," Hayden had said. Well, this wasn't New England. But Pasadena *was* east of Hollywood, and if Roarke were still a betting man, he'd have made a substantial wager that the dazed, attractive white-haired woman was Eleanor Lustig's mother.

He couldn't leave her, could he? Sure he could—hell, she'd committed herself. But that was over ten years ago, in the wake of a catastrophe. And since that time, the cumulative effects of Ridley's healing had eroded her free will. If Ida had the wherewithal, she might've screamed at Roarke for help.

Hunched, he stalked back across the lawn to the cafeteria. Over a radio, Toscanini conducted the "Blue Danube Waltz." The lights were dimmed, perhaps to keep inmates from becoming overstimulated. The room held about forty men and women, all looking both well heeled and disheveled at the same time: a weird mix of wealth and madness. Some were handsome, still—movie stars whose careers were derailed by morphine, cocaine, or chronic suicide attempts; others with the characteristic look of the dipsomaniac or the syphilitic; yet they walked and talked as though they were God's Favorites. It was like a perpetual black-tie New Year's party of the damned, and on top of it the food didn't look especially appetizing, and there was no champagne. Roarke stood in the doorway, searching for Ida.

She was just sitting down at a table in the middle of the room, among two elderly men and a woman young enough (but not nearly gorgeous enough) to be her daughter. Roarke didn't want Ida to get too caught up in her meal, or her dinner companions: she might make a scene. Anyway the ex-cop couldn't stand in the doorway indefinitely. So he strode across the dining room, right up to her table, looked down, and said, "Ida."

The white-haired woman looked up. "Do I know you?" Her voice was warm and welcoming, though her eyes were anxious.

"Of course you do," Roarke urged, and took her arm the way the orderly should have—as though he were leading her onto a dance floor, not hustling her off to a cell. "I'm a friend of Eleanor's."

"Eleanor." Ida Lustig brightened and, for a magic instant, ten years vanished off her face. She turned to her tablemates. "Ellie is my little girl. She's just going into the fourth grade." The old men and the young woman nodded and smiled, rotely and politely. It dawned on Roarke that everybody here was medicated, sedated. Whatever they were doling out was a potent brew. The effect seemed to be that nobody wanted to leave, even when they might've been ready to, even when they might've been "cured." Including Ida. She gazed up at Roarke with a pleading look, like a kid who couldn't bring herself to climb off a merry-go-round, though the music and the spinning had stopped.

"It's time to go now," Roarke told her. "You don't want to miss Ellie's first day of school, do you?"

Ida wiped her mouth with the cloth napkin and rose.

"So long, dearie," one of the old-timers hoarsely called.

"Send us a postcard," whispered the younger woman.

Holding hands, Ida and Roarke slowly, decorously exited the dining room. Then kept walking into the night, toward the wall.

It was cool, and quiet. Even the Dobermans were calm— they'd been fed their supper, too. When the pair strolled past the domed building, Roarke could faintly hear the German dialogue from that dreadful movie, but he ignored it. He was distracted with calculating his finder's fee. Mrs. Lustig was looking up at the silvery sliver of moon. Then she turned to Roarke and wondered aloud—shy but coy, flirtatious almost: "What are you, some kind of romantic gigolo?"

Roarke was about to respond with a joke, when he noticed the two white-coated brutes, waiting farther down the path.

"Those are not very pleasant men," Ida murmured.

"Y'mean Joe Palooka and Li'l Abner? We're just going to walk right past them," he assured her. "I'll tip my fedora and say, 'Nice evening, gentlemen,' and we'll stroll out together."

Ida looked confused. "You're not wearing a fedora."

Joe Palooka pulled a leather blackjack from his coat pocket as Roarke slid a Luger from his pants. Ida screamed. The scream threw off Roarke's timing, and the sap landed on his gun hand. It stung like a snakebite, but better his hand than his brain—or kneecap, for that matter. Because as Joe Palooka grabbed Ida and Li'l Abner reached down for Roarke's Luger in the grass, Roarke kicked Abner in the head, then ran. He reached a small building he hoped was a toolshed: maybe there were pitchforks inside, or shovels, or gardening shears.

It was no toolshed, it was a stable. The three horses inside started whinnying at once. "Good horsies" was the first phrase that came to the hopelessly citified ex-cop, and when that didn't help he tried, "Hi-yo, Silver," but that failed, too, so Roarke caught his breath, then ran out again and kept running.

"Behind the stable! Look! He's getting away!"

Now it wasn't just Joe Palooka and Li'l Abner in pursuit, but a pack of Doberman pinschers. To add to the excitement, a siren started to wail—the neighbors must have feared a squadron of Japanese Zeros had finally reached San Marino—and by the time a searchlight atop the main house swung around to blind Roarke, he felt much like Harley Hayden in *Perilous Passage,* shot down behind enemy lines. But alone: Errol Flynn was busy, committing statutory rape.

"Goddammit!" "Got your gat?" "Get that twerp!" B-picture dialogue to compete with that Nazi *schmaltz* in the mosque. Roarke reared and, dazzled by the thousand watts in his face, swung at something. Something swung back, and hit jawbone.

Roarke found himself on his knees, rocking like an Arab, praying to a dog. He was grabbed just before the foaming canine nipped off his nose, and hoisted up by the armpits.

"Sonuvabitching bastards!" Roarke snarled, careful to stay in character just like Joe and Abner as they dragged him across the lawn to the main house. "Get your stinking mitts off me!"

The leather sap came down—aimed, this time, at Roarke's skull. He'd sapped his share of uncooperative coons while on the job—but only after he'd exhausted other options. Roarke had always suspected it, and now he knew for sure: You don't hear tweeting birds, or "Listen to the Mockingbird," like in the Warners cartoons. You don't even see stars. You just head straight to Dreamland, though you're too tired for dreaming.

"Who are you?" came the voice. Serene. Gentle, even.

Roarke didn't open his eyes. He wasn't sure he could and, instinctively, was in no hurry to find out. "Fine, thank you."

A hand slapped his cheek, still sore from the earlier punch. "I said 'who,' not how." That voice again, oozing with bedside manner.

"Sorry," Roarke said. "Must've left my driver's license at home—but then again I didn't drive here, so why am I sorry?"

Now someone was prying open Roarke's lids. Joe Palooka.

They were in an examining room, Roarke thought. Everything looked white, reflective, sterile, hygienic.

"Your name." It was the little man with the thinning but carefully arranged red hair. Standing over Roarke, he actually looked tall. Now Roarke had no doubt they'd doped him up.

"You first."

Roarke girded for another slap, but the little tall man introduced himself, instead: "I'm Dr. Jasper Ridley. I run this facility.
Many wealthy and important people place their deepest trust in
me. Therefore I need to know your name, and I need to know
who sent you here to kidnap one of my patients."

"Too many questions," Roarke murmured. "If you want to
know so much, y'shouldn't make me all stupid on morphine."

Ridley smiled. "The morphine was administered to reduce any
discomfort you might suffer, as a result of Ray having to subdue
you." Ray, Roarke assumed, was Joe Palooka, the sap enthusiast.
"As to your difficulty in answering these questions, my clinical di-
agnosis is that you were born stupid."

Provoked, Roarke tried to sit up—and immediately realized
they'd taken the precaution of fitting him for a straitjacket.

Watching him struggle, Ridley proposed: "Restraints come off
when you start to cooperate. Till then we keep you bundled up
tight. It's for your own protection, really. Who are you?"

"Mike Hunt." *Slap.* "Dick Hertz." *Slap.* "Joe Blow-Me."

Ridley had the hypodermic ready. Perhaps he was squeamish
around needles; in any case he handed it to Li'l Abner. "Thank
you, Tommy," Ridley said, as Tommy-Abner pressed the plunger.

He and Ray peered down at Roarke. As the darkness started
closing in again, Roarke slurred at Ridley, "It's so damn cute—
you don't just dress your animals, you give them names."

Roarke awoke next morning—or was it next night? The room was
still sadistically white, painfully antiseptic. And maybe even a diabolical shade brighter: like paper cuts on his pupils. He tried to
go back to sleep, but Dr. Ridley wanted to talk.

"I really don't care to see you hurt," Ridley said. "I see so many people who are so badly hurt. It hurts *me* to see that, more than you can know. I have the gift of empathy, young man."

He was sitting beside the examining table, or operating table, or morgue slab, or whatever cold, hard surface they had Roarke laid out on, trussed like a turkey. Ridley's small hands were folded on his lap. From his vantage point, Roarke could admire Ridley's fingernails, the well-formed crescents, perfect cuticles. "But those two boys who work for me, Ray and Tommy? Are not to be trifled with. They've both got powerful physiques and fragile egos. It makes for a volatile and dangerous mix."

"Maybe they ought to be patients, instead of employees," Roarke suggested—rather sensibly, he thought.

"How long were you trespassing before you got caught? And aren't you aware that trespassing is a crime in California?"

"And forty-seven other states," Roarke reminded the doctor. "And since it's a crime, why not call the local cops on me?"

Ridley ignored this. "What did you see, while you were snooping? What—or who—were you looking for?" When Roarke didn't answer, he changed tack again. "If we have to continue to keep you under control by means of narcotics, you will soon develop a dependency. And you really don't want that. I've seen people climb walls. I've seen people *gouge* walls with their nails." This last recollection seemed to bother Ridley. He protectively petted the fingernails of his left hand with the fingertips of his right as he stared at Roarke, and waited.

"Okay," Roarke said, after a while. "You ask who I am? I'll tell you."

"Good," Ridley urged. "Then the straitjacket comes off."

"I need a better deal than that. I need to go home."

"Maybe," Ridley hedged. "Who are you?"

"The Lindbergh baby."

Dr. Ridley sighed. Then he stood, wringing his hands, but so gently. "Tommy? Ray? Come in here, please."

He hadn't a prayer of escaping so long as they kept him in that straitjacket. The morphine was pure, so it took a few days for this insight to dawn. After that, Roarke struck a bargain with Ridley: Let me have just one shower, and I'll tell you my purpose here. Not who sent me, but why. One thing at a time.

Ridley agreed, remarking that Roarke smelled rotten. "The body is the vessel," he opined, with his patented mystical air. "Rotten body, and the soul begins to spoil."

The night before the shower, as Roarke floated in the ether between heaven and earth, he tried to summon a telephone number. The digits danced on the ceiling, a racy rumba. There were seven of them, but they didn't seem quite in the right order.

Then, to his amazement, an angel flew in. Not Gabriel, a girl. How, Roarke couldn't imagine, since he was now held in a rubber-lined cell that Ridley called the quiet room—not even a barred window, only a padded and dead-bolted door. But the angel appeared nonetheless, with a face that resembled Eleanor Lustig's. She fluttered on gossamer wings and, though Roarke begged her to spend the night, she only stayed long enough to rearrange the seven numbers in an order that seemed familiar.

There was something extra in the mixture they shot in his veins that morning to promote good behavior. Ray escorted him to a private room, newly empty—a patient had checked out. It comforted Roarke to know that some people, at least, were allowed to leave, once in a while. Maybe when they ran short of money, or a close relative threatened to call the authorities?

Then Ray untied Roarke, with a boilerplate warning about not trying anything. "Such as what?" Roarke wondered, as there was nothing in the bathroom that wasn't screwed in or bolted down but a slim bar of Palmolive. Then Ray stood here, arms folded across bulging chest, while Roarke lathered up under the thin stream of tepid water. Ray tried not to look foolish, but he must have felt foolish, guarding a naked man covered with bruises and needle marks who was trying to wash himself.

Especially when Roarke turned and looked straight at him while soaping his groin. It seemed to bother Ray, as Roarke had hoped. Dr. Ridley might have diagnosed a case of homosexual panic. "Make it snappy, I'll be right outside," the orderly grunted as he slipped out. Ray left Roarke alone for two or three minutes, till the water was turned off. Then he reentered the bathroom, gruff and full of purpose. "Alright, let's—"

Either he saw that Roarke had unscrewed the showerhead, or he stopped in midsentence for the simple reason that Roarke clobbered his skull with said showerhead. In either case Ray crumpled without another sound. His blood looked shocking and lurid splashed across the bone-white tile. Still gripping the shower head, Roarke stepped over Ray, left the bathroom and padded down the corridor, naked and wet, to the nursing station. One nurse screamed, another let out an involuntary laugh.

Roarke picked up the nursing station telephone and dialed the numbers in the order that the Angel Eleanor had arranged them, the night before. A Mexican fellow answered: *"Hola?"*

"Enrico," Roarke said. Enrico recognized Roarke's voice and sounded glad to hear it. Roarke told him where he could be found—the city, and the street address, as best he remembered—then instructed Enrico to bring Mario and anyone else who wanted to have a swell time busting up a high-toned private loony bin in Pasadena. Roarke urged Enrico not to bother putting on a zoot suit for the occasion, just to make sure the pachucos arrived quickly, and were loaded for bear. Before Roarke had quite finished, Dr. Ridley and Tommy appeared. Both were upset, as evidenced by the high color of Dr. Ridley's cheeks, but especially by Tommy's rubber truncheon, and the crunching sound it made against Roarke's right temple. Roarke found himself resting on the nursing station floor, and Dreamland beckoned.

Next morning Roarke was shaken awake to find himself strapped into a wheelchair. Tommy perfunctorily spruced him up, then rolled Roarke into a large, bright community room.

There were twenty patients present, in chairs arranged in a circle. And Dr. Ridley, and one of the nurses—the one who'd involuntarily laughed when she saw Roarke's naked, soapy body.

Tommy was guarding the door, Roarke noticed.

"Let's all welcome John to our healing circle," Ridley said, gesturing in his direction. Roarke didn't mind being called John; as a longstanding patron of the Central Avenue whores, it was a name that felt familiar. Roarke gave a little smile, as the patients offered an encouraging round of applause.

Then a fastidiously dressed, white-haired geezer began:

"I'm starting to feel so much better. I'm eating well, sleeping well, taking my daily exercise. My digestion is excellent. I haven't felt the need for a drink in—months."

If they're pumping the same stuff into your veins as they are into mine, Roarke thought, well, brother, who needs booze?

"And I'm hoping," the geezer continued, voice trembling as he turned to Ridley, "that I might qualify soon for a day pass?"

Dr. Ridley peered at the handsome old gent. "What for?"

"Well," said the gent, with a sweet, shy smile that was frayed just a little at the edges, "I thought I might drive over to the Warner lot, look in on some of my producer friends and supervisors from the old days, to let them know I'm feeling strong again, and sober, maybe ready to get back into pictures." He fretfully tugged at his shirtsleeves, in a way that revealed his pale, bony, almost delicate and feminine-looking wrists.

Ridley nodded. Even Roarke could see (though this was only his first Healing Circle) that the nod didn't mean a day pass was forthcoming. "Ready to get back into pictures, Mr. Booth?"

Mr. Booth nodded back, but less certain now.

Roarke thought he recognized Mr. Booth. He thought he remembered Mr. Booth from an early John Ford Western. Mr. Booth had played the kindly sheriff who got shot down in the second reel while trying to bring in a cattle rustler. Roarke could have sworn that Mr. Booth weighed a good fifty pounds more, all muscle, when he'd played that role.

"I think you're far better off here, Mr. Booth," the nurse spoke up. "Where we all care about you. Where, to us, you're family. On the Warner lot, they may pretend you're family, but god knows they only care about one thing. The profit margin."

As opposed, Roarke wondered, to the Brotherhood of Man?

"Thank you, Deirdre," Ridley intoned.

"Personally I would hate to see you back in motion pictures," said an older woman. Roarke realized it was Ida Lustig. He hadn't noticed Ida in the room. As Roarke studied her, she smiled back—pityingly, he saw. Roarke suspected she'd already forgotten how he'd tried to escort her off the grounds. "There's nothing quite so terrible as motion pictures, Mr. Booth. Movies steal the souls of men," she added cryptically.

Roarke saw that Mr. Booth was about to say something, and maybe Ridley did, too, because he jumped in: "I think what Ida just offered is something very simple, and also very profound—though the terms in which she put it may be pagan, superstitious ones. Do you recall the thesis of *At War with One's Self,* Mr. Booth?"

Mr. Booth tried to look thoughtful. Instead he looked sad.

"Humpty Dumpty comes in many shapes and sizes. He may be ovoid, as even a child knows, or he may also appear . . . wasted." Ridley had chosen the word carefully. At the sound of it, Mr. Booth began to crumble. Dr. Ridley continued, smoothly: "But so long as Humpty Dumpty allows his essence to be divided— whether by a bottle of scotch, or a strip of celluloid film—he will continue to suffer from ego confusions, feelings of self-loathing, self-despair, even suicidal ideation. In other words, Mr. Booth, the very cures that you would seek are the keys to your own destruction. Do you want me to hand you a loaded gun? Or a syringe full of strychnine? If I gave you a day pass, Mr. Booth, that is approximately what I'd be doing."

Mr. Booth began to sob. "I'm so sorry," he sputtered.

Ida, sitting near him, leaned over with a lace hankie. Everyone else clucked as the pitiful old actor blew his nose then tried to pull himself together. Roarke couldn't watch.

"Who'd like to speak next?" Deirdre asked the circle.

A younger man, portly and prematurely bald, with an oddly self-satisfied air, turned to Roarke. "Why doesn't John tell us what brought him here, and how long he'll be staying with us."

Ridley turned to Roarke and fixed him with what Roarke had started to think of as the Kindly Glare. "How long John stays is entirely up to John."

Roarke started giggling. Because what Dr. Ridley'd said was, ironically, so true: Enrico and Mario and their heavily armed cohorts were coming, the only question was when. Maybe tomorrow, maybe the next minute. Exasperated by the giggling, Ridley signaled to Tommy, who wheeled Roarke out of the Healing Circle. Roarke laughed all the way back to the Rubber Room.

Roarke hadn't seen Ray since the shower episode, and he couldn't help but wonder whether Ray had pulled through. It didn't seem wise to ask Tommy about his partner, though; people tend to lose perspective about their partners, Roarke reflected—witness the Prince of Wales and that mangy Mrs. Simpson.

Roarke didn't have to wait long to find out Ray's fate, and his own. Late that night he heard the dead bolt pulled aside: the padded door to the Rubber Room slowly opened. Ray stood with his head swathed in bloodstained bandages. Roarke almost started giggling again—Ray looked like Karloff in *The Mummy*.

"I just stopped by to let you know." Ray took a single step inside the Rubber Room. Roarke had the sense he didn't like the smell in here. (Not only had there been no further showering since the Episode, but the staff had stopped escorting Roarke to the toilet as well.) "I'm still a little shaky on my feet. But tomorrow morning I'll be fine. And that is when I will administer one helluva beating, you crummy fairy boy."

Roarke supposed Ray's aim was to magnify the punishment by proclaiming it in advance. Maybe he assumed Roarke would stay awake all night, panicked. This was a fair guess, as there'd yet been no sign of Enrico, Mario, a single pachuco. Had Roarke given the gang leader the wrong address? Till El Hoyo arrived, he was just a straitjacketed ex-cop drugged on morphine (and, he suspected, scopolamine to make him talk), helplessly waiting for Ray to take his revenge. Roarke bathed in his own sweat from late night till early morning, when the door opened again.

It was Dr. Ridley, carrying a breakfast tray. He squatted beside

Roarke, poured fresh orange juice down Roarke's throat, then spoon-fed him oatmeal with raisins and milk. If the barnyard stink inside his cell bothered Ridley, Roarke couldn't tell. The doctor was as sweet and unstinting as Roarke's own sainted mother. He'd even brought coffee with cream and sugar.

"I know Ray's planning to retaliate," Ridley confided, as he raised the coffee cup to Roarke's lips. "And I can't blame Ray. The man was simply doing his job when you coldcocked him." Ridley brought a cloth napkin to Roarke's mouth and wiped him clean. "So I cannot in good conscience stop Ray from meting out his rough justice. But at the same time, I've come to think of you as another patient here at the Hacienda. Thus I have a conflict. And you have a problem. But we can help each other."

"By telling you my name, who sent me, what I saw?" Roarke felt coffee spill from his lips, drip down his chin as he spoke.

Dr. Ridley daubed him dry. "Or any two out of the three. You see? I'm a reasonable man, I'm willing to compromise. Answer any two, and I will release you before Ray even awakens."

Roarke closed his eyes and tried to imagine what Ray had in mind. And he questioned why in hell he'd risk more retribution for Harley Hayden, Bland Boy Wonder of the Big Screen? Roarke's eyes snapped back open. Who'd sent him? What did he see? "I was sent by Western Union. I tawt I taw a puddy tat."

Ridley rose. "I detest brutality," he muttered, "but when a man brings it upon himself, that's his business. His putrid destiny." The doctor left Roarke alone, again, to wait for Ray.

Who arrived a few moments later, freshly bandaged. He was hefting something as he let himself into the quiet room: a medical bag. When he started rooting around in it, Roarke heard clinks and clanks and strained to see the instruments within. He couldn't make out anything: Ray deliberately kept the devices—clamps, probes, surgical scissors, and other dreadful, more esoteric items—out of Roarke's limited line of sight.

"You ready for me?" he asked, making preparations. "Have you been waiting for me all night, you miserable nancy boy?"

"All night," Roarke assured him—then added, with a last burst of bravado: "Just one ground rule, Ray, before we start. Don't bother sucking my cock if you're not gonna swallow my jism."

"Keep it up, faggot." Ray was snapping something together, assembling an exotic medical appliance Roarke couldn't see—but could vividly imagine in his panicked reptile brain. A moment later Roarke flinched, feeling pressure on his abdomen, where it was soft and defenseless. In four-point restraints, he could only suck in his stomach, but the rest of him was immobilized. Pain hotly skittered up his spine. Roarke tried not to scream.

But he must have screamed because he was aware that, as his scream subsided, there were voices audible down the hall.

"What? Where?" The torture stopped, Ray turned around. "How many guys?" Then he went running off, leaving Roarke on the floor. Next, Roarke heard shouts. Then a gunshot. Followed by silence, followed by a shriek. Now more footsteps—a man, running. The squeaks of doors thrown open.

"I'm in here," Roarke called, sounding to his own ears like a tremulous cheerleader who'd just been gangbanged by the USC Trojans. Someone burst into his cell, whom Roarke didn't know.

"Are you the Interested Party?" The young man in the doorway was a foot taller than any pachuco. He was also blond and blue-eyed and had undoubtedly never seen Carmelita Street.

Roarke had no idea what was meant by "Interested Party," but he couldn't see the harm in identifying himself as such.

"Let me help you out of this contraption." The blond boy grabbed a scalpel, started slicing. "I'm Heinrich, by the way."

Heinrich? Why not? Superior Pictures couldn't have found a better bit player for the role of Young Grenadier, Waffen SS.

"Pleased to meet you, Heinrich." Then: "Who got shot?"

"One of their goons. The healthy one. The other one, Karl smacked on the head, where the bandages were, with the butt of his Colt." The kid laughed. "Pop goes the weasel."

"Sorry I missed it. Karl would be?"

"My brother." Heinrich tore off the straitjacket, trying not to retch at the mess.

Confused but grateful, Roarke got his bearings, limped out of the Rubber Room, and found his clothes stashed in a laundry bag in the night nurse's locker. After quickly dressing, he accompanied Heinrich down the hall to where Tommy and Ray were lying, at Karl's feet. (Karl was likewise the Compleat Aryan.)

Ray was out cold. Tommy was conscious, but there was a bullet hole in his thigh and his blood pooled thickly on the terra-cotta tile. There were no signs of Deirdre or Dr. Ridley. Either they'd run for help, or were crouched under a desk.

Roarke shook hands with Karl, then told the brothers, "There's a patient, a woman named Ida Lustig, white-haired, handsome. Try to find her. I've gotta go grab something."

The brothers went looking for Mrs. Lustig. Meantime, several inmates—though not Ida—were drifting around the grounds, unsupervised, at loose ends. Roarke avoided these slow-moving obstacles as he dashed toward the mosque.

There was a sign: MONDAY MOVIE NIGHT AT THE MOSQUE: "HEY, HEY, IN THE HAYLOFT" & "YANKEE DOODLE DAFFY." The door was locked, but Roarke kicked it open and ran upstairs to the projection booth. Roarke grabbed an unmarked can of film in the corner, hoping it was Seife's. As he came back downstairs with it, Ridley was coming up—Roarke nearly bowled him over. "Stop," Ridley demanded. "Think about what you're doing. Trespass, robbery, assault with a deadly weapon. If you plead incompetence, I'll vouch for you in court. I'll be your expert witness." Roarke was amazed at how collected Ridley was, in the circumstances. He held out his hands, and they were quite steady. "Just give it to me."

And Roarke gave it to him—that is, he smacked Ridley's face with the film can, a swing worthy of DiMaggio, knocking the doctor to the next landing. There Ridley sat, stunned, limp as Raggedy Andy, and not much taller.

Roarke stepped over him, down the last flight, then heard:

"You won't know what you're looking at."

The words sounded strangely garbled, distorted. Roarke turned around to Ridley, whose lower jaw had apparently been knocked off its hinges; he was trying, in his calm and delicate doctor's way, to set it right. "Is that so?" Roarke retorted.

"You'll only think you'll know . . . and you will only add more pain to this world." Ridley struggled to enunciate.

Roarke considered unevenly biting off all the doctor's beautifully manicured nails as a sort of coup de grâce, but on reflection that seemed an unsanitary revenge. So instead, Roarke sarcastically counseled: "Humpty Dumpty comes in many shapes. Not just ovoid. He can also be a half-pint, sawed-off blackmailing dope peddler posing as a caring psychiatrist—"

Ridley interrupted with a bizarre, savage, animal shriek.

Roarke left the mosque. Back in the main house, he picked up the phone and dialed. "Pasadena Police," said the operator.

"Yes, there's been some trouble at the Hacienda. You'll want to send an ambulance. We've got a bleeder from a gunshot wound, a possible skull fracture, a jaw out of joint, and—"

"Who is this, please? What is your name, sir?"

Roarke sensed someone behind him. He turned in time to grab Deirdre's arm and twist it, sending her rump to the tile. "And a sprained wrist. Have your flatfoots search the grounds for morphine, scopolamine, cocaine, opium, the whole shebang—"

He hung up when he saw Karl coming down the corridor with Ida stretched out in his arms, her white hair flowing freely.

"I think she's all doped up," Karl said.

"Specialty of the house," Roarke explained. Then whispered into Ida's ear, though he doubted she was listening: "We're checking out of the Hacienda, Mrs. Lustig, and about time, too."

They stepped outside as Heinrich pulled up to the portico in a lovingly maintained cherry-red Cord convertible. Karl deposited Mrs. Lustig in the rear seat, and Roarke climbed in behind and rested her head on his thigh. Meantime Karl jumped in front and the Cord sped out of the compound.

Roarke didn't look back, he just patted Ida's forehead with his left hand and clutched the film can in his right. There was the slightest dent in it, Roarke saw, left by Dr. Ridley's jaw.

It made Roarke smile, for the first time all morning.

. 12 .

Unsere Jugend

They were side by side in his convertible, her head resting on his shoulder as he drove along the windy, hilly streets above the Bay. It was sunny, cool, and clear, a perfect morning, and she seemed content with him, sure that he knew where he was going, what he was doing. He drove fast, with confidence, up and down streets he couldn't remember yet clearly knew well.

Soon he would have to stop somewhere. Park somewhere, go somewhere—and finally it would dawn on her, that he was lost.

To hide the fact, he would dump it in her lap. Trying his best to sound frivolous and gay, he announced, "The day is so fine, what say we just keep driving? You name the direction."

She seemed delighted, if surprised. "But, darling, don't you have to put in an appearance at the office?"

He laughed, as though at the preposterous idea of having to do anything. "Which way, Leora, Big Sur? Or back to Sonoma?"

"Sonoma? The very word makes the soles of my feet ache. But

I do miss my mama," she said, lightly yet with unmistakable poignancy as she lit a cigarette, then passed it to Tony and—

"*Cut.*"

Hayden knew what was coming. He could almost write Sykes's—Seife's—admonitions himself now. Something like "It's true this car will lead to the girl's death, but you, Mr. Hayden, are grinning the sardonic grin of one who is already dead himself!"

He girded for the tirade, wondering whether he'd be able to withstand this latest tantrum without an eruption of his own, at last. Hayden was a quivering tower of tension today (Day Seventeen) though he felt he was hiding it well, given that his anxiety had been steadily building since Saturday. It started when he didn't get a call or wire from Roarke over the weekend. It worsened when Sally conquered her fear to phone *him* at the studio, Monday morning; she was out of her mind with worry, not having heard a word since Friday. "Hell, he's taken a long weekend, maybe driven out to Arrowhead for some R&R," Hayden surmised, not even half-believing it. And now it was Tuesday afternoon.

As the stagelights came up, obliterating the panoramic San Francisco Bay on the rear-projection screen behind their car, which the teamsters had just stopped rocking, Hayden watched the impostor director approach. The strain on Sykes's face both mirrored and exacerbated Hayden's own. Sensing all this, Mary Oakley slid a hand (under the dashboard, out of sight) onto her costar's thigh. Not erotically or romantically, rather as a signal of solidarity between two actors in the same tough spot.

Sykes was ten yards away now, striding toward the process car. Harley squinted at Sykes's face—the camera wasn't rolling, he could squint all he wanted—and tried to read beneath the strain to some darker truth, some hidden guilt.

Did Sykes know what had befallen Roarke? Odds are, he did. *Odds are,* thought Hayden, *he did it.*

But what, exactly? Murdered the ex-cop, because he'd asked too many questions, seen too much, or merely had the temerity to shadow the secretive German? Maybe that sounded absurd, but Hayden wouldn't put it past Derek Sykes. As the director came ever closer, Harley felt his gorge rise. All it would take to set Hayden off, now, was a single no from Sykes. Who had finally reached the process car—on Harley's side, of course. Hayden felt ready to pounce. Just the *n* in no, the tongue on the roof of Sykes's mouth, and Hayden's rage would pour out, volcanic, setting Derek Sykes back on his bootheels, alright.

"Very good, Mr. Hayden. I think you are finally getting the hang of this, my boy."

There was no *n* sound to trigger the explosion. Hayden gaped—stupidly, he knew, but couldn't help it—at Sykes, who didn't notice, as he was now moving around the car to have a word (at last, Day Seventeen!) with Mary Oakley.

"My dear, you lit the cigarette like a schoolgirl. It was quite charming, but also quite wrong. You may be only a grape stomper, but you're a woman—no girl. Here, let me show you."

He snapped his fingers and Sam, the property master, was here with a Pall Mall that Sykes lit, then puffed on, with a certain continental savoir-faire. Mary studied his movements closely. Whether she could duplicate them, well . . . this was Mary Oakley here: not Dietrich or Garbo, or even Hedy Lamarr.

"Shall we try another take?" Sykes looked from Mary to Harley. This was the jauntiest he'd been, to date, on set—could it be because Roarke's body was securely six feet under?

"We got to talk, Mr. Sykes." This came out of Hayden's mouth almost involuntarily, as though he were being dubbed by another actor. Sykes looked surprised. So did everyone else within earshot.

"Yes?" the director responded.

"In private." Hayden climbed out of the car.

Sykes glanced at his wristwatch. It was already four P.M., but in truth the production was a half day ahead. "Very well," he muttered, then with a sigh followed Harley off the set. As he did, Sykes distractedly slipped the Dunhill lighter in his pocket as he reminded himself that Harley had top billing, and was only—for once—behaving like an actor who had top billing. How terrible a sacrifice would it be to indulge Mr. Hayden?

As they strolled together toward the farthest corner of the soundstage, Seife thought perhaps the discussion would have to do with Hayden's health. The tall young man had lost a bit of weight since filming began, and Seife was aware that the Hair and Makeup people had bitchily dubbed him Young Mr. Lincoln. A few more pounds off and Hayden (extending the Great Men of History theme) would cross the line from Lincoln to Gandhi. Lighting and makeup would become more critical and time-consuming. Hayden's whole wardrobe would have to be expensively altered. Seife hoped to address all this.

But instead Harley launched into a confused accusation—or series of vague allegations and contradictory innuendos—to do with an Interested Party who had apparently disappeared over the past weekend. At first, Seife was so perplexed by the phrase "Interested Party," he was unable to get the gist of Hayden's dark and hostile ramblings. But slowly he managed to make a kind of sense out of the actor's random questions and suspicions, hemmed and hawed though they were. And as Seife put together a picture in his mind, he made his face into a mask that he hoped was entirely inscrutable. "I have no idea at all what you might be talking about" was Seife's final word.

Hayden stared. "Do you deny that your real name is Dieter Seife?" he shot back.

"Why should I? It is the name I was born with." Then, in the mildest, most accommodating tone he'd ever used with Harley: "Now let's get that car scene in the can while you've still got it note perfect." No more was said about the Interested Party.

"Sykes" got the shot he wanted, and one more, before Day Seventeen was a wrap. He worked methodically, with far less fuss than usual. The crew was pleased with its calm captain.

But inside, Dieter was a roiling sea of doubt and remorse. Obscure, even crazy, as Hayden's complaints sounded, Seife couldn't dismiss them. His gut told him a grim truth: there must have been some connection between the disturbance outside the mosque he'd overheard as he'd watched *Hans Munson* and this mysterious Interested Party who'd suddenly gone missing.

Ach! Though Hayden had skirted the issue, it became clear to Seife, as he drove north on Highland, that the male lead in his own film was having him investigated! The outrageousness of it, the bitter injustice, went straight to Seife's bowels. He'd overheard talk on the set, of how Hayden was supposedly regurgitating in his dressing room after every setup—and dismissed it as gossip planted to win Seife's sympathy, maybe his mercy. Now Seife felt an urgent need to vomit as he made a left turn onto Camrose. He pulled the Buick to the curb and staggered out. Crouching, he began to spew hot chunks into the gutter.

"Herr Seife!"

What now? Seife wiped his mouth and turned to see Hilda, who'd been walking down La Presa Drive to the bus stop. Seife bitterly reflected that, on a film set, it would require a dozen takes at least to time such an encounter so perfectly. "Hilda?"

"You're ill. *Mein Gott,* you look terrible, Herr Seife!"

Before he could stop her—in truth, he didn't try so very hard—Seife was being helped into the passenger seat of his Roadmaster, and Hilda was driving the two of them up the winding hill to his house on Los Tilos. Here she insisted on helping the director onto the couch, pulling the shades, fixing him some warm tea with honey, and vigorously commiserating. "They are working you too much on that movie lot, working you half to death," she insisted, all in the (accented) English he'd asked her to speak.

Seife let her go on like this, let her cluck and flutter. He said nothing. In his mind, he replayed the scene outside *La Mezquita,* realizing now that the Interested Party must have trailed him there and been discovered. What then? Had Dr. Ridley's oversized, overzealous orderlies done something terrible, foolish, irrevocable? Seife leaned over the side of his couch, retched again. There was nothing left to bring up.

Hilda phoned her husband to explain she'd be staying the night with Herr Seife. She played nurse well past twelve, walking him upstairs, dressing him in pajamas, plying him with more tea and crackers when he thought he could take solid food, and finding just the right music on the radio-phonograph to soothe Herr Seife's frayed nerves. Throughout all this, Seife only offered grunts and sighs and an occasional groan.

Hilda finally fell asleep, sitting in Seife's rocking chair. She awoke before six to find the director still in bed, eyes open, staring at the ceiling. Seife had not slept, even a minute, all night. As soon as Hilda asked if there was anything he needed, Dieter confessed almost everything—about Hayden's Interested Party, the Hacienda, Dr. Ridley, and the Nazi films brought in from Berlin through Spain via Mexico by a pricey smuggler called Schmidt.

He spoke in German, and Hilda responded in the same language, and demanded to know why he'd kept all this a secret from her, and all Seife could exclaim, through hot tears, was:

"It's all too shaming! Too grotesque, and too shaming!" He looked so movingly like a lost little boy as he said this.

Hilda covered Seife's forehead in sweet matronly kisses, made sure his blankets were neat and straight, and then said she'd telephone her sons, Heinrich and Karl, and get them to drive out to Pasadena and see what in the world was going on.

Seife argued against it, but in fact he was in favor of the idea. He knew that Hilda's boys were brave and strapping lads who managed their own auto repair shop and didn't shrink from anything physical—including the use of firearms, for she'd told him how they'd recently been robbed (by a GI on leave, ironically) and took bold action. He hoped they could handle the Hacienda. He made negative noises, but didn't stop Hilda when she picked up the phone and dialed. In fact, he furnished the address of the sanitarium and detailed directions. His only condition was that his name be left out of it, that the Interested Party (if, please god, the Interested Party were alive) never know of Heinrich and Karl Biederhof's connection to Dieter Seife.

Then he remembered it was Day Eighteen, and he was due on the set. Hilda brewed coffee while he showered and shaved, looked over the day's script pages, and pulled himself together.

If Hayden glanced accusingly at him today, Seife resolved to stare haughtily back. "I may be weak, I may be flawed, I may be a poor and pitiful specimen," he reflected, as he donned his jodhpurs, "but in the grand scheme of things that young man is still only an actor—whereas I, Dieter Seife, am a director."

Reminding himself of this was roughly equivalent, in its restorative power, to six straight hours of peaceful sleep.

Hayden didn't glance at his director the next day. He didn't look at him at all. He gazed at his own shoes or at his mark duct-taped to the floor, whenever "Derek Sykes" consulted him about the next setup. Which worked fine for Dieter Seife, himself too fraught for even brief eye contact with his star.

The day dragged for both director and actor, at least till lunch, when Seife in his office had a call from Hilda. The news was disturbing perhaps (there had indeed been gunplay, two Hacienda orderlies were injured), but also good: the Interested Party was found in one piece, and freed. Seife kept this from Hayden—let the actor find out on his own. Dieter was still smarting from the revelation that Harley'd had him investigated.

Investigated!? He might as well be back at Ufa, in Berlin!

Ellie dropped by the set that afternoon for the first—and, as it turned out, only—time. She'd been visiting her father and remembered that Harley was shooting nearby, she said. Hayden suspected the real reason was Mary Oakley, Ellie's desire to take the measure of his girlish costar. But he acted pleased to see her, and he introduced Ellie to Mary as soon as they'd made the martini shot. The women shook hands and smiled at each other. Tense though this was, the proximity of his fiancée to the woman who played his fiancée proved a strange distraction.

After wrap, Harley stood Ellie to a steak dinner at the Vine Street Derby. They had cocktails before supper (Harley'd been teaching her how to drink, and Eleanor was proving an apt pupil) but then, over salad, they began to bicker. The fight was mostly about how little Ellie had seen of Harley since filming had begun, but Harley sensed that the unspoken subject of the quarrel was, once again, Mary Oakley. Never had such a sweet, unspoiled thing as Mary inspired such ugly emotion, he thought, but prudently kept this to himself. After dinner he invited Ellie back to his place to listen to some records. He'd just bought the new Artie Shaw disc, a Benny Goodman, too.

She followed in her Cadillac. As they parked, they heard Harley's phone ring. Harley walked Ellie slowly up the path, anxious to seem in no hurry to answer. Though he was dying to talk to Sally, dying for news of the private detective, he was terrified it was Mary calling, inviting herself over to run lines. He smiled at Ellie as he mentally rehearsed how he'd handle his side of the call, which he knew she'd be monitoring. For all his mental effort, he couldn't work out how in hell he'd pull it off. The phone still rang as they entered—and Harley ignored it, drifting into the kitchen to mix more highballs.

"Aren't you going to answer?" Ellie demanded, hands on her luscious hips. "It might be important."

"Might not." Harley tried to sound light. And then, to his horror, he heard Ellie grab the phone.

"Harley Hayden residence," she sang out, and Harley braced himself for the inevitable squall to come. But instead he heard "Yes . . . Alright . . ." and then a surprised "Oh!" from Ellie. Then a sustained silence—then an exclamation: "But that's impossible!"

Harley ventured into the living room with the manhattans he'd mixed. He tried to offer one to Eleanor, but she gestured for him to leave the room, indicating this was a private matter. Perplexed, Hayden drifted out—slowly, hoping to catch some fragment of conversation. But all he heard was, "No, no, that won't do . . .

No, that *definitely* won't do. Wait, I'll think of a place, another place where—hang on, give me a moment . . ."

Now Harley stood in his own kitchen, feeling as awkward and superfluous as he had in his first movie roles, playing the Best Buddy or the Extra Man. Then Ellie hung up, and Harley reentered the living room.

"Say, who was that?"

His delivery so flat, so false, he half-expected to hear "Cut" and would've gladly tried the line a few more times.

Ellie'd already grabbed her purse and was nearly out the door. "Oh! It was—" She stopped, flushed, flustered.

"You don't have to tell me," Harley offered, limply.

"It's not that. It's . . ."

He'd never seen her in a state of such reckless excitement. He knew Eleanor as measured, disciplined, self-possessed, wise beyond her years. His mind couldn't fasten on a reason, or a person, to throw her into a sudden tizzy. A lover, he thought, at a loss—but why would a lover call here, at Hayden's house?

"I'll phone you," she promised Harley, then dashed to her Caddy, forgetting even to give him a good-night kiss.

What could he do but let her go? He stood in his doorway as she drove away, thinking, "Ellie's going off in one Cad—to another . . ." Then wandered back inside and sat with the two cocktails. They looked so sad, these orphan manhattans, that Hayden momentarily considered giving Mary a call. She'd be here like a shot, and any social awkwardness would be smoothed over by the line running they could do—and, then, by the cocktails.

But getting Mary over here meant Harley wouldn't be able to spend the evening in a self-pitying funk, which seemed a more appealing prospect than his pert costar. He reached for a manhattan and drank it off in one quaff. Then stood, as the hooch warmed his blood, and put on the Benny Goodman platter. He listened to a few bars of the master's licorice stick, swaying to the hot licks, eyes filling with mawkish tears at Eleanor's abrupt run-out. Too many complex emotions had piled up between him and Ellie of late, grievances and resentments he barely understood. Maybe it was better she'd given him the brush like this. Maybe tonight was a clean break—unexpected, for the best. As though to sonically mark the break, Harley lifted off the tonearm: but he did it sloppily, scratching the virgin disk with an ugly ripping sound he barely registered.

He sat again, in silence now, wondering at the identity of Eleanor's new sweetheart. Was it someone Mr. L had set her up with, a boy of her own class, her own faith, a Hillcrest boy? (Someone Hayden had once pulled out of the pool? No, that was the MGM version, Superior would never make that movie.) Or a teaching assistant from the Psych Department, such as he'd mistaken Roarke for, back when? In short, had Ellie found someone she deserved, a boy she belonged with—as opposed to some boob from the Midwest who'd stumbled out to the Coast and into pictures with only a grin and a squint to recommend him?

The squint. It suddenly dawned on Harley that here, alone, in his own living room, he wasn't squinting. The squint had been drummed out of him on-set by Derek Sykes. And—dammit—without squinting in the slightest, Hayden realized he could see the room, and every object in it, with fantastic clarity!

Stunned, he reached up to feel his face, make certain he wasn't wearing his horn-rims. No, he was not—he'd taken them off when he entered the house, as he always did when he had company. He stood. He looked around again to make sure of the phenomenon. He read the titles off the spines on his shelf: *Penrod, Our Town*. He looked at the signature under Ellie's portrait, on the far wall: Hurrell, two *r*'s, two *l*'s, scalpel sharp. He studied the Benny Goodman platter, still sitting in the phonograph, and saw the new scratch . . . a long, shallow, gorgeous scratch! My god, Hayden thought, heart thumping like a Gene Krupa solo, a miracle! Somehow, none other than Derek Sykes—for all his evil scheming—had wrought a miracle here!

Enthralled, Hayden lost track of the two looming crises before him: Roarke's disappearance (possibly at the hands of his director) and the disappearance of his fiancée (possibly into the arms of a Junior Professor or Wealthy Young Jew). "I can see!" he exulted, knowing it sounded like a line from some sappy inspirational picture (the kind Hayden loved, actually, the kind Capra made—yes, Capra, who wouldn't deign to *audition* Harley). Euphoric, he grabbed the second manhattan and drained it—also in one quaff. He looked around his living room again.

This time the focus was even sharper. If Harley were a Roman Catholic, he'd have crossed himself. But since he was a Protestant, and not formally affiliated with any church, there was no ritual, no prayer, no genuflection—nothing, in fact, but a staggering walk into his kitchen to mix another manhattan.

Once he'd done that, he had a brain wave: Call Eleanor, tell her the fabulous news. He got as far as the phone, even dialed her number before it dawned that his fiancée would not be home, for she was busy trysting. Harley hung up, humiliated.

But only briefly. Because Harley had another bright idea, hard on the heels of the previous not-so-bright one: He would fetch his horn-rims, and snap the frames in half! Maybe stomp on the lenses for good measure! Talk about a meaningful, powerful ceremony! He lurched across the living room to the front hall table, where he'd set down his glasses. He grabbed them, started to bend them—then thought better of it. After all, those sturdy horn-rims had been a faithful friend, his boon companion, a facial feature, nearly. Perhaps one day they'd be worth something: "These belonged to Harley Hayden," he could hear a hushed docent of the future tell a tour group as she indicated the spectacles on a satin cushion in a glass display case. "Before God miraculously bestowed on him the gift of perfect sight." Ashamed, Hayden put the glasses back down.

Then he took the Benny Goodman platter off the turntable and snapped *it* in half, instead. (It was ruined, anyhow.) He carefully removed the Artie Shaw disc from its sleeve and put it on, lowering the volume, letting Artie's band "moan low." Then he dimmed the lights, kicked off his shoes, stretched out on his couch, and got comfortable. He'd wait up—all night, if necessary—for Ellie to realize she'd done him wrong and crawl back. At which point he'd dazzle her not merely with his perfect Christ-like forgiveness, but more thrillingly with his new powers of supersight (as Clark was sorely tempted to, when Lois seemed to stray with Lex). Right now, Hayden rested those rejuvenated eyes, letting his lids close. He slept deeply.

The doorbell rang. The living room was bathed in light, the phonograph needle was lazily drifting back and forth over the record label, and Hayden bolted up. He glanced at the clock, across the room. Its face was a blur. He came closer, squinted, saw it was just past seven, and croaked, "Who is it?"

"Philo Fucking Vance," he heard, muffled.

Hayden ran his fingers through his hair, hoping to tame the pomaded mess, then went to the door and tried again: "Who?"

"Aimee Semple McPherson. Open the goddamn door!"

Hayden opened, and could have kissed Roarke's bristly chin! He was so relieved, he didn't even dwell on the disappointing realization he'd woken up with double vision not X-ray vision. Seemingly, last night's supersight was a trick of last night's hooch, catalyzed perhaps by last night's heartache and dread.

"I thought you were—"

"I thought I was, too." The ex-cop, tough though he might be, was also superstitious: he couldn't speak the word "dead," either. Roarke was carrying something. He handed it to Harley. "You'll want to see this."

Harley looked down at the can of film. "A short subject?"

"Not short enough."

Hayden set down the canister then gestured for Roarke to take a seat as well. "Get you some orange juice?"

Roarke shook his head, and lit a Lucky.

"So what is it then?" Hayden indicated the Mystery Movie, now sitting innocuously on his coffee table.

"Tell ya the truth, I haven't watched it." Roarke shrugged. Blew a smoke ring. Then: "I watched another one, though. That was plenty. This one, I just held up a few frames to the light. That was plenty, too. Lustig'll want to take a peek, I'd bet. You should probably call Chester Dowling, reserve a screening room during lunch break. This is a doozy, this is dynamite."

"But not TNT?"

Roarke chuckled darkly. "No nitro, no plague. Not even smallpox. It's only a movie. No big stars. No box office draw at all, 'less you'd rather look at a swastika in the woods than Jane Russell on a haystack. I know one Kraut who'd prefer it."

"A movie." Hayden's gaze flicked to the film can. "So this is what Seife smuggled in, from Mexico? A *movie*?" After all the lively speculation, particularly his grave concern for the Golden Gate Bridge, Hayden couldn't help but feel deflated.

"Couple movies," the ex-cop corrected, annoyed. "And don't knock it, I went to a certain amount of trouble on your behalf."

"Okay, sure, don't get sore. It's just . . ." Hayden rose, then walked cautiously into the kitchen (skull throbbing from last night's unaccustomed bender) and poured himself some juice.

While pouring the juice, a thought struck him. He bounded back into the living room. "Say, maybe smuggling a couple of movies into the country was just for practice—a dry run, see?"

Roarke frowned. "Dry run for what?"

"For— I dunno, maybe"—okay, if it wasn't nitro, and it wasn't plague—"some new kind of death ray?"

"Y'mean, the kind that vaporizes people?"

Hayden nodded, but provisionally, sensing one of his legs being pulled.

Roarke leaned forward, stubbed out his Lucky. "I saw that movie, too. Brass Banfield versus the Diabolical Hun. We were both sitting in the Chinese, you clutching Ellie, me clutching my buttered popcorn, when was it, last year, last century? I can't remember anymore." He stood up, wearily moved to the door. "I think Seife just felt like watching a couple of movies. For the reason why, you'd have to ask Dr. Ridley, but Dr. Ridley might be retired by now, or lighting out for parts unknown." He started to leave, but Hayden stopped him, grabbing his arm.

Roarke winced. His arm was still tender.

"I don't know any Dr. Ridley," Harley said.

"And now you don't need to," Roarke assured him, removing Hayden's hand from where it pressed against his numerous puncture marks. "All you need to do is let Arthur Lustig know this film is the property of Dieter Seife, and let him watch it. The rest will take care of itself." Roarke took a few steps down the walk, then stopped. Turned. "I'll send you a bill. By the way, Eleanor's fine." Then, without further explanation, he strode to his car.

Eleanor's fine?

Hayden scratched his head, then reached behind him for his horn-rims, donning them just in time to watch Roarke drive away.

That's a hell of a note, Hayden thought. As he thought it, he realized the line came verbatim from a script he'd been reading.

"I've got no time for such nonsense—certainly not today."

Actually, Lustig was having an unusually pleasant day: he'd just watched preliminary color tests for *The Double* and was amazed at how Toland, the cinematographer, had tamed the usual gaudy palette into a brilliantly narrow spectrum that was close, in its way, to black and white! (Though he liked to tell overambitious cameramen to "call me Arthur, never *Art,*" Lustig was secretly thrilled by the bold look they'd achieved.) *And* he'd seen in *Variety* that de Havilland was suing Warner Bros. to get out of her stock contract. Any *tsuris* for Jack Warner was cause for Lustig's joy. But bedeviling his Boyish, Goyish Albatross had become a reflex for Lustig. "Can't this wait a few days, Harley?"

"Afraid not, A.L."

At this abuse of his initials, Lustig disconnected. And then, with some reluctance, he asked Agnes to make sure the executive screening room would be available at noon, and invite Dowling to join them. That way, when Lustig got bored, he could sneak out, grab lunch, let one gentile handle the other gentile.

"I haven't actually watched this myself" is how Hayden introduced the film, unpromisingly, as the lights dimmed. "But from what I understand, it's something you fellas want to see."

Like *Hans Munson,* the movie began with a dark screen and music, over. A stirring martial overture. Well, stirring if you were a National Socialist: Hayden recognized the trumpet theme as a melodic variation on *Deutschland über Alles.* Then the two-word title blazed, in a bold, jagged script meant to suggest lightning bolts. The two words were *Unsere Jugend.*

"What the fuck?" Dowling murmured.

"Our Youth," Lustig translated. He'd been born in Germany, a small village called Laupheim, and after immigrating to New York at nineteen to apprentice in the art of cutting calf-skin gloves, Lustig never spoke another word in his native tongue. Yiddish, often; German, never. "The title means 'Our Youth.' "

Then the first image appeared: A boy about fifteen, but tall for his age. Blond, proud, with perfect posture. He stood fearless near the peak of a craggy mountaintop, thick straight hair blowing in the alpine breeze. The camera captured him from a low angle, with a wide lens that stretched him to heroic, even iconic, proportions. He seemed to be gazing boldly at—

"Die Zukunft."

Hayden wondered: had someone sneezed?

"The future," Lustig translated.

The boy's name—his stage name, anyway—was Martin Volker, though none of the three people watching cared about this trivial detail. He'd also played the role of Hans Munson, but the men in the screening room hadn't seen *Hans Munson und die Hitlerjugend;* of course they didn't recognize the child actor.

Only Lustig understood the narration, but he'd stopped translating. It was all so much racialist bullshit anyway, mindless zealotry—a stinking crock, in short.

"How will we know Our Youth? We will know Our Youth by its strapping health, its eager soul, its cherished innocence. And, last and best, by its purity."

Now the camera pulled back to frame in a girl, also fifteen or so, also blond and straight and tall and pretty and proud. Her steely gaze was fixed on the future as well. The heated narration persisted, with the title phrase *Unsere Jugend* chanted over and over, and on the screen there were idealized images of fair-haired children at work and play, marching and swimming, leaping and studying. All the children were wholesome. All the exteriors were bright. All the angles were low. But presently these pictures were interspersed with contrasting footage of dark-haired young people huddled—whispering, conspiring. (Some of these swarthy performers had portrayed Communists in *Hans Munson*.) These exteriors were overcast. These angles were high, looking down upon the dark forms as an exterminator might regard a teeming nest of cockroaches at his feet. During this sequence, the narrator intoned: "We see a parallel in the itinerant routes of rats, which are the parasites and bacillus carriers among animals." The black-haired youths were skinny, sickly, stunted. Their hair wasn't only black, but oily and unkempt as well.

"They're repulsive," Dowling observed.

"They're Jewish," Lustig explained.

"What the hell're we watching?" Harley wondered.

Then the editing rhythms accelerated, and the apple-cheeked towheads swam naked in the Rhine while the sunken-cheeked Jews cackled in their shadowy cells, and suddenly a large family of rodents streamed en masse toward an open sewer as the narrator warned: "Wherever rats appear they bring ruin, by destroying mankind's goods and foodstuffs. In this way, they spread disease, plague, leprosy, typhoid fever, cholera, and dysentery. They are cunning, cowardly, and cruel." Then the blonds pole-vaulted and the Jews counted money and the rats copulated amid piles of rat-shit and the beautiful teenaged boy and girl clasped hands and marched toward the mountain summit—

"Stop. Enough." Lustig said this loudly, as he stood.

The screen went black. Then Joe, the projectionist, raised the houselights—not the usual classy fade-up, but fast, as though there was a fire and people had to get out.

Dowling was up, too, compulsively ruffling his brush cut, digging for dandruff.

Only Hayden stayed seated. "What the hell *was* that?" he wondered again.

Lustig's lenses appeared to have fogged. "This film is the property, you say, of Derek Sykes?" He spoke softly but glared at Hayden, daring him to confirm this.

Harley stood, finally. "Seife, actually, isn't it?"

Now Joe was down with the canister.

"Who belongs to this?" He held it out—but queasily, as though it were a large, round, metallic turd.

Hayden reached for the film can. "Thanks, Joe, I'll take it."

Lustig grabbed the canister, with more energy and strength than Harley'd ever witnessed in Mr. L. "The hell you will."

Fifteen minutes later, Chester Dowling walked onto the process stage, where rear projection shots were being completed. Here was Derek—Dieter—supervising the backlighting, which was a critical matter in this sort of illusion.

"You place a gobo right here, the shadow will take care of any kick," he advised, reveling in the technical minutiae of the occasion. "Someone bring in Mary, please. We're ready for her in five." Derek Sykes was relaxed, in his element—till he noticed Dowling loitering nearby. Then his manner changed.

"Chester," he said, with a smile. "So good of you to come and watch. But I'm afraid the camera has malfunctioned, and there won't be any filming for a while." This had been his standard ploy, dating back to his earliest directing days in Berlin, whenever a studio official should drop by the set. It always worked. The executive would leave within ten minutes.

Dowling smiled back. "That's okay, Derek. Actually, Mr. L would like to see you in his office, now, you don't mind."

The director backpedaled: "But we're about to take Miss Oakley's close-up. Can he wait for our next pre-rig, Chester?"

Chester mouthed the word no. When he saw that the production head would say nothing more on the set, Dieter knew—or thought he did—what this was all about. "Okay, we go. But quickly, yes?" He indicated the waiting crew, a machine that burned large sums when idling. Dowling nodded, led the way.

As they strolled to the Administration Building, Dowling stayed mum. So Seife—unusually voluble, now the Hacienda situation was resolved—jabbered: "I suppose Mr. Lustig has by now found a replacement for Mr. Hayden? The irony is, a replacement is no longer needed. I have finally gotten my young star to stop acting. And posing. He no longer makes speeches. Mr. Hayden now *says things*. Even his squint—not a mannerism, I realize. Harley has weak vision." As weak, Seife reflected, as Hitler's. But gods can't wear spectacles when they fulminate in public, so the Führer relied on cue cards with print two inches tall. And if gods could not wear spectacles, then neither could film stars.

Agnes sent the men directly in to Mr. L, who was standing behind his vast desk. Seife approached, his hand extended.

"Mr. Lustig, I appreciate your efforts on my behalf—and the film's. But the truth is, after more than three weeks—"

He stopped speaking, startled by a sudden, shockingly loud *thump* almost like a gun's report: the mogul had, unaccountably, dropped a full can of film onto the desk.

"What is this?" Lustig gestured at the can.

Seife looked at the can, then at Lustig, confused. He still hadn't fully registered that this wasn't a meeting to discuss a replacement for Harley Hayden. Dowling, anxious to move things along, opened the can, pulled out the reel, and handed it to the vexed director. Seife unspooled a foot, held the celluloid up to the light streaming through the window behind Lustig, and strained to focus on a row of frames. His face paled as he recognized the succession of tiny images.

"Why, this is . . . I believe the title is *Unsere Jugend*."

"We know," Lustig whispered, as one whispers when speaking of obscene things in front of children. "But what is it?"

Seife swallowed. As he lowered the reel back into the can, he noticed that, in dropping it, Lustig had dented the otherwise perfect surface of his otherwise gorgeous desk. "I believe this is a short film—the title would translate as *Our Youth*—that preceded the showing, in Germany last year, or so I am told, as you know I emigrated long before that, of a feature film—"

"What feature film?" Lustig cut him off. "*How Green Was My Valley,* maybe? *Only Angels Have Wings*? What feature film—by name, Mr. Seife?"

Seife tried to answer clearly, straightforwardly, keeping his gaze firmly trained on Lustig. It was not an easy feat.

"*Jud Süss,*" he said, presently. "I believe that was the—"

"*Jud Süs,*" Lustig echoed. "And what does *that* mean?"

"I—" Seife tried to frame a careful, accurate answer. "I have not seen *Jud Süss,* Mr. Lustig. From what I understand, Süss is a sort of shifty figure, a moneylender perhaps, and—"

"—a Jew." Lustig smiled. He held Seife's gaze.

"Well, yes. Obviously." As soon as he'd said this, Seife realized it sounded wrong, not at all the way he meant it. He quickly turned back to the short film lying on Lustig's desk.

"If you are concerned that I may have some connection with *Our Youth*—that perhaps I contributed to the screenplay, for example—let me assure you that nothing could be farther from the truth. I've no connection to this piece of Nazi kitsch."

"We're fucking well aware you didn't *work* on the fucking thing," Lustig muttered, still staring at Seife. "Whether you *worked* on the fucking thing is not under fucking discussion."

Seife looked to Dowling for help, or guidance. But Dowling was busy ruffling his brush cut. So Seife turned back to the mogul. "Mr. Lustig," he pleaded, "this crude sort of propaganda is of no interest to me! Please, sir—I am not in the least a political person! I am, at heart, a storyteller."

"A yarn spinner," Lustig reminded. And now, oddly, it occurred to Mr. L that he was looking across his desk at—his doppelgänger! Dieter Seife—Lustig's double. Not his twin, certainly there was no physical resemblance whatsoever.

But there was a deep connection, Lustig felt in his gut: Mr. Merrily and Mr. Soap, somehow they were the same. In a secret way, somehow. But *how*? For a moment, Lustig wanted to stretch across his desk and embrace Seife. Perhaps, in the embrace, both men might better comprehend the connection.

In the next instant, Lustig remembered that—were some connection confirmed, were it established that the two were doubles in some sense—one of them would have to die.

And Lustig was not willing to enter into such a contract: a deal in which the odds of his demise were even. He banished the bizarre impulse to embrace Seife and turned to the window.

"A yarn spinner, yes." Seife's arms hung limply, his legs bowed. In the jodhpurs and military jacket, he looked pathetic.

"Well, why in the world would you smuggle that . . . Nazi contraband into this country?" Dowling prodded.

Seife shook his head, either unable to elucidate or unwilling to do so.

"Was it your purpose," Dowling persisted, warming to his prosecutorial role, "to privately circulate this film among the silver shirts and Bundists, to give them aid and comfort?"

Seife remained silent, features frozen.

Lustig checked his watch, then announced: "We're wasting time. Let's come to the point, Mr. Seife. If you think we're keeping you on here at Superior, you've got another think coming. If you think I'll let you finish shooting *Big Betrayal,* well, my friend, I'm afraid you don't know shit from Shinola."

Seife looked up, peering at Lustig with incomprehension.

"Let me enlighten you." Lustig stepped clear of his desk, so the director could see the mogul's wingtips. "*This,*" he said, indicating their fresh coat of black polish, "is Shinola. And *this*"—he pointed at the film can on his desk—"is shit."

"I understand. Yes. Yes, Mr. Lustig. *Scheisse,* I agree."

But Seife the Trained Seal was no more endearing than Seife the Supercilious Prussian. Lustig turned to Dowling. "We suspend production till Monday." Then, to Seife: "You're out."

Seife pleaded: "What do you propose, I return to Berlin?"

"Why not?" Lustig shot back. "You were a big noise there."

"I'd be arrested. I—how do you say it?—skipped out on Dr. Goebbels himself. I hid for months in Paris, changing hotels every week. Then escaped to Lourdes, in the unoccupied zone.

Eventually I climbed the Pyrenees, in my dress shoes." Which is where and how he'd met the smuggler Schmidt, but Seife chose to omit this in today's recounting. "Then I had to bribe a Catalan soldier with what little I had left, and then I—"

"Save it for your memoirs," Lustig cut in. "You want, I'll write Goebbels a letter of recommendation, make it clear you're still a major booster of the Master Race. He'll take you back."

"And so will your wife."

This last comment came from behind Seife—who turned, startled, to discover Harley Hayden in a chair in the corner.

"Your wife's a card-carrying Nazi party bigwig, isn't she?"

"My wife?" Seife seemed to go blank. Then, exploding in a brittle laugh: "The She-Wolf? My god, you men have truly done your homework. But for your information . . ." He turned away from the actor, beseeched the studio head: "The Blond Witch and I have not lived under the same roof in more than a decade!"

"But you never divorced, either, isn't that right?" It was Hayden again.

Seife kept his gaze firmly fixed on Lustig. "If I'd divorced her," he stammered, "they'd have known—known how deeply I disdained them." No one was listening. But Seife added, anyway: "They wouldn't have let me make movies."

"Look, Dieter." Lustig sighed, sitting. He ran his finger along the fresh dent in his desktop. "I'm not out to destroy you. I just want you off my picture, and off my lot."

"But I have committed no crime. And I have a contract—"

"Get this straight." Lustig kneaded and tugged at an earlobe. "If you try to play rough, I will fuck you so hard there ain't a cushion in Hollywood you could sit on. You'll *walk* back to Berlin—in your dress shoes, all I care—and beg Adolf Hitler for the chance to shoot his vacation movies at Berchtesgaden. Or direct second unit for Leni Riefenstahl. Or load her cameras. Or wipe her ass." He lowered his hand again, thrust it in his pants pocket. "But if you go quietly, you can help decide what Superior tells the press about why you left *The Big Betrayal*. Family crisis? Exhaustion? Creative differences? Hell, I might even keep your name on the picture, as codirector. I might not get on the phone with Harry Cohn, Jack Warner, and Louis Mayer, and tell them about the memorable little short subject we screened here today. You might not be blackballed all over town. That depends entirely on you."

Seife blinked twice, trying to keep tears from flowing over his lower lids. "I so wish that I could explain," he murmured.

One lone teardrop streaked his cheek.

The other three grew restive. "We're past that, Seife," Dowling said. "It's time for you to pack up your office. I'll have Business Affairs cut your final check and deliver it up at your house. Thanks for all your hard work."

He offered a beefy hand.

Either Seife didn't see it, or couldn't accept it. He turned on his heels—Teutonic to the last, even with that teardrop—and, drawing himself to his full height, he marched out of the office without a glance back.

The room was silent. Finally Lustig cut a look toward Hayden, still sitting in the far corner. "Happy?" he asked.

Harley looked relieved. But happy was a stretch.

"What's the matter?" Lustig persisted, bolstering the actor even as he bullied him. "Don't you think we got five directors on the lot right now, sitting on their fat asses, drawing down jack, could do every bit as bang-up a job as old Fritz there?"

"We got *ten* could do it," Dowling boasted. "Maybe better."

"Sure we do," agreed Hayden, if only to be a Team Player—till recently one of his signature roles.

"Don't forget *Gone With the Wind*," Lustig added, now committed to rallying his male lead. "Selznick replaced Cukor with Fleming in the middle of production. And the picture came out pretty good all the same. Wouldn't you agree, huh? Harley?" Then, to dispel any uncomfortable feeling of pity for the proud figure who'd just been dismissed, Lustig added, "Sonuvabitch is goddamn lucky he's not in some detention camp for enemy aliens."

"Specially seeing as the sonuvabitch is living in a coastal area," Dowling put in.

Both men turned to Hayden, who signaled agreement.

It was odd. Though he'd prevailed—though everything had worked out, more or less, the way he'd hoped—Hayden felt an urge to run from the room, fall to his knees, and throw up again.

Lustig picked up the film can and held it out to Dowling. "Now what the fuck we do with this *schlock,* this *shtick dreck*?"

"We dig a deep hole," Dowling suggested, "and we bury it."

A nod from the mogul. "Then piss on its grave."

. 13 .

The Woman Who
Didn't Care

There she was, still passed out—but on his bed now. Funny: he'd fantasized a dozen times about Ellie on (or better, in) his bed. But never Ida. Yet here she lay, regardless.

Predictably, as Roarke had stumbled inside with a film can in his hand and a woman slung over his shoulder, Sally's relief at his return was overshadowed by hysterics about the "soused floozy" she assumed Ida Lustig to be. "I see you been out painting the town red," Sally shouted. "Plus yellow, purple, and green." Maybe she thought the can contained a stag film? While Roarke dumped Ida on the bed and pointed out that the floozy was fifty and not drunk but sedated, Sally was busy filling an overnight bag with blouses, panties, and her precious nylon hose.

"Calm yourself—or get an eye exam," Roarke suggested as he pulled off Mrs. Lustig's pumps. "This old dame, I brought her back here for strictly humanitarian reasons." Sally's response was to slam the front door shut and stomp down the stairs.

Leaving Roarke to attend to his stomach, the tender spots

where Ray had used electricity to sear his flesh. He searched his medicine chest for unguent. He found a tube of Pepsodent, a can of Burma-Shave, a bottle of Milk of Magnesia. In the end, Roarke settled for a stick of butter from the icebox.

Then he tried to reach Eleanor Lustig. She wasn't at home, she wasn't at Hayden's. So he put in a call to Enrico.

"Where the hell was El Hoyo?" Roarke groused. "Yellow-bellied Mex bastards. Turns out your big bad pachuco gang is just a *rumor,* Rico—the beaner cavalry that never came."

"Man, didn't you see the papers?"

"No, I didn't see the papers. I was busy sustaining second-degree—"

"I'd rounded up a dozen *vatos*. We were on our way!"

"But you got lost. Left your *Thomas Guide* at home?"

"Fuck the *Thomas Guide* and buy the *Times,* Roarke. Buncha sailors from the Chavez Ravine naval base, the shore patrol, too, came down to East L.A. and kicked our butts. They stripped zooters naked, stabbed a couple—the cops stood by, scratching their asses. Mario's in the hospital, man."

Roarke finally reached Ellie just after nine, at Hayden's house. After identifying himself and explaining he wanted her, not Harley, he said, "Eleanor? Sit down, I've got some news."

"Oh!" He'd thrown her into a panic. When what he'd wanted to do, he knew now, was delight Ellie with this unexpected gift. Yet, already, Roarke was having doubts. This particular gift, from this particular guy, would probably be as welcome as a limp mouse deposited on Miss Lustig's doorstop by a stray tomcat.

"I have your mother here. Found her in a luxury booby hatch locked up, key thrown away, so I took the liberty of—"

"But that's impossible!"

Roarke offered a brief, basically accurate if upbeat account of Ida's condition, then asked whether Ellie wanted him to drive Mrs. Lustig to Hayden's bungalow, while she decided—

"No, no, that won't do."

"Laughlin Park?"

"No, that *definitely* won't do. Wait, I'll think of a place, another place where—hang on, give me a moment."

She thought of the Malibu Colony. "We have a beach house up there," she said, "it's number . . . My god, I'm so . . . you've got me so . . . sorry, I'm having a mental block. Just drive up to the guard shack, ask the guard. We're next door to Merle Oberon."

Roarke hoisted Mrs. L again and humped her deadweight back down to the Packard, arranged her across the backseat, and drove out to the Colony. The guard, who (happily) didn't notice Roarke's prone passenger, nodded him toward the Lustig property. "Miss Eleanor is waiting for you."

"Nobody else's been around, have they? Looking for the Lustig place?"

The guard thought about it, then shook his head.

The private road was quiet, and the Lustig house—like all the rest—was dark. Roarke cruised down Malibu Colony Drive, cut his lights, and listened to the slap and crash of the surf. Then leaned over his seat and hoisted Ellie's mom again. Whatever gratitude he'd ultimately get for her return, Roarke hoped it would compensate for the chiropractor bills to come.

The front door opened before Roarke had a chance to knock. Ellie'd left a light on in the foyer, and as that light fell across her mother's slumbering face, and form, the younger Lustig woman let out a sort of gasp, mixed with a low moan.

"Mama." Ellie's eyes were wide, wet, glassy.

She led the way to a moldy-smelling upstairs bedroom. Roarke laid the dozing Ida down again on the chenille bedspread and tried to arrange her limbs so this looked like a nap, not a wake. Ellie opened a window to let in some air—and a shaft of moonlight came with it illuminating her mother's features.

"She's so beautiful," Eleanor whispered, and it was true—at rest, the older woman's face was unlined, not in the least bit withered, virtually unwrinkled. The daughter leaned over, stroked her mother's hair, patted her forehead, gently squeezed a hand. "How long has she been sleeping like this?"

"All day. That sanatorium, they handed out Nembutal like they were Sen-Sen." Then, his voice lowered, Roarke answered the larger question: "Off and on, she's been asleep about a decade. Eleanor, I have to warn you, time's stood still for your mom and maybe in a way that's a blessing . . . but bear in mind, she thinks you're still going into the fourth grade."

"Oh god."

Concerned that she might crumble on the spot, he suggested they go downstairs while Ida slept it off. Roarke gripped Ellie's hand on the staircase lest she stumble, swoon, or faint.

The living room had a row of French windows that faced onto the dark, roiling ocean. Its wildness suited the night, and Roarke's mood, and Ellie's, too, apparently. She turned on a few lights, then urgently rooted around in a dusty liquor cabinet. Roarke was concerned she'd come up with a bottle that predated repeal but, thank the Lord, some good soul had left behind a quart of scotch with a genuine label. Roarke cracked it open.

"Where exactly *was* she?" Eleanor demanded, pacing before the window wall, her silhouette seeming to glide in the gloom.

Roarke slumped down on a chintz sofa and sipped. "Out in Pasadena, high-toned funny farm run by a certain Dr. Ridley."

"Jasper Ridley?" Ellie stopped walking. She was standing by the wall that held a shelf of books. She turned and reached for a volume; she knew just where to find it. "*At War With One's Self.* A big best-seller, right around the time my brother . . ." Ellie trailed off, and chucked the book in Roarke's direction. He caught it, then set the volume on the floor behind him: he'd had enough of Ridley's nostrums to last a lifetime. "All the actors ate it up. Supposed to contain secrets to cure their neuroses and complexes." Ellie laughed softly. "They'll find a cure for cancer before they find a cure for actors."

Roarke let that pointed comment pass. Meanwhile Ellie plucked the bottle from his hand and took a healthy sip. "I think Mom hoped somewhere in the pages of that book was the secret that would stop her grieving. Anyway, I couldn't get her to look up from the pages, at *me*." She had to pause for a moment. "Then she disappeared. Father went to Europe to scout talent and locations while Mother went back East, to rest, was what they told me. How . . . strange, to think that all these years I pictured her on the other side of the country, the *moon* almost, unreachable, untouchable . . . You'll laugh, but when I enrolled at UCLA as a psych major, I had a dream I didn't dare tell anyone, that I'd learn how to save my mother—and then, with that special knowledge, I'd journey far and wide to find her, rescue her, like in a fairy tale . . . When the whole time, while I grew up without her, and studied late into the night to learn how to help this . . . vanished parent who'd become a myth, a fantasy, to me—she was twenty minutes away in Pasadena."

"Maybe your father never told you the truth 'cause if he spoke it aloud he'd have to face it, too?" Roarke suggested. "And if it was hard for you to live with the myth Ida was off in some faraway place, well—it was probably easier for your dad."

"I guess that's so." Ellie folded her fine strong legs, sat on the floor in a heap, and buried her face in her hands.

Roarke let Ellie cry awhile, happy to nip at the scotch till she'd pulled herself together again. Her cheeks glistened in the moonlight. She sniffled. From where Roarke sat, she almost *could* have passed for a kid going into the fourth grade.

"And he just kept her there, doped up, and . . . *Why?*"

"The way Ridley worked, he held these Healing Circles, where patients would reveal their dark secrets. Maybe it made good therapy, and maybe it made good blackmail material. When you get people talking about their pasts, their fears, the problems they've concealed, the vices and weaknesses that landed them in the booby hatch—especially rich people, you'll pardon me— that's like handing gold ingots to a certain type of creep. You know: leverage, to keep Ida at the Hacienda month after month, till years went by and your father forgot he had a wife, got used to scribbling that monthly check to the Pasadena witch-doctor while he was living alone with you in Laughlin Park. Ridley must've figured that Mr. L didn't want the whole world to know your brother drowned while his parents were busy getting tight and doing a foxtrot not ten yards away."

There was a shocked silence, and then: "How did you know that?" Her voice was low, but he heard a note of vehemence.

Roarke shrugged. "Not nearly as *secret* a secret as you and your daddy'd like to believe. Which is true of most secrets"—witness that goddamned grand jury—"but people don't want to face that, as a rule. Which is how blackmailers make such a comfortable living."

Eleanor flashed a thin-lipped admonitory smile not unlike her father's, though prettier. "If people didn't try to keep secrets, you'd be hard up yourself, wouldn't you, Mr. Roarke?"

Perhaps she'd sensed that Roarke was looking for a little recompense for his daring rescue of Mrs. L. If so, now was not the time for the ex-cop to claim his reward. Instead he nodded, amiably. "I'd have to find an honest line, like selling used cars or black market beef." Having made this concession, Roarke asked Ellie what he'd wanted to, for months.

"Why'd you keep it from Flip, all this time? About what happened, to make your family fall to pieces? I know it's been driving him crazy, but he doesn't want to push you, hurt you."

"You'll laugh at this, too," she said, ignoring the fact that Roarke hadn't laughed yet, "but I always felt it was—well, *ridiculous,* that my brother drowns and five years later I meet the love of my life, and what is he? A lifeguard! How's that for neat, how's that for sappy? Even a first-year psych student would cringe at such a coincidence. Even a hack Hollywood scenarist would know better than to plot his tale so baldly."

"Maybe so. But this is no movie."

"Are you sure?" Ellie asked. "Then why does it feel like one?"

She was getting tipsy, granted, but Roarke could see her point. Malibu beach house, moonlit night, gorgeous girl, pounding surf, and a lingering mystery solved in the upstairs bedroom. All that was missing was what Hollywood calls underscore—a swelling theme to target the hearts and tear ducts, make people say and do the most mawkish, maudlin things.

"Let's have a little music," Roarke called out.

Ellie had the same idea. She'd already crossed the room to fiddle with the phonograph. There was a stack of dusty records to choose from, and she must have chosen at random. Roarke heard Nelson Eddy dueting with Jeanette MacDonald from a picture that was dated and ridiculous when it came out five years earlier.

Once they'd stopped giggling, Roarke found himself holding

Ellie—and the two of them swaying to the banal song. Suddenly they *were* in a movie—not *Maytime,* but something better, richer, deeper, and more lurid, the taboo fulfillment of a fantasy Roarke had cultivated since that night in Barney's Beanery. Suddenly Roarke was determined to give Eleanor a memorable fucking. One that would erase the memory of her pursed-lipped head-shake, make her kiss-off the prelude to a kiss. Or better, he would put those pursed lips to work. And not so much out of animal lust. Not at all to compete with his movie star pal. Rather, out of a keen instinct that Eleanor Lustig hadn't had a memorable fucking yet and deserved one, if only for future reference, if only so she'd know what to demand from Hayden in their years ahead—if the actor had it in him.

Roarke held her tighter, closer. He sported a world-class hard-on, and he knew she was feeling it against her thigh. So far she hadn't slapped him, sprung away from him, or even stopped swaying. Roarke was about to place a hand on her breast when she spoke up, as the final chorus faded: "What do I owe you?"

Her tone was utterly cool, businesslike. If it was Ellie's intent to suck all the magic, the erotic possibility, from this moment, Roarke would not be a party to that—even if it cost every cent he'd hoped to earn. "Owe me for what?" he wondered.

Ellie gave a silky laugh that carried with it a note of condescension, if not contempt. "For bringing back my mother."

Roarke felt his cock shrink. "You were all paid up before the song. Our dance just now, that was my Christmas bonus."

She laughed again, perhaps mocking the part Roarke was now set on playing—and then, as though to heighten the humiliation, she tightened her grip: close enough to confirm that his manhood was as shriveled as his pride. The mood grew even more perverse as she laid her head on Roarke's shoulder—so that his whole world was dizzyingly suffused with the fresh scent of her hair—and said, "Shall we invite Merle Oberon, make it a real party?"

"Merle Oberon?" Roarke croaked, nonplussed, forgetting for a moment that Merle Oberon was the Lustigs' next-door neighbor.

Ellie sighed. "I used to sit on the porch for hours, just waiting to see her come out for a dip. I'd read *Wuthering Heights* twice, watched the movie ten times—I made my father run it again and again. I was obsessed with *her,* not Heathcliff."

Roarke took this as final confirmation that he was a far cry from Ellie's ideal bedmate. Squirming out of her grasp, the ex-cop managed, "I should get going. You and your mom have a lot of catching up to do. And you should try to get some sleep before she wakes. This won't be easy, El, you'll want all your wits about you." Roarke chastely kissed her cheek. "G'night."

"Wait, Mr. Roarke," she said. "You can't drive back to town, the condition you're in . . . You've had too much to drink."

Though her warning was pro forma, she was right: he was plastered. But Roarke was seriously out of his depth here, and he knew that now; it was more dangerous to be alone with Ellie in Malibu than brave Sunset Boulevard, stewed, in traffic.

"Stay in touch," he said, walking an exceedingly straight line all the way to the front door to simulate sobriety.

"Drive carefully," she said, and gave a goodbye wave.

Roarke rolled his Packard toward the guard shack slow and easy, so the do-gooder at the gate wouldn't phone ahead to the Malibu Patrol with his license plate number. Roarke had a smile and a nod ready for the guard. But the shack was empty.

Roarke shook out his last Lucky Strike and drove through. Simultaneously it struck him—soused though he was—that something was wrong. Roarke shifted into reverse, rolled back to the shack, got out of his car, and peered inside. The guard *was* here—but down on his knees and bleeding from one ear.

Roarke jumped out of his car without killing the ignition. He ran back to Ellie's place with remarkable swiftness and grace, given his elevated blood-alcohol level. He saw no one around front. He crept through the alley that led to the beach, crouching behind a garbage can while squinting into darkness.

Then he saw Ray. Roarke might not have spotted the orderly, but those white bandages around his head glowed dimly in the moonlight. This muscle-bound ape turned tarantula was climbing the wall via the drainpipe, and he'd almost reached the open window of the bedroom where Ida Lustig lay sleeping.

Roarke climbed up after him. Ray didn't hear the ex-cop (who had the Pacific to thank for that) or sense Roarke, as he reached the orderly's ankle. The skin was exposed here, about an inch of it above his sock. That's when Roarke realized the Lucky was clenched between his teeth, still lit. Tit for tat, he thought, as he stubbed it out on Ray's lower leg.

Lucky Strike has gone to war—for real, this time, at last.

If Ray screamed, the crashing waves covered that, too. In any case he dropped off immediately, like a burnt tick. Roarke dropped down, too—on top of Ray, as Ray writhed. Roarke punched his face with his right hand, patted him down for a gun with his left. Just as he found the gun, he got a bracing surprise—a huge wave splashed up and over: it took both men with it, rolling and tumbling them over jagged rocks and seashells.

They were submerged together, Ray and Roarke, both fully dressed, in heavy tie-shoes, smacking each other around as the waves smacked *them*. They grappled and gasped for breath. While gouging, biting, and brawling in the Pacific, Roarke struggled to kick off his brogans as the two sank, entangled.

If spotting Ray on Ellie's wall half-sobered Roarke, the shock of frigid water brought him all the way around. Roarke was thinking clearly as he socked Ray's nose, pulping it, but an instant later he found his own nose pressed into sand, and a few feet of water on top of him. And Ray, clamped to his back like a giant crazed crab, trying to tear his arms from their sockets.

Roarke kicked, twisted, gagged on the salt in his nose and somehow got to his knees—and then a monster wave whomped them both and, receding, dragged them out farther. Roarke lost his nerve, flailing wildly and stupidly like the drowning man he was. His terror only abated when he realized Ray wasn't on him anymore. Roarke calmed enough to swim to the surface.

As he came up, he saw Ray sinking. Roarke wasn't Harley Hayden; he'd had no lifeguard training. Nor was he from Ohio—not by a long shot. So he went limp and let a rip current carry him a hundred yards or so, then did a slow backstroke to shore.

And stumbled across the sand, Florsheims sloshing, back toward Ellie's. Then sat on the beach, catching his breath and waiting for Ray to resurface. Roarke coughed out what he feared was a lung, then saw that it was in fact a hunk of seaweed. After a while it seemed clear that Ray wouldn't be bobbing up any sooner than Brother Saul. Roarke hoped the sharks were fighting over him.

The Lustig house was dark now, and quiet—Ellie'd gone to sleep, Roarke guessed. He pictured her cuddled upstairs on the mattress next to Mama, like a schoolgirl who'd been troubled by a nightmare. Roarke made his way back to the guard shack and slapped the guard, enough to be sure he was still alive. Then he dialed the police for the second time in twenty-four hours. "Send a car out to the Malibu Colony. Someone pistol-whipped a guard. He'll be okay. Just bring a bottle of aspirin." Then he climbed in his Packard and drove back to Hollywood.

Though eager to get out of his sopping togs, Roarke parked down the block and walked home, to play safe. No orderlies loitered in the lobby, poised to pounce. And there was the film can where he'd left it on the kitchen table. Then he remembered he hadn't cracked at the Hacienda. They hadn't pried so much as a first name from him. Feeling good about that (if about little else), Roarke stripped off his clothes and showered. He'd track down Sally—at her sister's, most likely—and straighten things out. But first he'd drive to Hayden's with that can of toxic film.

The Big Betrayal was released in early 1943. The *Times* ran a mixed review: the picture's "Frisco scenery" was "swell" but the plot had "more twists than Lombard Street and left this critic feeling nearly as carsick." While Harley Hayden was judged "inconsistent" (and his character derided as a "weepy weakling"), Mary Oakley was deemed "a bright newcomer to watch."

Roarke took Sally to see it one night. He liked the movie far better than the *Times* had. Harley was the best he'd ever been: Roarke counted only two grins, as many head tilts, and one squint. (From the last weeks of shooting, after Seife was fired?) And the ex-cop was surprised at Hayden's bold choice of role: in the final reel, following the girl's suicide and a cascade of shocking revelations, Tony stumbles into the police station and, between sobs, snitches out all his rotten friends.

"Harley's a dreamboat" was Sally's verdict. She didn't think much of Mary—female jealousy, Roarke assumed, but maybe Sal was onto something: Mary Oakley never made another picture. Roarke's theory, based on their one handshake, was that Oakley either turned pro or took a vow.

The movie was out of theaters in a week. Maybe it was too dark for audiences that spring, with sons and brothers overseas struggling to wrest an unconditional surrender from the Axis. Or was it eclipsed by the star power of Bergman and Bogart in *Casablanca*? Perhaps the theme proved too elusive—*The Big Betrayal* was an allegory, Roarke recalled Hayden telling him once. Though an allegory of what, Roarke couldn't recall. Anyway the picture didn't catapult Hayden to the top of the A list. Or the middle, for that matter. The film was credited to Raymond Bannister, a director Roarke didn't know. He lingered through the credits but never saw the names Derek Sykes or Dieter Seife.

Meanwhile Roarke's business, never more than desultory, was in steep decline. This wasn't so much a consequence of recovering from injuries received at the Hacienda and in the Pacific Ocean (though that was part of it); Roarke had also gotten sidetracked by a resolve to identify the strapping German brothers who'd saved him, and repay them somehow. When, on the ride home in the cherry-red Cord, he'd asked the boys who'd sent them to the Hacienda, both had comically pressed their palms to their ears, repeating, *"Was sagen Sie?"* Roarke started seeing them in his dreams. But in waking life, he never found them.

Perhaps as a distraction from the professional doldrums, Roarke on a whim married Sally. After cooling down and listening to an account of his ordeal at Dr. Ridley's hands, she'd mothered him well. The wedding itself was convenient enough: Sally's job at the county courthouse was one floor above the corridor where newly licensed couples waited in line. The civil ceremony was accomplished over her lunch break for the bargain-basement sum of four bucks, even.

One day that fall Sally came home with a copy of *The Hollywood Reporter*. The boldface headline screamed "Screen Star Exposed Nazi Director"; the subhead read "Now Truth Can Be Told." The article, by editor and founder William R. Wilkerson himself, explained how, in November of last year, Harley Hayden, while starring in Superior Pictures' suspense-meller *The Big Betrayal,* had become suspicious of Derek Sykes, the "British" director assigned to the project. Hayden, whom Wilkie described as Tinseltown's Own All-American Boy, had followed the director on his days off and discovered him to be a "secret Fascist who, from his aerie high in the Hollywood Hills, was masterminding a planned Nazi attack somewhere on the West Coast, under cover of filming a motion picture." It was quite a yarn, making Hayden out to be a blend of Frank Hardy, Dick Tracy, and Brass Banfield; and Dieter Seife as a mixture Dr. Mengele, Dr. Frankenstein, and Mephistopheles. The piece concluded by revealing that, in the aftermath of his "unmasking," Seife had dropped out of sight—speculating that he'd either slipped back inside Berlin or was operating from a new clandestine lair elsewhere in California. The FBI, Wilkerson suggested, was investigating the matter.

Hayden was quoted: "I didn't do anything that any ordinary Joe wouldn't have done in my place. People need to be vigilant. Mostly, I have to thank Mr. Lustig for heeding my warnings."

Roarke looked from the *Reporter* to his bride. "How 'bout that?" he marveled. "Sal, we know a genuine national hero."

Sally wasn't mollified. "You don't rate even a mention?"

"I'm sure Flip mentioned me to Wilkie," Roarke said. "For a movie star, he's not one to hog the spotlight. You saw where Flip credited Lustig? Just, it makes a better story to—"

"—Leave out the main character? Of course he credited Arthur Lustig. The man is Arthur Lustig's indentured servant."

It's like a magic trick, Roarke reflected: You marry a giggling cutie-pie, and overnight she's a federal prosecutor.

"What would you like me to do, honey?"

"Call."

"Flip?"

Sally rolled her eyes, emptied Roarke's ashtray, and left—to spend the day shopping at Bullock's, he was sure. She wore a certain "Bullock's Look" that Roarke was learning to recognize.

Roarke called. At least he had a pretext. Hayden was home, "reading scripts," he said. (At least he didn't claim to be working through a *pile* of scripts.) The pretext, not entirely false, was Ellie and her mom, how things were going.

"Mrs. L is bunking with Ellie in Ellie's *casita*. They get along famously. They take walks around the park, swim together, play a little tennis, sit in the gazebo, drink tea, and talk."

And Mr. L? How was he adjusting?

Hayden chuckled. "Fine, I guess—once he got over the shock of his wife's opening line to him, when she came home."

Which was?

"This is classic. Ida walks in. Mr. L is waiting, nervous of course. She looks him in the eye and says, 'You got old.' "

Roarke laughed, noting that, somewhere along the way, Hayden had developed a flair for the anecdote and might one day make a good emcee.

"By the way, congrats on that item in the *Hollywood Reporter*." He hoped this seemed a mere afterthought.

"You saw that?" Harley sounded surprised, and abashed. "Jesus H. How that happened, I stop by Ciro's for a drink last week. Billy Wilkerson pulls up a chair and we get to chatting. 'Course, you have to be nice to old Wilkie, right? Anyway, after a while he brings up Dieter Seife. He knows the connection, somehow, and he starts asking questions. I tell him the story—some of it, anyway, about how I hired you to look into Seife's personal history. Turns out you two are buddies from way back?"

"Oh yeah," Roarke chuckled. "Pals since Prohibition."

"The point is, this whole thing is supposed to be 'on background, no attribution'—okay? Okay. Then I wake up this morning and read this story, makes me out to be J. Edgar Hayden or someone. Here I'm trying to read a script, and the phone is just ringing off the hook. Worst part is, there's not a line of newsprint about you, and if anyone's the hero of this thing, I mean . . . Thing is, if I thought you'd read the trades, I'd have called you to explain how it happened. You must be sore, huh?"

"Me, sore?" Roarke woodenly scoffed. "And you're right, Flip, I *don't* read the trades. I'm not in the picture business. A mention in the *Reporter* does me not a shred of good." Maybe it was pride talking, or perhaps he was trying to spare Hayden further embarrassment, but Roarke couldn't help embroidering: "Wilkie called me, yesterday, to check a few points. I asked him to keep my name out of it actually."

"No kidding?" Hayden sounded relieved.

Then Roarke said he didn't want to keep the actor tied up on the phone, what with that script. Hayden made noises about getting together soon for a steak or a highball somewhere, Roarke sent his love to Ellie, and the call ended. Though Los Angeles in the forties was still a pretty small town, there was a distinct note of finality: this time Roarke was absolutely certain that he and Harley Hayden would never cross paths again.

Meanwhile the story got picked up by the *Times* and other dailies—albeit less frenziedly, with Seife no longer scheming to bring about a domestic *Götterdämmerung*. Instead it was printed that he'd smuggled "caches of noxious Nazi propaganda" over the Mexican border (though Hayden's dubious conjecture that this was a dry run for future, more dangerous items did get some play).

By the weekend, Winchell was on the airwaves praising Hayden as "our foremost Home Front Hero" and, in print, Louella Parsons had dubbed him "the Nazis' handsome nemesis and a welcome rebuke to the likes of Mr. Flynn." *The Big Betrayal* was soon rereleased as the bottom half of a double bill with another Superior pic, *The Double,* a suspenser that had bowed six weeks earlier to raves and boffo biz, and was still drawing crowds. And, no, Roarke wasn't a part of this second publicity wave, either. Sally fumed, sulked, and threatened to phone various editors, publishers, and politicians.

Maybe—secretly—Roarke felt the slightest bit like a stooge, but he could hardly begrudge Hayden his day in the sun. Here was a kid who'd been denied his chance to shoot the Hun with a Browning automatic rifle, so he'd made do shooting training films for the troops—and Uncle Sam took that away from him, too.

Now, finally, Hayden got to be the brave soldier he'd surely have been, if not for those soft-boiled eggs God gave him. He even got another starring role: as a buck private stranded behind enemy lines again. But not the sidekick, this time. Single-handedly, Hayden foils the Nazi plan to build some kind of "super-weapon" (shades of the Inertia Projector) by ingenious use of items found in his mess kit. *Lonesome Hero* was a modest hit. Roarke was happy for Hayden.

Roarke was even happy when he read in the paper that Harley Hayden and Eleanor Lustig had been married the previous Sunday at Temple Israel of Hollywood, with a lavish reception at the Hillcrest Country Club following the ceremony. Oh, maybe he felt the faintest pang. He must have, because Sally didn't fail to notice. She figured he was miffed Flip hadn't sent an invitation, and Roarke let her go on thinking that. It was '46, America had beaten back darkness, the world was starting anew (so the songs and slogans said, anyway), and it seemed churlish to carry some trifling grudge into this bold new era.

Roarke told Sally to go down to Bullock's and pick out a little gift—tasteful, traditional, nothing extravagant. "The hell I will," she shot back. But in the end, she purchased a small, cut-crystal bowl. A few weeks later the Roarkes got a note back, on stationary *From the desk of Eleanor and Harley Hayden.* The note—signed by the couple but undoubtedly written by Ellie—read: *Thanks so much for the lovely bowl. We intend to fill it with food, flowers, and love. All best, The Haydens.*

"See!" Roarke crowed to his skeptical wife. "How's that for appreciative?"

"The bare minimum." But she put the card up on the counter, where houseguests might see it, and kept it there for months.

By the summer of '47, it was becoming clear that the world was new, but not necessarily different. With time on his hands (even Dowling had stopped calling—perhaps the production chief disapproved of the continued contacts with Hayden, "case notes" notwithstanding), Roarke had gotten into the habit of reading the paper from cover to cover. And he'd started to notice more and more items about the House Un-American Activities Committee.

Now the Nazis were kaput, it was necessary to find another peril—a more heinous one, if possible—and HUAC had come west to do Hollywood the favor of ferreting out pinkos in its midst. Late that spring, Jack Warner sat in a Biltmore hotel room and named a few Commies he'd met through the years. So, apparently, did Robert Taylor, Adolphe Menjou, and Ginger Rogers's mother. Who these fellow travelers were, exactly, no one knew or would say aloud. But it wasn't long before, by a quirk of fate, Roarke learned the name of at least one reputed Hollywood Red.

Once more, a call from Hayden set things in motion. Roarke hadn't heard the actor's voice for—what was it, now, three years? The voice had deepened, roughened, matured, yet retained that gee-whiz Midwest hitch. Roarke recognized him instantly.

"Flip! How's every little thing?"

Hayden was chipper as always, but more evasive than ever. He wanted to meet for a drink—this evening, if possible. Roarke suggested the Grove or Ciro's, two nightspots the ex-cop recalled as Hayden's haunts during the war years. But Harley demurred, explaining he'd prefer something quieter.

Roarke took this to mean he didn't want to be spotted by the press tonight. "There's a joint on Hollywood, just east of Vine, the Frolic Room," he told Hayden. "Very cozy. If Hedda Hopper shows up while we're hoisting one, I'll eat my hat."

Harley looked terrific, even by the lurid light of the Frolic Room: healthy and fit, at the right weight again. He made charming small talk about his wife, Roarke's wife, wives in general. "Best thing about marriage," he said, "you really get to know your partner." Roarke agreed, lit a Lucky, sipped his rye, and waited to hear the reason for this latest call.

It took Hayden two whiskeys. "You know how I've made all my pictures at Superior, all these years? And I've got no beef with Superior, god knows—except the boss is Ellie's father! And you know how people talk . . . 'The son-in-law also rises'?"

Roarke shook his head. "That's a good one, Flip. I never heard that one." It seemed to Roarke that Hayden believed him.

"Point is, I gotta start working for other studios or I'm a dead pigeon in pictures. Moe—my agent—he thinks so, too. So I've had him initiate discussions with Columbia, Metro, Warners,

Paramount, Universal, RKO, Twentieth . . . hell, every lot in town. And the responses we're getting, something doesn't feel right. Just going on my gut here, but . . ." Harley reached across the table, shook a cigarette out of his pack. His hand trembled.

What could Roarke tell him? That he was on the wrong side of thirty now and hadn't quite proved himself as a romantic lead? That the squint and grin had gone stale? What do you say to a fair-to-middling movie star whose star has started to fade?

"The offers aren't pouring in, is what you're telling me?"

Hayden gestured: more or less.

"And you think there may be some secret explanation, some hidden—what?"

Hayden inhaled, deeply, furiously, drawing the Lucky down a half inch in one puff. "Hey, I never got myself confused with Clark Gable—you know that. And I've made my share of stinkers, sure—but, then, so's Gable! And wouldn't you think, with all the press I got about the Seife thing, the public outpouring of gratitude, all the column inches, I'd still be a hot commodity in this town? I mean, honest, Roarke, wouldn't you think that?"

"Sure I'd think that. But as you've heard me say, I'm not in pictures. How the big shots make their decisions," Roarke admitted, "that's a bigger mystery to me than Amelia Earhart."

Hayden looked impatient. "Remember that funny feeling I had about Seife? Well, I've got it again. And I want you to look into the matter—discreetly, of course. Find out what, if anything, industry people might be whispering about me, okay?"

Perhaps Hayden was waiting for Roarke to quote his new, higher, postwar rates. Perhaps he was waiting to bargain Roarke down again. But Roarke was about to beg off, in fact; even a hard-up ex-cop couldn't imagine pocketing an actor's money, only to come back and report that a new crop of studio execs were calling him a has-been, yesterday's news, over the hill at thirty-one.

But Harley fanned three crisp hundred dollar bills on the tabletop before Roarke could think up a convincing excuse. And suddenly all Roarke could see was Sal's face when he fanned those bills in front of *her*. They'd have themselves a high old time, just Roarke and his bride. "I'll find out whatever I find out" was all he'd promise, pocketing Hayden's three hundred.

The first round of calls made, highballs bought and favors called in, a flabbergasted Roarke learned that there indeed *was* "some opposition" to Harley. It took a little teeth pulling to get someone to spill the rest of it: supposedly, Hayden had wound up on a HUAC list! Harley Hayden, who'd kept America safe from Dieter Seife! The scuttlebutt was that Harley'd said, or done, something, well, *suspect* . . . And until the matter was clarified, no one would touch him. (No one but his father-in-law, anyway.) Billy Wilkerson himself told Roarke: "I got it from a little birdie that Hayden's name is right up there alongside Eddie Robinson and Jack Garfield. They're saying the All-American Boy's gone pink—or just maybe he was pink all along?"

Roarke smelled a rat. So he kept phoning contacts, and buying drinks for ever more dubious characters. When he'd run out of favors to call in, he promised new ones. But his gears were grinding. Then he got lucky—Eddie Mannix, over at Metro, finally returned a message Roarke had left four days earlier.

"You wanna know about Hayden? I'll tell you. Sometime during the war, the bozo—I'm not saying he didn't mean well, but he had the bright idea of joining Tito's partisans in Yugoslavia! Which apparently led the dumb sonuvabitch to become a card-carrying Party member, in the fullness of time."

"Eddie, that's a load of crap! He never left these shores during the war. I don't even think Harley's got a passport!"

There was a brief silence at the other end, then Eddie sighed: "Well, buddy boy? There has been some confusion."

"Meaning what?"

"I thought we were talking about *Sterling* Hayden here."

And that was, in a nutshell, the big mystery: a mix-up of same last names. (Nancy Davis had an even worse problem, Roarke later learned: her pink double shared a first name, too.)

Though he'd found the solution, the case wasn't closed. This being '47, people were starting to act peculiar about the Red Menace. It took Roarke a few more calls, drinks, and favors to learn that, though there had indeed been a mistake made vis-à-vis his actor friend, Hayden still had to submit to an arcane process called "cleansing"—just as though Harley were Sterling.

Exactly what this cleansing entailed, Roarke wasn't able to learn, but it seemed to involve Hayden composing a letter to HUAC in which he'd spell out his allegiance to the good old USA. Also, perhaps he might find time to drop by the local FBI office for a quick chat—and maybe a personal appearance before the committee wouldn't hurt, either.

Roarke drove to Laughlin Park to deliver the news. (Harley and Eleanor were living on the Lustig compound while their new place in Holmby Hills was being renovated.) Roarke was sure Hayden would blow his stack—and, Christ, who could blame him?

The men met out in the gazebo. Not only was Ellie the frescoed angel hovering over Roarke's head, he could see Ellie in the flesh gracefully lobbing tennis balls with Ida, and for a moment he forgot he was married and why he was here—and then the moment passed, Roarke returned to his senses. He told Hayden what he'd come to tell him, then girded for an explosion.

"That's all?" Hayden laughed. "I'd be delighted."

"But it's a royal pain," Roarke argued, reflexively, "and there's no goddamn reason in the world you should have to."

"Hell," Hayden replied, "someone wants to know if I'm a patriot, then you bet I'll stand on a soapbox and shout 'Yes!' Anyway"—a gleam of little-boy mischievous fun in his eye—"I've always wanted to see the inside of an FBI office."

Roarke tried once more, as a friend. "It may be some kind of trap. Write a nice, sweet letter to the committee, next thing you know, by return mail, they send a subpoena. Last few days, phoning around, that's what I'm hearing: HUAC is starting to flood the town with subpoenas—on pink paper, no less."

Hayden sat back and laughed again. "What, tough guy like you losing his nerve over a piece of pink paper?" And when that failed to placate Roarke, he leaned forward and added: "Don't forget, they called me Flip 'cause I could turn the tables on an opponent just when he thought he had me pinned."

Roarke wasn't sure he'd heard right. "Superior cooked that up for a press release," he reminded Hayden. "I saw the old yearbook, remember? You weren't really *on* the wrestling team."

"You know that and I know that." Hayden shrugged. "And some studio flack." Then: "I'll write the letter. Can you contact the appropriate people, arrange the date and times for my visit to the FBI and the House Un-American Committee?"

Roarke stood, marveling at Harley's sang-froid—or acting skill. "Yeah, leave it to me. But only on condition you call your lawyer, have him advise you on everything you say, write, and do, and don't let him leave your side the whole damn time."

As promised, Hayden wrote the letter in which he affirmed his patriotic principles. Yes, the rhetoric has dated somewhat, and key lines read like the work of a high school valedictorian. But it was a heartfelt document, composed by Hayden himself—no help from studio ghostwriters, despite what's been written or implied in various historical accounts. The letter later formed the basis of Hayden's prepared statement at HUAC's Washington hearings that fall, and impressed Chairman Thomas enough to have it read into the record. The full text appears in most of the Harley Hayden biographies, both friendly and not.

Two days after their conversation in the gazebo, Hayden sent a carbon over to Roarke, who opened the envelope with apprehension, figuring that actors who write their own lines tend to favor quantity. But Hayden's statement was succinct. And as Roarke scanned it, his arm hairs stood at attention. When Sally came home, he read it to her. When he was done, her eyes glistened. This was the most lucid and inspired Harley'd been since the day, years before, when he'd breathlessly explained to Roarke what *The Big Betrayal* was really about.

By all accounts, Hayden charmed the FBI in their closed session. Afterward, they gave him a tour of the office at his request, even let him browse through confidential files on Errol Flynn, Bugsy Siegel—and, of course, Dieter Seife. As has been revealed elsewhere, subsequent to his highly successful visit, the Bureau stayed in close touch with Hayden. An unnamed special agent later recruited him; Harley was designated as T-12 in the sealed records of Hollywood informants. He got a tremendous kick out of this: "It's just like in the movies."

A side note on the informant issue: there is no disputing the fact that Hayden named names. Anne Revere, Canada Lee, and Larry Parks are three he acknowledged giving to HUAC. But Hayden always took pains to point out that he was scrupulous about only naming actors already on every pink list in Creation.

His meeting at the Biltmore Hotel with J. Parnell Thomas of HUAC went nearly as well as the FBI session. At Roarke's suggestion, his lawyer, Jack Diemer, sat at Hayden's elbow. But Hayden never resorted to asking Jack whether or not to answer a question. His responses were forthright and candid, his manner relaxed but respectful. When the session ended, Thomas invited Hayden to appear in D.C. as a friendly witness. This was just what Roarke had feared might happen, should Hayden get mixed up with these people. But Hayden shook hands with J. Parnell Thomas and promised he'd come to Washington "with bells on."

Roarke started to meet with him more often. Hayden knew the ex-cop as a man who could gather information, organize it, prioritize it, and disseminate it as necessary. "We're gonna need you," he said one night over drinks at the Frolic Room.

"*We?*" Roarke noticed that Hayden had grown more cagey and mysterious since becoming T-12, and liked to kid him about it.

"I've been talking to some other stars, on the Q.T.," Hayden confided, lowering his voice. "Robert Taylor, Ward Bond, Olivia de Havilland, people with a certain level of industry profile who recognize the serious nature of what's going on here." Off Roarke's look, Hayden launched into a commentary on what was "going on here" and the stakes, as he saw them:

"The politicians are sticking their noses into things they don't understand. If these HUAC boys have their way, they're gonna upset a lot of apple carts in this town. Nobody's safe, not L. B. Mayer, not my own father-in-law. Now, why is the committee here? Are they looking for some free ink, or are they genuinely concerned about Communist subversion? Who the hell knows? But it seems to me—and Taylor, and Ward, Olivia, and others— that the best way to keep these fellows at bay is to take matters into our own hands in a very public fashion. Show the world Hollywood is willing and able to clean its own house."

Roarke had no quarrel with Hayden's analysis. He only had one question: "Where do I fit into all this, Flip?"

"We've decided to form our own organization, that'll function as a clearinghouse for actors who've either been erroneously tarred, like myself, or who may have made mistakes in the past—appearing in movies like *Song of Russia,* attending the wrong meetings, even joining the Party—and now they're ready to repent. If that's the right word. Make a public apology, anyway. Ask for forgiveness. Your part of it would be to identify those people, preferably before HUAC does, so they can be brought in and cleansed. If we can stay one step ahead of Washington and demonstrate our commitment at the same time, then good and decent men like Mr. Lustig won't be at risk."

Even had Roarke's work not substantially dried up, this was heady stuff for a disgraced cop. It goes without saying he'd never been asked to join a council. He'd had business cards printed, but never with his real name or occupation. On top of that, Roarke was pushing forty. The pair shook on it.

Billy Wilkerson proved a big help and booster for the fledgling organization. He had his ear pressed firmly to the ground on account of his self-confessed fondness for dirt. Through Wilkerson and others, Roarke was able to quickly compile a comprehensive list of names in need of cleansing. And once the word went out, the actors came out of the woodwork: Eddie Robinson, Charlie Laughton, Jack Garfield, and more... They'd sit in front of Roarke, Hayden, occasionally Robert Taylor, and make a clean breast of things. Sometimes they'd weep and gnash their teeth—guys who played gangsters and contract killers would actually bawl. Roarke found it all very moving. Oscar-nominated actors would thank Hayden and Roarke for the chance to rehabilitate themselves, little realizing that Roarke, through this work, had miraculously found a path to self-renewal, too.

The kicker was that Sally was able to leave her job at the county courthouse and come work for her husband as the in-house stenographer. After typing up a movie star's tortured declaration of guilt, she'd ask for an autograph. Roarke, who never expected that he of all people would find himself in a professional partnership with his Missus, would jokingly compare himself and Sal (Roarke & Racine) to Alfred Lunt and Lynn Fontanne. " 'Cept neither of us could act our way out of a paper bag," Sally would point out, chortling. And then, as though to prove herself a show-biz flop, she'd do an awkward soft-shoe shuffle and warble like a road-company vaudevillian, "He takes confession, she takes dictation . . ."

Those were the happiest days of their marriage.

By the time October rolled around, Hayden's clearinghouse had generated a lot of press, most of it favorable. Hayden was surrounded by photographers as he and Roarke boarded the Super Chief at Union Station downtown. Jack Diemer came aboard, and a couple of Hearst columnists sympathetic to the cause: Vic Riesel and George Sokolsky. There wasn't enough in the budget to bring Sal, but Eleanor was included, of course. She looked a little thinner, paler, more stark and stunning. She wore black.

Arthur Lustig had passed away, unexpectedly, the previous weekend. It happened during one of those Saturday night games at Warner's house. Whether Joe Schenck was cleaning out the old man, nobody would say; in any case, around midnight Mr. L excused himself to use the powder room. He came back five minutes later looking drawn, according to some. But he continued playing—and drinking, and smoking cigars. At dawn, he con-fided to David Selznick that, on the toilet, earlier, he'd passed some blood. One Hollywood mogul didn't readily admit weak-ness to another Hollywood mogul, so Selznick knew this was a se-rious matter. As the sun rose he drove Lustig to his own cardiologist in Beverly Hills, who was asleep when Selznick pulled up. By the time the doctor stumbled to the door, Arthur Lustig lay dead in Selznick's limo. In any case, no cardiologist could have saved him: the coroner found that Lustig had been felled, not by a heart attack, but by an abdominal aortic aneurysm.

"Thank god we have Washington to focus on," Hayden mur-mured to Dowling as Lustig was interred at Forest Lawn beside his son, Saul. A moment later Ellie fainted and Hayden, sensing it, whirled, caught his wife just before she hit the ground. A news cameraman captured this extraordinary moment. The kinescope can be seen at the Museum of Television and Radio in New York.

En route to Washington, D.C., Ellie remained mostly in her com-partment. Jack Diemer and Roarke would sit with Harley, draw-ing up new plans and names for the council to consider, reviewing Hayden's upcoming testimony, and talking off the record with Riesel and Sokolsky. When Harley withdrew with his wife after supper and Diemer and Roarke found themselves alone, they'd hold informal drinking contests. Roarke was impressed by Diemer's ability to down a fifth of bourbon while laying out a co-gent argument to outlaw the Communist Party on grounds that violated neither the Constitution nor the Bill of Rights.

Hayden was scheduled for two days in front of the committee. Day One was mostly ceremonial, and it got off to a late start in the afternoon because some screenwriter was jawing and posturing about the committee's supposed "Gestapo tactics." Finally Hayden was summoned into the chamber. Roarke sat on his right, Diemer on his left (they'd tossed a coin and Roarke won). Hayden looked sensational. The costume department at Superior had pulled his business suit from *The Big Betrayal* out of storage, and a wardrobe mistress had subtly updated it.

He was given a hero's welcome by Chairman Thomas, and under the merciless movie camera lights, he effortlessly radiated a good deal of his own wattage. Unquestionably, Hayden had the straightest posture, the best projection, and the thickest pompadour in the room. It's claimed that, on the set of *Foreign Affair,* Billy Wilder had instructed Dietrich to "light herself," and here in the committee room Hayden was doing just that. He glowed as Thomas recounted the Dieter Seife affair, and didn't stumble when the chairman asked what had become of the "Nazi impostor" since Harley'd forced Seife to "break cover" back in 1942.

Roarke had anticipated the question, and done a bit of research. (Frustratingly, there was nothing conclusive to be found concerning Seife's fate, despite the exhaustive number of tipsters consulted.) Hayden, who'd brushed up with a cheat sheet Roarke had furnished on the Super Chief, responded:

"There are numerous versions of what became of Seife. Some contend that he managed to sneak back into Germany, where he anonymously cranked out the kind of filmic propaganda for Dr. Goebbels he'd tried to flood *our* country with. Others swear they've seen him on the streets of New York City, posing as an expatriate French national. One of the strangest stories—bearing in mind that, in L.A., a 'strange' story is often the god's honest truth...." He paused for the laugh he knew would come. "I hope this isn't too frank for the committee, but I'm told by one source that Seife remained in Southern California under a false identity but was reduced to directing pornographic short films, some apparently starring a washed-up Hollywood actress you've all heard of." This last was not in Roarke's notes; where Hayden came up with it is unclear. It caused some nervous rumbling, and he briskly wrapped things up by declaring:

"If you ask me, personally, what became of Herr Seife, I would answer in two ways. One, I believe he wound up a suicide, which we know is a sin, but would be a fitting end. My second answer is that the fate of Dieter Seife, whether a suicide or not, no longer matters—he represents a threat that's been soundly defeated, and in 1947 it is time to turn our attention to new, and ever more nefarious, threats to our way of life."

It was an elegant segue to the letter, which was then presented, in slightly altered form, as Hayden's introductory statement. As previously noted, it was read twice—first, and smoothly, by Hayden. Then by Chairman Thomas, less well, but somehow even more moving for the amateurish sincerity of it.

There was time for only one quick question before the session was adjourned. H. A. Smith, one of HUAC's investigators, asked Hayden to explain why he had failed to serve as an active member of the armed forces during the war.

Roarke glanced at Diemer, whose earlobes had reddened. Though he didn't show it, Roarke was steamed as well—why spoil a good day's friendly testimony with this sour closing note?

If Diemer and Roarke were rattled, Hayden was amused. "I know I appear to be a healthy specimen," he said, flashing his lopsided grin. "But, if it's not too impertinent, Mr. Smith?" He approached the committee. Roarke and Diemer traded looks.

Hayden pulled off his horn-rims, and held them out to H. A. Smith. "I invite you to see the world as I do, in reverse."

Embarrassed, Smith donned Hayden's glasses. And reacted to

their blurring, almost blinding, effect by whipping them off and handing them back while wildly blinking.

The committee room exploded in laughter again.

This was the only moment during the hearings that Eleanor, sitting quietly in the gallery, hands folded in her lap, gave a smile—as though some fond personal memory had been reawakened.

"Question withdrawn," Smith bellowed, for another laugh.

Back at the Shoreham Hotel, the Haydens dined alone in their suite. Diemer and Roarke ate downstairs, comparing notes on just how brilliantly their boy had done. After the requisite glasses of port and Cuban cigars, the two went up to their separate rooms. Roarke pried off his shoes and phoned Sally. "Flip's a natural at this stuff," he said, still marveling at the off-the-cuff jokes and charming asides the actor had sprinkled in amidst the stirring patriotic verbiage.

"Harley should go into politics," Sally noted. "He sure wouldn't do worse than the big shots who're running the show."

Roarke hung up, drew a bath, and grabbed for his Luckies—to find there was only one cigarette left, and it was crushed. Opposed on principle to paying hotel prices for cigarettes, Roarke tied on his wingtips again, went out to find a newsstand where he bought a fresh pack, then walked back to the Shoreham.

As he crossed to the elevator, he heard his name called out. Roarke turned, looked around—and saw someone waving from inside the lobby bar. Coming closer, he saw that it was Ellie, and that she was alone. "Fancy meeting you," Ellie said, smiling. Her eyes glittered—dangerously, Roarke thought.

It was the first time they'd had a moment alone together since that long-ago night at the Lustig beach house in Malibu. He'd never told her of his death struggle with Ray in the surf. And Roarke was sure that she, in turn, had never told Hayden of their private dance in the darkened living room. "Don't hover like some waiter," she teased. "Sit down. Have a drink. Keep me company, damn you." Roarke did as Ellie asked, of course.

And saw right away that she was already high. He ordered a scotch, offered a Lucky. They both lit up, and then Roarke began to tell her how sorry he was, about her dear, departed—

She cut him off with a dismissive gesture of her slim, exquisite hand. "I don't care to talk about that, not tonight."

"Fine. Whatever you want, Ellie." Then: "Where's Flip?"

Ellie frowned. He'd forgotten she never called her husband Flip and, lately, gave a little grimace whenever someone did. "He's upstairs, running lines for tomorrow." Her tight smile made it clear that "running lines" was not a random turn of phrase. A movie actor runs lines before filming a scene.

"Preparing Day Two of his testimony," Roarke corrected.

Far from appearing chastened, Ellie nodded at the glass in his hand. "Here's mud in your eye, now catch up to me, Roarke."

Roarke drained his scotch and, with the glass in front of his eyes, briefly studied Ellie's face through the refractions. By her frank, impatient look he inferred she wanted him to get as oiled as she, to minimize her risk in making a pass. Which, five years ago, he'd have accepted—then regretted. Now, all he wanted to know was why she was looking for a way to hurt Hayden.

"Waiter." Ellie was ordering another round.

"How can I catch up if you're staying one highball ahead?"

"One?" She fixed Roarke with a humorous but pitying look.

It occurred to Roarke that, under the circumstances, Ellie might have been better off back in safe, secure Laughlin Park. All the pressure on her husband, as well as the press scrutiny, must've unsettled her—she, with her nerves already rubbed raw by her dad's sudden death and a sick, needy mom.

"How *is* your mom?" Roarke asked. "Who's watching her?"

Ellie gave a dry chuckle. "Are you suggesting that, if my father were alive, he'd be looking after Ida in my absence?"

Roarke shook his head. "Just an innocent question."

Ellie drew deep on her Lucky, then blew out slowly, till the smoke enveloped her. "There are no innocent questions."

Roarke remembered the "blackish moods" Hayden had mentioned, years ago. He'd never witnessed one. Waiting to see how things would develop, Roarke felt fascinated and not a little afraid.

The next round arrived. Roarke sipped. Ellie talked. "You know the toughest thing about marriage?" she asked, and didn't wait for Roarke's reply: "You really get to know your partner." Before Roarke could tell Eleanor he'd heard that one, somewhere—not long ago, but a bit differently—she went on: "These last few months, Harley's given interview after interview to the press, and speeches at luncheons and dinners to just about every committee, club, and organization in Hollywood."

Roarke knew; he'd scheduled most of them. So the wife was feeling neglected. An old story, but not one to be casually disregarded. "True, he's been busy, maybe a little distracted, but we've been breaking our necks to launch this new council—"

"Yes," she said, curtly. "To keep my father safe. But Father's dead now, and he doesn't need Harley or you to defend him."

"It's about more than your father," Roarke reminded her, "though Mr. Lustig was always foremost in Harley's thoughts."

Ellie grimaced at this saccharine sop, then took up where Roarke had interrupted her, two exchanges back:

"And when they introduce him, before he steps up to the podium, they call him a war hero, and then do you know what he says—have you heard him? He starts reminiscing about 'when the war ended, and I came home.'" Ellie stared at her cigarette as it smoldered in the ashtray. Then repeated the words: "'And I came home.'" She looked up at Roarke. "I mean, this is a man who from 1938 till yesterday never once left Los Angeles."

"Never?" Roarke mumbled.

"Not even on a USO tour."

"I think Flip means 'came home' in the poetic sense of—"

"*Flip.*" She sneered. "No one calls him that but you. Haven't you figured that out, or are you just a perfect boob?"

"His people do." Roarke sounded defensive, exposed.

"His people," she parroted—making it plain this locution distastefully smacked of the backwater, the dustbowl, the hills, the swamps, the sticks. "I was so glad when that man yesterday asked Harley why he hadn't served in the army. Because I just knew he was about to start reminiscing about when the war ended and he came home. And this time, I thought I might start screaming." She gave a coquettish shrug of her slim shoulder, stubbed her Lucky, then drained her drink. "But, luckily, he—"

"Harley adores you. Why're you so—"

"He does, doesn't he?" Ellie laughed. "We used to fight about that costar who was always throwing herself at him: Washed-Up, Fucked-Out Mary the Virgin Slut-Whore. They called Chaplin the Little Tramp but the little tramp was Mary *Oakley*."

Roarke glanced around to be sure there was nobody listening in from the adjacent tables. "It's true Mary flirted constantly, but Harley never slept with her. He never strayed."

Ellie sighed again. "It's what we'd fight about. Why *didn't* he? She was a hot little number. Y'ever get a look at Mary's hands?"

Indeed, Roarke had—one look exactly.

"I think she gnawed on her fingernails," Ellie cattily surmised, "as a substitute for compulsive self-abuse. Don't I sound like a girl with an undergraduate psych degree?" Roarke fumbled for a response, but Ellie went on: "Anyway, poor Harley lacked the imagination, the initiative, or the drive. Before all this . . . hoopla, it was handball he preferred to sex. In his silly white shorts at the Hollywood Athletic Club. Now he likes to lie in bed and read the minutes of last week's meetings."

Me, too, for that matter, Roarke thought.

"Maybe I was trying to push him into Mary's arms. I'd started to wonder whether the love of my life wasn't, in fact, a schoolgirl crush that made sense at sixteen, not at twenty."

"But you stayed with Harley. I'd have figured you two'd be thinking about starting a family by now. Why so sore at him?"

Ellie sat back against the banquette and tried to get comfortable. "Sore? I'm not sore," she replied, almost kittenish. "Though— maybe I should be sore at you instead?"

"Sure, just tell me for what?" Could she still be angry about Roarke's having rubbed his hard-on against her leg, that distant night in Malibu? Peeved at his canine behavior?

"Oh, not much, just that bit of chicanery you two guys cooked up, to start this whole swell bandwagon rolling."

"Chicanery?"

"You're right, that's too big a word. And too dignified."

"C'mon, Ellie, please—I don't know what you're implying." Finding his palms getting clammy, he wiped them on his slacks.

Ellie swiveled to signal the waiter.

"I'm fine for the moment," Roarke said, before she could order more scotch. "And I think you should maybe slow—"

"Another round, please." Back to Roarke: "You'll need it." Then, abruptly: "Your bogeyman, your straw man, Seife."

Seife? That was it? Seife, he could handle, no sweat.

"What's your beef? I agree, the idea Dieter was smuggling those movies as a dry run for some Atomic Ray Gun of Doom was a little—overblown. I tried to tell Fl—" A quick correction. "—*Harley*, as much, but he got stuck on the idea. And yeah, the claim Seife was angling to blow up the Golden Gate Bridge, well . . . Harley's either been in too many movies, or seen too many."

"Both."

"Okay. But Jesus, El, I wouldn't call that chicanery."

"Nor would I." She reached across the table—Roarke thought, for an unsettling moment, to stroke his hand. But she was only grabbing his Luckies. She shook one out and lit it.

He tried again. "You mean Harley's pretext for hiring me in the first place, to nose around Seife's past . . . How some gaffers were gonna drop a klieg light on Dieter's head? I never took that seriously, anybody out of short pants would've known Harley'd hoked that up, but I don't get where that's so . . ."

Roarke could see by her look he'd once more missed the mark. And began to wonder: whether, far from being offended by his erection against her thigh, Ellie hadn't even noticed it?

"We're going in circles," he said, "and I'm getting dizzy. What terrible, horrible thing have Harley and I done?"

She flashed another rigid smile. "If you're playing word games with me, you can quit right now. You're not Jack Diemer, no classy bill-by-the-hour lawyer, you're just a scummy guy who by all rights should still be shoveling shit for the Chester Dowlings of the world and whistling while you do it. Instead, you stumbled on a gimmick, and now you're headed for the big time. Nothing wrong with that, Roarke, so long as you remember how you sucked somebody's lifeblood to reach the finish line."

Roarke raised both hands in surrender. "Shoot me," he said. "But first—please—tell me *whose* lifeblood I sucked and everything'll be hunky-dory and this scummy guy can die happy?"

The next round arrived. For an instant Roarke thought Ellie's drink might wind up dripping down his face, ice and all, as in a certain Hollywood genre: a so-called meller. But then something happened. Ellie kept looking at him—staring, peering, appraising. Roarke watched her swallow: not her booze, but whatever it was that had accumulated in her throat.

"Christ," she said at last, so softly he almost missed it. "You don't know. You really don't. Harley never told you."

"Told me what? And quick, before the sun comes up and this bloodsucker has to crawl back into his coffin."

Ellie laughed. Not at Roarke's dismal joke, but at the fact that he'd really, truly, had no idea of what she'd been getting at, these past ten minutes.

"He never told you. I wonder why."

"Told me what? Eleanor? C'mon, spill."

Ellie swallowed again. "Those movies."

"What movies? Harley's movies?"

Ellie shook her head.

"Ah! The two shorts Seife smuggled in?"

Ellie nodded.

Even as Roarke's pulse quickened, things seemed to move in slow motion, and the light was turning murky, brackish. "*Hans Munson? Our Youth?*" Another nod. "Okay, what about them?"

Ellie sipped. "Sometime during Weimar, Frau Seife drifted toward National Socialism. Eventually she became a favorite of Goebbels, who helped Seife get started making films in Berlin."

"I know that, Ellie. I did the research, remember?"

She didn't seem to hear him. "Seife despised the Nazis."

"Sure, that's why he went to all the trouble of smuggl—"

"Not so much for their politics," she coolly continued, "as for their production design. And he came to loathe his wife. But by then they had a son. A handsome, fair-haired son, named Martin. Whom Frau Seife brought before Dr. Goebbels, to show off to him what a perfect Nordic specimen she'd produced—the shining, healthy, proto-Nazi fruit of her own loins."

Roarke had a hunch that something was coming he might not want to hear. "Time out," he stalled. "Where d'ya get this?"

"My mother," Ellie replied. "My mother heard it all from Dieter Seife himself. He'd been at the Hacienda many times as an outpatient. Ida says he spoke about the past quite openly."

Now it was Roarke, nodding. "The Healing Circle."

"Goebbels put Martin in the movies. He got a new name, a stage name of some sort—because, by then, Dieter had disgraced the name Seife; he'd gone to Paris and never come back. But he couldn't get his son out with him; the Reich would never have allowed it, Hitler and his cronies *loved* their movies. Those drunks, dope addicts, and perverts took a film projector down into every bunker, they'd stay up all night watching Hollywood crap while some unlucky city was incinerated above. *Lives of a Bengal Lancer,* according to Father, was the Führer's favorite."

"Martin Volker."

"No, it starred Gary Cooper, I think, and—"

"Martin Volker," Roarke repeated. "A name. In the opening credits of that film I saw at the Hacienda. One of the films Seife smuggled in."

Ellie considered. " 'Volker'? Mm, that sounds like a fine stage name. 'Volker' like *volk*—'the people.' Right? A nice populist name for a Nazi child star." Her mouth was set in a sort of smirk. "Okay, genius. Can you fill in the rest?"

Roarke shrugged. "I'm a dumb bunny. You finish."

And Ellie obliged. "Goebbels plastered Martin's face all over the Reich, apparently, on billboards, posters, and banners for the German Youth Festival of 1941. He dragged the kid up on stage with him like a show dog, a prize schnauzer. Seife hated how Martin was being used by the Nazis. But there was nothing he could do from here. Most of all he missed his son, terribly. But the only way he could see him—see how he was maturing, thriving, growing up . . . was to look at those hideous films."

In a flash, Roarke knew whose idea that was. "Dr. Ridley."

"Under his close supervision and care," Ellie confirmed.

"His close supervision and care didn't come cheap."

"No. But he knew what was best for Dieter Seife, for Ida Lustig, for every lost, degenerate, desperate soul caught in his web. And Mama claims he was happy. Seife, I mean. After he watched that first film they smuggled in—*Our Youth*? He wept, she said, for what they'd done to Martin. Those sick bastards. But he was happy, ecstatic even, to see his son alive and well." Eleanor puffed her Lucky. Then: "Dieter Seife was many things—but not a Nazi spy. Mostly, he was Martin Volker's father."

Though the conversation had finally stopped circling, it seemed to Roarke that the lobby bar had begun to spin.

"You sure you told all this to Harley?"

"Of course I told Harley." She stared back at Roarke.

Was it possible she'd got it wrong—or Ida had? Or, addled by her father's death and the stress of a sick mother, and jealous of the success and attention Harley'd garnered these past months,

Ellie'd invented the story, whole cloth? And it was a *good* story, he'd grant her that—hell, she could write it up as a treatment and sell it to Superior in the high five figures. *But where is the proof?* came the voice of that persistent, contentious attorney inside Roarke's head.

"You don't believe it," she said, sounding pleased. "You can't. Because how could a perpetual Boy Scout like my husband, unimpeachably patriotic, with the best intentions always, be so . . . dead wrong? And then all this"—Eleanor gestured at the lobby, but Roarke knew she meant the hearings, and Hayden's new status as a Hollywood emissary, and Roarke's new status as the first lieutenant of a Hollywood emissary—"comes crashing down. Besides," she taunted, "what's done is done. You can't un-scramble an egg—right, Mr. Roarke?"

Waving for the check, Roarke remembered Ridley's words, as the doctor lay sprawled on the stairs in the mosque, fiddling with his busted jaw: "You won't know what you're looking at." And then Roarke remembered how Seife's eyes had shone as he'd watched the boy Hans Munson. Roarke was breathing hard now.

"You're distraught," he began, by way of suggesting that El-lie'd been under a terrific strain lately, and that the Seife business was perhaps more complicated than she could imagine.

"Distraught?" Ellie spat out both syllables. "Sure I am. And don't forget 'hysterical.' After all, I'm a woman."

Her delivery was as arch and acerbic as Bankhead's. Once more it felt to Roarke that he and Ellie were costarring in a movie. But the lounge pianist was playing "The Girl That I Marry," which was the wrong song for the sound track—it helped Roarke stay rooted *in the moment* (per Derek Sykes) as well as the loca-tion for this scene: a hotel bar in Washington, D.C. He laid a twenty on the table, took Ellie's arm, and escorted her across the lobby to the elevator bank. As they rode up, he asked: "You plan on talking about this, Ellie? To the papers?"

Ellie stared at him and shook her head. "Take away your serge suit and your leather briefcase," she replied, "and you're still just a flatfoot at heart." Then the car stopped on the Haydens' floor and she stepped off. The elevator door shut.

Back in his room—which seemed oppressively small, and stuffy—Roarke's first thought was to call Sally. But what, exactly, would he tell her? His second thought was to pack his bags, check out, hop the next train home. Roarke got as far as unzipping his valise. Then, abruptly, he grabbed the phone and dialed the Haydens' suite. To Roarke's relief, Harley answered. "You had a chat with Ellie, huh? Hang on, I'll be right down."

Three minutes later he was at Roarke's door, with a bottle of scotch from the minibar. He crossed to the bed, kicked off his shoes, and settled back on the mattress. Roarke began, falteringly, to recount the conversation downstairs, but Hayden cut him off: "Yup, that's Ellie's mom's story, alright. But here's the catch: Ellie's mom, god bless her, was locked in a loony bin, doped out of her tree. So, buddy: do we buy it?"

Roarke cleared the phlegm from his throat. "Well—"

"I got an even better one for you. It's about Mr. L, how he died. The all-night poker game at Jack Warner's? Pure hokum. Ellie cooked it up by herself. Then she got on the phone with her father's cronies and worked 'em till they agreed to circulate it around town. How's that for a smart cookie?"

Hayden went on to describe the actual circumstances of Arthur Lustig's death. "Seems the old man, god rest his soul, would on occasion visit a certain lady of the evening. A special one: apparently this girl bears a striking resemblance to the young Theda Bara. With the black hair and the black bangs and the kohl rings around the eyes. The nymphomaniac raccoon look, if you go in for that. Remember The Vamp, Roarke? 'Kiss me, my fool'? 'The Woman Who Didn't Care'?"

Hayden lowered his voice an octave and, portentous as Welles in Mercury Theater mode, intoned, "Born in the shadow of the sphinx . . . Unscramble her name, and you get 'Arab death.'" Back in his normal register, he chuckled, "*Arab* death, sure. But *Jew* death? Anyway, the old guy's gut ruptures in *flagrante delicto*—and, apparently, Theda panics and waits too long to call someone. A. L. might've been saved."

Roarke wondered why Ellie'd concocted a cover story that, inconveniently, required the collusion of so many cronies. Then he realized: in Hollywood nothing was true until it had been made true by consensus, ratified by committee. And the fact that so many important figures were now written into his death scene gave the old man's passing some stature, weight, a place in movie history. Meanwhile Hayden was shrugging, getting to his feet. "Gotta grab some shut-eye before tomorrow."

Roarke nodded. A decent night's sleep was important. Only after Hayden left did it strike him that the question of Ellie's Dieter Seife story, and whether it was true, had been raised but not debated. Roarke resolved to take it up with Hayden on the Super Chief, heading home to California.

Roarke lay down. But sleep eluded him. He got up and paced. He turned on the radio in its fancy console, ran the dial from end to end, had an earful of static and clicked it off. At two, he took a hot bath. At three he beat off, just to kill a few minutes. By four he felt so caged in he got dressed and started walking the dark streets of D.C. For the first time in seven years he craved the pungent release of reefer. Roarke thought, if he meandered far enough east toward Capitol Heights, the colored slums, he'd maybe stumble on a tea pad like the long-gone one on Central Avenue back home. As he wandered, the Nat Cole song "I'm Lost" played in his head: *"I walk around in circles doing things I shouldn't do."* After a while, feeling foolish and afraid, he turned around. As he reentered the Shoreham lobby, it was just Roarke and the hotel dick. The detective didn't stir—he must have recognized one of his own kind. Roarke went upstairs, stared out the window, ordered breakfast when the sun came up at six: bacon, eggs, grits, and toast. It smelled delicious, and Roarke was ravenous. To his surprise and irritation, he couldn't eat a bite.

Hayden's testimony on Day Two was even smoother than Day One. He had the rhythms down just right. He'd testify in solemn tones, then tell an anecdote, then get serious again. The committee was amused and entranced. The press was, too.

He hit a tiny speed bump only once, when Congressman John Wood, from Georgia, inquired about his religious affiliation. Hayden licked his lips while calculating whether the question hid some insinuation about his Jewish wife, and her late—but prominent and influential—movie mogul father. When he answered Congressman Wood a moment later, it was with a brilliant leap in time, the sort of dramatic flashback dissolve he'd learned from movie scripts: "Dad was a night watchman, even worked Saturday nights, so he always slept through church. But Mother was . . ."

Roarke, though seated at Hayden's elbow, hadn't been paying close attention. Now he perked up. After all these years, he was about to learn whether Hayden's mother had been a Christian Scientist, as the actor had once claimed, or Episcopalian.

"What they used to call a meliorist. It was a sort of church of boundless optimism, even through the darkest days of the Depression. I can still remember Mom repeating—and she trained me to say it, too, each morning before school—'Every day, in every way, I'm getting better and better.' " A shrug. "I don't know if you'd call it a religion. But that was Mom's credo, got her through some trying times. Mine, too, I guess."

The room rang with applause.

Roarke was exhausted. He knew at that moment he wouldn't be bringing up the Seife matter on the return trip to Los Angeles, after all. Instead he would sleep for three days straight. And as Hayden's testimony wound down, Roarke knew something else. He'd never discuss Dieter Seife again. What was the point? Even if Roarke *was* inclined to reopen the inquiry, how would he do it, five years after the fact? As cold cases went, this was Iceland. And even if it were current, how could he reliably confirm or rule out Ellie's story? By giving Ida Lustig the third degree? By hooking her up to the electrodes Ray'd used on him, keep cranking the juice till she recanted?

In fact, the story of Martin Volker and Dieter Seife was a can of worms, a blind alley and, yes, a scrambled egg. And on the off chance it was true, what could Roarke possibly do about that? Turn his world inside out and upside down in deference to a father's enduring love for his fascist-icon kid? Fuck that.

In the cold light of day, Roarke's guess was that Hayden had asked himself the same questions, and reached the same conclusion. From the moment actor and director became aware of each other's existence, only one of them was destined to survive, to prevail. What American can sincerely regret that the winner of their bitter, fatal struggle was Harley Hayden?

As Hayden made his final remarks to the committee, Roarke realized he'd have to cede one point only, to Eleanor. Harley was, indeed, playing a part, acting a role, as she'd implied with her "running his lines" remark. But looking around the HUAC hearing room at the senators, congressmen, reporters, investigators, and concerned public, Roarke may have been too distracted to register Harley's every word, but he could clearly see Harley was *knockin' 'em dead,* Harley was *killin' 'em*—and that was what counted, wasn't it? In the cold light of day?

> Perhaps I am writing this as a form of expiation—but that is for the head shrinks or historians to decide. In any event I trust that you and Superior Pictures will never make these Case Notes public or at least not till both Harley Hayden and I have been deceased for twenty years. As to my lifelong silence about Seife, well, it dawned on me finally what Ellie meant by what she said to me in the hotel elevator going back upstairs that night in D.C. A cop—even a former cop, a retired cop—he will try to get at the truth at least some version of it. Maybe try to do something about it even. Whereas what we were doing (what Ellie was doing, filling me in about Seife and his son, I mean) was basically what the "smart" people (the lawyers, business executives, the politicians) who run the world do, which is get our stories straight in case someone asks. I count myself lucky, Mr. Dowling, that no one ever asked.

.14.

Mit **Martin Volker**

He wasn't sure whether they were scabs from shrapnel to the face or dried sores from malnutrition, maybe disease? But they frightened him. Even more so than the man with the rusty kitchen knife—though he thrust it forward repeatedly, and with relish.

He dreamt it would be different. There was a film he'd seen back in '34 that made a big impression: *The Prodigal Son,* it was called. A young man boldly leaves his homeland, journeys far in search of freedom. Instead he finds hell. And hell is so hellish, the young man (Tonio) doesn't even realize for a while that he's among the damned. There is a kind of deadly seduction: the illusion of abundance, of luxury—but no peace, and no love. It is a lonely, chaotic, and foreign place, a devil's playground tarted up as a paradise, and soon the man yearns for his mountain peaks, his Alpine village, the spa in the forest. Finally he returns. He feels diminished and ashamed. But the town is forgiving, happy to have him back.

And here, after years of exile, Seife was back in the homeland, the Fatherland. Not some mythical hero he was watching up on the screen, at the splashy premiere in Dresden, this handsome fellow Tonio whom Seife so hotly envied—for his adventurous spirit, his daring, his pluck . . . having no presentiment that, only four years later, Seife would set off, too, for the West, as a fugitive, and not in the spirit of pluck or daring, either, but clammy fear and nauseous loathing. Now it was Dieter Seife's time to come home. But the homecoming did not play at all like *The Prodigal Son*. If he'd left a metaphorical inferno, he'd returned to a real one. And there was no one here to forgive, comfort, or greet him.

Unless you counted the two men moving toward Seife. One with the scabs, or sores, on his face. The other clutching the kitchen knife. "Wait!" Dieter cried. As in a nightmare, they kept coming. "Stop," he said, voice catching. The knife edge flashed in the sun as it slashed air, aimed at Seife's heart.

He'd waited out the war in the Biederhofs' garage. Where once Seife had lived off the largesse of Arthur Lustig, he was now the reluctant charge of Hilda and Gary (formerly Gerhart), emigrants from Hamburg now relocated to Tarzana, California.

All he'd brought with him was the cash from his final Superior check, and the meager savings he'd withdrawn, right away, from the Bank of America. (Seife had an idea that forces he couldn't name might freeze his assets, so he was waiting in front of the bank on Hollywood Boulevard next morning when it opened.) Also his clothing and few personal effects, and the Dunhill lighter he'd distractedly slipped into his pocket and inadvertently carried off the studio lot. He'd burned the diaries and notebooks in his fireplace. The entries, he feared, were too open to misinterpretation and altogether "too German."

The garage was a far cry from Los Tilos, but endurable. Hilda had thoughtfully carpeted it for her lodger, and installed a small refrigerator and butane stove. There was even a tiny window. When Hilda wasn't in here, straightening up and urging Seife to get some air, he kept the window covered with a towel. He secretly feared that agents of the FBI would peer in at him as he listened to the radio for war news. Perhaps they would suspect this was a shortwave radio, not a decrepit Magnavox that Gary had thrown in the trash and Dieter had furtively retrieved. And then he'd be arrested, tried—perhaps convicted, hanged. . . .

Hence the towel, a small aesthetic sacrifice, considering. (In point of fact, the FBI never paid a visit, nor did the local police.) Meanwhile Admiral Dönitz and his wolf packs were sinking almost eight million tons of Allied ships and supplies. Britain would soon begin to starve. Seife could only imagine the movie in production, at this very moment, in Berlin.

A U-boat commander in the Atlantic. He's badly wounded in a skirmish with an American battleship that damages the sub as well. The crew is demoralized, literally adrift. Into the breech steps a handsome young enlistee whose courage outweighs his inexperience. He quickly assumes command of the crippled U-boat. Though the men are doomed, the boy resolves to take a Liberty ship down with them. He is played, of course, by Martin Volker. We fade out on the image of the submarine in ruins at the bottom of the sea—alongside a thousand American sailors and tons of their munitions. The final frame shows a thatch of blond hair, waving like seaweed. The body of Martin Volker has come to rest on the ocean floor—drowned but not bloated, nearly naked, the muscular arms thrown wide in a watery crucifixion.

Seife had to imagine this movie, because—even had it been shot—he couldn't see it. Contact with Schmidt the smuggler was severed. Perhaps *L'Affaire Seife* had made the Madrid papers? And no one answered when he dialed the Hacienda. The name Jasper Ridley had been expunged from the Pasadena phone book. There would be no more private screenings. Meantime, Seife was mad with missing Martin, anxiety magnifying his longing to see the boy on celluloid. How tall was he now? Had his hair begun to darken, like Seife's, at sixteen? Was he still making movies, or had he been conscripted? The thought of his son bogged down outside Stalingrad made it tough for Seife to sleep, sometimes for three days running. Still and all, there was some comfort, some hope for Martin's continued safety as, even into '43, U-boats off the American coast kept up their deadly mischief.

But then what did Hitler do? The brilliant strategist, the military genius? The Greatest Field Marshal of All Time? He moved the sub reserves to Norway! Norway! And then, of course, the tide began to turn. Meanwhile Gary—Gerhart—wanted Dieter out. "The man makes me nervous," he complained to his wife.

All this, Seife monitored from the garage: the terrible war news, and Biederhof's increasing discontent. Perhaps Gary was distressed about the fate of Hamburg. Among the local German Americans, there were whispers of two hundred thousand dead in the air raids, perhaps more. They called it carpet bombing. In Hamburg, it was said, incendiary bombs had turned the asphalt molten, and citizens were swallowed by it just the way Dieter had once fantasized La Brea would engulf him: the men and women and children of Hamburg boiled alive in a molten asphalt lake.

Occasionally, past midnight, Seife would be jolted awake—in terror—by a bomb exploding nearby. But no, it was just a dish or bowl that the master of the house had flung at Hilda.

Then came the Allied invasions of North Africa and Sicily. By the time of the Normandy landing, Seife could no longer imagine how a current Martin Volker film might look, what the story might be, unless it were a narrative of utter extinction and Martin had signed on to portray one of the Apocalypse's Four Horsemen.

There was a brief reprieve. Von Braun launched his wonder weapons at London, the nominally cute "doodlebug" V-1 rockets; the Nazis wrecked, sacked, and booby-trapped Cherbourg before the Allies sailed in. Was Martin starring as a brave young saboteur left behind in France, or the green but selfless de facto leader of a chewed-up Panzer division, sacrificed on the Western front?

Then the Battle of the Bulge and after that, phosphorous, fire-bombs, high explosives dropped by the RAF and USAF. Seife crouched by the radio (he kept the volume low—almost inaudible, like the murmurs a madman hears only in his head—for fear of G-men snoopers, and Gary's wrath). Not just Hamburg: Dresden, Essen, Düsseldorf, Nuremberg, Frankfurt, Berlin, all bombed to rubble.

It's strange. You hear the word "rubble" and it means one thing—in your mind's eye, you see a pile of stones. You hear "bombed to rubble" and what does that conjure? *Many* piles of stones, whole streets strewn with broken, blasted stones. You pick your way through the stones, toward your old house if it is still standing. Or to your son, if he has survived somehow.

May 7, V-E day. Churchbells tolling. Whistles, sirens, gun salutes, fireworks at the Hollywood Bowl (Stokowski coconducting again, with Mickey *and* Donald). Seife missed the revelry. A month before, sensing the end, he packed what was left of his money, a few changes, the Dunhill (for good luck), and crept out of the garage at midnight. Cabbed to Long Beach Harbor. Here, under the name Raymond Bannister, he bribed a quasi-legal passage on a tramp steamer bound for the Panama Canal. A week later, Seife was aboard a commercial vessel that sailed from Honduras, bound for the Gold Coast of Spain. Though Seife appeared to be the only crypto-Nazi aboard, he detected a colorful variety of fugitive rapists, killers, con men, and other lovelies. From Barcelona he flew to Arnhem, in the Netherlands.

Getting back into Germany, inside the fallen Fatherland, was no simple matter of proclaiming "I am the Prodigal Son!" to sentimental border guards. In trying to cross into a besieged country that a half-million refugees were trying to leave, Seife attracted a certain amount of uncomfortable attention. More bribery and subterfuge were required. Almost all his money and most of his provisions were bartered or pilfered between Kassel and Nauen.

Perhaps he walked halfway across his homeland. Sometimes he had company: stragglers, foragers, putative survivors, all with the same look: beyond dazed, beyond empty, even. "Empty" would seem to presuppose a bottom, and sides: something hollow, at least. There was little talk: mouths were saved for gobbling chicken guts. Seife ate a crow, uncooked, for lunch one day. He gagged, kept the crow down, trudged on.

The main thing was to stay clear of the Red Army, those hated Mongols on their Cossack ponies. "The Russkies," he was told, "despise our *Deutschland,* they call it *Die Weisse Hexe.*" This brought a smile to Seife's face: 'The Blond Witch' was one of two nicknames he had for his wife (the other was 'She-Wolf').

At Babelsberg, Seife met witnesses to, and victims of, Ivan's atrocities: gang rapes, summary executions. They could elaborate upon these terrible deeds for hours, but didn't know the time of day, for electric power was cut and the Soviets had stolen every wristwatch in the Reich. Seife continued to put one bleeding foot in front of the other until finally—it was late spring, perhaps June already—he reached the pine forests of Grünewald, at sunrise. He was alone by then. Some of his companions had been forced to stop, weakened by dysentery and typhus. They would simply lie down by the side of the road in the grass. (If they were very hungry, they might try to eat the grass.) There was a suicide in their group, a girl with bloodshot eyes, who, carrying the child of a Cossack who'd defiled her, filled her pockets with stones and threw herself into the Wannsee one day before dawn.

Moving through the pine forests, Seife was slowed by the sandy soil and the hundreds of dead soldiers still strewn (difficult to dig graves in such soil) alongside their slain horses. Seife could see that most mortal wounds were caused by jagged splinters rained down from the treetops above. He knew the trees were shattered by aerial bombardments but it looked, eerily, as though the forest, the very tree limbs, had of their own volition destroyed the Ninth Army as it tried to retreat.

Seife slipped through Schönberg, feeling that he was drawing closer to his son, and energized by the fact, though he'd consumed nothing more than a potato and two bites of stale *dauerbrot* (he'd purchased both with his last, crumpled, nearly disintegrated American dollar) in the past forty-eight hours.

The motorways were jammed with automobiles abandoned when their tanks ran dry, cannibalized for spare parts. Seife kept to the roadside to avoid these, as well as the mines he'd been warned about, and the fire trenches, and gun pits. Finally he reached the Landwehr Canal, clogged with empty schnapps bottles.

One could smell Berlin—"the lair of the fascist beast," according to Soviet sloganeering and graffiti—before one saw it: the stench of many dead mixed with cordite, smoke, soot, and brick dust. Here was the Reich's funeral pyre. Seife was home.

Just outside central Berlin he stopped and hunched behind a stack of cordwood to survey the scene before him, his keen eye searching the gloom for roaming Russians. He thought he might rest here awhile, but then he saw that the cordwood was in fact a pile of blackened corpses, shrunken and mummified in a firestorm. He reeled backward, retching, and in this way Dieter killed his first rat, crushed it with the thin sole of his shoe.

The closer he came to the Reich Chancellery, the more numerous were the rats. Not just numerous, but brazen. They swarmed you as you walked, and when you stopped (as you had to, to avoid bodies hanging from lampposts, with placards around their necks reading "I was a coward") the rats would climb up your legs, biting and clawing your flesh. Seife killed dozens of these rats barehanded, not even looking, as he called out:

"Martin Volker? Martin Seife?"

He discovered that the zoo had been smashed by incendiary bombs—the same zoo where, ten years ago, a llama had devoured an entire paper bag stuffed with peanuts from his son's hand. Martin had been frightened at first, then vastly amused. Now there was a dead elephant in the street, and vermin were crawling inside its exposed entrails. Seife had to presume that the belly was opened by citizens foraging for fresh meat. He himself might have approached the great capsized corpse of the pachyderm but for the poisonously sweet reek surrounding it.

The Kleiner Tiergarten, where Martin had romped as a toddler, was a rubble-strewn arcade in which emaciated girls, garishly made up to look older, were selling their bodies for cigarettes. There were campfires here, and a bullet-riddled Volkswagen that was improbably fitted with a roof rack for antitank rockets.

"Bombed to rubble." No, it was not a matter of rock piles here and there. Seife saw, with a growing sense of wonder, that the scale, magnitude, depth, intensity—however one might wish to describe it—of the destruction, was something that had about it a magnificence. The devastation, complete as it was, carried with it a whiff of the sublime. Probably, this is what Hitler and his cohorts had yearned for all along: a cleansing, yes, but not a hygienic one, for that would be too easy, too banal. No, it was clear to Seife that the National Socialists had wanted, had willed, a crucible. Here was the cult of death, the honor along with the blood. You had only to study one of the hundreds of cadavers littered like jackstraws across the Alexanderplatz, bodies cooked in their own fat, which had then been boiled off, leaving human beings transformed into black, petrified sticks. Not pretty, perhaps, not clean in any conventional sense—but, in their macabre new state, very pure.

And wasn't Purity the watchword, all along?

"Martin Volker? Martin Seife?"

Faces, grimy and stubbly, turned to him. None was Martin.

Seife moved on, licking his teeth, trying to remove the stubborn grit.

The flies were everywhere, the air was filled with their angry constant buzz, and they made no distinction between the living and the dead, harassing both the bodies and stupefied Berliners picking their way around and over the bodies—some searching for relatives, others rifling for rings and coins. Seeing that the flies made no distinction helped Seife resolve to make no distinction either: whether one was upright or lay sprawled and desiccated in the sun, whether one's organs were functioning still, or being fed upon by rats, cats, and dogs, there was no difference in the New Necropolis. Seife was starting to feel better, now—exhilarated, almost. As though he'd died and come out the other side, or been crapped out of death's own asshole. And maybe Martin was nearby, somewhere, wandering as well, and soon they'd be reunited across all the years, the kilometers, the firebombings, and those films.

Once across the Weidendamm Bridge, Seife found himself disoriented, and had to ask for directions to the soundstage where Martin's films were made. A man of indeterminate age, his hair long, greasy, and lice-ridden, face covered in scabs and open sores, pointed him in the right direction (all the city's street signs had been blown down by bombs) then demanded payment, his black eyes blazing. This was the only light Seife had seen in anyone's eyes since reentering the Homeland. He handed over all that he had left: the Dunhill cigarette lighter. It looked miraculously shiny and deluxe, and Seife felt it appropriate payment for the man who'd directed him to the place Martin might be found.

Maybe that had been imprudent. For, after he'd hiked past a long row of roofless shops selling junk that didn't even qualify as junk, and reached the area where the stage had been (it now looked like the dark side of the moon, all that was left to mark it as a movie soundstage was a twisted, melted catwalk thrusting up out of the debris), the man with the scabs on his face was here, too. He'd followed Seife, apparently, along with a friend. The friend was the one wielding the kitchen knife.

Seife didn't hear them crunching across the wreckage, not at first. He was standing in the midst of shards, parts, detritus, dead bodies, live rats, blackened planks of wood—in short, nothing that wasn't broken, destroyed, scorched, or pestilential. And he was calling, "Martin, are you there? Can you hear me?" When he noticed the footsteps behind him, he turned, thinking he was about to see his son. But it was the scabby man and the man who waved the knife, and they were coming toward him. "Wait!" he cried. "Stop! I have nothing left."

They didn't stop, or wait. They were going to rob and kill him. And when they found nothing on his corpse to steal, they'd surely pry the gold molars from his slack mouth.

Seife knew all that, and he felt strangely, almost giddily, impassive about the fact. But then it dawned on him that he mustn't die in such a random, sloppy, disorganized, and ugly way.

Because he was, after all, a director! And not simply "a director," but *Der Phantasie Erzähler* himself! Perhaps one or both of these men had heard of him? It wasn't impossible. He raised his hands to his mouth to form a sort of bullhorn, and shouted: *"Cut!"*

Startled, the two men stopped.

Seife continued: *"Nein,* this is not the way! You are not properly backlit, and you are not elegantly framed. You there!" He turned to the Scabby Man. "I want you to walk—but slowly, deliberately, to that hunk of wood split down the middle. Do you see it? *Then* stop, *then* turn to your friend. Yes, *you."*

Now he was addressing Knife Man. "You don't reveal the blade yet, it's too soon, you must keep us in suspense for one beat longer, do you understand? And then you stop right here—" Indicating a pool of muck and gore that had dried, crusted, and darkened in the sun. "That will be your mark. *Verstehst?* Go back to first position, and begin only when I call Action."

At this, the two men just stood and stared dumbfounded at Seife, who explained, "There are many ways to end a story, one can be hackneyed or absurd or just plain arbitrary, but I don't choose to end my story that way. I choose to end it *this* way!"

Scabby Man scratched his scabs, as though discouraged, and

began to walk off. "Stop! Come back, we cannot do the scene without you!" A moment later Knife Man turned, to follow his accomplice. Seife stood alone, perched high on a pile of charred paper that might have been a mountain of carbonized film scripts. "Where are you going?" he cried out. "Why are you leaving?" His arms windmilled as he gestured at the wreckage all around. "After all," he shouted to the vanishing figures, "is this not the most magnificent movie set you've ever seen?"

Epilogue

The Light

Dowling squinted at the forty-year-old case notes, painstakingly hand-lettered by the crooked Irish cop whom seasoned strategists had forced out of the Hayden organization in the midfifties. (The unfortunate Roarke was dead of cirrhosis only a few years later.) The ink had faded—and now, the retired production topper noticed, the line *I count myself lucky, Mr. Dowling* had gotten smudged under Dowling's thumb, still greasy from the grilled chicken sandwich some college intern had brought him from the studio cafeteria.

He turned to the barrel-sized garbage can labeled TO BE RECYCLED. In Dowling's day the word "recycled"—the concept—didn't exist; when you were done with something, it got thrown away: forever, for good. Hunched here in the subterranean gloom, Dowling decided that to send Roarke's case notes to the Hayden Library would only result in confusion, consternation, and questions—too many questions—and it would fall to Dowling to answer them. Perhaps Helen Prater would insist on flying him to Ohio, where he'd be asked to talk into a tape recorder. The process would take days. Dowling was too old and tired for that.

In his prime, when the production chief came across a bum paragraph in some hack scenarist's treatment, he would scrawl in the margins: *Does not fit the story line!* And he would draw thick, wavy lines through the problematic paragraph. Roarke's faded jottings did not fit the story line either. Dowling dumped the whole pile into the barrel.

So what did that leave after a day's digging? There were some never-before-seen makeup tests for Harley in the role of Tony, a Daily Production Report specifying that Hayden had not required glycerin for his big breakdown scene, and a mimeo draft of *The Big Betrayal* with notes from Edward Dmytryk (the director who'd pseudonymously stepped in after Seife). These he'd send along. Dowling was under no illusion that this modest grab bag of movie curios would do shit for the legacy. He only hoped they'd be enough to get the Hayden Library to leave him alone.

Harley's character in *The Big Betrayal* might once have been described as a snitch, stoolie, pigeon, or canary. When push comes to shove in the picture, Tony breaks down and spills everything. He even sniffles, a little, during the last reel—in a police station, no less. In the forties this was a risky career move for a leading man—and, initially, it must be noted, Hayden's ambitions backfired. After a quickie rerelease, the picture disappeared, forgotten for thirty years.

But sometime in the midseventies, after Watergate, in the wake of Nixon's resignation, snitches got *recycled* as whistle-blowers. Distrust of government was so intense for a season, the divulging of its secrets came briefly into vogue: Benedict Arnold reborn as Paul Revere. And thanks to Women's Lib, weeping men were admired for their supposed sensitivity. So it was with Tony—now conflated with Hayden as he worked to expand his political base beyond Southern California. Still, not till '78 did Hayden get any traction on the national stage—owing (so Dowling believed) to the American Film Institute's restoration of *The Big Betrayal,* which was screened at Lincoln Center, opening week of the New York Film Festival that year.

In his *New York Times* review, Vincent Canby called it "less than a masterpiece, perhaps, but much more than an antique," and Stanley Kauffmann in the *New Republic* hailed the film as "bold and underrated social realism cum noir, ripe for rediscovery." Hayden's big confession scene now played not as some tawdry *mea culpa,* but rather as a cleansing, a catharsis, a symbol—somehow—of political purification and transcendence. *Betrayal* subsequently became a steady rental in the nascent home video market, and by the time the party elders were searching for a face both new and known, Harley Hayden was perfectly positioned on the cusp of a rediscovery himself. His last line of dialogue in the film, coughed out between contrite sobs in that dimly lit station house, briefly became a campy catchphrase of the era: *"No more lies—we'll all sleep better."* The words were oft quoted, till they were supplanted by *"Where's the beef?"*

Dowling smiled as he pictured the script displayed beside the item he'd been told was the most popular piece of Hayden memorabilia at the library: those horn-rim glasses (resting on a satin pillow, like a saint's relic) that Harley'd hid as an actor but proudly worn as a politician. (Detractors liked to bray that the glasses transformed Harley, in more or less a wash, from Handsome Moron to Four-Eyed Mediocrity. But then the detractors always found something to bray about. Their favorite—those pointy-headed East Coast pricks—was a variation on the Hitler-painter premise: If Harley had only been a half-decent actor, the country would have been spared eight years of Hayden, Haydenism, Haydenomics, etc.)

There was one item left at the bottom of the box, surely the final item—for, by the early fifties, Hayden had stopped making movies altogether. It was a *Photoplay* profile, dated June 1950, one in a series on how the male stars of the forties forced to suspend their careers during the war were now faring. The series was titled "What's Become of the Class of Forty-five?" This article bore the cutely alliterative heading "At Home with the Harley Haydens of Holmby Hills." Squinting, Dowling skimmed:

> . . . a spacious, gracious house that, despite all the homey touches supplied by Mrs. Hayden, still feels a bit quiet, a little empty. Eleanor pats her tummy. "Don't worry," she whispers, out of earshot of her husband, who's in his study, penning his upcoming speech to the Motion Picture Industry Council. "I was an only child—Harley, too. We have every intention of filling this huge house with noisy children."
>
> Just then Hayden strolls in. He's maturing, filling out, there's a hint of salt-and-pepper in his sideburns (though not the famous pompadour!) but he's still every inch the sweet, thoughtful dreamboat, apologizing for starting our interview ten minutes late. "You're probably wondering what new hobbyhorse I'm riding," jokes the public-spirited star, as Mrs. Hayden excuses herself. "Well, I'm happy to tell *Photoplay* what's been getting my goat lately: the low esteem in which actors are held by the public. This crazy idea that we're nothing but a bunch of spoiled, overpaid children, and dope fiends to boot! When the truth is that Ellie

and I go to church every Sunday. Heck, almost everyone we know does. If a bomb were to go off at Beverly Hills Presbyterian, why, they'd pretty much have to rebuild the movie business from the ground up."

Eleanor reenters the room with a pitcher of iced tea (her own special, refreshing blend). As she sits, with an affectionate glance at her husband, he continues, "But enough about my fellows-in-greasepaint, there are bigger fish to fry in 1950. Let's skip the fancy phrases like 'private enterprise,' or 'constitutional guarantees.' Increasingly, what it all comes down to, for me, can be summed up in one simple word: 'Americanism.' *That's* what I stand for now. And Ellie, too. And all our friends here in Hollywood."

Meantime Mrs. Hayden pours iced tea for her husband and for Harley's spellbound guest—Your Correspondent.

"When I came home from the war, so much had changed. Our freedoms felt more dear to me than ever, and more fragile—and the enemies of those freedoms more numerous and determined to subvert them than *before* the conflict."

Eleanor squeezes Harley's hand. "That was a period of adjustment for us—but we got through it." It's all she'll say on the subject. Must have been a scary time for a girl in love, worried about her future husband's safety.

Impatient, Dowling flipped to the final page:

". . . other night, I attended a private screening of a new film by a very talented director, Mr. Billy Wilder. It'll be out soon, I guess. It's called *Sunset Boulevard*." (Mr. Hayden is too modest to mention that he'd been approached by Paramount Pictures to play the male lead, a terrif role eventually filled by his bosom pal Bill Holden.) "Now don't get me wrong, it's a wonderful picture and I'm sure it'll be a big hit. But there was something at the end that bothered me, a line of dialogue I couldn't shake."

Harley strolls over to the window and parts the curtains, to gaze out onto his lush green lawn. "Gloria Swanson plays a big star from the silent days, a real grande dame. I don't think I'm giving away any secrets here. Anyhow, at the end of the picture, Miss Swanson talks about her life in the movies. It's a very touching speech, very well written by Mr. Wilder, beautifully directed, as Gloria thanks the fans who've stood by her through all the years. Just as I thank *my* fans."

Mrs. Hayden quietly puts in: "Harley answers every letter himself. Though I've *begged* him to hire someone!"

Harley grins, shakes his head, then continues: "Miss Swanson talks about 'all the wonderful people' she's entertained through her career, those happy faces looking up at the big screen 'out there in the dark.' And it got me thinking, maybe it's high time for me to take my message beyond the motion picture palaces. Whatever I've got to say, whatever example I might be able to set—so I'm not just talking to people 'out there in the dark' anymore."

He glances at his wife, as though not quite ready to spill the beans. "Why not say what's on your mind, dear?" Eleanor prompts her famously self-effacing hubby.

"Well, I'm ready to get out there in the *light,*" Mr. Hayden states, with more than a bit of movie star mystery.

No mystery, reflected Dowling as he dropped *Photoplay* back in the carton—rather, the prelude to Hayden's maiden run for

Congress in '52. And no, it wasn't true that on the campaign trail, when asked what sort of congressman he'd be, Harley said, "I don't know, I never played a congressman." Sure, that made a funny story, one the Hayden detractors never tired of *recycling*. But Dowling knew it was apocryphal; he'd personally supervised a feature only six years earlier in which Hayden *had* played a congressman, the 1946 Superior laffer *When V-Girls Vote*.

Having lingered all day in the basement, Dowling had lost track of time. He suffered from macular degeneration and was warned against night driving. He limped upstairs, anxious to return to the safety of his ranch house. The Sparkletts man might come in the morning. Dowling wanted to be in bed at a decent hour, rested, ready in case the doorbell chimed early.

He was taken aback—even a bit frightened—to find that everyone was gone! Dowling shambled past dozens of eerily empty carrels. The impossibly young girl had left for the day, as had the college intern who'd brought his chicken sandwich. As he reached the exit, Dowling felt like the Last Man in Hollywood.

There was one more surprise: The sun, though no longer high, still blazed down. After all the hours belowground, Dowling stepped outside and lurched toward what he hoped was the parking lot where he'd left his sedan. The light was blinding.